Michael Arnold lives in Hampshire with his wife and four children. His interest in British history is lifelong, and childhood holidays were spent visiting castles and battlefields – a passion he now inflicts on his own kids. He is the author of the acclaimed Civil War Chronicles; one of which, *Devil's Charge*, was chosen as a *Sunday Times* Book of the Year.

THE SAVAGE ISLE

Michael Arnold

CANELO

First published in the United Kingdom in 2025 by Canelo

This edition published in the United Kingdom in 2025 by

Canelo, an imprint of
Canelo Digital Publishing Limited,
20 Vauxhall Bridge Road,
London SW1V 2SA
United Kingdom

A Penguin Random House Company
The authorised representative in the EEA is Dorling Kindersley Verlag GmbH. Arnulfstr. 124, 80636 Munich, Germany

Copyright © Michael Arnold 2025

The moral right of Michael Arnold to be identified as the creator of this work has been asserted in accordance with the Copyright, Designs and Patents Act, 1988.
All rights reserved. No part of this publication may be reproduced or transmitted in any form or by any means, electronic or mechanical, including photocopy, recording, or any information storage and retrieval system, without permission in writing from the publisher.
No part of this book may be used or reproduced in any manner for the purpose of training artificial intelligence technologies or systems. In accordance with Article 4(3) of the DSM Directive 2019/790, Canelo expressly reserves this work from the text and data mining exception.

A CIP catalogue record for this book is available from the British Library.

Ebook ISBN 978 1 83598 037 8
Royal Hardback ISBN 978 1 83598 236 5
Paperback ISBN 978 1 83598 036 1

This book is a work of fiction. Names, characters, businesses, organizations, places and events are either the product of the author's imagination or are used fictitiously. Any resemblance to actual persons, living or dead, events or locales is entirely coincidental.

Cover design by Becca Thorne

Printed and bound in Great Britain by Clays Ltd, Elcograf S.p.A.

Look for more great books at
www.canelo.co | www.dk.com

For Becca. We did it.

'We are the last people on earth, and the last to be free...'

Tacitus, *Agricola (XXX)*, H. Mattingly trans.

CHAPTER ONE

Britannia AD 42

The waxing moon played guide as the men threaded the woody defile. Stooping trees, a gauntlet of jagged, moss-clad rocks, the clawing grasp of shadow-cloaked briars.

The men funnelled onto a narrow track, steps muffled by a blanket of leaves. From up high, on slopes choked by the lush canopies of oak and beech, an owl's hoot pierced the sounds of their rasping breaths. Further off, amongst the deeper, darker realms, wolves broke into mournful song.

The men pressed on, following a leader gleaming in winged helmet and exquisite mail. Spear points caught and twisted the pearl-grey light above their heads.

They came from the north, these war-givers.

Raised from every village and farm, every modest steading, and every ridged and fortified hill, they had gathered in their masses beneath the banner of the twin white serpents and surged like a great tide onto the tracks and fields that would lead them to their enemy. Through the moon-gilded hours they had swept, crossing ditches choked by holly and foxglove, over rolling fields and spirit-haunted forests, beseeching the gods to favour their endeavours. Now dawn approached, and still they flowed, like an iron river, ever southwards, and with them came blood and horror.

Cullen moved in a half-crouch, slowly, with great care, one shadow amongst so many beneath the whispering boughs. Above him, the canopy was thick enough to blot out a sun that dazzled the flower-dotted meadows beyond. Within this forest-world, only a dim, greenish twilight illuminated the track of gnarled roots and tangled underbrush. The air was thick with damp and decay, tinged with the bitter tang of toadstool and nightshade, but underneath it all, he caught the scent – acrid, pungent, unmistakable.

He halted, braced on the balls of his feet, heart quickening. His knuckles bone-white where they clasped his spear.

The wolf was close.

He stooped lower, fingers brushing the ground. The soft earth yielded to his touch, and there, pressed into the mud, was the fresh imprint of a paw, larger than his hand. The breath caught in his throat, his mouth instantly parched. He twisted his neck, keeping the rest of his body utterly still, searching the deep murk, senses dagger-sharp. The shadows were long and twisted, the silence heavy, unnatural.

A breeze stirred the branches above. Cullen's hand tightened around the spear haft, the rough wood grounding him, reminding him of his purpose.

Another scent reached him, sharper now, mingling with the wolf's musk. Blood. He moved painstakingly forward, driven by a morbid curiosity, his body taut with anticipation. As he pushed through a dense thicket, the forest seemed to close in around him, the trees leaning closer, their branches like skeletal fingers clawing at the sky.

Then he saw it – a patch of disturbed earth, the leaves stained dark, almost black in the dim light. The remnants of a kill, but the body was gone, dragged away. Cullen's stomach lurched. The wolf had been here, had fed here, but where was it now?

A branch snapped in the distance, and he froze, the sound ricocheting through the silence like a thunderclap. His eyes darted towards the noise, but the gloom revealed nothing. The dark seemed to pulse, the forest holding its breath, waiting.

He stood still as stone, every muscle tensed, straining to hear past the pounding of his heart. But there was nothing, save the caw and cackle of crows beyond the high, latticed branches, tumbling on the breeze, ignorant to his hunt. Cullen swallowed hard, the wolf-stench and blood still ripe in his nostrils. He knew he had to keep moving, to find it before it found him, or, more crucially, before it found his goats.

Even as he started out, he heard it. Fragments on the breeze. A whispering sound, nebulous and indistinct. But this gave him pause, for the noise was not what he had expected. Words, though muffled and shapeless. Human voices.

He scrambled off the animal track and slipped through brambles and ferns, the wolf forgotten for now, making his way to the treeline some two hundred paces away, ears straining to catch the sounds again. A ditch formed the wood's edge, before the trees gave way to a flower-strewn meadow, and Cullen slid down into its rocky base. It was shallow, gouged from the chalk by long-dead hands to mark a long-forgotten boundary, but deep enough to conceal a whip-thin youth dressed in pale yellows and greens that made him blend with the forest.

He crawled up to the brow. The ditch brimmed with lush stands of bracken, limbs of ash and lime, and the tangled, leafy talons of dogwood and elder, concealing all. Yet, with arms locked straight, Cullen could elevate his head beyond the lip to look out across the meadow. Deer, three or four, grazed far off, meandering carefree through fetlock-high grass. A pair of buzzards circled lazily, wingtips splayed like stretched fingers, ruminating on their next meal with high, mournful screeches.

Voices again, away to his right. Louder now. Closer.

His guts convulsed. Something large slid, almost imperceptibly, through tall grass and gnarled branches at the field's edge, tracking the treeline. It was well camouflaged, and he might have considered it the movement of a stag or even his wolf, but for the speech of more than one man, reaching him in unintelligible scraps. He almost stood up, waved his arms, called out a greeting. But something was not right. Something in the tones, the accents. It screamed of the unusual. The foreign. He swallowed down fear.

Where were the goats? Cullen pictured the stand of trees, too far away for comfort, in which he had left them to graze. Could bandits have come to steal the herd? He silently swore. His mother would flay him alive.

He slunk back, slid further into the recess, and set down his spear, pulling the leather strap and pebble-pouch from the waist-tie of his braca. He regarded them, feeling suddenly devoid of knowledge, as if he no longer knew how to sling a stone, his mind empty.

More voices. Louder, closer.

Icy fingers dabbed at the nape of his neck. He wanted to retreat, to sink back into the embrace of the wood and find a hollow in which to curl. But there were strangers abroad. He could hardly ignore it. He had seen sixteen winters, after all. Almost a grown man. Gritting his teeth, he resolved to discover the identity of the strangers. He returned to the crest, palms tormented by bits of twig, dried leaves and shards of bark, and inched aside the bracken fronds, stems parting like a curtain, their rustle achingly loud to his ears. He held his breath. Eased forward on hands and knees until his face and shoulders brushed the outermost ferns. Directly ahead, the meadow, painted in brilliant colour, hummed with life. Except the deer had gone. And the buzzards, still calling, soared far higher than before, mere specks before the blue vastness.

He looked to his right. Nothing.

When he looked left, what he saw almost made him cry out. It was indeed a man, but not one he had ever before seen. He was tall and lean, with short hair the colour of dark gold, sculpted with hardening paste into sharp spikes. He was no farmer or smith. Cullen could not see his face, for the man strode away southwards, down the meadow's gentle slope in the direction of the town, but a want of features did not alter what was instantly clear. He wore not a stitch above his waist, and his back and shoulders writhed with fantastical beasts, painted in a deep blue by an expert hand so that they coiled and struck with the shifting of his muscles. In his left hand a long, oblong shield scraped the edges of the ferns, causing them to sway and whisper. As it turned with his gait, twin serpents were revealed above and below the iron boss, daubed in white, jaws wide and fangs long. In his right hand he gripped a tall throwing spear, while at his midriff, suspended from a chain of linked iron rings, hung a long sword, its scabbard nestled against the wool of braca chequered in red and brown.

Pulse pounding, Cullen glanced to the right as he made to leave. He was forced immediately to screw up his eyes before a low bank of dazzling light, as if the sun had fallen from the sky to hover just above the grass. Even as he shrank away, he knew that Belinos had not condescended to walk the mortal realm. Rather, it was the brilliant play of summer rays upon a mass of polished metal. So much metal. The air caught in Cullen's lungs, knotting and twisting, as though vines crept about his ribs, paralysing him so that he simply stared, dumbstruck. Men – a lot of men – were emerging from the trees.

Spear tips bobbed high like shimmering banners. Most were bare chested or leather-clad, but some wore breastplates and mail shirts, reflecting the sun in beams, while ornate hilts and chapes, armlets and torcs glittered like jewels. These were men like the first, but more, so many more. More straight swords, more long spears, belts slanted over hips under the weight of scabbards and daggers. There were bows hooked over shoulders and leather slings dangling from palms.

They all came this way, dozens upon dozens, stepping out from the forest as if the Underworld disgorged all its demons at once. A high, droning call rolled out from their midst. It made Cullen's skin crawl. It was the call of the carnyx. Chilling, lingering, doleful. The song of war and of death. And, as he slunk back into the ditch's embrace, he heard someone shout. They had seen him.

Cullen ran like a hound-harried fawn, terror giving wings to his feet. He would not stop; could not. At his back he could still hear the shouts of his pursuers and the awful drone of the carnyx. The tribe bearing the twin serpents were the Catuvellauni, the most warlike of all the nations. They were here for war. For blood. The knowledge turned his bowels to water.

He smothered the thought, crushed it savagely, unwilling to face it as he crashed and stumbled and cursed his way out through the last of the trees. He bounded a pair of shallow gullies and tore into an open slice of meadow. A flock of sparrows erupted from the tall grass on all sides, making him swear in fright, though it did nothing to slow his legs, and he pumped his knees high against the rasping blades.

He ran ever westwards and soon drew near the dun of Calleva. He looked to his right, searching for signs of movement. That was where the great road lay. A conduit joining his people's territory to their neighbours' in the north. That was where the warriors would be. Because it was those very neighbours who had come for blood. Those neighbours who had come this brightest of days with darkest intent. Their emblem, daubed on shields and bodies, had told him as much. The Catuvellauni enthusiasm for vicious bloodletting was well known. And now they had turned their ire upon the Atrebates. Cullen's people. Tentacles of fear crept up his spine.

Cullen moved nearer to the road, hanging back in the low branches, ignoring the needling of brambles at his flanks. The broad thoroughfare, first cut when the tribe had crossed the sea from Gaul to escape Caesar's ire, but widened and metalled in recent years by King Berikos, vanished southwards in a sweeping bend. It was patched with horse dung and marked by the deep grooves of cartwheels. A gutter ran down the nearside edge, finished in smooth river cobbles, and he crouched beside it, listening.

There was nothing but birdsong and the incessant chirrup of insects. Stillness reigned amongst the trees and on the road and in the air. Perhaps, he thought with a surge of hope, the men who had so cruelly stumbled upon the morning's secret tryst had been nothing more than bandits. Catuvellauni, for certain, but a rogue company, stranded or banished. But that, whispered a nagging voice, belied the full battle-paint and their brazen proximity to the capital of a rival tribe. Nor did it explain the presence of a carnyx player. The instrument was a *war*-horn.

And yet.

Cullen prayed to all the gods that would spring to his racing mind, and to all the gods he promised to recall later. He begged them to make this morning an aberration. An hour of horror that would prove to be little more than waking nightmare. The kind of blood-dream the Wise Ones spoke of when they emerged from those magical stupors induced by brews of flower and fungus. Because the Catuvellauni were not here. The road was empty.

Feeling a swell of relief, he ventured out into the open, and sprinted for the town, leaning into the curve of the road as he rounded the forest-flanked bend, and almost careening headlong into the rearmost rank of the Catuvellauni horde.

Cullen hauled himself to a stop, skidding, clamping a hand across his mouth so as to stifle the yelp that surged up from within. They were a multitude. A serpent made of flesh and iron and bronze, with spines fashioned from spear tips, stretching away to disappear around the next bend in the road, all clouded in the dust that roiled up from hundreds of pounding feet. Somewhere a drum called out the pace, low and constant, and more carnyxes brayed like the beasts after which they were ornately fashioned.

Cullen thanked the gods and the forefathers, the spirits of the road and the sprites amongst the bracken. Because, in the midst of their marching, the warriors had not noticed him. Nor did they see him return to the trees, plunging through the branches on the opposite side with breath held to burning point and heartbeat raging. And then he was running again, concealed from the road but parallel to it, desperate to reach Calleva's gates before the bristling rows of painted killers. Slaughter was coming, and his people had to be warned.

Slaughter had already arrived.

He had sprinted. Crashed and stumbled and cursed, bounced from tree to tree, all the while rehearsing the warning that would be delivered in breathless but authoritative style to the watchmen at the gates and maybe, just maybe, in the presence of Berikos himself. But he had taken leave of reality, he realised, as he crossed through the eerily desolate outer earthworks. A ditch and rampart that would, on any other occasion, present a formidable obstacle to any incomer larger than a mouse. Arrogance, he told himself, as he ran past a twisted corpse that still clutched a shield bearing the horse-mark of the Atrebates, had fooled him into thinking that this scrap of a lad, too meek to take his tribe's warrior tests, could somehow affect the way the day played out. He plunged through a little orchard and knew that he was too late.

Of course he was too late. Of course the Catuvellauni had reached the town before the scampering boy, and of course King Berikos's patrols had long since raised the alarm. There was a joke in there, somewhere, Cullen suspected. One about a delusional child who thought he could act the hero.

All he could do was climb an expansive, spiral-trunked tree and silently curse his own hubris as he watched the attack unfold in slack-jawed impotence. In the clearing that separated orchard from town, a score of chariots criss-crossed the scrub, bearing the enemy's leaders. The charioteers, status marked by metal circlets about their heads, steered deftly, while behind them, conspicuous on the wickerwork platforms, their crowing lords seemed like bizarre beasts to Cullen, torsos gaudily decorated, hair adorned with painted feathers, and necks and wrists heavy with thick golden torcs. They barked orders at messengers who ran forth to convey word to the invaders, who were already at the main gates. And those gates, painted with the sacred symbol of the three-tailed horse, yawned wide.

Cullen leaned in, pressing close to the tree for better concealment. He wrapped an arm around the trunk, parted a clump of leaves with the other, and pushed his face to the opening. He could see a good deal from here, all the way to the grandest structures that dominated the centre of the town. What he saw put an icy grip around his heart. He had always considered the great Calleva nothing short of a miracle. He knew there were larger and more impressive settlements. Traders often brought news of ports to the north and west, teeming with men and ships and goods more exotic than a youthful mind could begin to invoke. They described the bustling cities – grander than any dun to be found in the Isle of the Mighty – that dotted the great empire across the sea, the home of strange creatures, impossible innovation, and exquisite works of art. And the itinerant poets would weave elaborate tales of Rome itself, the very centre of the world, conjuring magic in word and song across his mother's blazing winter hearth. Cullen and his sister would huddle in the crisp cold, revel in the heady wood-smoke, and hang on every word. Yet Calleva remained the most inspiring place in his small sphere. The expansive enclosure of roundhouses, great halls and swarming streets seemed so incongruous, so very unlikely, set as it was within forbidding and endless woodland, that he felt sure that the first building posts must have been driven into the soil by the very gods who dwelt amongst the leafy boughs. The lands of his people were ancient. Far older than the Atrebates themselves, who had come in desperation, generations before, with a voracious Rome expanding at their heels. As those ragtag fugitives had found shelter from their enemies, they had coalesced under the leadership of ambitious kings, and as the tribe had set down strong roots, so Calleva had sprung like a sapling from the earth, thriving with the tribe's natural talent for trade and their links with far off peoples. A village, then a town, then a fortified city, honoured with the status of a chieftain's dun.

This great hub, then, was a meeting point for any with wares to trade. A junction where news, goods and coin were exchanged in a perpetual blur. A beacon in the darkness. And Cullen would come out of the pastures to simply stare. To drink the place in. Its smells and its sounds. Life, unbridled and unabashed.

It was his Rome, and now it was burning.

He looked out from his high vantage, wide-eyed and scarcely breathing. The huge settlement, ringed by a deep ditch and spiked bank, was already shrouded in poisonous smoke, white, black and yellow. Folk screamed. They scattered; ants from a kicked nest. They dashed through door skins as thatches lit up, one to the next, in a contagion of flickering flame, and crashed into one another as they scrambled to find a place of safety that did not exist. Cullen could see children hiding in nooks and crannies, behind cartwheels and at the foot of fence panels, but the gates – those great, redoubtable gates – gaped invitingly, their sentries cut down in the first throes of the attack. Warriors lay twisted and bloodied in the streets, the flotsam of a fight, but whatever defence had been offered had been snuffed out in short order. The totems of the twin snakes, cast in iron and fitted to long staffs, swept through the acrid miasma, bobbing like the prows of ships in morning mist, and the invaders snarled and jeered, drunk on killing. They strutted like cockerels as they swung iron and spilled blood, pouring through the broad thoroughfares in a raging torrent. Past the din of the animal pens, livestock maddened by the stench of smoke. Past the storage pits, the homes and forges and workshops, as rooftops began to collapse, one after another.

These were places Cullen knew. He could picture the faces of those whose livelihoods depended upon the stricken buildings. A red-haired swordsmith. A one-eyed maker of fine chariots. A woman whose expertise in the working of leather was famed for miles around. The white-bearded bone and antler carver, the portly grain seller, the heavy-jowled merchant whose wares ranged from metals to slaves to the very finest jewellery.

All was chaos. All was fire. All was noise.

Cullen shifted his gaze to the Grand Path, the greatest of the roads, aligned with the sunrises and sunsets of midsummer and midwinter, and bounded on either side by massive, carved stones. He traced its route into the haze. The story was the same. The sea of roundhouses, large and small, spewed a terrified population with nowhere to go. The enemy bands roved and chased and cheered. After so many years of wrangling on the borders of their territory, stealing cattle and launching small raids in retribution for minor slights, the tribes of this part of the world had settled into a period of relative stability. The Atrebates butted up against the Dobunni and Durotriges to the west, the Catuvellauni to the north, the Cantiaci to the east. They held dominion over the Belgae and Regneses and a dozen smaller clans on the south coast. All the borders were held in a tense state, often in continual flux, but held they were. Yet even one so green as Cullen could see that this was no raid. No simple application of pressure. It was conquest. Pure, simple and brutal.

He let his gaze drift across the rooftops, to the long halls that marked Calleva's beating heart. The large salt-seller's premises, with its pile of broken briquetage out front, and the Roman oil-trader's house, its phalanxes of curved amphorae just visible through the noxious fug. Beyond them, flanked by twin guardposts that now appeared to be vacant, was the huge, rectangular hall that contained the very throne of the king. Around it clustered the grand temples to Epona, Taranis, Belinos and Lugus. All now under attack. All disgorging their human contents for the waiting blades.

Cullen shuddered. Tasted salt where tears collected at the corners of his mouth. His eyes tracked the chariots again, alighting on one that was finer than the rest, gold leaf reflecting the sun like hot iron sparking. Its passenger had long hair, dark as raven feathers and braided with coloured beads. As Cullen watched, the warrior bounded from the platform, deftly avoiding his driver, and ran along the traces to balance upon the yoke, his throwing spear poised at his shoulder. Cullen was mesmerised. The skill, the balance, the raw power.

A magpie settled in the canopy near his head, its jarring cackle making him start. He glanced up. The beady blackness of its eyes bore into his own. The spark of blue on its flank caught the sun, shimmering as it skittered along the branch. An evil omen, meant for him alone. Why, he wondered, when he was lucky enough to be outside of Calleva's boundary? Why would the creature pick Cullen out when so many faced immediate peril?

The magpie sprung out suddenly, a smear of black and white upon lush green. Cullen watched it go, and the realisation struck him as sure as any spear thrust. He hugged the rough bark of the trunk and descended to earth in one grazing slide.

—

The undersides of his forearms smarted as he ran, still wet and fresh from the skinning they had taken. He paid them no heed whatsoever. Nor did he care for who might have seen him cross the wide road. Calleva could fend for itself – or not. All that mattered now was reaching his mother's steading, away to the south, and he raced through the woods not even bothering to check for pursuers. If the Catuvellauni were already at Berikos's seat, then the tiny hamlet occupied by Cullen's extended family would be the very next place they would reach. It was no longer a matter of raising the alarm, but purely of survival. The magpie omen was clear as crystal.

The trees gave way to dusty scrub, patched with tall stands of purple-topped thistles, their spiny clutches snagging his clothes, even as the braying of a dozen distant carnyxes gave wings to his feet. He prayed the gods would open his mother's ears. That she would hear the war-horns and know to run for the hills. Even so, he needed to see it with his own eyes. Walk into an empty village and know for certain that every soul had long since fled.

Chastising himself viciously for the tiredness that crept up his legs, he leaned into his strides, pounding the soil, demanding vigour they did not possess. He leapt over a stream that babbled its amusement as his landing foot found a knot of slick dung that dispatched him halfway down the bank. He scrambled up, slinging a filthy curse over his shoulder at whatever sprite dwelt amongst the reeds. Then he was through a row of distinguished alders that he knew well, their conical, fissured trunks like old friends, beckoning him home, and into a dense stand of oak that cast him in immediate shadow. He slowed. A sudden sense of dread gave him pause, and he scanned the gloom. He could feel them now. Moving in the trees, wraiths in the watery light. The land – *all* the land – was crawling with Catuvellauni. Infested with them. In his mind he saw them as demons. Minions of some ancient and terrible magic, though that did not change the reality. They were behind him, certainly, but also to the front.

A few paces ahead, the land dropped sharply, forming the side of a lane that had sunk through centuries of use. He made for the slope, sliding on his side, all the way to the foot, making to cross the lane and scale the far bank. He glanced back up at the oak and alder. Moving between the ageless trunks, silent as wildcats, he caught a flash of metal and woad. They were coming.

CHAPTER TWO

Cullen's lungs were bursting as he laboured into the village. He stumbled to a ragged halt as he crossed the shallow ditch, doubling over between the gateposts to clamp hands on wobbling knees, leg bones suddenly turned to water. He had found the gate open, which had given concern, but he was overcome with relief to see that no smoke choked the spaces between the buildings. No killers stalked the grassy paths. No one screamed.

Gradually, he edged into the compound. Eight roundhouses huddled together within the stockade, his mother's, the largest, at the centre. There were grain pits along the inner edge of the defensive ring, glistening dew-ponds, fly-clouded middens, and livestock pens that would normally be guarded by small boys with large dogs. None were to be seen. The place was empty, and as silent as the burial ground on the far side of the stockade. He closed his eyes, whispering thanks to each and every deity that sprang to mind. The Atrebates were being put to the sword at this very moment, but at least his family had survived.

He twisted to glance up at the sloping meadow, topped by the dark treeline through which he had come. There was a low hump halfway down. A natural feature that would, in winter, shield the compound from bitter winds. In summer it would host a lookout, though it was vacant now, left for the gently swaying grass. He guessed whoever had been in position that morning had done their job, for the alarm had clearly, thankfully, been raised.

With that, he made his way into the village. The first two houses were small, perched either side of the main path leading from the gate. Home to families of four apiece, kin on his mother's side, their walls were decorated in rich red and yellow swirls. One had a goat's skull nailed above the door, the other's lintel etched with a detailed carving of a hammer. Cullen made for the latter, the smith's mark declaring his cousin's mastery at the forge. He thrust his head beyond the door skin, taking a moment for his eyes to adjust to the gloom. Empty, save a small fire, remnants glowing orange. He pulled away, blinking in the sun, searching for signs of life. They had not been gone for long. Then he heard voices further off. Deeper into the settlement. Fearing they were the words of invaders, he ducked in close to the smith's house, pressing against the cool wall beneath the overhanging thatch. He held his breath and squinted along the line of the path, a tongue of brown bisecting the grass, beyond the largest roundhouse to the collection of smaller huts at its far side. He noticed a ripple in one of the door skins, then a small head emerged. A child. A little girl, with a daisy-chain strung about her neck. His half-sister, Fi, waved uncertainly. Cullen's heart twisted in his chest.

He burst from his hiding place and lurched into a run. He was tired still, dog tired, but he screamed all the same, bellowing at the people gathered within the house to flee immediately. The skin rumpled as it was hauled back. More faces in the doorway. All children he recognised. He read concern on their features, but not fear. Not the blanched look of abject terror the day deserved. Whatever they were hiding from, it was something they assumed – they had been told – would eventually pass. So he screamed again and again as he drew closer, beseeched them to get out, to run for their lives, and gradually they were coming out into the open. Five, ten, twelve little bodies, more. But he realised they were no longer listening to him. All those wide eyes had shifted to another place. Somewhere above him and beyond. He slewed to a halt, twisting as he did, still ten paces from the group.

Up on the meadow, spreading rapidly across the low ridge like spilled oil, were men. Painted men, armoured men, savage men. Huge, loping, slavering hounds wove between and beside them. On one flank, a skinny youth with a mop of fair hair clutched a long brass tube vertically before his face. Its ends were curved, forming something akin to a serpent. The central portion was straight, while the flared lower mouthpiece and upper bell were horizontal, thrusting in opposite directions. He put the mouthpiece to his lips. The bell, outward facing, was styled like the gaping maw of a roaring beast, and through it came the sound that chilled Cullen to the marrow. It was loud and long and mournful, like the call of a stag, and at its behest, the warriors of the Catuvellauni surged down towards the village.

The children screamed, scattered like mice before an invasion of cats. Cullen reached for Fi, but her little hand was gone in an instant, her body whipped away amongst the others as though it had been snatched up by a whirlwind.

Begging for Belinos to protect her, Cullen went instead to the big roundhouse. His mother's home. His home. The place where his heart felt warmest, where his dreams were best. He had known other boys, those with the rarefied blood of chiefs in their veins, who were not raised at their mother's hearth or father's knee. Sent instead to the territory of distant kin, or that of an honoured foe, there to see out the years of fosterage to learn valuable skills and forge new alliances. But that path had been closed to Cullen. His father had died, his uncle too, and duties about their steading had fallen at his feet while still a stripling. He did not mind, of course, for it was his mother's land, held by her line for generations, since the time before the great migration from the kingdoms across the Narrow Sea. She was a Dobunni, of the ancient blood, his mother. A people as old as the oaks and the groves and the rivers. It was his father, with those deep chestnut eyes and darker complexion, that bore the blood of a foreign line. His forebears came from the lands the Romans called Gaul. They had settled here generations ago, eased the natives out of the area and established their own kingdom, in time becoming as much a part of the soil as any of the island's diverse peoples. But that was ancient history. What Cullen knew was that his father had been smitten upon first laying eyes on his mother. He had brought a dozen goats and five head of cattle to the match. She had brought the land upon which they staked out their roundhouse, their animal pens, their grain stores and their future. Her family had come. His father had taken more wives and whelped more children, and the little community had thrived, even after their gruff patriarch had returned to the soil. Thrived, that was, until now.

He dragged aside the heavy skin and peered into the black maw of the house, blinking hard as he scraped fingertips over the totems of stag, bear, eagle and horse that were sunk into the doorpost. When his eyes had adjusted, he stepped in, quickly scanning the interior. There was no one home. He half jogged into the wide space. Smooth cooking stones and a trio of scuffed iron pots circled a still-warm fire that was bridged by a large and elaborate fire-dog. Bowls were positioned about the edges, unwashed and left for the flies. They had vacated this place in a hurry. But where were they now, the adults? As if he did not know.

The sound of battle provided the answer. He wrenched himself round as the clashing song of iron and bronze played suddenly outside. Of course, his mother had not abandoned the children to their fate. He should have known better. They had been hiding somewhere within the stockade. Beside a ditch, perhaps, or in one of the grain pits. And now they had emerged to defend their homes, and tears pricked hot at Cullen's eyes again, because he knew that they would all die. They should have fled. Should have taken what belongings they could carry and dissolved into the wilderness. They had underestimated the raid, assuming it was a matter of simple theft, of cattle or slaves. But they had not been to Calleva. Not witnessed the sheer numbers committed to its sacking. He could see it now. His proud mother, leading her sisters and the few remaining men, would have planned an ambush that would be simple, bloody and swift. Utterly ignorant of the reality. He froze behind the door, a statue in the darkness, and listened with rising horror as shouts turned to screams and the fragrant scent of wood smoke rapidly soured to the acrid fug of burning thatch.

Footsteps passed across the front of the roundhouse, scraping the dust, a shadow skittering through the bar of light beneath the draped skin. The sound jolted the inertia from his bones. He turned back. He would hide. There was no point fighting. Even so, his eyes went up and to the right, roving the stout crossbeam where the family's weapons should be. The hooks and nails were mostly empty. His father's old sword and throwing spears, half a dozen knives and a club of knotted blackthorn; all gone. Only the spare axe remained, its haft smoothed by years of use, but it was another made for his father. The iron blade was fearsome, but far too heavy for Cullen to swing, while the haft was as long and thick as his own arm. The rest of the weapons were outside at this very moment, he knew. His proud mother, rich red hair, long and unkempt, dazzling in the sunlight, would be wielding them as expertly as any man, snarling and grimacing in the eye of this savage storm as she hurled and thrust and hacked, teeth bared like a crazed animal. They all fought when necessity called. Any man or woman who could lift a spear would be expected to play their part. Cullen shuddered at the thought, fear zinging through his body. At sixteen, it was almost two full years since he had begun to practise the war games at which he was expected to become adept, yet he was still too scrawny to heft a full-bladed sword with any efficacy. He was useless, and he knew it. He was old enough, though, to earn his place at the fire by watching over the precious herd. Sharp eyes and a penchant for his own company had sealed him the role, and life had been acceptable enough. The other children would tease, and his mother would suffer the occasional barb from his father's other wives, but out in the woods Cullen was his own lord. He talked to the goats, pissed in the brambles, and watched the clouds drift by. As ambivalent to the ways of war as he was to the skills of the smith or the songs of the poets.

He skirted the fireplace and scrambled over a row of low wooden benches, diving into the piled pelts of the sleeping area behind. He sprawled over the deep nest of fleeces and furs that so recently kept snug his kin, noting with a sickening pang the exquisite cloak of thick beaver pelts that was his mother's favourite. Scrambling on hands and knees until he reached his own space, undisturbed this past night, he lunged for the dark void beyond, the gap between the tightly rolled cloth of his pillow and the house's broad posts, groping in the dirt with both hands. Cullen did not possess many things. No bright coins or valuable trinkets. But the few treasures he could call his own were stashed here, away from prying eyes. He fumbled for a breathless moment, fingers scrabbling from item to item, probing two pieces of curiously shaped antler, a rock that sparkled like a sky full of stars, a half-finished bead necklace, and the intact skull of a polecat, until finally they settled on what he sought; a skinning knife, gifted to him to mark the birth of his youngest half-sister, Cora. He plucked it from the shadows, freeing the blade and tossing the sheath away. It was a length of slender iron, light and curved, sunk into a hilt of smooth bone bound in leather. It was not a weapon so much as a tool, the impossibly sharp blade forged to slip beneath the hide of an animal, but far too thin to withstand any kind of blow. He turned it in his grip, the dying fire's meagre embers dancing along its length. The smith had forged it at his father's request, pressing the emblem of the three-tailed horse, the symbol of the Atrebates, into its heel. That image now shimmered. The horse seemed to gallop. A sign, if ever there was one. Cullen kissed it as he lurched about, diving under his mother's cloak, covering himself in the stitched pelts that smelled so strongly of her. He was lying on his belly, facing into the room, and he used the tip of the knife to lift the cloak's heavy hem a fraction, affording sight of the expansive doorway. Here he would wait out the tribulation. He would hide for as long as it took.

Almost immediately a flood of light filled the roundhouse as the door skin was torn violently away. Even as Cullen instinctively clamped shut his eyes the light was eclipsed by something altogether more sinister, and he was compelled to peel open his wavering lids. In the doorway was a man, his bulk an undefined black mass. At the sides of the silhouette were the more regular lines of spear and shield. He could have been anyone. Could have been Atrebates, had such unlikely fortune amused the gods. Cullen knew better. He had never been favoured. Why would they start now?

The man stepped inside, letting in light and revealing more of the village beyond. The roundhouse opposite, painted dark green, was aflame. Burning thatch spewed acrid smoke that smeared the sky. The stifling stench was already coming in. The warrior advanced carefully, taking on more shape the closer he came, and drew up before the dwindling fire, nudging the ash with his toe. He hawked up a wad of phlegm and spat, causing the embers to hiss, then clanked the spiked butt of his spear against the iron frame that stood like a sentinel over the charred circle. It had been a gift, the fire-dog, from a neighbouring faction. A centrepiece to the great roundhouse and a point of deep pride for his mother. It had two terminals, gorgeously shaped like boar heads, on the ends of long iron shafts, which were, in turn, joined to a thick horizontal crossbar. The whole thing was a work of high art, and an object of tremendous weight. So when the warrior casually kicked it over, Cullen wanted to clutch at his ears as well as his broken heart.

The big man dropped his shield and went to the room's edge, rooting through pots and chests for the promise of loot. Cullen kept still as rock, a shrew cornered by an adder. Only his eyes were exposed to the smoky air, his heart thudding madly at his ribs.

And then it was over. Just like that. He was finished. Because the warrior noticed him. Perhaps the flames outside reflected on his eyes, causing them to twinkle like stars beneath the dark furs.

Maybe the warrior, inured to the smoke, caught the persistent whiff of goat shit that ever clung to Cullen's skin. Either way, he was betrayed, and the big man's helmeted head tilted slowly up, the broad face rotating, glaring directly at the sleeping space. At the boy concealed within. That boy, ever the disappointment, pissed his braca, warmth flowing down his thighs.

The warrior grunted as he sidled across the roundhouse. His feet crunched and embers flew as he stepped straight through the fireplace. Cullen, rapt in his terror, pushed up onto his knees, shedding his mother's cloak, brandishing his blade in a hand that violently trembled.

'Come, little friend,' the warrior said, flashing a grin that was a crescent of glowing white below the thick whiskers of a black moustache and prominent nose in which a big, golden ring shone. He spoke in the common tongue, though his accent was not of the Atrebates. Without his shield, he had a free hand, and he held it out, gesturing with flicking fingers for Cullen to join him. 'Put down the weapon, little friend.'

Cullen gripped the knife so hard his knuckles ached. 'I... I'll stick you,' he managed to blurt, though he knew the threat was absurd.

The warrior laughed. 'If you come without a fight, little friend, I can protect you. Do the right thing, and you will be spared, on my word.'

'Your word?' Cullen hissed through his teeth, remembering what had been done to Calleva. Yet the ropes of twisted bronze at the man's neck and wrists were not lost on him. Nor was the mail vest that covered a fine red tunic, or the bronze brooch at his burly right shoulder, fastening a long cloak of dark green. At the right hip hung a long sword in an elaborately decorated scabbard, dangling from a belt of bronze hoops that winked as he moved. This was no foot soldier. These were the trappings of authority. Of nobility, even.

'Come, boy, I am losing patience. I am a known man. A man of renown. Branna is my name, and these spears,' he twitched his wrist so that the point of his own spear jerked back in the direction of the doorway, 'are mine to command.'

'You'll spare me?' Cullen murmured, his words constricted by the weight of fear pressing cool and remorseless upon his chest.

Branna took a tentative step closer, the horse master and the skittish colt. Cullen, paralysed by indecision, remained rooted to the spot, as unable to fight as he was to flee. All that moved was his gaze, and it drifted to the light beyond the warrior, to the outside world he knew he might never again see. Smoke still roiled there, bodies criss-crossing in the haze. Screams still rent the air, metal still clashed. Then one figure came out of the dirty mist, swaying alone by the building's entrance. It was Fi, his half-sister, gaunt-faced and strangely unbalanced, faltering. Her eyes seemed sleepy and unfocused, as though she strolled in the dreaming realm. She still had the daisy-chain about her neck, but it had been joined by a ragged slash in her belly. Those bleary eyes drifted down to stare, blinking, at the wound, her hands clutching at either side as though she tried to keep the contents from spilling out.

And in that moment his horror distilled into something utterly pure. The gods were laughing. And he hurled the skinning knife.

He had been taught what to do. Hours in the dust circle with blunted blades, hours in the forest spotting boars for the hunters, hours in the paddocks, striking invisible marks from the ground and from the saddle. Every member of every tribe was taught to fight as soon as they were old enough to lift a weapon. Even with so modest a blade, he should have given an account of himself. Perished in such a way as to impress the ancestors with his bravery or skill. But all that had gone. All the practice and preparation. Seared to ash in the time it took for the Catuvellauni to stalk past the post carvings, the cinders scattered on a breeze made of white-hot grief as sweet Fi had clutched hopelessly at her guts. He was mindless now.

Unthinking and uncaring. A cornered animal in the gloom. So he threw his feeble knife for all he was worth, and he leapt from the beaver cloak like a crazed dog, hurling himself at Branna as he screamed the little girl's name.

And Branna moved.

He was quick, the warrior. So quick, in fact, that both Cullen and his knife missed their mark. As he lunged, he sensed only the great hulking form as a malevolent presence at his shoulder as the Catuvellauni side-stepped, sprightly as a stoat. Cullen braced himself, even as he blundered past, expecting the bright spear tip to explode through his chest or stomach at any moment. But the blow, when it came, was blunt and hard, behind and above his left ear, and he knew he had been felled by a cuff from Branna's meaty palm. Down he went, tumbling in a welter of limbs and grunts, kicking up sparks as he careened through the fireplace. He collided with the compacted earth, dust tainting his mouth and nose. There, at arm's length, was the skinning knife, gossamered in grey ash and impotent as its owner. He snatched it up, much good it would do. Footsteps scuffed the floor, heralding Branna's advance. Cullen twisted onto his back as his skull thrummed. Outside, the fires licked up, roaring like beasts, filling the roundhouse with new light, and he could see his own death in Branna's glittering eyes. Up went his arms, as if they might shield him from the killing thrust, the knife in his hand looking suddenly like a toothpick as the great spear trained on him in reply, the leaf-shaped point gleaming like molten gold.

'You had your chance, little...' Branna's words faltered as he lurched suddenly, skittering forward as if performing an impromptu dance. But his legs were running away with him, one over another, and his body, weighted as it was by weapon and mail, seemed unable to catch up. And then he was toppling, down and down, like a felled oak, the spear clattering away to the side, its intricate carvings of birds and cats grimy with ash, and Branna kept coming, until what light there was had been utterly eclipsed, and Cullen thrust out his arms, screwed up his eyes, and tried to shrink into the earth, turning his head away from the inevitable crush.

The air left him, pummelled clear in a heartbeat. He was sure his arms had snapped like dry twigs. He felt like the grain beneath a quern stone, such was the press of man and armour, the life squeezed slowly from his body. His ribs crackled, echoing the burning thatch outside. His mouth opened and closed like a landed fish, though no breath would come.

Branna was slumped across him. Impossibly heavy. Rough whiskers grated against the fresh skin of Cullen's face, the smell of ale and garlic wafting from the Catuvellauni, pungent at such close quarters. The cheek piece of Branna's helmet dug into Cullen's temple, the stout terminals of the big man's torc pushed like knuckles into the flesh below his chin. There was liquid around the torc, the junction of their necks sticky and wet, and he wondered if the braided bronze had pierced him.

Cullen waited for the warrior to push himself away. Hoped for it, though he knew it would spell his death, for at least he would be afforded one final breath. Yet Branna did not move. He lay, inert, like a massive log.

The slickness at Cullen's neck, increasing by the moment, provided assistance, for it greased the moving parts, letting him extricate first his head, then shoulders, sliding gradually out from under the warrior. It was painstaking and painful, so crushed had he been, but that first lung-full of air might have been taken on a snow-capped peak, so fresh, so crisp did it feel. Three or four huge gasps later and he was able to complete the task, digging his nails into the dirt and using his arms as levers. He hauled his lower body from beneath the big man, a fraction at a time. Finally, with an almighty heave and a jolt that almost compelled Cullen to knee himself in the mouth, his legs were free. All of a panic, he rolled onto his front and up onto his knees, remembering as he went the wetness at his neck. He looked down. A dark stain had spread like blooming petals across his chest. He noticed the odour for the first time. The metallic tang of fresh blood. He patted himself frantically, probing the contours of throat and collar and sternum, panting uncontrollably, expecting to lose consciousness at any given second. Only when his searches proved fruitless, when he understood that the blood was not his own, did he manage to rein in his reeling mind, and force his gaze down to Branna.

The warrior lay where he had collapsed. His head was turned to the side, facing Cullen, and his eyes were closed, his face serene, so that he looked, for all the world, like he had drifted into a pleasant slumber. Cullen might have believed it, too, if it was not for the slender skinning knife that protruded from the soft flesh beneath Branna's chin. And the blood. So much blood. It was the same blood, he now understood, that daubed his own chest, but it had not stopped leaking from Branna's thick neck. It coursed, hot and dark, like a river of the underworld, filling the cracks in the compacted earth, its long fingers creeping round the strewn debris of the fireplace. Bloody rivulets extended about pots and cooking stones, curled round lumps of charred wood and the utensils now scattered like so many augury bones. It stretched out to touch Cullen's knees, and trace crimson lines about Branna's still limbs, and it seeped beneath the iron fire-dog. Cullen stared at the black object that had stood in the room's epicentre, and suddenly reality dawned. The warrior had tripped on the fallen frame. He had advanced so rapidly to the kill that he had not noticed the fire-dog and his toe must have snagged, causing the pell-mell stumble that had ended in an accidental stabbing.

The gods were indeed laughing. Cullen scrambled to his feet, his mind slow to clear. Blood everywhere. A dead warrior. A dead sister. But he was still alive. He slapped himself – once, twice – across the cheek, trying to clear the daze that had taken hold. Time to flee. He stooped quickly, grasping up Branna's long spear, and turned for the doorway. The light was dimming again, the sky clogged with blackening smoke as more buildings were torched. At least he might use the filthy haze to screen his escape. Hope flared within him.

He heard the blow as much as felt it. A wail that echoed around and around the high beams, dissipating only when he crumpled, and he realised the sound had come from his own mouth. The floor was rising towards him. He made to bring up the spear, but it had gone, loosed by inexplicably numb fingers to clatter upon the hard earth. He was on his knees now, then on his side, curling about a pain that enveloped every morsel of his flesh. He felt snot cascade out of one nostril in a gelatinous line, watched it dangle, dabbing the dust before retracting with his suddenly strained breaths. His stomach lurched, the world spun. Darkness descended.

CHAPTER THREE

Cullen stared into the dark.

He felt himself sway from side to side, weightless, floating, and he imagined giant hands cradling him, conveying him, surely, to the Otherworld, there to await the next life. His father had been there these past years. Perhaps he had already moved on. The prospect of a reunion, in the warm and endless realm of the gods and the ancestors, made him smile as he gently rocked. Up and up and up.

His mother came into focus. She smiled, a loving, reassuring gesture. She could be a hard woman, had iron in her veins, was born to the saddle, trained to the hunt, and skilled with shield and spear. A matriarch, leader of their little tribe-within-a-tribe, respected by nobility and known to the king himself. Yet the smile she reserved for Cullen was marked by warmth and affection. Her green eyes glimmered against the red curls of her long hair, and every weathered line of her face crinkled with happiness as he grinned back. Still smiling, she threw her arms wide so that she could gather him up, and he let the rocking motion move him, desperate for her protective embrace. But her hands closed too quickly, clasping instead at either side of his face. Her long fingertips pushed into his hairline, palms cold on his cheeks. She pressed, gently at first, kneading his flesh, then harder, beginning to squeeze at the bones beneath. Cullen grunted, slightly surprised, and he made to pull away but found himself helpless. His mother was still smiling as her grip tightened. Cullen heard himself yelp, but she did not falter. The fingers pressed harder still, grinding at his temples as though they made to burrow into his skull, and now he was crying, begging her to release him, but still that smile, that implacable smile, beamed down, unflinching. The pressure was immense. He felt his eyes burn and knew that they would be crushed to jelly as the sockets gave way. He imagined his brains spattering his clothes.

He screamed. Or at least he tried to scream. All that came out was a muffled groan. Then she was gone. Thin air. Darkness remained, and the pain in his head, and the persistent swaying.

A jolt shuddered through his whole body. The sense of floating vanished. Now he could feel his own weight. His head pounded, searing and relentless. He tasted the tang of blood on his tongue. It was all so real, so stark. And the swaying started again, except this time he knew that he was not being lifted to the clouds, but drawn on the back of a cart, the stink of the horses ripe in his nostrils, the bouncing of the wheels jarring his bones.

One side of his body felt free, touched by the air, while the other pressed upon something hard, and he realised he was lying on his side. The cartwheels rumbled through ruts or over tree roots, traces jangling, and stabs of pain beset him like a hundred bee stings. Voices, gruff and low, carried to him from all sides, but he did not look up. Understanding had dawned. The smell of his burning village was ripe in his nostrils. The memory of little Fi tumbled into his mind. The daisies hanging at her neck as she wandered amid the chaos, her short life leaking onto the ash-dusted grass.

The cart lumbered on, and Cullen lay there, numb. He clutched at his knees, curling in on the pain, and on his hatred, fostering it, nurturing it, vowing revenge.

It was still dark when he woke again, though this time there was a rawness to his senses that told him the fog of dreams had lifted. Thoughts continued to flutter, difficult to catch or harness, but the pain and the cold and the twinkling night sky were real enough. He lay there, ankle, hip and shoulder numb against the base of the cart, head tilted up so that he could see the stars. Occasionally those bright specks would vanish, obscured by treetops, only to wink again, constant in their places as he had thought the elements of his own life had been constant. He could have laughed at that, at his own pitiable naïvety, and a knot of sickening grief twisted deep in his guts. It had all changed. All been shattered, utterly. He recalled his mother coming to him. It had been a dream, he knew, but if he had learned anything from the Wise Ones it had been that the dead speak to us in our dreams. The dead. The dead.

A ragged shape loomed over him, startlingly close, and he saw that a man walked beside the cart, his hand resting on the high side. Even in the dark, Cullen could make out long hair, a forked beard and a spear bobbing high.

'She died,' Cullen croaked, 'didn't she?'

The man's head turned, his eyes flashing bright in the moonlight. 'Who?'

'My mother.'

'In the village? Many died.' Grunts of acknowledgement greeted the words, betraying the presence of many more warriors, set just back, moving in the deeper dark.

'She was tall,' Cullen persisted. 'Her hair was long and red. She wore gold.'

The head nodded. 'I know the one. Fought like a fiend.'

'Dead,' someone else offered from the murk. 'Speared in the neck.'

Fork-beard shrugged. 'On the pyre with the rest. All the rest. It's on to the next life for them.'

Cullen expected to cry but found he could not. He was empty inside. A husk. Numb and dry. 'Why not...?' he tailed off, rendered mute by a sudden lance of guilt.

'Why not you? I clubbed you hard enough to scramble your brains, that's for sure, but I ever was the merciful kind.' That last was met by raucous laughter, and the warrior allowed himself a low chuckle at what was evidently a fine jest. 'And the fact that you killed the Slayer, boy.'

Cullen had touched fingertips gingerly to his throbbing skull. A lump, the size of a quail's egg, protruded above his right temple. 'Slayer?'

'Branna the Slayer.'

All at once Cullen's mind was assailed by fragments of memory, flapping from all sides like rooks startled from high boughs, loud and frantic and blurry. Branna's face resolved before him. The hard eyes. The disbelieving grimace as Cullen's knife plunged home. The weight of the massive Catuvellauni, pressing down on him like a landslide. The concoction of ale and garlic and blood.

'A named man,' Fork-beard was saying. 'One of Caratacos's chiefs.' He laughed again, evidently incredulous. 'The gods favour you, boy. The Slayer was a terrible force. Ferocious as a bear. Named for his fame, for the heads he has taken.'

'I did not mean it,' Cullen mumbled. 'It was an accident. A mistake.' His head throbbed so powerfully that it was a struggle to pin down the words, but he knew the truth of them nevertheless. He had shown neither courage nor skill. A lucky coward, that's all he was. By rights, he should clamber out of the cart and throw himself down before the horses' hooves. Pulverised to a deserved death. *But then I am too cowardly even for that.*

'Did not mean it?' the warrior scoffed in the crisp dark. 'You are guided. We all are. By the gods of war and of blood and of pride and of the earth and the wind and the afterlife.' He thumped the side of the vehicle with a ring-encrusted fist. 'Of course you did not mean it! Branna the Slayer was a great man. Until that moment you were shit on his shoe. But the gods play games beyond our understanding, and you have slain the Slayer. The kill is undeniable, and it is yours to own.'

—

Deep night, and the harsh stench of smoke and corruption hung like a heavy blanket as they entered Calleva. Cullen, sitting up now, had to swallow hard against the sourness settling at the back of his throat. He peered into the streets, abetted by well-placed braziers and by the bright face of a rose moon, resting his chin against the side of the cart. Even in the gloom there were unmistakable landmarks. The roundhouses, long halls, warehouses, wide junctions and carved way-stones that had always made this place so sophisticated, so vital. A hive of industry and commerce. Except now the irresistible buzz had diminished to a low, almost heart-breaking drone. Faces of a defeated people peered nervously from amongst the debris and from narrow alleyways, like lingering ghosts, eyeing the cart and its escort of grim spearmen with deserved worry. Every few paces there were the charred shells of once-proud buildings, reduced to black monsters, clawing at the stars. In places, where the fight had been fiercest, whole areas resembled slaughter yards, so thickly were the corpses scattered. They were piled and tangled, large and small, in various twisted poses, macabre monuments to the power of one tribe and the humbling of another.

'Destroyed,' Cullen muttered to himself, struggling to keep his jaw from lolling with the shock of it. As if to push the point home, he noticed they were passing the Roman trader's house. Lines of amphorae, large and small, stood outside, as fastidiously arranged as ever. Except the Roman himself was there too. Sprawled before his wares, bathed in his own entrails.

'Hardly,' the warrior's voice answered, just behind. Fork-beard was still walking beside the vehicle, strides heavy and rhythmic on the crunching gravel of the road. 'Calleva's a big place, boy. Not as big as Camulodunon, mind, but name me somewhere that is. You know how long it would take to torch everything here?' He flashed a wolfish grin, a white crescent in that slab of a face. 'And why would Togodubnos burn his new town?'

His new town. The words reverberated in Cullen's head like a hammer blow. This was enemy territory now. A day's work, and the old empire of the Catuvellauni had been reborn. He had been right, though, Fork-beard. For all that Cullen's eye seemed inexorably drawn to scenes of destruction, there were incongruous patches of serenity in between. Cooking fires still smouldering inside untouched homes, wagons laden with goods that would never make it to market, a pair of shoes arranged neatly beside a doorway, freshly scraped skins hung out to dry. Echoes of the life before. Life that had been suddenly, catastrophically, interrupted. But the reminders, too, that it would resume in time. The homes would be rebuilt and reoccupied, the traders would return.

'Besides,' the warrior continued, 'we must take care of our fresh livestock.'

'Livestock?'

'We always have need of slaves, boy.' He indicated the shadowy shapes of the houses, from whence the ghoulish faces still peered. 'Your people will fetch much over in Gaul. The Romans pay well.'

They rumbled into Calleva's heart. Everywhere, the victors roamed, making sure of their prize. Some cleared the streets of battle detritus, others gathered the dead. Spearmen prowled here and there, alive to trouble, and Cullen imagined they would be out on the banked walls too, staring fixedly into the surrounding woods. Guards would be glowering at junctions, standing sentry at the temples and halls, erstwhile bastions of Atrebates authority. Scouts would be further out, scouring the surrounding countryside, flushing stragglers from the undergrowth.

They celebrated, too. The Catuvellauni, having risked all to strike at the very heart of their enemy, were in the mood for song, and the tangled sounds of revelry wafted in and out as the cart crossed the mouths of streets, wide and narrow. In looted homes they imbibed what strong drink they could find and recounted the day's heroism with brash voices and braying laughter. In ransacked yards and gutted brewhouses and merchants' stores. Most, though, congregated at the palace of King Berikos, the very centre of Calleva, there to hail the man who had brought them so dazzling a victory. Cullen saw all this as the swaying, bumping cart drew to a halt within the shrub-lined, half-circle enclosure that fronted the great rectangular hall. That building was unusual in its size and shape, in the apexed roof and the massive timber doors. Outside, a pair of big braziers flickered, throwing mellow light that cast long shadows up the walls. A huge stag's head, antlers protruding like the branches of a silver birch, was nailed to the lintel, empty eye sockets glowering at the scene of its master's demise. He felt suddenly cold. Casting his gaze about the cart, he noticed a dark pile of skins an arm's length away. He recognised the bundle immediately for what it was, and reached over, biting down on the pain as it rolled like a thunderclap through his head, and unfurled the beaver cloak that had once been his mother's.

'What happened to the king?' Cullen asked Fork-beard as he pulled the cloak about his shoulders. On one side of the enclosure, beyond the manicured plants, the roadside was clogged with unmanned and unhitched chariots. On the other, he noticed a pile of milky white corpses, already stripped of anything worth having. To which tribe they belonged was anyone's guess.

'Old Berikos has gone, boy.' The warrior snapped fingers and words at the rest of the escort. The spearmen and the wagon driver faded into the streets. One younger lad, with a pronounced limp and a scalp shaved close, scuttled through the open doors, plunging into the darkness of the hall.

'Dead?'

Fork-beard shook his head. In the trembling flamelight, Cullen saw that he had a flat nose and wide-set eyes. There were feathers dangling from his earlobes and woven into the cloak at his shoulders. 'Clean vanished.' He turned to wave a meaty hand at an unspecified target. 'Damn these woods. Thick as swill, black as tar. You could hide a whole army in there.' He slapped the side of the cart, tilting back his shaggy head in a bark of laughter. 'By all the dead, that's exactly what we did!'

Cullen felt a sliver of hope. He had never met Berikos, only ever seen him at a distance, but the man was the figurehead of the Atrebates, and suddenly his survival meant a great deal. A last act of defiance in the face of the murderers of Cullen's loved ones.

'No matter,' Fork-beard went on, ignoring the look of triumph Cullen feared must be plastered across his own face. 'Caratacos will snare him in the end. Always does. He's a clever one, see?'

The assertion stirred something in Cullen, conjuring the image of the open gates, the battle raging within the walls of Calleva instead of out beyond the ditch. What were the earthworks for if not to keep an enemy without? 'How did he do this?'

Fork-beard grinned. 'Caratacos had men inside, posing as traders. Opened the town at the right time.' He looked up at the hall. 'Now Berikos is gone, and we all of us have new kings. Togodubnos and Caratacos, may the gods keep them strong.'

'Is not Cunobelin your ruler?'

'Crossed to the next life, boy. Last winter. Togodubnos, the eldest son, rules in his father's place, out of Verlamion. High king of all the tribes, that's what we work towards.'

'And Caratacos?'

The limping warrior with the shorn pate emerged from the hall and exchanged a meaningful glance with Fork-beard. 'Ask him yourself!' He looked, almost fearfully, up at the baleful skull, then back at Cullen. 'Gods go with you, boy. You'll need them.'

Just like that, Cullen found himself alone in the light of the hall's torches, save the whickering palfreys and the piled dead. He stared into the guttering gloom. Were they mad, these Catuvellauni, or merely so arrogant that they believed he might simply be discarded like one of the corpses? Left to his own devices and yet incapable of the initiative to escape. It was true that his head still hurt, but he would be damned if he was going to take his ease on this abandoned vehicle and await his fate.

He shuffled on his rump, cursing viciously as his tender skull made clear its desire for him to stay put, and let his legs drop over the back of the cart. There they dangled for the time it took for him to bridle his fear and steady his resolve. He knew Calleva well enough. Even though its conquerors seemed to swarm the streets, they could not possibly hope to cover every yard and pen and alley. He drew in a deep, almost painful breath, patted himself down, checking for missed wounds that might slow his run, and slithered down to the hard earth. The pain seemed to fill him, as if a sluice gate had opened in his head, letting it run in agonising rivulets all the way to fingers and toes. His guts churned and his head swam, and he gripped the cart, bracing legs that suddenly seemed empty of bones. But the nausea ebbed as quickly as it had flowed, and, panting sharply, he forced himself to stand tall.

The magpie's black eye twinkled in the brazier's glow. It was watching, judging him, from the far side of the bushes, perched upon the wicker mesh that formed the side of one of the chariots.

'What do you want from me?' Cullen hissed, flapping a hand that the bird duly ignored.

'The creature recognises one of its own.'

Cullen wrenched himself about so violently that the pain in his head seemed to distil to a needle of white-heat that lanced, eye-wateringly, from temple to temple. He gasped, the world rolled again, but this time he clung tight to his wits, grinding his teeth and refusing to crumple, though the urge threatened to overwhelm. Because even in the feeble, tremulous light, he knew who had spoken. A matter of instinct, perhaps, or a fatalist's presumption following a day of compounding doom. Or maybe it was the magpie. That denizen of the afterlife had followed his lurching path to this place. Its presence now could mean only one thing.

And that was why Cullen, with his eyes clamped shut against the pain, managed to utter one word.

'A murderer, am I?' replied Caratacos of the Catuvellauni. 'Personally, I prefer conqueror, but a man cannot please everyone.'

Cullen forced himself to straighten. He gripped the back of the cart as he rounded it. There, beneath the stag's head, was the man himself. A man Cullen had never laid eyes upon, but whose identity was not in question. The magpie's appearance had foretold it.

Cullen pushed away from the cart. A score of bristling spear points followed him. They had emerged from the hall at their master's back. Shorter, heavier throwing spears too, and slings and axes and swords. A battle-standard bearing writhing bronze snakes atop a long pole, bobbed from a pelt-carpeted shoulder. It was as if Berikos's palace, offended by the interlopers, had decided to vomit up the entire invading army, and out they poured, to the left and right of their leader, hard men with fame on their names and blood on their hands and death in their eyes.

At the centre, tall and lean, Caratacos, son of High King Cunobelin, took a forward pace. The rose moon cast a thick pall of shadow over him, and the braziers threw light at his back, so that he was more silhouette than flesh. 'They tell me you bested my man. Branna was his name.' He cocked his head to the side. 'Come, do not be shy.'

Cullen forced his gaze to rise. There was something familiar about Caratacos. He nodded.

Caratacos came closer. The shadows slid away, detail flooding the shape in their wake, and Cullen found himself looking into the face of a man around the age of thirty. His hair was long and black, braided at the sides, into which had been woven black feathers, small and large, the crow and the raven both. His black moustaches curved around a wide, thin-lipped mouth, running down as far as his square chin, and protective symbols, in blue and red, had been daubed across his cheeks. He wore no cloak, instead displaying an exquisite corselet of mail that encased his entire torso, the plaid tunic of blue and grey beneath only discernible by his sleeves. Deep blue swirls coloured his neck, their meanings obscured at the throat by a thick golden torc, and at the left side by the pale line of a vicious-looking but long-healed scar. He was as magnificent to Cullen's eyes as he was hideous. A battle-god made flesh. A spear-commander. A death-giver. Beloved of Andraste, the war goddess. Cullen saw again the man at Calleva's gates who had pranced adroitly along his chariot's traces to balance on the yoke.

'Branna was my shield-man,' Caratacos said, resting a hand on the pommel of his sword's ornate hilt, its long scabbard engraved with snakes at the chape. 'My right hand in the charge.'

In that moment Cullen was sure he would die. Certain that the great blade would sweep free and make an end of his miserable existence before he had so much as a chance to close his eyes.

But Caratacos pursed his lips, as if considering some answerless riddle. 'Why the gods see fit to touch you, I know not, but then I am merely a humble farmer.'

Hatred. It was all Cullen felt. All he could imagine feeling for this creature who had caused the deaths of his entire family, his entire clan. He should have been terrified in the face of Caratacos, like a mouse quaking in the shadow of a cat, yet the natural instincts to run, to weep, to beg, were overwhelmed in this instant by something so much stronger that it rendered him utterly, surprisingly mute. Loathing, pure as mountain water, keen as a freshly sharpened blade, blunted the stabs of fear.

'You are no farmer,' he heard himself say. 'You are a murderer.'

Caratacos grinned at that, showing neat, white teeth. 'We are all of us murderers when the need arises. We till our fields and hunt our meat and raise our children.' He glanced at his warriors in evident amusement. 'And, every so often, we deal with our enemies.' That last was met with a chorus of gravelly laughter.

'You killed my family,' Cullen said. He had nothing to lose now. He would die, one way or the other, but he would not go to face his mother, to face little Cora, and tell them that he had failed to speak truth to the man responsible for their slaughter.

'War kills many,' Caratacos answered flippantly.

'Children.'

'War does not discern adult from child.'

'Men can discern,' Cullen retorted, tears hot in his eyes as he imagined Fi scrabbling to keep her guts in her belly. 'Men know the difference.'

The only thing sharper than Caratacos's sword was his stare. Those eyes, pale in the flames, burned bright with intelligence and scorn. 'By rights, this land belongs to the Catuvellauni. The pretender, Berikos, was emboldened by his ties with Rome. By my father's ties, also. Those ties have now been cut.' He swept an arm expansively towards the road beyond. 'Come, you think me a villain? Do you hear the screams of your women? I protect them. I am a man of honour. Calleva will rise again, under my authority.' He raised a broad palm to render Cullen's bitter retort stillborn. 'And I honour the gods for placing victory in my grasp. The blood you spilled today was portentous, have no doubt.' He turned to one of his men. 'He comes back to Camulodunon. Arthmael will wish to see him.'

With that, he turned and stalked away, plunging into the smoky night, leaving the injured and heartbroken boy to stare impotently at his back. Caratacos of the Catuvellauni. The man Cullen despised above all others. The man who had overthrown his king and subjugated his tribe. The man who had slaughtered his family as though they were spring-feast piglets. In that moment, before the moon and stars, hatred bloomed within him, pulsating and raw. He let loose a howl of pain, and wept.

CHAPTER FOUR

Dawn saw the Catuvellauni on the move. Parties of spearmen, arranged into groups of nine, went out into the countryside in the wake of mounted scouts, there to scour the ditches, trees and lanes for wounded friends and regrouping foes. A substantial garrison remained behind the rampart to stamp the authority of Great Cunobelin's line upon the beleaguered Atrebates, but most of Caratacos's horde marched north and east, beginning a trek that would have taken the better part of a quarter moon in comfortable conditions, and was now hampered from the first by a sudden, violent downpour that seethed upon Calleva's thatch and formed deep pools at the roadside. They pressed on, nevertheless, a cavalcade of warriors, the painted snakes upon their shields beginning to blur and slide in white rivulets like melting snow. They leaned hard into the rain, amongst chariots and lumbering wagons, knocking shields, miserable hounds, clanging iron and whickering horses. The commanders snarled oaths and barked orders, and whips cracked on the flanks of steaming livestock, and the banners of stag and badger and boar and eagle bobbed high above it all, as if surveying the land ahead.

Cullen was as drenched in grief as he was in drizzle. They were a thousand strong, he reckoned, though his mental tally was padded by significant guesswork, given the restrictive view from the back of the swaying cart. Whatever the true number, it was the most awesome demonstration of power he had ever witnessed. Growing up just south of his nation's capital, he had seen hunting parties, royal escorts and warbands aplenty. This was something else entirely. An army of conquest. One whose assembly would inspire song and verse for generations to come. It would have been magnificent to Catuvellauni eyes. As it was, Cullen stared at the noisy procession with a mixture of sour resignation, bubbling hatred and, as the vehicle rumbled through one of the main openings in the outer rampart, growing trepidation. He was leaving his home, perhaps for the final time.

There was a press of bodies around the gates. The elderly mostly, for the young men had been slain or driven into the forest, while the children and younger women had been corralled like cattle in some of the larger buildings, there to be bound, inspected and divided between Caratacos's nobles, or driven like so many geese, bound for one of the slave markets on the coast.

'They fled to the edges,' came a voice as dry as the rustling of fallen leaves.

Cullen twisted round. He shared the back of the bumping vehicle with two others, an adult and a child, but that was as much as he could ascertain, given their silence and the deep hoods they wore against the rain. Now, as the larger figure pulled back the oiled cowl, Cullen gaped in astonishment. The face leering back at him seemed positively ancient. The man's cheeks were blotchy, lips thin and mottled purple. The lines around his mouth had deepened to crevasses over the years, and his snow-white hair was thinning in clumps, revealing a piebald scalp beneath. But none of that had accounted for Cullen's surprise. The old man, he now saw, was blind. More than simply blind. There were hideous, puckered caverns where his eyes should have been. Where his eyes had indeed been, before something – someone – had gouged them out of the skull like mussels from a shell.

Cullen knew his mouth lolled open, though he was unable to shut it. 'Edges?'

'Of town,' the old man said, hunkering deeper into the embrace of the heavy cloak that was fastened at his reedy neck with a large oak-sprig brooch. 'The gates were guarded, the buildings were burning, so they fled as far from the centre as they could.' He shrugged, making the saggy skin at his throat quiver like a chicken's wattle. 'Now they're gathering to return.'

'To be slaughtered,' Cullen said bitterly.

'To what end?' the old man asked. 'No, they will return. Folk must live here for it to thrive. Caratacos will not lay waste to a sturdy settlement. It'll bring him wealth. He'll be hammering his own coins here before long.'

'How can...?'

'How can I see all this?' The blind man brandished a grin that was more gum than tooth. 'The moon told me. The moon and the trees and the beasts, they all whisper their secrets.'

Cullen could not help but rise at that, peering over the side of the wagon, beyond the empty outer earthworks, to the impenetrable woodland that clogged and darkened the land. Did those brooding branches really watch over everything? Really share their knowledge with a chosen few?

'But mostly I tell him,' the second of Cullen's new companions said, in a thickly accented version of the common tongue. He drew back his own hood.

Cullen slumped down, sweeping a hand beneath his rump to flatten the folds of stitched beaver pelt. He looked at the one who had spoken, though it was not easy to tear himself away from the ghoulish visage of the ancient's empty eye sockets. What he saw struck him dumb. Since being lifted into the vehicle in the hoary first light, the second person had remained concealed, face utterly submerged in shadow. Now that more of him had been revealed, it was plain that this was no child. Young, certainly. Early twenties at most, to judge by the freshness of the round face and the wispy fluff at the end of his blunt chin. Yet he was tiny. Cullen wondered if he might be a dwarf.

The little man pushed stubby fingers through black hair that was tightly curled. 'Born of a human mother and a piskie father,' he said with a sardonic grin, nut-brown eyes bright as they fixed on Cullen. Then he pulled up the hem of his cloak to reveal braca that had been stitched at the cuffs and folded back where nothing filled them. 'Born without legs.' He waggled thick eyebrows. 'The rest is good, believe me. Ask the girls in Camulodunon.'

'Becan,' the old man chided, 'mind that impudent tongue. What has your mother told you?'

'She tells me a lot, Drest, and very little is of use.'

The sightless fellow, Drest, tutted softly, turning to address Cullen. 'I apologise for my friend, here. He was in the service of Cunobelin, no less, and it made his head grow somewhat.'

'But not my legs, alas,' Becan said, winking.

Cullen could not help but smile, though the gesture brought an immediate pang of guilt. 'You were at Cunobelin's court?'

'As a slave,' Becan said, sourness coming into his tone.

'The high king,' explained Drest, 'revered those touched by magic.'

Becan patted one of his stumps. 'What's more magical than half a man?' He laughed bitterly, as if the notion were risible. 'It's the only reason he kept me alive. A thing. Not a person. Not an animal. Not a spirit creature. A product of all.' He glanced up at the slate-grey skies. 'Of the very earth.'

Cullen recognised the accent from seasonal traders at Calleva. They would come with furs, cheeses and weaponry, distinct for their curls and swarthy complexions. 'You are from the far west?'

Becan nodded. 'Silures. Beyond Sabrina's Sea. We had raided inland, navigating the waterway as we sacked Dobunni settlements. The Catuvellauni had the same idea. They came from the east and we met one black night. Blundered into one another.' He laughed mirthlessly. 'The gods are capricious.'

'You,' Cullen could not keep the incredulity from his tone, 'raided?'

'I was only there as a talisman,' Becan explained, 'to bring luck to the venture. Next thing I know, I'm in the presence of

Cunobelin, the Sun Hound, chieftain of more tribes than he could count.' He spread his hands in a gesture of resignation. 'But he treated me well enough. After all, a half-man appearing from the chaos of battle? If that is not a gift from Morrigan herself, then what is?'

'If only Caratacos granted you the same reverence,' Drest muttered irritably. 'We would travel in comfort.'

'Peace, Drest,' Becan said, before his large, brown eyes shifted back to Cullen. 'I am kept to honour his father's memory.'

'Kept like a pet,' Drest said scornfully. 'He serves now as my eyes, the lucky little fellow.'

Becan shook his head, grinning, and it was plain that this was not the first time they had debated his evidently waning importance at the court of the Catuvellauni. He leaned forward suddenly, eyes narrowing. 'Tell me. Did you really kill Branna?'

'Yes.'

'Good,' said Becan, eyes spangled. 'A piece of toad shit, that one.'

'I did not mean to,' Cullen began.

'Do we ever mean anything?' Drest intoned archly.

'Hold this,' Becan said, thrusting a hand at Cullen, 'against your head. It looks like a spider's woven her egg sack above your ear.'

Cullen glanced down at the scrap of cloth lying flat in Becan's palm. Its surface had been smeared with a moist-looking paste of pale green, white and yellow. 'What is it?'

'Poultice of daisy blossom, olive oil and butter,' the legless man replied. 'It will reduce the swelling. We are charged with putting you back together, Drest and I.'

Cullen took the cloth and plastered it against his head. There was an instant cooling sensation. 'For what?'

'For that which awaits.'

And what might lay in wait gathered like a black cloud in Cullen's mind as the days took them eastwards, into the ancient lands of the Trinovantes. Those lands were flat in the main, so that Cullen could see for miles in the column's wake, to the distant lines of hills they had crossed, appearing now like vast black serpents beneath the brooding sky. The kind landscape meant the roads were good, too. Many of them straight as spear hafts and wide enough for traffic to pass in both directions. These stretches, conjured from the minds of the Wise and carved from the raw wilderness through the toil of slaves long returned to the mud, were underlaid with a mesh of hazel fronds, tamped with chalk or flint, and paved with smooth river cobbles that would withstand the worst winters or the heaviest hooves. It meant Caratacos's great and cumbersome procession, in spite of the occasional interruption by gurgling stream or ageless track or woody gully, made good progress, devouring the miles with a renewed gusto. Thus, after a further two days, a deal more rain, and a patchwork of fenced and hedged arable fields, tell-tale columns of smoke smudged the eastern horizon. So many columns, indeed, that their provenance was clear.

'Camulodunon?' Cullen asked, rising onto his knees to get a better look beyond the driver of their cart. Perhaps a mile ahead, through a gap set in a high palisade of sharpened stakes that bristled on the crest of a formidable earthen bank, he could see scores of thatch-work cones, the rooftops of what had once been the capital of the Trinovantes.

'What you see is a mere tick on the cat's chin.'

It was Drest who had answered. Cullen looked down at him. The words were a surprise at first, but he imagined himself becoming suddenly blind. He supposed he would forever remember Calleva in all its detail, however faded the memory became. 'A tick?'

Drest brandished his empty gums. 'These homes you see form the western edge of my city. Look to the left and the right.'

Cullen did as he was told, and saw only the earthwork, rising above the dark line of a ditch. It stretched away, seemingly unending, to both the north and south. 'I see only the bank.'

'Our great walls. They hide a multitude.' He grinned again. 'You'll see, boy. You'll see.'

So it was with great interest that Cullen took his first proper sight of Camulodunon. The cart had stalled in its place in the great column, waiting as men and horses, wagons and chariots, oxen and baggage carriers all filed cumbersomely across the flat, open space of the greensward and through the gap in the high outer earthwork. But eventually it was the turn of the mud-caked vehicle with its incongruous burden. Blind man, frightened boy and legless talisman held themselves up against the soggy timber sides and absorbed the slowly unfolding tableau.

It was a fortress city, the like of which Cullen had never imagined, let alone seen. The earthen banks shielding that initial cluster of roundhouses were, in essence, part of a system of deep dykes, facing westwards, running as far as the eye could see, and pausing only for natural defensive features like valleys and dense patches of woodland. There were more gullies beyond, set parallel to the first, the spoil from their excavation used to construct sheer escarpments on the inner edges, so that any attacker foolish enough to find himself at the foot of the ditch would look up at a defender looming some twenty feet above. As Cullen's cart rocked and lurched through these sequential lines of defence, the road deliberately squeezed to control traffic at each crossing point, he noticed more ditches, placed laterally to the west-facing dykes, some blocking the way entirely so that the cart had to negotiate a sharp corner to keep to the roadway. The presence of spearmen at these junctions made it clear that their purpose was to control the entrances to Camulodunon. He imagined one of the war chariots making a mad dash into the city. No straight lines, as had been the case at Calleva. Each kink in the road would offer a torrent of trouble and slow a thrashing gallop to a precarious canter. The thought made him shudder.

'She lies,' Drest said, breathing deep of the air, 'on a bountiful stretch of land between two wide and fast-flowing rivers. One to the north and east, the other to the south.'

Which explained, thought Cullen, the extensive works to the west. The dykes' function was to plug the only gap left by nature. 'Can the rivers not be crossed?'

'In certain places,' Becan put in, 'but there are more ditches where the water can be forded.'

The column funnelled through the various checkpoints, turned the necessary corners and snaked under every spear-bristling platform atop every staked bank, until finally they were allowed through the last, biggest gates. Set on either side, leering down, were a pair of heads, each topping a tall spike. Flashes of white bone showed through the beak-stripped skin. The eye sockets were as empty as Drest's, and the hair had been torn to scrappy tufts, but they were fresh enough to have come from Calleva. Cullen stared up at them. The undertone of creeping dread that clung to his every thought like a second skin began to resolve and harden in his heart, knotting his guts. He pressed a finger to the lump at his temple, letting the pain overtake every other feeling, and forced himself to focus on the dun as it gradually came into view.

Those first thatches, the ones he had glimpsed from a mile out, fell behind as the rest of the sprawling settlement was revealed. The smell struck him first, like a hammer-blow to his nostrils. After days in the damp, open countryside it seemed as if he had shoved his head into a bucket of rich spices in a room full of animal dung and woodsmoke. The roads were empty, on account of the incoming army, but Cullen could see enough folk in the doorways and side streets to know that the city teemed with life. To his palpable disbelief, the city was clearly larger – much larger – than Calleva. A fact he would have considered preposterous only days earlier.

Drest and Becan chattered as Cullen gaped. They told him about the industry and agriculture that flourished on the fertile banks of the twin rivers. And of the houses and workshops and temples that had sprung up in between. Becan explained that the northern river, flowing deep all the way to the sea, was regularly crammed with vessels of every kind, bringing trade and coin to the heart of the settlement. Which was why, Drest continued, a note of regret souring his tone, avaricious eyes had quickly fallen upon the city. He rattled off the names of the old kings of the Trinovantes, telling the tale of how they had claimed the place for their own, establishing a great dynasty that was, for a time, the leading tribe on the island the Romans called Britannia. But, like the Atrebates, they had eventually fallen to a greater power, and now Camulodunon, though still perhaps the greatest dun in all the land, was in the possession of the Catuvellauni.

Drest was warming to his theme, regaling his companions with tales of the fall of the hapless Dubnovellaunos to the warmonger Cunobelin. Cullen let his mind drift, for he had heard it all before during the long, wet miles, and the imagery of the conquered Trinovantes began to meld with his own, painfully similar memories. Dubnovellaunos became Berikos. Drest's martyred ancestors became Cullen's mother and sisters. The brutal picture of Cunobelin wavered and shifted in his mind's eye until the features resolved into the very real visage of the dead king's son, Caratacos. That was why, when he glimpsed a gaudy chariot up ahead, its wheel-spokes chased elaborately with veins of silver and gold, he initially assumed it was all part of the daydream. But then the man standing on its wicker platform made a half turn, nodding to someone familiar, and Cullen knew that he was staring at the reason for it all. The very object of his hate.

The man shone in polished mail, a fist on his belted hip, the other gripping the rail of the gorgeous chariot as the driver coaxed the large grey horse around a pen of quarrelsome geese.

The horse was decorated in the same greens and reds as the chariot, its plaited tail and mane shot through with fine golden wire.

'A god of war,' Becan said, following Cullen's gaze. 'Caratacos,' he added, evidently for Drest's benefit.

The blind Trinovantes nodded. 'The fates decree his greatness.'

Cullen's chest was suddenly tight, a lump snagging in his throat. He wanted to say something, but the words – the very air – would not come. Tears erupted at his eyes, hot and unquenchable.

CHAPTER FIVE

A busy wind whirled the fire's sparks.

It came through the doorway, which was only shielded from the elements by a thin woollen drape that had seen better days, and it whipped about the little roundhouse with a soft whistle. At the room's centre, the flames leapt madly, faded, and leapt again. Embers sprang up about the small cauldron dangling above the fireplace, dancing and twirling all the way into the thatch. Outside, the sky above Camulodunon was a uniform grey, dimming by the hour.

All had been bright when the victorious horde first reached the deep earthworks to the south and west of the settlement. The sun had glittered on the far sea and lone clouds had thrown fast-shifting shadows over the flat lands to the north. But three nights in, and those dark shapes had multiplied and come together, until the land was beginning to suffocate in the gathering gloom that presaged encroaching storms.

The first days in Camulodunon had been a waking dream. The marching column, so loud and vibrant on the road, had dissipated almost as soon as the great gates had groaned open. Fighters had returned to their families and their trades. Farmers had gone back to the outlying fields, there to nurture life instead of end it. The high king's brother had eschewed his war-chariot for matters of state, and the spoils taken from Calleva had been shared out, squirrelled away or melted down. For Cullen, it had been a question of recovery. The lump on his head had throbbed, compelling him in and out of sleep, and in those fitful dreams he had relived what had come to pass at Calleva.

But the pain had eased, and the dreams had gradually receded like summer mist, though an undertone of creeping dread still clung to his every thought like a second skin he could not shed.

He found himself ushered into a house near the centre of Camulodunon. It was a small affair, set in a clearing surrounded by two concentric circles, the outer ring formed of pale standing stones and the inner of wizened trees, painted in tar to keep them frozen for eternity, each a black claw, draped in colourful charms. The area was an old nemeton, according to Becan. A grove of the gods, once known as Avalloc's Shelter, where the Wise practised their rites and the spirits shifted unseen, but since his arrival it had hosted no more activity than a couple of rooting pigs and gangs of children kicking an inflated sheep's bladder between the trees.

It was a half freedom, this new existence. He was not a prisoner in the strictest sense. Could walk, take the air, see the sprawling town, but always he was observed, always the spear-shadows snaked the ground behind. Still, the greatest dun of the Isle of the Mighty did not disappoint. Like Calleva, it was an outward-facing sprawl of the new age, its eyes on the continent beyond the Narrow Sea. It was a place where folk of different creeds walked. Where traders from Gaul and Rome crossed paths with the mountain folk of the far west and the barbaric clans from the cold north, here to trade their whale oils and seal skins. Thus, the roads were not all mud, and the houses were not all round, and the people ate away from the floor, raised up on benches, sideways to the fire instead of directly before it.

Yet here, in his unfurnished little hut, with a modest flame and guards outside, Cullen felt as though he had travelled back in history, to the time when the Isle of the Mighty was the very end of the world. He pulled the beaver cloak tighter about his neck as he watched the glowing specks settle on the straw, each snuffing out in turn, like stars smothered by cloud. One day an ember would burn just that little bit longer than its siblings, and the roundhouse would be a blackened shell by morning. But not this chill night, he thought. Not when the wailing shee rode the breeze in the deep dark. He listened closely as the mournful keening came again, and he knew the spirit sung to him of his slain mother and sisters, consoling and grieving. He whispered silent thanks.

The door flap bunched to one side. 'Is it ready?' Becan asked as he swung into the room on a pair of fine blackthorn crutches.

Cullen looked up and smiled. 'Shall we see?' He pushed off his haunches and peered into the pot, fingers of fragrant steam curling about his face, erased in a heartbeat by the vagary of wind that squeezed through the open slit at the side of the door flap. The stew was dark and hearty. Hunks of venison mingled with pale onion slivers, tumbling together amongst the noisy bubbles. He unhooked a wooden ladle from the cauldron's iron frame and dunked it deep, stirring the thick mixture, puncturing the patches of skin forming on the surface. Purple carrots turned and eddied, rising and falling, glimpsed and gone. He raised a ladle-full to his lips, blowing and sipping almost simultaneously to avoid a scalding.

Becan did not wait for an invitation. He hobbled the few paces to the fire and dropped down eagerly, setting the sticks on the tamped earth. They were polished along the shafts, intricately carved faces grimacing from the handles. 'Pass me a bowl.'

'Where is Drest?'

'Sleeping,' Becan said as he took the steaming meal, cradling its warmth, 'though it is hard to tell.'

Cullen spooned himself a portion and sat back. 'I cannot imagine something like that. Having your eyes taken.'

'The risk a fighter takes, capture. He was first shield, you know. To Grendor the Cruel.'

Cullen looked up in surprise. 'Our poets sung of him.'

'The Eceni hated Grendor,' Becan went on, pausing only to blow upon the stew. 'Despised him. Of course they did. A man does not earn himself such a name without making enemies.

Drest seems a mild old bastard now, but to be a named man in Grendor's band? That took some doing.' He shrugged. 'The Eceni were never likely to treat him gently. When they took him, they took his sight.'

Shaking his head in astonishment, Cullen set to the meal, slurping the viscous concoction with gusto and ignoring the heat that seared the roof of his mouth. It was a fine, filling repast, one of many he had enjoyed since arriving in the great city. Indeed, it had been a surreal time, all told. Swept along on a tide of fear and grief and desperation that had threatened to drown him just a week ago, he had somehow found himself washed up in this rambling settlement, with a roof over his head, a fire that never went out and a belly that was never empty. He had been given a new tunic and braca. Plain and undyed, but well made for all that. His weary body was well rested, and his skin was cleaner than he could remember. He looked down at his hands. No grime or flaking blood crusted the nails, and the scrapes on his forearms had mostly thickened into reddish brown scabs.

'Why am I here?' he asked after a short while.

Becan looked up sharply. 'Why are you here?'

Cullen stared fixedly at the man whose very presence set him on edge. They had become friends – or something like it – in the days of travel and rest. But the mere fact that he was Silures was unsettling, his obvious incapacity and jovial nature making him an unsuitable candidate for a jailer. So Cullen had watched and listened, bided his time, and now he lunged with the question across the flames as though it were a blade, his objective this precise reaction. The knee-jerk echo of his own words was dissemblance enough. 'Why,' he repeated slowly, 'am I here, Becan? In this house.' He plucked at his tunic with his free hand. 'With clean clothes and good food. Why? What kind of imprisonment is this?'

Becan's eyes wrinkled, but the smile was clearly an effort. 'You are no ordinary prisoner, Cullen. You stared into the face of death and grinned.'

'I pissed my braca,' Cullen answered bitterly, unable to curtail his shame. 'Branna tripped. I meant none of it.'

'It matters not.' Becan jabbed the air between them with his spoon. 'Yours is not a soul to be crushed under foot. It must be revered.' He laughed suddenly, a high-pitched fox-bark of a sound that still spoke of unseen strain. 'Not bad for a goatherd, eh?'

Cullen could not help but share a rueful smile. 'Not bad.'

'I watched the flock in my youth,' Becan said.

'You did?'

'I did.' Becan grimaced. 'A mind-melting business, if ever there was one. By the ancients, I could have thrown myself off a cliff. Specially when it rained.'

'I enjoyed it,' Cullen said. 'Out in the pastures, I was chief.'

Becan snorted. 'One way to look at it.'

'The only way. Or I'd have thrown *my*self off a cliff.' He leaned in while Becan laughed, stirring the pot slowly. 'I kept myself busy. Hawks and buzzards to scare off. Even the big fish-eagles from the coast would fly overhead sometimes, spying an old nanny or new kid. Had to keep my eyes on the sky.'

'Wolves? We had them. Bastard things.'

Cullen dished himself some more stew, fishing out a large shard of bone, sharp as a blade, and setting it on the ground by his foot. 'Always. I made traps. Ditches, covered with branches and lined with spikes. Kill the leader and the rest fade away.'

'Sounds like a lot of work to me,' Becan muttered, replenishing his own bowl.

'I had plenty of time.'

'They were your father's livestock, the goats?'

'Mother's,' Cullen said. 'She was village leader. Father died when I was young. I barely remember him.' He tipped back his head and gulped down the last of the stew. 'He was senior huntsman. Could spear a boar from twenty paces, so my mother always said.'

Becan whistled softly. 'Quite the pair.'

Cullen nodded. 'In our little village, yes. I practised with blade and spear, as we all did. Slings, too, for the protection of the goats. But I never had talent. Not with weapons, not at the hunt. My uncle was our smith, but my hand was never steady enough.' He laughed, a bleak, empty sound to his own ears, self-loathing sitting where mirth should have been. 'I watched the goats.'

Becan grinned, showing neat, square teeth, a single gap splitting the upper front pair. 'To goatherds across this whole misty land,' he proclaimed, raising his bowl like a trophy. 'The humblest of folk, yet the noblest.' He tilted the vessel towards Cullen. 'It is good stuff. Perhaps your role should have been the village cook.'

'My mother made a good stew.'

'You dwell upon her.'

'I cannot believe she is gone.'

Becan raised the bowl again, looking at the ceiling. 'On to the next.'

'On to the next.' He felt hollow, desolate. Thinking of her, of his sisters. He tugged the beaver cloak tighter. 'Do you miss your family? Your homeland?'

'The black mountains, my people call them,' Becan said wistfully, 'though they're green until the snow comes.'

Cullen made to ask him something, but voices broke through the wails of the wind. The words dried up before they could take form. He found himself cocking an ear towards the doorway. There were guards outside, he knew, and he often heard their chatter, but this was something different. The voices were strangely strained. Twitchy and nervous. Drums started up, too. Somewhere in the distance. He might have dismissed it as thunder, but for their undeniable rhythm.

'Our village was nestled in their great shadow,' Becan went on, oblivious to whatever transpired beyond the confines of the roundhouse. 'The mountains, I mean. Protected by the spirits dwelling amongst those high crags. You could not imagine such a place, my friend.' His eyes had grown glassy in the flamelight, so dark it seemed the colour had been devoured by the pupils. 'The valleys are choked with trees, abundant with life. The biggest bears, the noblest stags. Martins with fur so soft you could swaddle a babe in their pelts and leave them in the snow. Our rivers run fast and clear.' He blinked suddenly, returning to the room. 'Do I miss it? How could a man not long for such a place?'

'Why don't you leave?' Cullen asked. 'You are free to come and go.' The thought somehow dragged his gaze down to the crutches which shone black in the tremulous glow. He was again struck by how fine they were.

'It is a long way,' Becan said dismissively. 'Should I ask Caratacos to loan me his horse? Or perhaps the Dobunni will send an escort through their territory?' He shook his head, setting down the bowl and pressing the balls of his hands into his eyes with a deep yawn. 'I am content enough here. They treat me well.' He reached down to pat his truncated legs. 'They revere ones such as I.'

'Touched by magic.'

Becan smiled again, but this time the creases fell far short of his eyes. He swallowed. It sounded thick and difficult. His face seemed ashen. 'Or condemned by it.'

'What do you mean?' Cullen said, and his skin was prickling, turning to gooseflesh despite the fire's warmth. Outside the drums were getting louder.

Thunder, real thunder, rolled across the sky, shaking the earth, making them both start. It seemed to jolt Becan from his trance, so that his eyes jerked up from the flames, bright points of light glimmering within the dark. 'Cullen, I—' he began, only to falter when the drums – very close now – switched their beat to a slow, pulsing thrum. The lowing of cattle, made loud by palpable fear, carried to them on a gust wind that was laced with bitter smoke.

Cullen moved to his knees, the sudden urge to run almost overwhelming. 'What is it? Becan, tell me!'

But Becan, gathering up his crutches, would no longer meet his eye. His face a blank mask, turned to the shadows. A feeling of dread formed in Cullen's belly, like a hundred tiny snakes, knotted and writhing. He reached for the bone shard that still lay at his feet, folding it in his palm, squeezing tight his fingers to prevent them from trembling. Becan was already at the doorway, easing aside the skin with one of his sticks. They went outside.

—

The lowing had risen to a shrieked crescendo. It was a strange and incongruous sound, too high pitched, too urgent to come naturally from such a creature, and yet it came all the same. There were human voices too, shrill and whooping, like the caws of birds above the rib-shaking beat of the drums, and all of it mixed, melded, like a toxic potion for the ears.

The night air was warm. Too warm, given the vigorous wind, and Cullen turned to the centre of the clearing to see huge tongues of flame lap at the stars and the gathering clouds and defying the thin rain that eked its way to earth. Those flames climbed beyond the standing stones and the tarred trees, illuminating them against the sky. The shapes of the stones were black against the writhing yellow-red giants, and the trees were like taloned fingers, and embers scattered upwards, swirling into the rain and vanishing, dowsed, high above. More shapes came and went, movement of people around the fire. Cullen started for the clearing, sensing the guards accompany him at a distance. He ignored them, gaze transfixed on the grove and what lay within.

Thunder rolled, deep and lingering, and moments later a fork of brilliant white rent the eastern sky. Yelps of surprise and delight greeted it, and he saw that a large number of bodies were inside the ring of stones, gathered in clusters around the edges of the nemeton. The noise of the cow had ceased now, he realised, and already he understood, for the smoking air was laced with the smell of roasting meat. He stopped between a standing stone and a painted tree. Despite the encroaching night and the gathering storm, the fire bathed everything in a querulous glow, and he could see now that those roaring flames were consuming a vast cage, inside which were the blackened remains of a horned bullock, slumped now against the diminishing timber bars.

The nearest folk turned to Cullen, faces strangely haunted as they beheld him. They parted wordlessly to let him through, forming a short corridor into the ceremony's inner sanctum, and he wanted to ask why. But the crackling of the fire was so loud, and his own curiosity had him by the balls, and so he entered, taking his place at the edge of the ring.

He braced himself against the wall of heat as it seared his face, squinted into it, drinking in the otherworldly scene. It was a sacrifice. Even an orphaned goatherd from Calleva could see that. The nemeton was not as dormant as he had assumed. Nor as he had been *informed*. The lie struck him, and he looked around for Becan, intent on challenging him, but the legless man had vanished.

The onlookers were ordinary folk, watching in twos and threes or family groups. Spearmen stood by, stationed at intervals, the flame-light transforming their accoutrements of bronze and iron to so much liquid gold, and Cullen quickly realised that the ceremony had been patronised by more than just Camulodunon's lowest. Real gold glittered amongst the baser metals. Torcs and brooches and scabbards that spoke of nobility. The great and the good of this place that was the heartland of two nations, made one by Cunobelin and consolidated by his sons. Cullen watched with mounting surprise as the grove continued to fill, a steady stream of people filing inside the rings of stones and trees, coming up from the town in a sombre procession, the reverence of the night revealed in expressions that were sober and watchful.

And around the burning cage, the Wise Ones danced.

Cullen counted ten, half men, half women, though it was hard to pin down the shifting, whirling forms. They circled and wailed like gulls about a fishing boat, mad-eyed and oblivious to the heat. They capered and pranced, all high knees and wide elbows, and the bells that were attached to their hair and hips and wrists formed a discordant chorus that can only have been meant for unearthly ears. Two of them, both men, were stark naked, their bodies scrawled in charms, thick metal rings inserted through their noses and earlobes, while the rest donned the full-length skins of wolf, bear, deer, and more, all decorated with broad feathers and clanging toe bones. Their faces were painted black and white, half and half, and Cullen thought again of the magpie that seemed to be his personal shadow.

'I once saw a giant burn,' an elderly man said to someone in the crowd.

'A giant?' came the response, the disembodied voice of a child.

'When I was a boy,' the older voice croaked. 'The first Caesar's failed invasion was fresh in the memory of our elders. Rumours of another were rife. The people were nervous. The Wise chose to invoke the deepest magic they knew. That which comes from the time before the gods. At the very birth pangs of the world. The most brutal magic, but the most potent.'

'What kind of magic?' the child asked.

'The wicker monster. A great structure of timber and hazel. They caged a score of sheep in one arm. A handful of calves in the other, and three young men in the chest. Burned the whole thing above the waves. The smoke blotted out the moon. The screams I hear to this day.'

More lightning streaked overhead, the boom of thunder quick on its heels, and those white sheets brightened all to reveal the old man. His head turned. It was rain-soaked, pasty and deeply lined, ghoulish in the writhing shadows cast by the ever-shifting light, and he was looking directly at Cullen. 'The rumours have started again. The sons of Cunobelin must protect their people. Must call up the deep magic, as their forebears once did.'

Cullen tried to look away but found he could not. The drums had stopped. The Wise had become still. And he had the strange notion that all those faces, out in the dark, had turned to behold him. It was not true. It could not be. A mere goatherd from another land. Yet a sickening knot pulled tight in the pit of his guts.

He remembered hearing the cry on the wind. The shee's lament. He had thought it a song for his mother and sisters. 'It was for me,' he tried to say, though his lips and tongue were dry and stuck fast. Out of the corner of his eye, he saw a man approaching. One of the Wise. A tall man, draped in a cloak layered thick with feathers. Massive antlers protruded from his head, lashed to his bald pate with leather straps. He drew close, within an arm's length, and Cullen sensed the crowd shrink back. He tried to go with them, but the spearmen stepped up, blocking his escape. The Wise One's charcoal-lined eyes were wide. So wide and so black that he was surely peering directly into the next world, that window opened by some potion known only to those of his creed, and on his cheeks there were star-shaped scars, so neat and precise that they must have been the work of hot brands. His tongue slid out over a long chin that was painted in black vertical lines, and Cullen saw that it had been sliced at the tip, giving it a serpentine fork. He lapped at the air with it, tasting something unseen, and then threw back his head so that the antlers clattered to the ground, revealing a scalp that was marked in crescent moons and wavy-edged suns. He held his hands aloft, as if calling some power down from the stars, and, sure enough, two, three, four bolts of lightning stabbed the blackness above. His body shivered in response, and the feather cloak slid from his shoulders to reveal a torso that was thin as a withy and etched in the same symbols as his head.

'You see here, a messenger of the gods!' the Wise One called in a voice that crackled like dry twigs, waving long, thin arms expansively at the crowd. He spun about, striding back towards the flames at the centre of the grove.

Just as Cullen began to let out the breath he had not realised he was holding, the spear tips were nestled at the small of his back, prodding him forward. Without time to understand what was happening, let alone react, he found himself taking faltering steps into the heat-hazed ring. And then the skinny man with the forked tongue rounded on him.

'Who here can believe a meek and craven child was able to defeat Branna the Slayer?' The Wise One extended a long, bony finger at Cullen as he screamed the words. 'I think not! This whelp has not the strength or skill or guile to best the first shield of Caratacos in single combat!' He twisted on feet Cullen now saw were bare, and both had short stubs where the smallest toe should have been. 'This boy I bring before you, has been imbued with the power of the Otherworld. Only with that power could he have achieved such a feat!'

Lightning sheered the sky directly above them, bathing Avalloc's Shelter in a bluish glare. A great thunderclap shook the earth beneath their feet. The onlookers yelped and gasped with one voice, every leering face thrown into rictus relief. For the merest flicker of a heartbeat, Cullen saw the entire, ghastly tableau. The blackening bull and the ranged warriors. The wild-eyed Wise and the awestruck townsfolk. The dozen chariots at the edge of the grove bearing exalted passengers, present to witness this most ancient rite.

'Hear it!' the Wise One bellowed, tilting back his bald head, mouth split in a euphoric grin as the rain began to pelt down. 'Hear it, I say! Taranis comes this night! The thunderer, in all his pomp, all his glory and power.' More thunder, more lightning. He laughed maniacally. 'His battle chariot rumbles across the sky! Those magnificent wheels strike sparks as they spin! He comes! He comes! He comes!'

Then he was away, running now in a loping gait as one leg dragged, towards the flames that were beginning to ebb, the bullock and its cage all but consumed. Cullen watched, dumbstruck, feeling his heart would surely give out there and then. His body was numb with terror, and he wondered if he had soiled himself, but he could not move his head to look down. Could not do anything at all. He heard himself whisper for his mother, his father, but only silence met the plea. The hatred he had harboured for these people. The grief in which he had wallowed and the vengeance he had sworn. It was all as nothing. Ground to dust by profound, cloying, suffocating fear. Revenge? He would have laughed if he could draw enough air into his lungs. Revenge was irrelevant now. Only survival.

The other Wise Ones, the bears and the wolves and the rest, were bringing up another cage, setting it beside the first, and they were banking the edges with brushwood faggots and bunches of straw, and the spearmen poked and cajoled with their razor points and Cullen stumbled forward.

'Oh mighty lord, Taranis!' the chief of the Wise was shrieking again as he stooped to snatch up another cloak. This one was as plain as the other had been ostentatious. It was pale yellow, like a fresh-scraped buckskin, and so thin it looked worthless against the rain. Except that when he tossed it about his narrow frame, the dancing flame-light gave it a glaucous glow, and the shapes of fingers and mouth and eye-holes were thrown briefly into horrifying relief. Cullen understood that it was no animal pelt, but the death-skin of a sacrificed man.

Now he vomited. He bent double, bracing his hands on his knees while his guts twisted and lurched and purged themselves of every shred of food, every drip of bile that could be scoured away. After that his stomach kept pulsing and his chest heaved dryly, but nothing came, and he thought his ribs might crack under their own convulsing, but then the spears were at him again, pricking his back, so that he was forced to stand and take in a scene he could not quite believe.

'Yes, I feel you, lord! Arthmael senses your power!' the skinny Wise One was shrieking wildly from behind the stolen face as the lightning shredded the sky above Camulodunon into jagged strips of white and black. He pranced towards the burning cage that contained the twisted black carcass. In his hand there was a staff, its point bound in rags, and he dipped that bandaged end into the flames, which roared furiously alight. As he held the torch to the crowd, he shifted on the spot, one foot to the other, like a child desperate to urinate. The new flame illuminated the pale cape he wore, and he looked for all the world like a giant snake, shedding its skin. Cullen, walking falteringly towards the grotesque sight, might have laughed, if he was not wondering whether his own skin was destined to become the shrieking man's next garment.

But then, muttered a nagging voice within, that cannot be possible. Because they are going to burn you.

Realisation dawned. It clanged in Cullen's mind like a smith's hammer, reverberating about his skull and into his innards and down to his feet in a moment of resounding clarity, as if he had not truly been awake until now.

'Receive this offering, mighty Taranis!' Arthmael wailed, and he twirled like an acrobat, the torch tracing a blinding circle as he went. In a moment he was beside the second cage, looming over the stacked faggots with a manic grin bathed in ceaseless light and shadow. 'Accept this gift as thanks for our great victory over the Atrebates! Be pleased with this sacrifice and send your storms to dash the might of Rome, which turns envious eyes upon the Isle of the Mighty once more! Let not the foreign foe send their legions to these shores, for with them will come their own false gods!'

The crowd bellowed agreement. They would see him burn to keep themselves safe. He could hardly argue with that.

The spears prodded. Cullen stumbled on.

The Wise Ones in their flowing pelts opened the cage, stood aside, and beckoned him with a low, droning chant. Something about Otherworld protection against worldly threats. But Cullen was not listening. He was casting his gaze about Avalloc's Shelter. The flames that had consumed the bull, the flames that danced from Arthmael's poised torch, the empty cage that was intended to hold his own charred remains, the tar-daubed trees and the standing stones and the gasping, open-mouthed throng. There was nowhere to go. No escape. Arthmael loomed above him now, leering and laughing and chanting all at once, the symbols that adorned his body seemingly given life by the flickering torch.

An ear-splitting crack drew a collective scream from the gathered onlookers, and the blinding light that followed had eyes buried in hands. Even Arthmael shied away, wrenching his face from the source, shielding himself in the crook of his free arm. One of the bare black trees had been split in two, straight down the middle, both halves now ablaze. Smoke wafted up from its base, where the bolt had slammed into the ground and fried even the deepest roots. It was a message. Clear and concise. Taranis gave his blessing.

But to whom, asked the voice in Cullen's mind?

So he ran.

It felt like that was all he had done these past days. Run from the woods as the warband had descended on Calleva. Run from the rampant armies of the Catuvellauni, run to his mother's steading, run from Branna. All that running, to no avail. No real objective. Like a headless cockerel, he had dashed, pell-mell, from one catastrophe to the next. This time it was different. This time he had purpose.

That was why he ran at Arthmael. He ground his teeth and cursed his fear and he ploughed every shred of strength into those few paces. His was not a heavy body. He was tall enough for his age, but he had yet to thicken, yet to put brawn on his bones, and he had a pang of dismay as he leapt forth. A sudden sense that he might simply bounce off the Wise One like a stone tossed at a shield. But Arthmael was himself a study in willowy brittleness. His feet were planted flat, his arms outstretched, eyes averted. Over he went, like a rotten branch at the butting of a stag, and the torch spun loose and the ground surged up and up and up. They came down in a welter of limbs and cries,

Arthmael grunting heavily as all the air was smashed out of his body, Cullen's arms tangled about the cape of human skin now mired in dirt and ash. The crowd brayed and gasped. The pelt-swathed acolytes screeched like outraged gulls all around them, and Arthmael flailed with those long arms like an upended spider, snarling his astonished fury to the smoke blotted moon.

Cullen had only moments before the full wrath of the Wise Ones descended upon him. He heaved himself off the prone magic-man, letting Arthmael's desperately shoving arms propel him up and away. He rolled to the side, scrambled up to his knees. The jagged shard of deer's shoulder was in his grip before he knew what he was doing. Arthmael came up too, sitting with long legs stretched out, bewildered and gasping. Whatever powerful potion the Wise One had imbibed, Cullen was thankful for it, for the wide, black eyes, hitherto so terrifying in their otherworldly stare, now seemed to roll and glaze, as if they would not let Arthmael's mind sharpen. An arm came out, reaching for Cullen, grasping haphazardly with spindly fingers like talons. Cullen recoiled, swaying out of range, then back in, bringing down the fragment of bone to stab the Wise One in the thigh.

Arthmael screamed. A sound that was querulous and pitched so high it made Cullen wince. He lunged, taking the dazed man at the neck with his free hand and scrambling round to kneel behind him. Arthmael pawed at his leg, trying to stem the welling blood, but he froze when he felt the tip of the bone-shard pressing against his bobbing throat.

Cullen held Arthmael close, firmly, like a sheep he was poised to sheer. The world seemed to slow. The Wise Ones descended. The gaping maws of wild beasts slavering atop their skulls. A bear, a badger, a boar, a ram, a lynx. Teeth and tusks and glittering eyes, all bearing down on a callow boy who should never have left his goats. New light quavered to his left, bathing the advancing creatures in flaring reds and yellows, and surging heat told him that Arthmael's dropped torch had found the stacked faggots about their empty cage. That cage, constructed for Cullen, was alight now, empty, the roar of the climbing flames like an impotent howl of rage.

Cullen braced himself. The Wise Ones came on as their leader babbled an incoherent stream of half-formed words while blood welled black from the scrawny flesh of his punctured thigh. The crowd seemed to swirl at the edges of Avalloc's Shelter, their vague shapes melding and parting from moment to moment. Cullen screamed at them. Beckoned them to come on, for he could do little else. It was a scream of rage and of futility and of endless sadness. He had lost it all. His life would end, if not in Arthmael's flames then at a dozen spear points, or the tearing hands of a righteous mob. One way or another, it was over for him. So he held the Wise One, and pressed his jagged deer bone against his persecutor's neck, and wondered if he would have the guts to dispatch the man who would have killed him without a shred of hesitation.

'Hold!' a voice boomed out in the dark. A powerful, sonorous voice that brooked no dissent. 'By all the gods! Hold, I say!'

And the crowd seemed to hush, and the Wise Ones stalled, suddenly uncertain, and into the centre of Avalloc's Shelter strode a figure. A half-silhouette, one side bathed in firelight, one hand resting on the pommel of a full battle sword, the blade longer than Cullen's arm, its sheath chased in twisting serpents. The face was one he recognised, but altered by shadow, eyes sunken, nose and chin stretched long in the golden glow. Caratacos. Son of Great Cunobelin. Brother to the high king. Greatest warrior in all the Isle of the Mighty. The man Cullen despised. The man he hated above all others. The man who had just saved his life – for now.

CHAPTER SIX

Cassia watched in silence as two callow boys stretchered a groaning man out of the cave. She waited for them to pass beneath the skull pyramid and into the watery light of dawn, then pressed the bloody scalpel into the skin just above her left wrist. The whiter flesh of the underside of her forearm, red-stained up to the elbows, smarted at the blade's razor kiss. A lance of pain told her the skin had broken, and the sensation, shocking at so tender a spot, made her inhale sharply.

She held the breath for a few moments, bending her thoughts to the new wound, focusing all upon it. She placed the scalpel on the low bench, inserting it in place amongst the neat row of probes, retractors, bone saws, forceps and needles, then exhaled slowly, letting the air leak through gritted teeth. There was nothing else now. Just her and the pain and the patter of blood on the rushes.

A voice outside. Footsteps echoing at the cave mouth. A shadow extending up the wall as its owner strode past the flickering braziers that threw light over shelves cluttered with herb jars, mortars, pestles, leather flasks and bowls full of coloured powders. The voice again, coarse and lisping as it echoed with the approaching steps. 'Girl, where are the dried ferns? Cassia! You in here?'

Cassia blinked hard, clamping a palm over the wrist, smearing her own blood with that of her patients. 'One moment!' she called, speaking the common tongue for the benefit of her mistress, though she knew her accent was jarring to their ears. She crossed the few paces to one of the other benches set around the edges of the cool chamber, upon which had been set a bowl of clean water. She dunked her filthy hands, catching her breath all the same as she immersed them fully so that the cool liquid turned immediately opaque. As she dried them on the linen apron that protected her cherished cream tunic with its embroidered purple knots, she stared back towards the opening. 'Here!'

'By the ancients, girl,' the woman called as she emerged into the torch light, 'you got cloth stuffed in your ear holes?'

'I was tidying after the last patient.'

The woman sniffed, a typical display of incredulity, planting spindly hands upon bony hips. She threw a glance back at the cave mouth. 'Will he live?'

'I closed him up and splinted the leg.'

'Hooded Ladies preserve me,' came the exasperated reply, 'but I could have done that. Is there no Roman trickery you can employ?'

'Not for a fractured shin, Critheanach, as well you know.' Cassia took a cloth to the table upon which she had operated on the stricken man, mopping up the bloody pools. 'Why do you need the ferns?'

'Maidenhair,' Critheanach said. 'When mixed with honey, ground to a pulp, strained, scorched and cooled, it may be applied to a patch of skin.'

'To what end?'

Critheanach's shrewish face, angular and harsh, crumbled under the burden of wrinkles. 'Hair will grow like weeds.'

Cassia stopped the wiping motion and faced her. 'You're curing baldness? Now?'

'We are paid now,' the woman retorted in a tone too petulant for one who had seen more than fifty winters, 'so the cure will be now.'

'The wounded come by the day,' Cassia argued.

Critheanach offered what was presumably meant as a sweet smile, though the prevalence of empty, rotten gums detracted from its charm. 'And that is why you are here, my dear Roman flower.'

'I am here because I have no choice.'

Critheanach scraped fingernails across the silver stubble covering her pate. 'I do not consider you a slave any longer.' She wafted an arm in the direction of daylight. 'You may vacate my cave any time you wish, girl.'

'And go where? I cannot swim the Oceanus Britannicus.'

Critheanach's leathery face folded over on itself in disapproval. 'I am not suggesting you swim the *Narrow Sea*,' she answered, labouring the name the Britons often used for the channel of tumultuous water separating Britannia from Gaul. 'But you are not chained in this place. You're free to forge a new life elsewhere. Plenty to do in Verlamion, after all. Tis a magnificent city.'

Cassia almost laughed at that. As cities went, the whole place, capital of the new over-king, Togodubnos, smacked of the primitive to her eyes. It was large, certainly. Wealthier than any other settlement in this far-flung island, save Camulodunon. Yet Verlamion, the ancient seat of the Catuvellauni, boasted not a single stone building. There were no hypocausts here, nor glazed floors. No tapestries, exquisite mosaics, or veinshot marble columns. The halls were timber and thatch like everything that had gone before. They were simply bigger. Indeed, she might have laughed, were she not so utterly exhausted.

She barely managed to stifle a yawn with pink-stained knuckles as the pair of assistants grunted their way into the chamber, a prone form suspended between them on a wicker hurdle.

Critheanach moved to intercept them. 'What do we have, Harrol?'

At the hurdle's front handles, Harrol, a mealy-mouthed eel-catcher's son yet to make his final life choice, announced solemnly, 'Axe blow, lady.'

'Get him to the healing space,' the old woman commanded.

Cassia went to the hurdle, casting her gaze over the patient, whose upper arm was swaddled tightly in layers of darkly stained bandages. 'Another from Calleva?' She directed them to set the wounded man down on a table upholstered in dense furs near the small fire at the cave's centre. The patient might not have needed the heat, but Cassia certainly required light and flame. She knelt before the stricken man, whose short tunic and braca, in matching brownish plaid, bore the stains and snags of a fierce fight. His cheek symbols, painted in charcoal, had been reduced by sweat and blood to undefined smears. She leaned in to sniff the wound. He squirmed, consumed by pain, but did not acknowledge her presence. She looked up at Critheanach. 'It has started to turn.'

Critheanach knelt beside her, beckoning Harrol. 'Then let us see what's what.'

Cassia let her gaze slide back to the writhing, delirious man amongst the furs. He was a reed-thin youth, barely old enough to fight with the horde, with a thicket of messy brown hair and the beginnings of a moustache that was mostly fluff. The three of them commenced the painstaking process of peeling away the groaning patient's dressings. The second assistant, a rotund boy in his early teens, hovered near the tool bench, eyeing the array of fiendish-looking instruments in expectation of the next instruction. Cassia teased at the blood-caked strips, each layer crusted to the next so that they tugged against the stinking flesh below. Mercifully, she could see that the poor wretch was not truly in the room. His mind had fled to the realm between this world and the next, leaving a moaning, sweating shell that gave only perfunctory resistance as she revealed the chasm beneath the final coil of blackened fabric.

Cassia muttered an oath in Latin as she took in the severity of the damage. The warrior half opened his eyes at that. They were as cloudy as the sky outside. Then they rolled back into his sweat-drenched head and he sighed deeply, slipping into unconsciousness again. 'We need to work quickly. Maccos, the lamp.'

She squinted as the second assistant brought up the oil lamp, a hand-held clay device in the Roman style, the faint earthy smell of burning linseed oil inflecting the air. The stricken arm was in a poor enough state, a whitish blue, marbled and cold, made starker by the gaping wound that glittered like a polished ruby just below the shoulder. She ran her hand down to the mottled hand, pressing fingertips to his wrist. 'There is no pulse.'

The warrior's head lolled to the side as Cassia spoke, his face a mask of sudden horror as he caught the foreign flavour of her accent. 'Enemy,' he whispered. 'They have me.'

'Easy there,' Critheanach crooned, mopping his brow with a balled rag. 'Easy.'

'Mother?' the warrior muttered.

'She's not here, my little hero,' Critheanach said, 'but you have Critheanach the Healer, the next best thing.'

Cassia looked across at her mistress. 'Her voice is soothing as honey.'

The old woman sneered back. 'Least Critheanach the Healer can speak the common tongue without sounding like her lips have been chewed by a dog.'

Cassia smiled at the irony, looking again at the wound. The axe had cleaved a chasm of destruction through layers of skin and muscle, splintering the bone within. To make sure her gut instinct was right, she fingered the oozing maw as gently as she could. The warrior screeched like a snared eagle. His arms flailed so that Cassia was forced to leap out of range, while his eyes bulged, flickering madly, desperately, from one face to the next. They waited.

Eventually the young fighter grew calm, his breaths shallow. He looked at Cassia with sudden surprise. 'Are you Ceridwen?'

'War goddess,' Critheanach prompted, knowing Cassia would have no clue as to the name.

Cassia shook her head. 'No.'

'This is not the Otherworld?' His murky eyes regarded the rook-dark ringlets of Cassia's long hair. 'But your—'

'I am from Rome.' That elicited a new panic, and she placed a hand gently upon his heaving chest. 'Hush. I have been here these ten winters. I know the healing ways of my people. Critheanach knows the ways of yours. We work together, join the two. You are in good hands, I promise.'

He closed his eyes. Critheanach took her turn to sniff the wound, looking up dubiously. 'Irredeemable.'

She had whispered, but something resonated with the delirious youth, for he bucked at her assessment, clawing the air with his good arm as if he might fly right out through the bedrock ceiling of the cave. 'Not my arm! Not my arm, I beg of you!'

They were already bent to the task, despite his frantic pleas. Cassia and Critheanach made space as Harrol and Maccos fastened the bucking and writhing patient to the table with broad ropes. One of them took a chunky strip of visibly pitted leather and thrust it into the patient's mouth. His eyes looked as though they might pop straight out of his skull and he spat the leather out so that it flopped like a landed trout on his convulsing abdomen.

Cassia turned away, scanning the tool bench for the instrument she would require. As she took it up, she could not help but wonder how on earth a Roman girl so dedicated to healing had found herself wielding a grimy knife in the backwater of the world. She thought of her father as she worked. She had wanted to be a physician, like him, ever since she could remember. It had happened, she supposed, and for that she could be grateful. But nothing else had come as she might have expected. The throbbing flesh of her own forearm was a constant reminder of the strange fate that had befallen her.

The patient brayed as she leaned in, tracing with the small knife her intended line of cutting in the air just above the ruined limb. She made a couple of practice sweeping motions to ensure her eye and hand were in tandem, shutting out the stricken warrior's fettered jerks. He was terrified, and her heart went out to him, but she could not afford to allow sentimentality to dent efficacy. Speed was key.

'Almost chopped right through,' Harrol said in something like admiration as he pinned the patient by the legs.

'That would have been preferable,' Cassia replied.

'Would he not have bled out?' Maccos asked.

'Maybe.' She looked up from the arm. 'But when the limb is cut right off, cleanly,' she paused, trying to select the right words in a language not her own, 'there is less chance of poison in the flesh.'

A small earthenware bottle had appeared in Critheanach's hand. 'This will dim the pain.'

They all watched as the liquid contents were tipped from its slim neck into the mouth of the warrior. The man gagged and spluttered, took a moment to catch his breath, and gaped for more. Already his eyes were beginning to roll, his struggles losing their vigour.

'Tie the arm,' Cassia said when the bottle was nearly empty.

Maccos appeared in her peripheral vision, knotted strips of cloth bundled in his hands. She indicated the required location, just above her intended incision point, and he went about threading and fastening the ties with the practised dexterity that came with healing this most warlike of tribes. The warrior opened his mouth to scream, then passed out.

'They've gone to Camulodunon,' Harrol was saying as he dashed sand across the floor. 'Caratacos and his horde.'

'He does not like to linger here,' Critheanach said. 'In big brother's thrall.'

Cassia was ready. The knife was bone-handled, gently curved and as sharp as iron could possibly be. She leaned over the prone patient, thrusting her free left arm underneath the warrior's upper arm, so that she cradled the limb in the crook of her elbow. Then she brought the knife down, cutting deep in a sawing motion, pushing the blade forcefully through the flesh just below the shoulder until it met with resistance from the bone. Then she brought it back towards her chest, tracing the curve of the arm all the way around the bone in a single sweeping cut through skin and fascia and muscle. When it was done, blood seeping rather than pumping to form a crimson paste with the sand at her feet, she discarded the knife and held out a hand without taking her eyes from the arm. 'Saw.'

The cool solidity of an iron handle immediately filled her palm. She took a deep, lingering breath as she positioned the instrument's jagged teeth above the incision, then pressed it into the livid gulley, wiggling it firmly as it snagged on tissue until it hit upon solid bone.

The warrior woke. He screamed like Vagitanus, his entire body juddering and bucking, and Cassia could only dip her shoulder to the task, ignoring his agonised pleas as she began to cut. The saw bounced at first, slipping on the surface of bone greasy with blood, but then the teeth bit securely, and she found her rhythm and confidence, increasing the speed of her arm with each successful sweep.

'There's a good man,' Critheanach was saying. 'All over soon. You'll earn fame for your courage. The girls will be all a frenzy for you. Garn Grey Boulder has one hand, mark you, and his name is sung at every hearth in the land.'

The arm fell way in a matter of seconds. As it did, the patient slipped from consciousness again. Cassia wasted no time, tossing the saw aside and reaching for needle and thread. She gathered up the flaps of muscle and skin, folding them over the raw bone with as much care as time would allow, and immediately set about suturing them tightly into a stump that would, with the gods' grace, heal in time.

She sat back, giving Critheanach room to apply a poultice of chewed oak leaves to the angry, puckered stitching. The warrior was so still that he looked dead, but a quick check of the pulse at his neck confirmed otherwise. She wiped her bloodied hands on her apron and indicated for Maccos and Harrol to unfasten the straps and bind the wound.

The whole thing was over in significantly less than an hour. To Cassia it might as well have been a week, so exhausted was she. With the conquest of the Atrebates only days old, the next wounded individual would come soon enough.

—

The storm had broken just before first light, giving way to a thin, sorcerer's mist, white fingers curling about Camulodunon's trees, groping its defences and homes. Through that shifting miasma came the great and powerful, gathering as they did the night before, but this time at the Hall of Serpents, an imposing rectangular structure of timber and thatch, a vast edifice that loomed over the clustered roundhouses. They had come because word had spread through town like a disease. Word of fire and blood, of tradition confounded and of the humiliation of the Wise. The very air, still laced with the smell of ash, was alive with anticipation.

The sun climbed steadily from behind the hall's apex, flooding the dun with new light, bathing the huddled circles of smaller roundhouses in warmth. Between the impromptu congregation and the ancient throne room of the Trinovantes, a lone boy knelt and muttered to the gods and to the souls of those of his line who had come before. He begged for deliverance from the inevitable revenge that must only be moments away. Yearned for the earth to open up and consume him there and then, for, while he pleaded for a swift death, no such mercy could be expected.

Behind him the crowd warped and shivered like shoaling fish, taut with expectation. Whispered rumours slid between them, mouths pressed close to tilted ears, tunics and cloaks tugged furtively by eager tale-tellers. Those who had witnessed the night's failed ceremony attempted to outdo one another for tension and embellishment. Those who had not seen the spectacle for themselves did not let facts prove any kind of obstacle.

Cullen, knees damp as he stared fixedly down at the sodden earth, could hear only fragments, but it was clear that the stories grew wilder with the telling. It made him cringe. Yet what exactly had transpired? He was, himself, not entirely certain, for it had all ended so swiftly, in a maelstrom of orders and accusations. Some folk had wanted to tear their intended sacrifice limb from limb, toss his shredded remains into the flames for which he was destined. Others, disembodied voices out in the dark, had bellowed their defiance. Calling for his courage to be honoured, at least until a council of elders could gather to consider the situation. Arthmael had squealed like a gelded hog, and his pelt-adorned followers had spirited him away to some mysterious place of healing that only they knew of. Caratacos, that massive silhouette against the flames, high on his glimmering chariot, had trundled nonchalantly into the night after issuing his blunt decree, as though the whole fiasco had been an inconvenient diversion. And Cullen had been conveyed back to his hut, with a Wise One's blood on his hands and his own piss drenching his legs.

The night thereafter had been like a great wheel, its twin spokes of fear and relief turning over and over. He had waited, unsleeping, every vein, every sinew charged, as though Taranis's lightning had lanced his own body instead of the tar blackened tree. He had stared into the embers of his little fire, watching them flicker and falter, and not lifted a finger to stoke, for what would be the point? The taint of roasted bull lingered in his nostrils, the image of a burning cage – intended for him – seared indelibly onto his mind, along with the sight of a bleeding, spitting, cursing sorcerer, dragged off into the shadows by his dumbfounded brothers and sisters. The smells and the sounds of the ritual, the dread of final understanding, knowing for certain that death had come for him, grasped him, and then suddenly loosened its grip. It had all been like a dream, but not a dream.

In the end, with the likelihood of immediate retribution leaking away with the hours, he had slumped, exhausted, on his bed of straw, hearing only the spit and pop of the dwindling fire and the scraping footsteps of the sentries outside. Then the summons had come. Death, Cullen supposed, had come back for another try.

There was movement in the hall now, for he could hear low voices and dull clunks on the far side of the massive timber doors. He stared blearily up at the vast stag's skull nailed to the high lintel. It glowered back, black-eyed and implacable. With deep, lingering creaks, the white symbols painted on the doors began to move. A hush descended upon the crowd. Cullen stared as a figure stepped out, and his skin rose like gooseflesh. It was Arthmael, first amongst the Wise Ones of Camulodunon.

He had expected Caratacos, as befitted the great man's dignity, but he supposed the war chief was not strictly king. A king, by any account, but a lesser variety than his brother. And that put the leader of the Wise Ones on almost level footing. Certainly, Arthmael's status allowed him to walk first from the hall without causing offence. And that realisation alone put the fear of all the gods into Cullen. What manner of enemy had he managed to make? He wondered if he might have been more sensible to embrace the flames.

Into daylight lurched Arthmael, barefoot and mad-eyed, leaning heavily on a blackthorn cane and grimacing like a crow-picked corpse. Whispers rippled through the onlookers. Even the mist seemed to shrink back at his baleful presence. Cullen resisted the urge to vomit, though it was a close-run thing. He forced himself to look up at the man he had so enraged. A sheen of sweat made the moons and suns glisten on Arthmael's bald pate. He wore plain grey wool on his thin legs, and fastened at his neck was a striped cloak of many rich colours. Cullen counted those strips, as he had been raised to do, and saw that they numbered six. The simple fact sent another wave of fear washing over him. Petty chiefs wore no more than five colours.

Without a word, Arthmael had made crystal clear the station he held amongst the Catuvellauni.

The cloak itself hung open, exposing Arthmael's bare chest, displaying the host of markings that shifted over the cadaverous ribcage as he breathed. Some were bright and blue, their lines a finger's width, freshly painted that morning. Others were clearly older, faded with the years, and he supposed they had been etched permanently into the skin. Cullen found himself staring. One image was a wheel, the same as the one painted on the door. The life wheel that was the emblem of Taranis. Another, just below Arthmael's left nipple, was that of a long-necked goose. He wondered if Arthmael had had them needled by the teachers at Mona, that sacred island far to the north and west, the very epicentre of religion.

The Wise One hobbled out from under the hall's deep eaves. His face had been cleaned of the ceremonial paint, the black lines that had bisected his chin were gone, revealing a dusting of silver bristles, and his eyes, without their charcoal edging, seemed so much smaller. They were blue eyes, Cullen saw, but so pale that they were almost translucent, and he found he could not hold that gaze, for it burned with such hostility that he felt himself physically quell. Instead, he studied the moist soil and focused on the manic beating of his own heart. Behind him, a new murmur rose through the crowd.

'What we witnessed last night,' a resonant voice broke across everything like a sudden tidal surge, 'was an act of the gods.'

The people fell deadly silent. Cullen did not dare stir, but he knew the voice well enough. Indeed, he had been so girded to hear Arthmael's sneering condemnation that the smooth confidence in the words felt like a kick in the ribs. He curled in on himself like a balling hedgehog, but the speaker went on regardless.

'No less a sign,' Caratacos of the Catuvellauni said, 'than a frozen river or a blighted harvest. Taranis marks you out, boy. That is why you have been summoned.'

Every one of Cullen's sinews tensed, as if his own body refused to obey, but he had been addressed directly. His situation was precarious enough already, without adding disrespect to the list of offences. So he looked up. Caratacos, greatest battle-chief in all of the Isle of the Mighty, son and brother of high kings, stood, solid and implacable, like one of the standing stones of Avalloc's Shelter, as magnificent as Cullen had expected. The long, black hair elaborately braided, the rest of him wrapped in exquisite fabrics and adorned with black feathers and precious metals. Blue etchings and an old, deep scar fought for territory upon his oak-bough neck, while he carried no weapons, save the ceremonial dagger fixed at his hip. His arms, though, filled the sleeves of his tunic in a manner that suggested they might be deadly without the need for sharpened iron.

Cullen opened his mouth to speak, but Arthmael cut off his words like a scythe through wheat. 'He tried to kill me, lord!'

There was astonishment in the tone. Disbelief at the memory. All coloured by a shrill desperation that spoke of an argument unresolved, and Cullen realised they must have been debating his fate behind those formidable doors. The tiniest shoots of hope sprouted deep within. Perhaps, he dared wonder, no consensus had been reached.

As if acknowledging the thought, Caratacos lifted a meaty palm, first to cool his advisor's ire and then, more broadly, to hush the crowd's growing murmur. To hammer home the point, his free hand moved to rest on the dagger at his belt, the handle veined in impossibly fine threads of gold. 'Good people,' he spoke loudly, for all ears, a matter of spectacle as much as justice, 'you have come to hear my word on this most unusual occasion. Then listen well, for this will be an end to the matter.' He turned to the Wise One. 'Arthmael the Learned is hale and hearty, thank the gods.'

Arthmael tilted up his chin as he regarded Cullen, as if he was attempting to avoid a bad odour. 'It will take more than this scrap of gristle to push me on to the next, lord.' He dropped his voice to a low sneer. 'But I will ever limp.' As if to evidence the claim, he sidled awkwardly forward a step. The cane was strung at its head with an array of wooden dowels, which gave a discordant rattle as it jammed deep into the soft earth. 'Let me slit his belly, lord.' He ran a crooked thumb over his own midriff, licking his thin lips, speaking slowly, relishing each word to pass that unnaturally forked tongue. 'If he is a harbinger of Taranis, I will read the great one's message in the manner of the spill.'

Cullen's bowels clenched viciously at that, but Caratacos simply raised an eyebrow. 'And what if Taranis's will is to keep him alive?'

Arthmael shook his bald head furiously, breathing hard through his nose as if girding himself, and it was a few tense moments before he was equal to replying. 'It cannot be, lord. That is not the way.'

Caratacos held up a staying hand, as though calming an excitable child. Arthmael's mouth continued to flap, but he managed to curb his diatribe. There was a hush as the people waited.

'What I witnessed,' Caratacos began, before correcting himself to wave inclusively at the crowd, 'what *we* witnessed, was remarkable. Tell me, my friends, have any of you beheld such a thing before?' He paused as a ripple of agreement travelled through the mass of bodies. 'This boy defied the gods in their very midst,' he went on, warming to his theme. 'Defied me!' A bark of incredulous laughter. 'Twice!'

Now the crowd started up, for this was news to many, and their leader let them chatter like sparrows in a hedge for a time, pacing slowly back and forth, basking in the effect the revelation had caused until the noise began to fade. 'Aye, it is true,' he called out. 'Branna, who was named Slayer on account of his battle-fame, fell to this lad's blade! Can you countenance such a thing?' Cries of 'no' came in reply. He jabbed a thick finger at Cullen. 'You all know that Arthmael the Learned, wisest of the

Wise, almost met the same fate. I confess, there is something – ' he hesitated, glancing up, as if the suitable word were flitting about his head like a dragonfly – '*unusual* in what has transpired.'

With a rattle, Arthmael pivoted on his stick to face the chief. 'Lord, I ask – I beg – of you. This *thing*.' The blackthorn was up now, jabbing the air in Cullen's direction as though it was a deadly weapon. 'This worm. He mocks us. Mocks the gods.' His voice grew steadily shriller as the sentences toppled out, as uncontrollable as startled horses, for he was losing the people and he knew it. 'He must die. By all the powers of the next world, he must die, lord!'

The staying hand came up again, bringing a new hush. Arthmael might have been the wisest of the Wise, but he knew when to keep his serpent's tongue in his mouth, and he braced against the cane, hanging on to it with bone-white knuckles, as if his own fury threatened to drag him to the ground. Caratacos looked down at Cullen coolly, cocking his head to the side as though he were appraising a sow at market. 'Calleva was his time to die, my old friend,' he said to Arthmael. 'Branna, who has sent more souls to the next life than any man here, should, by rights, have crushed him like the tiniest insect. Have you stopped to ask yourself why that was not the case?'

'He must—' Arthmael began a protest that was abruptly aborted when he received a sharp look from the great warrior.

'I have not the wisdom of Mona,' Caratacos said, 'but last night's ceremony should have laid this matter to rest, would you not say? And yet...' He waved a hand at Cullen, leaving the words hanging, as heavy on the air as the bitter ash.

Evidently sensing the floor had been handed back, Arthmael leapt to retrieve the initiative, stabbing the blackthorn up at the clear skies. 'He insulted Taranis!' The Wise One took a few lurching steps closer, so that he loomed above Cullen, playing to the crowd as his master had done. 'Taranis answered our call and brought his lightning and his thunder.'

'And his rain, for that matter,' Caratacos interjected, eliciting laughter from the onlookers.

The sinews convulsed in Arthmael's thin neck as he bit off every word. 'Taranis graced us with his presence, lord, and was cheated! By this whelp!'

'It pleased him to let the boy live,' replied Caratacos levelly. His eyes raked the scene, from Cullen to those gathered behind. 'Therefore, it pleases me to do the same.' Shouts of assent rolled up from the sea of people.

'It was a betrayal,' Arthmael protested, his voice wheedling in its desperation.

Caratacos pursed his lips thoughtfully, then considered Cullen for a lingering moment, as if trying to extract his deepest thoughts from behind his eyes. 'I confess, boy, I have never seen the like. You are favoured. I need no representative of Mona to tell me that.' To the crowd he called, 'This stripling killed Branna the Slayer, my first shield. He wounded Arthmael the Learned, foremost of the Wise, while escaping Taranis's cleansing fire, under the god's very nose! There are no coincidences.'

Arthmael's face quivered as he gritted his teeth. 'You risk the ire of the gods, lord,' he said softly.

A smile pulled at the corner of Caratacos's mouth. 'I like to live dangerously.'

'Humiliation,' Arthmael said softly. He drew a lingering breath, then shrieked, 'Humiliation, I say!' A smattering of cheers and jeers vied for supremacy at his words, the crowd torn in two.

'He humiliated *you*, my friend,' Caratacos said pointedly, 'not Taranis.'

Arthmael's little eyes bulged from that cadaverous face. 'You cannot—'

'I cannot?' Caratacos echoed, calmly enough, his expression inscrutable. But there was a subtle vein of threat in there, almost imperceptible. The effect was utter and immediate silence.

With visible difficulty, the Wise One managed to bring his ire under control. His left eyelid gave a butterfly flicker, betraying the rage beneath the surface. 'Lord, I—' he stammered, tailing off when he read the finality in Caratacos's expression. He glared down at Cullen instead, nodding almost imperceptibly. 'Then I curse this boy.' He waited, then. Perhaps for the crowd to lend their support, or for his master to intervene, but when Caratacos did nothing, he licked his lips slowly, and smiled. 'I curse you by the earth beneath your feet, and by the sky above your head.' His voice was rising as he spoke, as if he poured all his pent-up rage into the very syllables as they formed on his forked tongue. 'By the sacred hills and the whispering trees.' He stooped, clinging to the cane but getting as close to the prisoner as he could manage, fetid breath pulsing in waves over Cullen's dipped face. One of his legs, the one Cullen had stabbed, kicked at the compacted soil. 'I curse you by my life's blood, spilt at your hand, and by all the gods of my people and yours.' He recoiled, straightening, and his spindly arms rose up, as if to embrace the sky. There was spittle foaming at the corners of his mouth, and his ears had reddened at the tips. 'I curse him! Hear my pledge! May his skin wither and his sight fail and his heart stop! May he choke on his food and drown on his drink and shit out his own guts!'

With that, Arthmael the Learned, wisest of the Wise, councillor to chiefs and kings, lurched about in a whirl of his colourful cloak. He stalked, hissing like a cornered adder, back into the Hall of Serpents. And Cullen of the Atrebates was free.

CHAPTER SEVEN

There was a feast that night. A hunting party, led by a fearsome-looking woman with a shock of flame-red hair and a thick necktorc of twisted bronze, paraded through the gates of Camulodunon with a dozen boars, trussed and dangling beneath massive wooden poles, and the warriors who had the honour of spearing those proud beasts could be identified by bloody smears under their eyes and tusks dangling from string at their necks.

The hunters entered the town with great ceremony, an excited procession expanding in their wake. Braziers were lit at intervals along the middleway, through the layers of battlements, guiding the heroes into the heart of the town, and out into the precinct before the chieftain's hall. Pyres greeted them, blazing hot and wild, the surrounding buildings draped in a quivering tableau of tremulous shadow and liquid gold, and there the people gathered as the boars were gutted, skinned and spitted, and the Wise Ones capered and chanted, and the flames began to hiss with steadily dripping fat. There was a sense of anticipation and of joy. Families mingled, laughed and shared news.

Cullen absorbed every sight and sound, revelling in his inward pretence that the celebration was for him, his survival against all odds. In reality it was a triumph in honour of themselves: the Catuvellauni. A grand revelry to celebrate their own supremacy over one subjugated people, taking place in the greatest settlement of another. Yet the bitterness Cullen felt could wait a while. He was, at least, alive, and he could hardly believe it.

There was fighting while the boars cooked. Armed and unarmed; men, women and those youngsters in training for the autumn warrior tests. The crowds whooped and cheered for their champions as wiry wrestlers grappled within circles scratched into the soil, and muscular fighters slipped and jabbed with knuckles bound tight in leather. Blunted spears vied with wooden swords, shields cracked and clattered like felled trees, and always the ceaseless drums thrummed like the heartbeat of giants. The hunting party took pride of place, as was the custom, at the edge of the fighting space, feted by all, their cups never allowed to run dry.

Caratacos entered the throng, heralded by drums and harps. He made offerings to the Wise, then drank a broth made from the carcass of the sacrificed bullock that had expired just before Cullen's entanglement with Arthmael. The broth, he announced, would bring fertility and strength to him and his people, and they duly bellowed their joy. After that, the great warlord moved amongst them, his wives, advisors and named men in tow, receiving bows and pledges with equal parts solemnity and bellowing laughter, cowing and charming all at once. He toasted those who had brought the feast from the forest, paid due respect to the Wise Ones who oversaw the various points of tradition, and loudly backed his favourites in the mock battles that rang out to thunderous applause, especially when a move showed skill or a blow drew blood.

Then peace floated in on the lilting notes of the harpists, who accompanied the poets in the telling of their great sagas as the meat was carved and passed through the revellers on ornate platters. The people listened as they chewed. To the story of Casivellaunus and his defiance in the face of the first Caesar. Of the giant king Bran and his beautiful sister Branwen, and of the divine waters of Danu, that great mother river across the sea, from whence all life sprang. And now, of course, came the newest tales; those of the sons of Cunobelin. Of Togodubnos's new empire, and of Caratacos's humbling of the Atrebates. That last tale, its freshness only adding to the poet's natural dash and verve, cut Cullen to the quick, even as all around him gasped and cheered.

Caratacos was the centre point around which the night swirled. Together with his royal party they formed a tight knot of colour and wealth, of feathers and charms and precious metals. They slid through the people at the edge of the fires, harvesting words of fealty and flattery as they went. The sight of the great lord transported Cullen, as if on an eagle's wings, through time and place, from the dancing flames of Camulodunon to the ditch where he had concealed himself, cowering before the warriors of the Catuvellauni. Off again, soaring above the heads of painted spearmen and dust-clouded chariots, to Calleva's open gates and terrified people, then on, over field and tree and holloway, to his own village, thick smoke funnels turning the air acrid and stifling. The images swirled before him, soaked into his bones, coalesced in the pit of his stomach, weighing heavy, as if he had swallowed a quern stone.

'Do not sneer so,' someone said in the dark, 'lest you drive away the women.'

Cullen returned to the present with a jolt. In that instant, the unexpected voice cut the ensnaring threads of unbidden memory, and the whole web fell away, leaving Cullen blinking and dazed. Becan sidled out of the shadows with impressive dexterity, given the pot of ale he somehow managed to carry. Drest shuffled along behind.

Cullen glared, stepping in close. 'I should kill you.'

'You should,' Becan said, 'but you won't.'

'Why?'

'Because you have precious few allies here as it is.'

Cullen gave a scornful grunt. 'And you're my ally?'

'We're your friends,' Becan said, tilting his ale jug at Drest. 'Besides, they'll string you up if you hurt me.'

That seemed an unlikely outcome to Cullen, but an internal voice reminded him that he was still in an enemy town. He relented a touch, moving out of Becan's space. 'You should have told me,' he said bitterly. 'Warned me.'

'That they were likely to kill you?' Becan answered incredulously. 'Was that not obvious? Besides, what would you have done? Walked back to Calleva? Meanwhile, it would have been my skin bubbling from my bones in that cursed cage.' He took a sip from the cup. 'I am sorry.'

'*We* are sorry,' Drest added.

Becan gave an enthusiastic nod. 'Let me make it right. Let me show you this great dun. Help you make a life with the Catuvellauni, as we both have. By the ancients, Cullen, you have a second chance.' He smirked. 'Third chance, even, seeing as Branna should have gutted you.' He handed Drest his drink and plunged his hand into the folds of his cloak, bringing out a small but heavy-looking bag. 'Here.'

'What is this?'

'A token.' Becan handed the bag over. 'Of my regret, and of my friendship.'

Cullen closed his fingers about the bag. It was full of coins. More than he had ever seen in one place. He hefted it in his palm, instinctively luxuriating in the weight. He looked up. 'How did you—?'

'Look,' Becan said, levelling his crutch through a gap in the bodies. 'Does he not look every inch the god of war?'

Cullen turned to see Caratacos, who stalked the crowd, milking their adulation. 'They honour him as king,' he said in a low voice. 'Is he king?'

'Any man can call himself king if he has a scrap of land to defend and enough spears to do the defending.' Becan took back the ale and leaned heavily on one crutch so that he could drink. 'When his brother shares the room,' he said after a lingering draught, 'he is king no longer. But here, tonight, there is no one higher.'

'He is not my king,' Cullen said, hearing the sourness stain his words.

'He is the man who could have had you killed,' Becan chirped brightly, as if discussing the weather. 'On the journey here. At the sacrifice. During the night. This morning before the audience. He might snap his fingers at any moment and have you back before Arthmael's blade before you can say *Taranis protect me*.'

'Then why hasn't he?'

Becan shrugged. 'Your death does not please him.'

'He tests always,' Drest offered in that desiccated tone. 'Gauges the people. Keeps their favour. He knows his power comes from them.'

'I thought it came from his spears.'

Becan beamed. 'I like you.'

Drest sighed. 'Conquest and administration are different beasts altogether. But he must harness them both.'

With a lurching stomach, Cullen noticed the wisest of the Wise loping amongst the courtly group, blackthorn in hand and striped cloak on his bony back. 'Is that why he indulges that bastard?'

'Arthmael the Learned was a favourite of the high king,' Becan answered, pointedly emphasising the name for the blind man's benefit.

'Togodubnos?' Cullen asked.

'Great Cunobelin,' Drest corrected him. 'The Sun Hound.'

'The decision to keep him as advisor,' Becan said, 'is partly a matter of honouring his father's memory. Partly a matter of custom.'

Drest nodded. 'The Wise of Mona send their representatives to every corner of the Isle of the Mighty. Every village is graced with their poetry, their healing and dreaming, their philosophy and judgement. Some of the grander chiefs keep their own Wise Ones, as advisors. And the especially powerful of Mona's children become part of the high king's court. His right hand.'

The strands were beginning to entwine in Cullen's mind. He thought of the morning's audience. The sense of the dramatic, of display. 'Caratacos would behave in the manner of a high king so that his people become accustomed to it.'

'A shrewd thought,' said Drest. 'You witnessed first-hand the way he issues pronouncements. Judgements. He is the power when Togodubnos is not present.'

'He is a rival to his brother, then?'

'Not in any overt way. But he must be ready for whatever may come. The life wheel turns inexorably.' Drest waved a wizened hand in the direction of where he supposed Caratacos might be. 'He will behave like the over-king, for perhaps, one day, the fates will align—'

The statement had been left dangling, but Cullen caught the intimation well enough. After all, had his own world not turned on its head in a matter of hours? 'But if Arthmael is the greatest of the Wise, why does he not sit at Togodubnos's right hand?'

'Because Togodubnos has his own favourite,' Becan put in. He lowered his voice conspiratorially. 'And besides, the king is no friend of Arthmael's. Never has been. In truth, neither brother is fond of the old stoat. The Wise Ones are a law unto themselves. Only the blood royal may command them. But is the privilege enjoyed by any member of that line, or only the one at the very apex?'

'Much depends on the people themselves,' Drest interjected. 'Their strengths and their guile.'

Becan laughed. 'They butt heads as often as they agree, Arthmael and Caratacos. One the wisest of the Wise, the other a king, but not the high king. Arthmael calls Caratacos lord but sees himself perched on a branch of similar height. Caratacos reveres Arthmael, but he is not above the odd jibe when the mood takes him.'

'Is that what I am?' Cullen said, anger rising. 'A jibe?'

'By the ancients!' Becan exclaimed. 'Between the second most powerful lord in all this island, and the most feared of the Wise? Yes, that is precisely what you are!'

Drest laid a calming hand on Cullen's forearm. 'You are beloved of Taranis, that much is undeniable.'

'But,' Becan cut across him, lurching out a hand to grab a new ale from a passing lad's over-full tray, 'if you think your pardon gave Caratacos no pleasure, you are mad as a barrel load of polecats. He'd do it ten times over, just for the look on Arthmael's face!'

'I am not their plaything,' Cullen retorted, hearing the anger swell in his tone but unable to stifle it.

Becan laughed, shaking his head as if stunned by what he was hearing. 'We are all their playthings, you slop-witted goat-fiddler. All of us. Before gods and kings we are nothing.' He handed Cullen his ale pot, indicating that he should drink. 'By the ancients, be happy that you are still alive!'

'Happy,' Cullen echoed. He could feel himself becoming distant again, like water seeping through cracks in parched soil, his mind going to Calleva once more. The faces of his family danced in front of his eyes. Happy. Such a simple word. It felt strange now. Incongruous. As if it were no more than a pair of syllables, devoid of all meaning.

'It will ease.' It was Drest who had spoken. 'That feeling of your innards dropping to your feet. It fades.'

Cullen stared at the old man, at the ruined hollows of his face, filled now with shadow, his white hair like moon-touched ice in the dancing flame light. Evidently the incredulity was writ large on his own face, for the description of Cullen's suffering was more apt than he cared admit. 'I do not see how.'

Becan, leaning on one stick to free up a hand, tipped his newly purloined pot steeply above his mouth, draining the last vestiges of whatever had been within. 'By the ancients, but this is good.' His chest convulsed in a silent belch. 'We will help you, goat-fiddler. On that you may depend.' He let his eyes track to the purse weighing heavy in Cullen's fist. 'That'll prove a tonic, too, I'd wager.'

Cullen closed his fingers about the packed coins, feeling them chink and slide in his grip. 'Why? Why will you help? Why give me money?'

'You are one prong,' Becan mused, 'on the trident of life's detritus.' He waved the pot at the three of them in turn, finishing with Cullen. 'Blind, lame, and damned. That makes us allies.'

'Am I damned?'

'So says Arthmael the Learned,' Becan said, effecting the Wise One's sneering lilt.

'I saw a magpie at Calleva, during the attack.'

Becan shrugged. 'I saw one yesterday.'

Cullen shook his head. 'It almost perched on me during the battle. Then again, it came to me after my capture.'

Becan clicked his tongue softly. 'A bad omen.'

'Was that a question?'

'Would you like it to be?'

'I was always taught to beware magpies,' Cullen said. 'We did not eat them or sacrifice them. We did not take their feathers.'

'White and black,' Drest intoned. 'The living and the dead. Good and evil, made one.'

But it was more than that, Cullen thought. Their way of looking at you, those beady little eyes, shining like precious stones, alive with guile. They were more than birds. Malevolent spirits dwelt within them. Snare a raven, it will fight you. Climb for a hawk's eggs, she will tear the very scalp from your skull. But never antagonise a magpie, the most sacred of birds, for her revenge is taken in the dreaming realm, the Otherworld, where souls drift after death.

'Yet you cannot choose your totem,' Becan said.

Cullen looked levelly at him. 'And if the magpie has chosen me? What can that mean, except that I am doomed?'

'Seems a waste.'

'Waste?'

'If your fate is to die, goat-fiddler, then why would he bother with you?' He beamed as he noticed a serving girl's approach, though whether that was due to the girl herself, or the huge ale jugs she hefted, it was unclear. The liquid slopped frothily as she picked a stunting way through the revellers, and Becan raised his pot as high as he could without losing balance. 'Here, my sweet enchantress!'

Cullen said to Drest, 'How do you know this feeling will fade? You live among your enemies, as I must do. How is it possible?'

'Time passes. People accustom themselves to all manner of hardship, in ways they never imagined possible. Feelings fade. Edges dull.' The old man shifted his stance slightly, so that he now faced the grandest building in this grandest of precincts. 'Take the Hall of Serpents. Are you looking?'

Cullen stared across the crowd at the mighty structure. 'Yes.'

'Its posts were not set into the sacred soil by the Catuvellauni.' Drest spread a withered palm before him, indicating the hall's great doorway. 'Those symbols are not the original symbols. Indeed, it was the Hall of Addedomarus long before it bore the name serpent. *My* people built that place. This whole town. Dug out the defences which transformed it into the great dun that you see today. The Trinovantes. A mighty people. But we have been edged out over the years. Subjugated and weakened. We are still here, but you would hardly know it.' His thin lips cracked in a wistful smile. 'Ours was the sign of the galloping stallion, marked upon those very doors, and it watched over that hall, fierce and proud.' He shook his head, as if the memories were cobwebs to be rid of. 'There was a time when I vowed to slay every Catuvellauni I encountered. Burn their steadings, kill their cattle, do to them what they did to us.' A sigh, long and heavy. 'Time passes. Skin thickens. It becomes easier to bear. You ask how I can live among my enemies. Well, now you will learn to do the same. For what alternative do you have?' The drummers were whipping themselves into a frenzy now, their background thrum climbing to a crashing din, and Drest laughed, tilting back his head, as if drinking it all in. 'Welcome to the Catuvellauni, Cullen, beloved of Taranis!'

'Beloved?' Cullen echoed incredulously, as Becan thrust an ale pot into his grip.

'What other explanation do you need?' Drest said.

'You are beloved of him,' Becan cut in, 'for he has kept you safe, in spite of that old weasel-swiver.'

Cullen caught the intimation and followed Becan's gaze. Arthmael hovered at the edge of the royal party, deep in conversation with one of Caratacos's named men, a thickly bearded warrior with forearms like oak boughs.

'Now,' Drest went on, oblivious, 'you must walk tall as a new man.'

'New man?' Cullen said absently, unable to tear his gaze from Arthmael.

'By the ancients,' Becan spluttered into his ale, 'do you intend to repeat every word he utters?' He quaffed several gulps, foam whiskers overlaying his stubble, then belched prodigiously. 'What our friend means to say, is that the old Cullen of the Atrebates perished at Calleva. What you have come through is nothing short of rebirth.'

Drest poked Cullen's shoulder with a bony forefinger. 'Taranis peered into your soul, boy. Marked you for a different path. Your time was not yet at hand. Perhaps you'll join the Wise. Journey to the schools at Mona.'

Becan winked at Cullen. 'With Arthmael's blessing.'

Drest cackled. 'Smith, then? The metal workers enjoy the esteem of the gods. With fire, water and art, they are able to breathe life into hard metal. It is magic. They are the highest of all people after kings, chiefs and the Wise.'

'I cannot imagine they tasked him with babysitting goats,' Becan said, 'on account of his famously steady hand.'

Drest threw up his arms, exasperated. 'Something else, then!' Again, that jabbing fingertip. 'How many years do you have?'

'Seventeen,' Cullen replied, 'come the festival of Calan Gaeaf.'

'Then your time of choosing fast approaches.' The old man gestured at the ember-flecked sky. 'Taranis knows. He will guide your choice. But you *are* new, boy. No longer Atrebates. Nor Catuvellauni. A new breed. You must beat your own path.'

Over near the fire, Caratacos and his court had gathered in a half-circle to face one of the Wise. A priestess, to judge by her bare legs, which were long, lithe and lily-white. The rest of her was entirely enveloped by the thick pelt of a bear, its gaping maw encircling her face, as if it had devoured her whole. She swayed before them, like a reed in the breeze, muttering an incantation that was lost to the drums and the revelry, and when Caratacos acknowledged her efforts with a bow, she dragged her toes through the soil, sketching out a rudimentary circle. She produced a small bag from which she drew handfuls of something pale and granular, scattering it liberally within the circle.

'Seeds?' asked Cullen.

'Salt,' Becan answered, 'and herbs.' He leaned across to Drest. 'Artio performs the rites.'

'The bear goddess,' Drest said. 'Caratacos begs her for strength. For her wisdom as he scours the wilderness in search of glory.'

Hardly wilderness, Cullen thought. More nations would fall for the man's ambition. 'He has more than his fair share.'

Becan shrugged. 'His father's ghost casts a very long shadow. He means to prove himself worthy of the Sun Hound.'

Artio incarnate was gyrating now, flailing and whirling through the salt, kicking it up like white dust. One of the Wise, a thin man wearing nothing but layers of bone necklaces, stepped out of the shadows and handed her a limp mass of what looked to be feathers.

'The winning cock,' Becan said. 'Most savage of the night. His body will show the way.'

The priestess stooped, pinning the bird between her knees and wrenching hard back its head. A knife flashed in the firelight, and she was sawing out its throat, expertly angling the cut so that blood drenched the earth in black gouts. When the flow began to ebb, she hacked at the carcass, eviscerating it, then dropped it like a dirty rag. She pranced on the balls of her feet as she skirted the remains, prattling at the slaughtered cockerel, as though it would answer back. The naked subordinate poked the entrails with a long stick, drawing them out in careful lines, though he was careful not to step onto the salt. Artio stooped lower, running the tip of her reddened blade through the mix of soil and salt, blood and herbs, reading the future therein. She whispered, a rapid patter of words, and the man beneath the necklaces spoke in turn, translating for Caratacos and his hangers-on.

Cullen thought of the caged bull's death. 'Caratacos means to make sacrifice to all the gods?'

'All the powerful ones,' Becan replied.

'Our king, Berikos, made the same offerings,' Cullen said. 'It did not help him in the end.' He was about to say more when his skin prickled with the discomforting sense that he was being watched. Almost immediately he noticed Arthmael's baleful glare from across the precinct. The dark eyes gleamed, hard and unforgiving. He had broken off from the bearded warrior, reserving his gaze now for Cullen alone.

'By the ancients,' Becan said, his own eyes flicking between Cullen and the Wise One, 'you've made an enemy there.'

'He was an enemy before I stabbed him. He tried to burn me alive.'

'But then he was only one of the Wise. Performing a ritual on his master's behalf. You were no more to him than that fighting cock. A captured foe, to be presented as blood-gift to the gods. Now you are so much more. Now he knows your name.'

'I do not fear him,' Cullen lied.

'You should, goat-fiddler,' Becan warned. 'He'll not forget.'
'Nor will I.'
'I'm sure he's quaking in his braca.' Becan laughed. He reached out to flick a finger against Cullen's temple. 'Wits. Keep them about you. Keep them sharp. This is no game.' With that, he lofted one of his crutches to catch the attention of the serving girl. 'Now then, goat-fiddler. Let us drink!'

CHAPTER EIGHT

Cullen woke. Or, at least, he realised he had been awake for some time, staring listlessly up at the beams. At the cloud of unmoving smoke, suspended beneath the thatch, filtering slowly through. Each half-baked thought tumbled over the next, like so many newts in a bucket.

The world spun gently. His head swam and his mouth tasted of the grave. He felt grim, for certain, yet somehow there had been change overnight. A shift in his mind, unseen but unmistakable. The heavy cloak of grief had slipped just a fraction. In his stupor he had dreamed of the past. No surprise there, but now something new, something unexpected came with those flashes of death and a community lost. He had dreamed of the future. Of his own future. One he thought had not existed. Beloved of Taranis, Drest had said. It seemed too good to be true, yet here he was. His heart breaking, but still beating.

'By the ancients,' Becan groaned. He was lying on the opposite side of the hut, a pale face in a pile of furs. 'Is this the Otherworld? Have I finally moved on to the next?'

'I have made my choice.'

Watery light filtered through the cracks either side of the door skin, making Becan's eyes glimmer as they widened. 'But a few nights ago, you were Arthmael's latest blood offering. Now you've made your life choice?'

'Beat my own path,' Cullen repeated Drest's words.

Becan sat up. 'And you must.' He shrugged off the furs and slumped heavily forward on his hands, blowing hard upon the pile of white ash at the room's centre. Sure enough, orange embers peeked through the billowing smoke. He persisted until a little flame danced into life, then eased back, screwing shut his eyes and slapping a palm against the side of his skull. 'By the Shining One's lustrous face, I swear my brains are about to leak out of my ears.' Without opening his eyes, he said, 'I'll indulge you, goat-fiddler. Which path do you intend to walk?'

Cullen opened his mouth, but the words never came. The sound of war horns shredded the dawn.

—

The streets were a hive of activity. It was early still, and many folk looked as woolly-headed as Cullen felt, but there was a communal hurriedness nonetheless. Horses were brought up from stables, chariots hooked to traces, wheels checked and reins fastened. Boys and girls carried armfuls of tack, weaponry and clothing up to the main thoroughfares, handing them to the waiting men and women who snapped barbs intended to quicken their efforts. They grunted and muttered as boots were pulled on and cloaks fastened with brooches. They shared tales of how badly their heads pounded or how song-sore were their throats, but they shouldered spears and slung shields and sheathed swords all the same, with nods of good cheer when their lords came by. Some – the nobles and the named – daubed their bodies with symbols, letting the wet woad dry in the sunshine beneath a sky that was ice-clear and blue as chicory petals.

Cullen, draped in his beaver cloak despite the day's warmth, dragged himself blearily along the road, trying to make sense of the sudden activity. He looked back intermittently to see if Becan had caught up, but his friend had not been as eager to leave the hut, preferring to wallow despite the incessant cry of the carnyxes. Cullen, however, needed to see what the commotion was about. Because he had asked the gods for retribution, and perhaps this was it. Perhaps an army of conquest was, even now, sweeping through the outworks of the great dun. For a fleeting moment he imagined Berikos at the head of an avenging army, intent on the restoration of the Atrebates, but what army did the old king have left? He was probably hiding in some fox hole deep in the woods, enfeebled and terrified. Besides, if Berikos intended to recapture Calleva, he was in the wrong city.

Not Berikos, then. Still the carnyxes whined in earnest, like a swarm of angry hornets, their drone underlaid by drums as the call to arms travelled far and wide. Still the warriors assembled. Yet the place was strangely devoid of fear. Instead, the air seemed almost to crackle with a frisson of expectation. And then the people were moving, westward as one, in the direction of the great gates and the greensward beyond, a swelling tide of bodies and chariots. Cullen found himself going too.

The greensward was a large, open expanse of land located between the first layer of earthen barriers and the main western gate. Entirely flat, save its blanket of tufty grass, and empty of tree and building, it was a ceremonial area, reserved for festival and pageant. Or easily transformed, Cullen noted as he clambered up to the rampart with scores of others, into a killing ground if the need arose. In response to the thought, he looked along the line of the palisade to see what horrors Caratacos had prepared for whoever came to threaten his seat. But there were no spearmen here, nor archers or slingers. The entire rampart was full of common citizens. Bakers and merchants, woodworkers and smiths. Not a warrior in sight. All the fighting men and women had gone to the low ground, pouring out onto the greensward en masse, and now they formed a bristling, formidable block, fronted by a double rank of horsemen, spears in the centre and chariots arranged in sections on the flanks. Caratacos was there, at the very front of it all, mounted on a vast black horse with white fetlocks, his named fighters close at hand. At his back the formation curved in the shape of a vast bow. It was a bizarre sight. An entire army placing itself with practised efficiency into battle formation, yet possessed of a languorous, almost comfortable nature that did not speak of impending conflict. Nor, Cullen came to realise, did the mood of the onlookers, who seemed interested rather than apprehensive.

Before he could quiz someone, he noticed movement in the distant treeline, as if a swarm of bees hovered around a point where a track made its cutting. Cullen stared as riders emerged. A hundred or thereabouts, double-file, straight-backed and at a rapid canter. They wore long cloaks that billowed across the rumps of their proud mounts, and helmets of various design, many bearing the elaborate devices of wing, plume or spike. A gasp rippled along the crowded rampart, then a collective hush as the approaching column kicked into a gallop, dust roiling up in their wake, plaited hair and cloaks, manes and tails all flung back by the rush of the wind. Yet there was still no apparent panic, no shrill calls of alarm, and Cullen shielded his eyes with a palm and squinted down at the road as the new arrivals negotiated the outer defences with evidently little difficulty. It was more than simply the helmets that spoke of finery, he noted. These riders had donned their full regalia. Battledress, for certain, but with an extra layer of adornment that spoke of high pomp and solemn ceremony. As they emerged onto the expanse of the greensward, he saw painted shields, glistening with bright colours at the sides of saddles, the dazzle of precious metal glinting along their line like winking stars, hinting at torc and hilt, chape and clasp, bridle and brooch. Then they broke ranks, suddenly and expertly, fanning left and right so that they bore down on the waiting army in a broad line.

And the army of Camulodunon did not respond. Not a chariot moved. Not a spear twitched. Cullen turned to ask someone – anyone – what the supposed defenders were about, but a new ripple of chatter interrupted him, for Caratacos, alone, save a dozen named men and women, urged his mount forth. He sat straight-backed, formal, but relaxed in the confines of his four-pommelled saddle, holding the reins loosely, casually, guiding the horse with imperceptible movements of hips and thighs. The newcomers surged on at pace, as if they intended to trample him without breaking stride, but he barely flinched at the centre of his little knot of warriors. Instead he drew to a halt and waited, taking deliberate care to place his long war spear in its saddle loop. A gesture of peace, Cullen now understood. No, it was more than that. A gesture of submission.

It was only when the greatest leader this side of Verlamion – black hair shot through with war-feathers and oak-strong body encased in battle-iron – dipped his head in marked subservience, then dismounted, that Cullen realised the true nature of this meeting.

The galloping horsemen wrenched hard on their reins and the horses whinnied and reared and swirled like a torrent about Caratacos and his group, who, by now, had all slid out of their saddles. The newcomers drew up in a half-circle, a bevy of sharpened weaponry, furs and feathers, but they took care not to cut off any retreat, for this was no act of aggression. And Cullen saw that what they wore was indeed a matter of display over substance. Tunics were favoured over breastplates, while none of their faces carried the curse-marks of the Wise Ones. Their helms were gilded and polished, to attract the attention of spectators, and to catch the brilliant glory of Belinos's rays. Some of their mounts had yellow plumes tied to their manes, and many of the warriors carried shields that were long, rectangular and intricately decorated, speaking of a penchant for beauty over function. Cullen let his gaze rake across the greensward for the one figure that mattered, half holding his breath. Just as he began to think that that man had not come after all, one amongst the new arrivals abruptly swung a leg across his saddle and alighted before Caratacos. From his head he pulled an eagle-winged helmet to reveal a strong, broad face, with florid cheeks, a large nose and a head of thick red hair that had been expertly woven into a dozen plaits that sprung like rope from the sides of his skull, woven with many feathers. Encircling his throat was the thickest torc of twisted gold Cullen had ever seen, its ends like a pair of balled fists. It was something only a king would wear.

Togodubnos, eldest son of Great Cunobelin, de facto High King of the Isle of the Mighty, embraced his younger brother. There they stood for a few lingering moments, utterly oblivious, as if they were the only two people in the world. They slapped one another's backs hard, swaying sideways as though they were about to wrestle, but both laughed loudly, easily, when words were exchanged. Caratacos enveloped his older sibling, for he was taller, his tree-trunk limbs all bulk and unconcealed strength. But Togodubnos held him up, despite his lack of obvious brawn, the metal adorning arms and necks clinking like the inside of a busy smithy. Around them the warriors chatted amongst themselves, old comrades all, and the people on the rampart began to cheer.

—

Inside the dun the roads were lined with people, from the meekest to the mightiest, all clamouring for a closer view. Togodubnos did not disappoint, riding an immaculately groomed dappled grey stallion at the head of the procession, the torc of leadership his ostentatious banner. Beneath his golden cheek pieces, he grinned broadly, accepting the adulation of Catuvellauni and Trinovantes alike, while occasionally glancing back to throw a word to his brother, who rode half a length behind. Cullen finally understood the traditions at play. If Caratacos received Togodubnos in the great hall, it would offend the senior brother's dignity. Honour dictated that the younger of the two needed to greet his lord out on the greensward, with all due ceremony, so that Togodubnos might enter the town as king. Now that the pleasantries were done, lord, nobleman and warrior could begin to relax, for they were one people under the sons of Cunobelin.

Cullen made his way back through the traffic, watching the royal progress but thinking about his grumbling stomach. As if the gods had read his mind, a smell soon slipped in on the air, creeping between the ever-present woodsmoke and the decaying stink of sun-warmed middens. He followed the aroma like a hound, sniffing his way to a row of tables set out beside one of the larger roundhouses. There, a man with a twitching left eye and prodigious belly was selling strips of preserved boar meat that were drying on large hazel-wood frames. Cullen stood for a time, exchanged one of Becan's coins for some scraps of meat, and absently watched the procession rumble past. The royal party, its ranks swelled by Caratacos's wives and attendants, slipped into the distance, heading for the long halls at the centre of the dun. With them went the majority of the crowd, and as their numbers thinned, he spotted Becan threading his way through the remaining traffic, making heavy going as his sticks were clipped and knocked. Cullen hailed him.

'So,' Becan said as he came to a panting stop, puffy cheeks red with effort, 'you have seen our greatest lord. Over-King of the Catuvellauni confederacy.'

Cullen ate some of the boar meat, the saltiness surprisingly satisfying. He handed a hunk to Becan as a family went by, little children balanced on their parents' shoulders. 'Not as fearsome as his brother.'

'Older,' Becan said, popping the meat into the side of his mouth. 'Cleverer too.'

Cullen nodded mutely, distracted by the children lofted high, giggling as they swung at one another with imaginary swords. Though he tried his best to put on the cold face that was now his constant companion, the sight summoned memories of his own kin. The loss of them hit him anew, an almost physical blow, and he found himself fighting back tears. To quell the feeling, and deflect the inevitable questions, he said, 'Why has he come?'

'You expect me to read a king's mind, goat-fiddler?' Becan answered, noisily chewing. 'Two kings', for that matter.' He shrugged. 'Paying his respects to Caratacos, who has expanded upon their territory. He'll be keeping a close eye too. Ensuring little brother does not covet a throne of his own.' He beamed broadly as he swallowed down the meat. 'Either way, there'll be celebrations, praise be to Belinos.' The thought of more feasting did not fill Cullen with excitement, and he supposed the expression on his face must have reflected the thought, for it earned a withering look from Becan. 'You can sit in a corner and ponder your strange and undeserved good fortune, while I drink.'

Fortune. Cullen could not prevent a bitter smile at the word. The idea that it might best describe the past days still seemed perverse, and he was intent on saying as much when a knot of weathered-looking warriors tramped past, catching his eye. Quite apart from their hard eyes and scarred faces, they were exceptional for the sheer amount of metal on display. Bronze, copper, iron, silver and gold, in rings and bracelets, buckles and torcs. In the lead was the formidable woman with red hair from the night before. 'She led the hunt,' he said. With the benefit of daylight, he could see that she might have known thirty winters, many of them grim, to judge by the lines on her face. Her eyes were dark green and intelligent, and the deep groove of a long-healed wound formed a vertical gorge in her chin.

'Aoife the Dread is her name,' Becan said. 'From Inisfail, the Isle of Destiny, that last scrap of land on the far side of the Clear Sea, before the watery abyss at the end of the world.'

'What brought her here?'

'She left her tribe under a cloud, so they say. Crossed the sea to seek a new life. Now she is one of our most trusted fighters. A blade-wielder of renown. A woman of fame.'

Cullen watched Aoife, unable to tear his attention from her tall, sinewy form, but all the while praying she would not turn her baleful gaze upon him. 'What kind of cloud?'

'Caught her husband ploughing the wrong furrow,' Becan said with a wink, 'if you follow me. Wounded him and his lover.'

'Wounded?'

'Let us merely say that the plough in question is now blunt.'

Cullen felt his jaw loll loose. 'Was she not punished?'

'Revenge for unfaithfulness is permitted, so long as it occurs within three days of the original offence.' He grinned maliciously. 'And three days she waited. Till the very last moment, so her unfortunate mate was off his guard.'

Cullen shuddered. 'By the ancients.'

'Not an unusual response,' Becan laughed. 'She is a warrioress. A blood-letter of the highest order. But her name she earned in the bedroom.'

'By the ancients,' Cullen muttered again. He stared still. At the tall frame, swathed in blue tunic and red cloak, that moved with the languid smoothness of a predator. At the huge sword at her waist and the heavy bracelets on her wrists, and the woad snakes coiled around bare, sinewy forearms that were latticed in veins and knotted with lean muscle. 'A named woman.'

'Never seen one before?'

'I am from the fields and forests. The wilderness. My mother could fight – *did* fight – when raiders came.' He shook his head slowly, unable to keep the awe from his tone. 'But I have not seen a woman with a full battle-name, no.'

'Then feast your eyes upon her,' Becan said. 'Everyone must fight when their homes are threatened. A pair of tits does not prevent the throwing of a spear. Some are too good to retreat to the cooking fires. They take the tests with the boys. But still, such a woman is rare enough, even amongst the Catuvellauni.'

Cullen noted the group around her, fearsome to a man. Each looking more cutthroat than the next. 'She commands them?'

'Magnificent, is she not?'

That was one way to describe her, Cullen supposed. Another would be to say that she made his own formidable mother look like a field mouse. The way she carried herself smacked of latent threat, as though her every gesture was a thin veneer, concealing the violence beneath. The way she seemed to cast her gaze was ever watchful. Even the rings on her fingers were more akin to weapons than baubles, so thick and ridged were they.

'Now that is more like it,' Becan was saying.

Cullen hardly registered the words, until he caught sight of what his friend was looking at. The warriors were gathering around a long table, outside what was evidently a wine-seller's shop, to judge by the Roman-style amphorae that were swiftly brought out. Aoife the Dread perched on the end of one bench, taking a whetstone to a long, slender dagger, while the men under her command began to set to the wine, offered with obsequious deference by the owner of the establishment. A steady stream of women, like gulls trailing a boat, emerged from the nearby roundhouses and lanes. They called to the younger warriors, threw flowers at their feet and took up seats between them at the table. The warriors drank with gusto, laughed like mules and flirted shamelessly.

Cullen was enthralled as he studied the scene, noting the confident bearing and gruff banter, seeing how they commanded respect by mere presence. They feared none, and were feared, in turn, by all. They chatted to the girls in confident, ribald fashion and received none of the contemptuous rejections to which he would have been treated. Rather, coquettish giggles and winks were the order of the day. They were heroes, all, these named men.

'I want that.'

'Don't we all?' Becan remarked ruefully.

'Not the girls.' He had woken that morning with a resolution on his mind, and this moment only served to strengthen it. 'I want to fight.'

Becan looked up at him. 'Who has earned your displeasure, goat-fiddler?'

'I do not want to fight *now*,' Cullen said impatiently. 'I want to *be* a fighter.'

'You'll do just fine in a scrap, none could deny it.'

Cullen shook his head. 'A full warrior, with renown.'

Becan drove one of his crutches hard into the ground, adopting a mockingly deep voice. 'Cullen Goat-Worrier!'

'I'm serious.'

'Lightning-Tickler, then.'

Cullen punched him on the shoulder, hard enough to make him stumble sideways. 'You do not think I could do it?'

'Did you take your tribe's tests?'

Cullen pictured the event in his mind's eye. Twice a year, at the winter and summer gatherings, all the clans that made up the Atrebates tribe would gather together as one nation, and the young would take the tests. They would face challenges, with weapon and shield and horse, and only those who performed to the demanded standard were given their warrior's spear. This would not earn them a name – far from it – but it would elevate them within the tribe. Allow them to take their place in the battle line when their people were threatened. Set them on the warrior's life path if that was to be their decision come choosing time. But Cullen had been too busy. At least that is what he had told the others. Told himself. Every testing time that came and went, he claimed the herd needed him. Claimed he would take the challenges come next summer. Come next winter. And so it went. Eventually he would take them. Of course he would. Except now there was no one left to test him. He looked at Becan, forming the excuses on his lips but never managing to voice them. In the end he just shook his head and hoped the humiliation he felt was not as clear on his burning cheeks as he feared.

'There is a reason the Catuvellauni find success on the field,' Becan said gently, 'and it is not because their tests are a simple thing to pass.'

Cullen puffed himself up. 'I used to set wolf traps to protect our goats.'

'Go and see Caratacos immediately!' Becan barked with sudden enthusiasm. 'He will probably lend you his own shield. The goat-fiddler sets traps! Put him in the front rank and see my enemies flee!'

'What else can I do?' Cullen hissed, acutely aware that the warriors were almost within earshot. 'I am trained for nothing. You mock me, but I am lost here. I rely on the good graces of Caratacos, the very man who slaughtered my kin. I watch my back for Arthmael's dagger. I have nothing to trade, nothing to give but the coins you provide. In the end, I will beg or I will starve.' He shrugged. 'But I could fight.'

Becan waved his crutch in Cullen's face. 'Cease your whining, goat-fiddler, it is hurting my ears. I have means. Enough to keep you fed.'

'And how is that?' Cullen bit back, not intending the hostility in his tone but powerless against the frustration bubbling to the fore. 'How do you have means, and why would you share it with me?' He stepped away, the sudden tremor of suspicion running through his body. 'Who are you, Becan? He who cannot walk and, by his own admission, has no purpose in the tribe. He who is not my guard yet follows my every move.'

Becan arched an eyebrow, amused. 'Consider me your guide, goat-fiddler.'

'You speak in riddles,' Cullen countered angrily. 'By the ancients, if you do not answer I'll take that crutch and—'

Becan stepped closer, so abruptly that it killed the end of Cullen's sentence. He let his voice drop to a conspiratorial tone. 'There is a woman,' he began softly. 'Moranna of the Silver. One of the Wise. She senses things. What a soul desires. Or, at least, what it needs, in spite of its desires. She will reveal all. Help you see the choices you must make.'

Cullen shook his head, exasperated. 'But you told me I must beat my own path in this new life.'

Becan's knowing smirk widened, revealing the gap in his teeth. 'And you must.' He raised a crutch. 'Moranna will hand you the stick.'

They went as evening crept in, its slate-grey tentacles slithering round tree and thatch alike.

Went where? Cullen had no notion, save Becan's nebulous but enthusiastic pleas. 'Trust me, goat-fiddler,' was as much surety as he would offer. Yet Cullen went, because, like so much of this new, surreal life of his, there was little alternative. He was stumbling from moment to moment, hour to hour, like a blind man in a strange room, only too willing to be led, whatever the destination might be.

The sounds of civilisation faded with the light. Only the hoot of an owl and the skin-chilling shriek of a vixen accompanied the crackle of leaves and twigs beneath feet and crutch. The path – a tangled track barely deserving of the name – seemed to burrow into the earth, sinking with every pace so that the land loomed above them on all sides. The moon, rising and brightening somewhere far off, was choked almost to nothing. Unwelcome on this highway to the underworld.

Becan, though, knew what he was about. At a dense barrier of vicious brambles they stalled, cocking ears to the hidden sky at the mournful, skin-prickling howl of a wolf. It lingered, dying slowly on the balmy air, only to be echoed by another and another.

'Far off,' Cullen said, for he had gauged such cries more times than he could remember. 'It is not us they hunt.'

Becan pulled an expression that spoke of abundant relief. For his part, Cullen felt the same. Not for the wolves, but the realisation that he could see his companion's face. He glanced up, realising that the canopy had thinned, letting the moonlight in once more.

Becan grinned. 'Almost there.'

They rounded the thicket and came to a place where the land fell away steeply. Cullen peered along the trajectory of the track. Beneath them, perhaps a hundred paces down, it began to curve, widening as it went. It seemed to shift too, as if molten gold, by some miracle, had replaced the forest floor. He blinked hard, fearing the strain of recent days had finally caused his wits to crumble. There was a creeping suspicion too. One that whispered of gateways to other worlds, hidden deep in these timeless woods. But which one was this? A realm above, or one below?

They descended, faltering as they negotiated scrub and root, eyes always on the trackway that still quivered like a moon-gilded stream at the foot of the slope. Halfway down, picking his way over snagging brambles, Cullen realised that that was exactly what it was. The track had not turned into precious metal, but the moonlight played upon a large body of water.

'Come,' Becan urged. 'She awaits.'

CHAPTER NINE

'No, girl, she must be in heat.'

'In heat?'

'That is what I said.'

'And that will make all the difference?'

'So claimed my mother.'

Cassia sipped her beer in an effort to conceal the smirk that threatened to overwhelm her mouth. The taste was bitter, despite the overtones of spice and honey. 'And what say the Wise?'

Critheanach snorted disgust, screwed up her face and lifted her own pot. 'How would I know?'

Now Cassia could not prevent a laugh. Baiting her mistress was a long-cherished pastime and talk of the old woman's strained relations with the esteemed Order of Mona often proved fertile ground. 'Perhaps I should ask.'

'You ask, girl, by all means,' Critheanach muttered testily. She sank the rest of her beer, then set the pot down in a manner that suggested she would not have mind if it shattered. 'But, mark you, my dear mother's remedies were as effective as any those puffed-up cockerels can conjure.'

Cassia laughed as Critheanach twisted on the bench, clicking fingers for a serving girl to bring up two more pots. The huge roundhouse was full of long tables arranged around a blazing fire, above which a cauldron of porridge bubbled.

'Let me be clear,' Cassia said. 'To stop a dog barking, I must flay a bitch hound, make gloves from her skin, and wear them wherever I go.'

'So long as the bitch—'

'Is in heat.'

Critheanach nodded firmly. 'Precisely. Mother said it would work, and that's the final word on the matter.'

Cassia drank from the newly brimming pot, thanking the girl, who scuttled quickly to serve a gang of hard-looking men. The air in here felt hot and sticky, the heady fug reeking of smoke and beer and bodies, fat droplets of salty sweat dripping like rain from the high beams. 'I don't understand why you failed to join the Order,' she said, eyeing the warriors as they sang and jostled at one of the tables. 'You have a great talent for pronouncing the final word on things.'

'By the ancients, you are an impudent pup,' Critheanach replied, though the twinkle in her eyes was bright. 'And ignorant too.'

'Oh?'

'A maker of potions does not make judgements. The Wise Ones have a hierarchy, just like every other part of society.' She took a moment to sup. 'We have kings, nobles, creators, farmers, slaves. The wild places of the world have nymphs and piskies, who bend the knee to the spirits of forest and river. And those, in turn, depend upon the good graces of the greater gods. So it is with the Wise. Seers and healers and the makers of sacrifice.' She counted the roles off on her bony fingers. 'Poets, who know the songs and the stories, whose task it is to protect our traditions and see that they are handed down through the generations. Finally, all work under the authority of the philosophers and judges, who answer to none but chiefs and kings. So, you see, my significant ability to weigh and judge a situation,' she went on, apparently oblivious to her companion's reappearing smirk, 'would have nothing to do with my work as a healer, were I to don the robes of Mona.'

'Fortunate that such a confusion will not arise,' Cassia muttered.

'Quite so, girl, quite so. The schools of the Wise attract pompous fools as a sheep's arse attracts flies. I'm better off without them.' She sat back, appraising the warriors. 'Good men, those.'

'Like bears,' Cassia said, 'down from the mountains.'

Critheanach grinned toothlessly. 'Smell just as bad too, but heroes all.'

Cassia thought of the wounded coming up from Calleva. 'Will there be more fighting?'

'Togodubnos is not the over-king his father was,' Critheanach said with bleak resignation. Almost at the hour of Cunobelin's death, the patchwork of tribal unity, stitched so carefully with the twin threads of diplomacy and force, had begun to fray. Lesser kings, strident warlords and petty chiefs, all chafing under the Catuvellauni yoke and each harbouring their own chariot-load of long-simmered grievances, were eyeing their chances. 'Berikos of the Atrebates was the first to flex his muscles and I would not bet on him being the last.'

'Do they not see that their weakness will play into Rome's hands?'

The old woman shook her head. 'They never see beyond their cocks or their swords, until it is too late. Until their people are dead and their lands conquered.' She brightened as one of the warriors strode across the room towards them. 'The Grey Boulder, as I live and breathe.'

The man was big. Huge, in fact. With shaggy silver hair and a thickly plaited moustache of the same shade, tied off with silver wire. He gave Critheanach a broad, lascivious grin. 'Now this is a fine example of womanhood. Clever, kind and built like the goddess Branwen.'

For a moment Cassia feared her mistress was in the grip of a seizure, but, as she watched the colour flood the old woman's narrow features, she realised it was the beginnings of a blush.

'Garn, you old charmer,' Critheanach was saying. 'You never change.'

'I'd like to charm you out of that tunic and no mistake,' the big warrior replied, evidently trying to smooth out the gruffness from his tone, but nevertheless sounding like a waterfall after torrential rain.

'Stop,' Critheanach said, touching his massive forearm as he planted the spiked stump that served as a hand at the edge of their table. 'I'm surprised there's any snap in the old wolf's jaws.'

He winked. 'You'll have to find out, won't you?'

Cassia stared, astonished, at the exchange. Not because the combined age of the pair was almost beyond counting, but rather because she knew she was watching her mistress flirt with a living legend. Garn Grey Boulder had earned his fame. In the endless fight for territory, for water, for fertile soil and for livestock, he had defended his nation as well as any. Made himself a name to be feared. He had flushed Coritani sheep rustlers out of Cunobelin's pastures, killed Eceni in the deep fens and had his left hand lopped off by Cornovii raiders in the high hills. The wound had nearly sent him to the next life, but he had won that fight too. When the raw stump had healed to a mass of leather-thick scar tissue, he had bound it in tough bull-hide that was studded with iron spikes, and the injury had only added to his repute.

Folk still talked of Grey Boulder with awe. The poets sang at fuggy firesides of the days when he had been a brawny monster. No man faster with the broadsword or heavier with his fists. A mountain bear in man's clothing. But Cassia saw little more than blubber on legs. The muscle had run to fat as the years had seeped by. The studded club remained in place of his left hand, but the huge arm itself did not flex, so much as wobble.

'You're staying in Verlamion?' Critheanach asked. 'I hear Togodubnos has gone to see his brother.'

'That he has,' Garn boomed, 'but he'll be back. We hold the capital while he is away. Ulla commands.'

'May Belinos protect him.'

Garn regarded Cassia with interest. 'And who is this?'

'My ward,' Critheanach said, 'Cassia.'

The silver brows arched. 'Roman?'

'A slave, strictly speaking, but one of us in the sight of the gods and the ancients.'

The face that loomed above Cassia was wide, the eyes shrewd and blue. The bulbous nose was webbed in livid lines which became a myriad of long-healed scars as they reached his cheeks. 'Speak the common tongue?'

Cassia nodded. 'I do.'

'Well met, then. I am Garn. The Grey Boulder, they call me.'

'Your name carries with it the fame of your deeds.'

'So it does. Your name carries with it the knowledge of an empire. Tell us, will they come?'

'The legions?' Cassia asked. She did not need to think upon a reply. 'Eventually. Given the right reason.'

Garn pulled his spikes out of the tabletop and flicked bits of wood from the fiendish looking points. 'Rumour has it that Adminios begs the emperor for aid. Wants him to rid this island of his brothers so that he may rule. What say you, Cassia of Rome? Is that reason enough? Will your people invade?'

—

It was a pond, silent and stagnant. A thin skein of mist hovered over the black surface, turning gently, obscuring all notion of size or shape. Trees grew all around the pond's edge, not that Cullen could see very much of it. Yet what little he discerned immediately struck him as curious, for out to his left, where the water and bank should be hardest to distinguish, everything seemed to shine like polished bronze, affording a view of the bank in profile, complete with its divots and roots, its reeds and bull-rushes and leaning trees, all guarded by bristling ranks of teasels.

'There,' Becan said, indicating that very place, which was perhaps forty or fifty paces distant.

Cullen realised why that spot seemed so much brighter than anywhere else. 'Someone has lit a fire.'

They traced the curve of the bank, like a pair of moths drawn to the light. Sure enough, at the water's edge, there was a bright, flickering flame. Not a campfire, but a thick stick, one end wrapped in oil-soaked rags that blazed madly. It had been propped in a loose pile of smooth stones. Cullen glanced at Becan. 'For us?'

Becan indicated that he should take up the torch. 'For any who seek guidance.'

As soon as Cullen pulled the light free, more of the pond's edge was thrown into stark relief. Immediately he saw a large, black shape amongst the foliage, incongruous for its regular lines.

Becan had already hobbled to the land's frayed edge by the time Cullen understood what he was looking at. The Silures leaned on one crutch and used the other to probe the water, snagging a length of something, like a black snake lurking just below the surface. He hooked it up, hauled it in, and out on the pond the large shadow began to drift closer. Cullen swung the torch down, throwing light on what he saw was a crude little raft, lashed together with slime-tinged vines. It hissed along the edge of the reed beds, sliding against cloying mud, dull thuds betraying the presence of exposed tree roots beneath the water.

'Get on,' Becan instructed as he set about unfastening the rope from one of the stooping trunks that stood sentinel.

Tentatively, testing the robustness of the planks with prodding toes, Cullen slid into the centre of the raft, inching to the fore as Becan clambered aboard. It was a precarious and ungainly manoeuvre, which had the raft bucking like a colt, but, to his credit, he was able to prop himself expertly on his stumps, so that he appeared in the gloom to be kneeling. As soon as the raft became calm, he set down one of his crutches and used the other as a punting pole, shoving away from the side with an initial lurch, the splash and slop of water seeming unnaturally loud in this still and ancient place. They were moving swiftly in no time at all, crossing smoothly into the middle of the pond despite the grasping attentions of unseen debris.

Cullen held the flame high. Misty wraiths turned languorously above the patches of plants that floated like black oil slicks on the surface. All around them the waters eddied and swirled.

'Almost there,' Becan said.

'What is this place?'

Becan simply brandished an enigmatic smile. 'Look.'

Cullen looked, lofting the torch a little more. From the gloom, new shapes gradually began to resolve. Low-hanging branches at first. Willow and hazel, brushing the tops of reeds, a curtain drawn across the land beyond. Then the more certain line of a bank, covered in a gnarled web of exposed roots that reached down below the waterline.

He saw another flame. Modest and tremulous, but clear as a precious stone on a charred log. It was low, the flame. Close to the ground. A fire to heat a pot, rather than light a path. It told of a camp. A base, perhaps, though its permanence was a matter of guesswork.

'Someone lives here?'

'This is the Seeing Pool,' Becan said, a note of unexpected reverence hushing his tone. 'The island at its heart is the lair of Moranna of the Silver. Pay her respect.' He turned then, his round face a greyish leer in the murk. 'Forget your manners and I'll be fishing your bones out of this stew.'

The rushes and weeds thinned now as they traced the contour of the island for another twenty paces or so, until a scrap of ground emerged that was clear of the dense detritus, allowing access for a craft to moor. Becan switched his crutch to the opposite side, pushing hard against the pond bed beneath them, and they slewed inward, the water bubbling and frothing at the bow. In a few moments the foremost timbers grazed the sticky earth hidden by the waterline and Becan deftly guided the bow home so that the side of the raft kissed the mud and roots of the bank.

Cullen looked back at his pilot, but Becan shook his head. 'For your ears alone.'

Alighting was an unsteady and graceless affair that had the raft lurching violently, but Becan kept it against the bank with a wedged crutch. 'Find your truth, goat-fiddler!' he called, waving impatiently towards the light, as if whatever waited would wait no longer. 'Find your truth!'

'You're the one,' a voice came from the dark.

Cullen spun so fast he almost toppled back onto the raft. 'I—' he blurted, peering into the gloom with palms raised to shield whatever blow might come.

'It was not a question, red crest,' came the voice again. A female's voice. Slow, almost lazy. 'You *are* the one.'

His eyes strained, discerning the outline of a round face, some ten paces away. The woman stood to the side of the little fire, but she took a few barefooted steps towards him, so that he could see a pale countenance, ethereal in the moonlight, with narrow eyes and a snub nose. Her hair was long, straight and silver, and woven into the strands were a score of items, from carved totems to little bones to bits of metal bent into various shapes. That gaze, almost translucent, was as penetrating as any venerable grandmother he had encountered. Over what he guessed was a wiry frame, she wore a plaid cloak of many colours, and about her neck hung a heavy-looking chain of wooden dowels.

'He who vanquished the Slayer,' she said. 'He who turned Caratacos's votive to chaos.' She grinned, then, as if the notion brought her great joy, and Cullen saw that her teeth had been filed to sharp points. He felt an involuntary shudder, though she seemed not to notice, or perhaps not to care. 'Beloved of Taranis. Scourge of Arthmael the Learned.' She spread out a hand, indicating the island. 'You are most welcome here, red crest.'

She took another step towards him, through the mingling mist and smoke.

Cullen swallowed thickly. 'You are Moranna of the Silver?' When she nodded, he said, 'The Seeing Pool. What does it see?'

She fingered one of the dowels at her throat, caressing it between thumb and forefinger. 'It is a meeting place for men and gods,' she said, in that strangely off-kilter way, the words coming to her in fits and starts, punctuated by elaborate pauses, as if she pondered ceaselessly upon their appropriateness. 'Thinkers... and dreamers.'

He braved a glance away, taking in the arrangement of the land. It was flat and low-lying, for he could see the glimmer of water on the far side. In the centre was the fire, and beside that a pair of trees. One was wizened and old, tarred and bare, like the ones at Avalloc's Shelter. The other had been curtailed at the height of a man, its stump carved with deep, swirling marks that took a few moments for Cullen to identify as a bearded face, topped with ostentatious antlers. 'Cernunnos.'

'The horned one,' she agreed. 'He gives this place its power.' She turned to glance at the carving. The moonlight shifted over her face to show the pits of old pockmarks, some of which had been permanently dyed in charcoal-black. Her ears, he now saw, were woven all the way up the sides with silver thread. 'Cernunnos, of the oldest gods, who dwells in the great nemeton, the grove of all worlds, connecting earth, sea and sky.'

'And pond,' Becan chirped from somewhere behind Cullen, making him start.

The woman's face became taut as her pale eyes left Cullen's to skewer the man in the raft. 'Hush, legless toad!'

'It's a nice enough puddle, you old she-wolf,' Becan said casually, 'but the grove of all worlds is a stretch, if you ask me.'

'By the ancients, Becan Half-Man,' the woman jabbed a beringed finger at him as though it were a dagger, 'I'd offer your sorry carcass to the gods if I didn't fear they would take offence.'

Bemused, Cullen asked, 'Is this your home?'

Becan laughed. 'Her lair.'

She shot him an acidic look, then shook her head, the dowels rattling in response. 'My home is wherever the king may choose. Here, there, it matters not. But this place is where I dwell when we come to Camulodunon.'

'King,' Cullen echoed, as if the word were new to him. He said it again, slower, sounding it out. Then, 'You are the king's Wise One?'

'Indeed.' She shrugged. 'One of them. His counsellor, as I was his father's before him. Advisor in all things.' She held out a bony hand, beckoning Cullen. 'Now step forth, red crest. The Seeing Pool is a powerful gateway, the water a conduit. A passage,' she pointed skyward, then down to her feet, 'betwixt thither and hither. I dwell at its edges. Listen to the whispers of the unseen. Others come. The Wise. To have their eyes opened and their dreams enriched. We discuss the heavenly bodies, the size of the universe, the properties of the earth, the movement of the stars and the power of the gods. Old knowledge has coalesced about the rushes. Caught there, perhaps, like fish in a net. New knowledge is gained and shared, by those deemed worthy.' She broke off to stare pointedly at Becan. 'And which are you?'

This time there was no equivocation. With a nod more solemn than Cullen thought possible, Becan pushed away from the island, the raft drifting out into the dark water.

Moranna of the Silver led Cullen into the island's interior, where the fire flickered beside the trees. Nearby he noticed a rudimentary shrine of painted seashells and the skulls of cats. Incense burned out of the tops of those skulls, lacing the air with a sweet scent. The nature of the shrine stood to reason, Cullen supposed, for even a fool knew that skulls were venerated above all bones, the soul of a person residing in his head. Even so, he found himself absently contemplating whether the soul of a cat went to the next life like that of its human counterparts.

'Your friend brings you to me,' Moranna said abruptly, shattering his train of thought, 'because you seek guidance. What burdens your heart?'

Cullen opened his mouth but stalled when words were sought. There were a thousand things pressing down like quern stones. So many that he could not find just one to utter in this surreal moment. So it was, from out of the confusion, an image resolved in his mind's eye. 'I am followed by a magpie.'

She frowned. 'The black and the white.' A pale hand went up to her necklace, fiddling furiously with the clattering dowels. 'Death and life, intermingled. A bird venerated and feared in equal measure.' Moranna's brow furrowed yet further. 'Did you kill one?'

He shook his head. 'I would never. It is forbidden.'

'Strange, then. If it comes not to haunt, we must consider another purpose. A message?' She offered what he took to be a smile, though the thin mouth twisted hard so that one corner went up and the other down. The sharp teeth flashed as though she were about to devour him. 'Let me look at you.' Her hand shot out, pressing his chest firmly as she gauged his heartbeat, as if the very rhythm spoke a secret language known only to her silver-sewn ears. 'I see. Yes, I see. Your will be done, lord.' The glassy eyes bore into his, black pupils suddenly contracting. 'Taranis dwells here. He preserved you for a purpose, red crest. That is why he has sent the magpie.'

Cullen thought of his dead family. The burned-out shell that had been his village. 'His purpose was to torment me.'

'You are selfish,' Moranna said sharply, 'and foolish.'

'My kin—'

'Your kin were slaughtered,' she interrupted. 'A tragedy, to be sure, but no more or less than a thread in the great cloth.' Evidently, she saw his mouth work as he tried to assemble a coherent protest, for the fingers that had conversed with his heart, now found themselves pressed to his lips. 'Take this cloak,' she said, and with her free hand she tugged lightly at the material that enveloped her body. 'One garment, yes? A single item. But how did it come to be? Where from do its colours derive? How does it provide such warmth? Layers. Lining. Individual threads, beyond counting. All connected. Mingled and mixed and woven to make one. Some strands are dyed. Some are long, while others have been cut away. Brutal – tragic on some level – but all part of the design.'

He stared incredulously. 'My family's slaughter was part of a design?'

'Life's design,' Moranna said, her slow timbre unsentimental. 'The world's design. Those who plant, those who cook, those who forge and those who fight. The men and women of Mona, sent to gain knowledge. Our singers, our teachers and our dreamers. Those marked out for their deeds of valour, given names higher than the rest. Those whose bodies take them upon uncommon paths, by age, like the elders, or by birth, as you see with your friend, Becan. We are all of us part of the great cloth. All of us threads in the design. All of the living, and all of the dead. It was time for the strands of your kin to be cut.'

'And mine?'

'You killed a named man, little red crest, and you embarrassed Arthmael the Learned.' She bore the fangs again, relishing the words as though each one tasted of honey. 'There is more thread yet to unravel.'

'You dislike Arthmael?'

'Dislike?' Her wolf's grin only broadened, reaching her eyes for the first time. 'He has two shadows, that man. One for him, the other for the demon sitting on his shoulder. Oh, he is wise, have no doubt. His power is great. But he is also cunning and dangerous and imbued with a malice that is as cold as the mountains of the Brigantes.' She winked at him. 'And he is as pleasant as a badger's back passage.' That broke the spell, and Cullen could not help but laugh. She cut him off with another raised palm. 'Beware his wrath, red crest. Fear him or fall foul of him. Your thread is special, but that does not mean your enemies will not try and cut it.'

'Then where does my thread lead?'

She licked her lips slowly. 'Your past has been devoured by fire and soaked in blood. So shall your future be. Use it. Embrace it.'

'War,' Cullen said. 'I am to be a fighter?'

'If that is the path you wish to tread, the most-high Taranis will guide you.' She canted her head to the side, silver twine shimmering with the movement. 'And you seek revenge. It is etched upon your face.'

Cullen inclined his head. 'I do.' Calleva's gaping gates flashed before his eyes. 'I—'

She curtailed him abruptly, almost slapping him with that raised palm. 'I cannot know. I must not know. All that is clear is that to move forward on your life path, you must first purge the bitterness you feel. It is a poison to be extracted.' She lowered her hand and stepped closer. 'Listen carefully.'

—

In the clear blue dawn, Cullen of the Atrebates, alone in the cacophony of joyous birdsong, walked to the forest outside of Camulodunon. His clothes were still damp from the journey back to the mainland, but now they steamed as the sun began its inexorable climb. It was a scene in complete contradiction to the hours that had passed, as bright as the Seeing Pool had been dark, and yet the night's tasks remained incomplete: this one morning trek the final hurdle.

Cullen walked. Further and further. Along a track barely worthy of the name, marked only by the occasional carving set in a high bough, or the soft tinkle of chimes. The language of the Wise.

A dozen black smudges twirled high above, and he whispered his thanks to Taranis, for he knew the rookery meant that he had arrived. She had told him. Moranna of the Silver, Wise One to King Togodubnos, had instructed him in this. Placed the steps before him that must now be followed. Could she be trusted? Perhaps not. But she was an enemy of Arthmael, which made her a friend of Cullen's, and so he walked the track and watched for the signs and now he was here. The rookery, and after that, his destination.

The nemeton was still shrouded in shadow, for its perimeter, enclosed by ancient yews, was a mess of entwined limbs doing their best to resist the onset of day. Tiny birds erupted from the dense canopy as he pushed the branches aside, jinking away to alight somewhere higher, their beady eyes ever watchful. There would be spirits up there, too. Whispering, laughing, and taking what transpired back to Moranna. No matter, he thought. It was not for him to trouble himself with the ways of the Otherworld.

Thus, he crossed the bounds of the sacred space. The ground was marked by deep grooves, etched by the hands of the Wise to describe mystical symbols. He moved beyond them, incanting apologies as Moranna had said he should do, until he reached the arrangement of pebbles that were laid out in the oval shape of an eye at the very centre of the grove. The filed teeth and pale eyes skimmed across his memory. 'Thrice round, little red crest,' she had said. 'Thrice, for the three phases of the moon, and for the three parts of the middle world; earth, sky and sea.'

And so he stepped, carefully, softly, around the eye that peered sightlessly back at him, and when three passes were done, he took a knee before it. The ground was mossy and moist. There were toadstools in patches all around. At the base of one of the yews, he saw a little wooden door, made, presumably, for the piskies to enter. He took a breath, deep and steadying, and then unsheathed his knife.

'Three words,' Moranna of the Silver had said. 'Uttered three times, for three is the most powerful of all the numbers. It will unlock the magic you seek to harness.'

He bit his lower lip hard and drew the blade firmly over the white flesh under his forearm. The metallic tang of blood came into his mouth too, as his teeth dug in, but he stifled the cry that welled in his chest. Instead, he hissed, 'Strength, strength, strength.'

Three words, uttered three times. 'Say them aloud, red crest. Make them binding.'

Another cut, beside the first, the blood showing black in the gloom. 'Courage, courage, courage.'

The pain gave him pause, but he had come this far. He cut again, a third line opening in the soft flesh, dark liquid beading, welling and falling in a rivulet to patter the pebbles that formed the eye's staring pupil. Through gritted teeth, Cullen said, 'Vengeance, vengeance, vengeance.' He rocked back, looking up at the canopy and the scatter of blue shards that peeked through. 'I am Cullen, voice of my ancestors. Gods of old, take my blood. Take my sweat. Take my pain and my tears and my sorrow. Replace them with courage. Crush my fear. Smother my shame. Grant me the power of death and of doom and of damnation. Give me the will to smite my enemies. All fear be gone. All hesitation be buried. Until my family are avenged.'

Then he fell back, suddenly exhausted. And he cried. A welter of grief, for all he had lost. But amongst the tumbling tears were those of hope. The vow had been made; solemn, binding, magical. He would learn to fight. Learn to become a warrior. Because he was going to murder a great lord. He was going to kill Caratacos.

CHAPTER TEN

Oars rose and fell as the longboat cut its way across the harbour. Behind them, the mainland grew distant, trees, buildings and jetties melding to become a single, long smudge.

'Gods, but it is filled with thorns, this rain,' the old man muttered, pulling the cowl further over his head and staring grimly out at the blue-grey depths that seemed to boil under the bitter shower.

On the opposite bench, the boat's captain grunted as he chewed. His quick, dark eyes flittered skyward. 'Won't last.'

Berikos, venerable statesman of the Isle of the Mighty, rightful ruler of the Atrebates nation, and hunted fugitive, fiddled again with his hood, as if he could somehow tease out more of the fur-lined material by sheer perseverance. 'By the ancients, I hope you are right.'

The sailor flicked a scrap of something out of his salt-crusted beard, then spat a jet of green juice over the side. 'Not often wrong.' He spoke in the common tongue, though it was heavily laced with the accent of the Aquitani tribes of southern Gaul. 'Crossing the Oceanus Britannicus with us?'

Berikos nodded. He would have put his host's age in the mid-forties, but winters were hard to count on faces that had seen hardship, and this face had had a lifetime of battering by the elements. 'The port at Ratumacos.'

The sailor spat again, leaving beads of leaf-dark spittle clinging to his beard. 'Rotomagus,' he said, 'we can manage.'

Berikos tucked the damp plaits of his white whiskers into the cloak's folds. 'Call it what you like, as long as we get there in one piece.' He squinted through the sheeting rain at the big ship anchored out in the deep water. Seagulls swirled above its masts, a chaotic mass of wings and screeches. He felt sick with trepidation as he studied the sleek lines of the huge vessel, for he was utterly reliant on its seaworthiness, and on its crew.

'In a hurry, I hear,' the sailor said.

'I would prefer not to tarry, that is true,' Berikos replied sourly, the understatement jarring to his own ears. In truth he had never been in more haste. His future, his very life, depended upon this crossing.

A grin, bright with avarice, the clever eyes lingering briefly on the thick gold ring with its carved green stone that encircled the middle finger of Berikos's right hand. 'It'll cost.'

'I've no doubt,' Berikos answered, knowing that the grizzled sailors had already eyed the few treasures with which he had managed to escape Calleva. He glanced across at the man seated at his side. The warrior propped his shield between his knees and patted one of the saddlebags with whose safekeeping he had been charged. It chinked meaningfully. The sailor's jackdaw eyes sparkled, and he could not help but let them drift over the other bags held by the rest of Berikos's half-dozen retainers.

Berikos sat back, relaxing a little now that there was some distance between himself and the mainland. All around him the benches creaked as the oarsmen pulled and the watchful warriors twitched. He wiped rain from his bushy brows, then fished in the folds of his cloak for a scrap of stale bread, chewing it until the pain stabbed his jaw. Damn this tooth, he thought. It was rotten to the root, the gum black and foul tasting. He had been meaning to get it seen to. Meaning to summon the brutish but effective tooth-puller from his hovel in the shadow of Calleva's western earthwork. But that had all been before the calamity. All been forgotten as he galloped south with his handful of named men, as if bloodthirsty hounds were on his heels. Which, to all intents and purposes, they had been. Hounds in human form, painted with white snakes and empowered by the heady mix of ambition and victory. The hounds – the Catuvellauni – had not caught him, thanks be to all the gods. Which meant it was time to go to work.

He spat the half-chewed remains of the bread over the side, jaw still throbbing. 'How long from *Rotomagus*?' he asked, intentionally using the Roman name to avoid riling the mariner.

'To Rome?' The sailor whistled softly. The ship was looming above them now, its massive, weed-draped hull a floating fortress. Sailors lined the rails, tossed ropes, hurled insults at their compatriots. 'Little short of a month, if you take another ship and sail through the Sinus Cantabrorum, down the west coast of Gaul, all the way south to Burdigala.'

'And then?'

'Land, north of where Gaul meets Hispania, until you reach the port of Narbo, then by sea once more to Rome, over the Mare Nostrum.'

A month, mostly at sea, did not appeal. Perhaps in his younger days, but Berikos was in his sixtieth summer and for the majority of those he had remained steadfastly on dry land, his bed warm, his rump dry and his belly full. 'What if I take the road?'

'Good roads through Gaul,' the sailor agreed, 'but your problem will be the terrain. Mountains, see? Big ones. Call it two months, assuming the weather treats you kindly. More, if not.'

Berikos glanced again at the retainer seated adjacent. It was a lot of wealth to be bringing with them, let alone for three months, over unknown roads with untold dangers.

'So be it,' Berikos said. 'And I'll need an interpreter.'

'I know men who will serve, for the right price.'

'Give me names.' Just then, Berikos noticed the warrior at his side, staring down at his shield, watching silently as the three-tailed horse, the symbol of the Atrebates, melted in the rain. 'Gods be with us,' Berikos said. Because now was not a time for timidity. His throne had been stolen. His legacy lay in ruins. It was a time for action. For vengeance. He would go to Rome. He would meet an emperor.

The brother kings, high and low, spent the hottest weeks at Camulodunon. It was their headquarters as they roamed with warbands between the great dun, Verlamion and Calleva. Sometimes they strove south into the territory of the Cantiaci, there to remind subordinate chieftains of the unassailable force that lurked on their borders, and sometimes north to keep the ever-raiding Coritani at bay. Every so often they would all arrive at Camulodunon at once, and a vast feast would be joined, the Wise would prance and prophesy, while the poets would sing tales of slaughter. Caratacos would take up a throne on a high dais. Togodubnos would do likewise, only slightly higher. Slightly more magnificent.

Summer slipped towards its twilight, the days, yet mild, gradually shortening, the air becoming fresher. The crops were still full in the valleys, swaying and lush, and the hillside grass was a dry yellow, but the hawthorn hedgerows were no longer white, and the drone of bees had begun to fade, and some of the birds had already vanished, flying south for the Narrow Sea and the mysterious lands beyond. The season was leaching away, changing as the first gods had decreed, time moving inexorably forward.

Despite the evidence of his eyes, Cullen felt that he somehow lagged, like the dregs at the bottom of an ale pot. He woke each day with dread. A nameless, formless empty feeling in the pit of his stomach, as if his innards had been scooped out as he slept. He had made his vow with Moranna's help, hardened his resolve, but already he felt himself drifting. Had he expected revenge to come so soon? On the contrary, he knew it must be the work of a lifetime. But perhaps he had hoped mere existence would become easier with the making of the pledge. Yet it changed little, day to day. He was nothing in Camulodunon. Hardly more than human detritus. He had been permitted freedom, and that was more than he could ever have wished for. But to what end? What was freedom to a boy ripped from his tribe? A tribe subjugated; a family killed. Now he felt like a pot of fertile soil, planted with the twin seeds of sorrow and lethargy. One nurturing the other. Both showing green shoots. The beginnings of what would be a wasted life.

And yet, here he was, undeniably at liberty in this most vibrant of towns. He could walk the colourful streets unmolested, despite the odd flicker of recognition in a face or the excited pointing of a child. There was liberty, and there was food and warmth, thanks to Becan. But what was he to do in the end? Where was he to go? Society was built on purpose. From the farmer to the cattleman to the metalworker, and all the way up to those of royal blood. On the day of choosing, a life with meaning was embarked upon. But what if that choice had never come? What if that pivotal moment had been violently torn from a person's grasp?

Cullen had made his vow. Moranna of the Silver had told him to harness the strife that had engulfed him. Embrace it and use it to hone his future, like a whetstone against a blade. But time nagged at him, gnawed on his belief. He did not doubt the power of Taranis. But how could he not question the god's will? Why would such a deity trouble himself with so lowly a creature as an orphaned goatherd from the hills south of Calleva? It made no sense. And as the days slipped into memory, so did his ambition. Moreover, who would teach one so loathed by the wisest of the Wise? He might have wished to learn the ways of the warrior, but who would have the temerity to provoke Arthmael's wrath? That fork-tongued sack of bones and bile was ever present. A spectre, lurking at the fringes of Cullen's awareness. His threat palpable, if yet unspoken.

He found respite from the white-hot glares of Arthmael's minions by offering a hand to Solidu, who made most of the

Catuvellauni weaponry at a forge on the very edge of the dun. The smith was a stout man with ruddy jowls, slits for eyes and oak-boughs for forearms, and he was only too happy to dispatch his willing volunteer into the wild woods, where the land was cleaved deep by the wide river. Cullen would collect lengths of alder, beech, birch and oak, stripping and stacking them in a conical pile that the smith's gang of burners would cover with bracken and mud, and char, slowly, for days at a time, producing the invaluable material that could burn hot enough to melt iron.

It rained in those shortening days, grim and persistent. Becan proclaimed it a sign, suggesting Taranis had deigned to visit his protégé, and that offerings must be made. But Cullen, no longer inclined to dwell on the predictions of others, preferred simply to stroll in the drizzle, focusing his efforts on the perpetual quest for Solidu's charcoal.

It was on one such morning, when the air was too close for comfort and the rumbling skies began to open, that he watched a drift of ponies come up from the river valley, corralled by whistling men on horseback. They laughed and sang under the ensuing shower, calling to one another as they checked each beast and separated the foals, selecting which were to be trained for work and which for battle. The best would be sent to the charioteers and a life of pomp and prestige. Cullen stood under a dripping willow, half watching the ponies while he rifled through his sack of foraged elderberries, plantain leaves and nuts, all of which were intended for the evening's pot, but only the tough leaves likely to make it that far.

It was as he crammed a palmful of hazelnuts into the side of his mouth that he noticed the figure standing away to his left, shielding from the rain beneath a soaring, deer-scarred beech. It was a man, to judge by the height, though the cloak – which was now little more than a heavy wedge of sopping folds – obscured frame and face from sight.

'A filthy day!' the figure called when he caught Cullen's eye. Indeed, a male voice, deep but unnervingly smooth. A tone clear as a bell, with not so much a quiver of uncertainty.

Cullen indicated the expansive willow canopy. 'Drier here, friend.'

'Summer is on the wane, I am sad to say,' the man said, approaching. He held palms up to the branches, acknowledging their stifling effect upon the drizzle, then accepted some of the proffered hazelnuts gratefully. 'We must prepare for the dark months.'

Cullen nodded, thoughts turning back to the goats and the anxiety that would come at this time of year. 'Wolves are at their hungriest. Their most brazen.'

The man grunted, tugging at the strands of an auburn beard. 'You know my struggles.'

'I would dig traps when the leaves began to fall.'

'Hard to catch them out in my experience,' the man said, 'so wily are they.'

'Find a piss-post where the wolf marks his territory,' said Cullen. 'Get a dog to cock his leg against it. The wolf will not resist the chance to reply with his own dowsing.' He paused as the man laughed. 'Beside that post, dig a deep hole with flat sides, spikes at the base. Bait it and cover it with branches.'

'You catch many?'

'Many, aye.'

'I will have my men follow your advice.'

Cullen looked out at the riders, saturated as they laboured. 'Your men?'

The fellow laughed, revealing a flash of neat white teeth amid the depths of his cowl. 'We, indeed.' He waved his hands expansively towards the horses. Hands, Cullen noted, that were heavy with rings. 'I oversee.'

'The drift?'

Now the hands came up and the hood went down. 'Everything.'

It was the first time Cullen had looked a king in the eye. In fact, he later reflected, it was probably the first time he had looked any truly powerful noble full in the face, for he had failed to entirely meet the predatory gaze of Caratacos, or, truth be told, the vicious stare of Arthmael. The oldest of the sons of Cunobelin had a kindly face, all told. As broad and florid as Cullen remembered from the day he first glimpsed the king at the greensward, but now, up close, he saw a certain openness to those green eyes. A sense of decency behind the bright intelligence. Not that he would ever say such a thing, for the scar that blighted Togodubnos's nose hinted at the capacity for violence he must surely have possessed. The elders of the Catuvellauni tribe would hardly have upheld a weakling's claim.

'In truth,' Togodubnos said, 'I am here to meet a particular person.' His green eyes were twinkling as he spoke, almost playful. 'All the talk is of a boy. A humble goatherd, no less, taken captive at the fall of Calleva.'

Cullen felt himself quell. 'I—'

'The talk,' the king went on, as Cullen gaped like a suffocating pike, 'says that boy is touched by Taranis. Favoured, even.' He brandished that disarming smile again. 'This is no chance meeting, Cullen of the Atrebates.' He scratched at something in the tawny beard, turning back to the gathering herd. 'They say you killed my brother's named man. They say you would become a warrior yourself.'

They say a lot, Cullen thought. Then it hit him. 'Becan? He is your spy?'

Togodubnos gave a grunt of amusement. 'Becan does not spy on you, Cullen. He spies on my little brother. But he informs me, time to time, of matters he deems worthy of my ears. I trust his judgement.'

'Because he is kin to Moranna of the Silver,' Cullen replied, his narrow existence opening up before him like petals on a blossoming rose. 'And she is your Wise One.' So much had been explained, in this single instant. Becan was no mere cripple in a tribe of warriors. No scrap of human surplus, as he would have folk believe. He had power of his own. The ear of the Wise and, it seemed, of the over-king himself.

'Becan was taken in by Moranna,' Togodubnos was saying, 'when he came to our tribe. She is his mother, or the nearest thing to it. I trust them both.' He turned from the astonished goatherd to stare out at the pony drift, the beasts steaming in the rain, their whinnied complaints snatched by the breeze. 'You are surprised? A king must know all the goings-on in his kingdom.' He shrugged. 'After the events at Avalloc's Shelter, Becan saw fit to have me informed. Moranna and I believe there is something special about you. Something only the gods can see.'

'I do not understand it. Any of it.'

'What is there to understand? The gods are capricious. You are Taranis's latest plaything, like as not. To be cast off when the whim takes him. But why should that make you any less grateful? He has seen fit to shine his glory upon you. Bask in it.'

'How, lord?' Cullen answered, doing his best to ignore the desperation in his own voice.

'Forge a life. Make Taranis see the worth in his decision. When is your time of choosing?'

'It would have been this coming harvest.'

'Would have?'

'My family are all gone, lord.' Cullen shook his head, battling the hot tears erupting at his eyes. 'What does it matter?'

'You remain.' Togodubnos tapped a finger against his own temple. It was thick, proportionate with the meaty forearm, and for the first time Cullen was aware of the raw strength this man exuded. 'Your memories are locked away in here. Your loved ones live on while they are remembered. You owe it to them to make of yourself what you can. You reach the age of choosing as a Catuvellauni, albeit a reluctant one. So what will be your choice?'

Cullen's pulse raced. Now was his chance to beat the path the others had spoken of so readily. It had all seemed so impossible, so far out of reach. Now, astonishingly, he glimpsed a way forward. 'I would take the tests, lord.'

The king's auburn brows rose in unison. 'The warrior tests?'
Cullen inclined his head. 'I want to fight.'
'The tests are no easy thing.'
Cullen felt his heart tumble into his stomach, reality levering its way back in. 'You are right, of course. I wander the forests, collect sticks for Solidu the smith. I eat and I sleep and when I wake I go back to the forest.'

'You have given Solidu much assistance, come rain or shine. He tells me you worked like a dog for precious little reward. Tells me you are eager to learn and as diligent as any apprentice. Our mutual friend, Becan, tells me you are clever and humble, and the poets already sing of your courage.' The king offered a conspiratorial wink. 'When Arthmael is not present.'

'Then what, lord? What must I do?'

'Come to my court. Where you will learn what must be learned.'

A croaking sound came from a low branch nearby. Cullen squinted into the foliage. Black and white plumage shifted behind the green. Beady black eyes fixed on his.

—

Everything had changed, though it took a deal longer for Cullen to grasp. He had walked into the rain as a gatherer of twigs. When he went back to Camulodunon, he was a member of the high king's household.

'Why?' Cullen had asked that night over a greasy repast of roasted wood pigeon. 'Why would he help me?'

'He is helping himself,' Becan replied. 'Moranna says it will curry the gods' favour.'

'And will it?'

'Does it matter?'

Cullen supposed it did not. Which was why it was with renewed optimism that, the following dawn, he gathered the new knife, bought with Becan's coins, and his mother's beaver-skin cloak, and clambered onto a cart with Drest and Becan.

The same cart that had brought them here from a shattered Calleva. Except this time, it was bound for Verlamion.

The king rode at the front on his dappled grey, shadowed closely by Moranna of the Silver, mounted upon a shaggy pony whose mane and tail rattled with wooden carvings that matched those adorning her own neck. Flanking them was the ever-present wall of grim killers that were the king's named men, led by the flame-haired fury, Aoife the Dread. The rest came after in a sprawl of animals and leather, mud and dung, spears and slings and chariots and the seemingly endless hangers-on, of which Cullen was just a tiny part. The rain abated, though the air seemed to cool by the hour, and soon they had left behind the great dun, its spiked earthworks fading to scars on a distant horizon. Into the west went Cullen. Into a new future.

—

'Halt!'

The hulking greybeard sidled along the line of young men, every eye nervously tracking his progress. Until a moment ago, two of their number had been engaged in a furious duel, but they disengaged as he jabbed a short, oar-shaped club between them, forcing their bodies apart.

'Three words, you spavined half-wits!' The old man shouldered the darkly seasoned club, its filigree of nicks and gouges showing pale in the noon sun. He glared furiously with the only eye he possessed. 'Shield, shield, shield!' He reached out with a thumbless free hand and knuckled the long shaft of ash that was levelled in the grip of one of the duellists. 'The spear gives us range. That is why we use it.' He glanced at the spearman's opponent. 'So how do we counter?'

'Block, Master Farrad,' Cullen of the Atrebates panted, looking instinctively, and diffidently, down at the rim of the shield that now hung limp in his left hand. It was thin and light, made of green willow bark, sweat droplets pattering the inner face as they fell from his forehead.

'And?'

'And move, Master Farrad.'

'By the ancients,' Farrad brayed, a sudden outburst that had Cullen flinching, 'he can be taught!' He stepped in, hip rolling awkwardly as it dragged a near-lame leg in its wake, and shifted Cullen aside with his bulk. Then he was facing the erstwhile – and half-terrified – opponent, twisting sideways, and brandishing the club defensively. 'Get him to stick his spear into your shield and move the point aside.' With a little coaxing, the lad with the spear, which was, in fact, a blunt length of ash, caught his meaning and prodded the weapon towards Farrad's considerable midriff. The big man grunted as he turned the point easily, pirouetting in the same fluid movement to shorten the range. He had a dagger in his other hand, a real one, and the lad blanched when he saw it coming towards him. Farrad grinned as he lowered it, a toothless, fleshy expression that was more terrifying than most people's fiercest scowl. 'Like so.'

Around them, watching nervously, Farrad's pupils shifted their feet and murmured assent. There were twenty-two of them, including Cullen. Some as raw as him, others marginally better, but all green as cabbage and scared witless by the named fighters with whom they now crossed paths. One such being, their war-master, Farrad, was known widely as Skull Splitter. It was that club, horrifying in its primitive brutality, that had given Farrad his name, for he had once been a devil in its wielding. Famous for cracking Eceni heads and Cantiaci spines, or so the legend went. Cullen feared the very ground upon which the grizzled old campaigner limped, but he could not deny the man's expertise. And that, after all, was why Cullen was here.

Summer had bled almost imperceptibly into autumn. The leaves were beginning to lose their vibrancy, and the swallows were gathering in the high boughs, ready for that mysterious annual migration to the lands beyond even the reach of Rome. The king and his huge retinue had arrived in their capital just as the harvest began in earnest. It was a time to make use of the last of the long days, work from dawn till dusk, let the sun burnish faces, cram storerooms to the rafters and fill grain pits to the brim, and Cullen had helped where he could. Verlamion, like every other steading, village and fortified dun in the land, was a hive. Smaller than Camulodunon it may have been, but it remained the ancient centre of Catuvellauni power, the seat of Togodubnos and his most influential nobles, and multitudes were drawn to it as the days shrank away. Just as the stores were filled for the colder times ahead, so the outbuildings were occupied by ards and sickles, coulters and ploughshares. Pens were crammed with sheep and cattle driven down from the hills, their lowing drifting in deep echoes across the hilltop settlement. Life in summer's twilight was lived in haste, for the sense of impending winter was palpable. There was merriment amongst the gloom. The swelling population meant gatherings of long-separated families, and friends, new and old. Somewhere in Verlamion, on any given night, there were feasts and dances and games. When the ale barrels were dry, the air quickly filled with spellbinding stories, richly told by the itinerant Wise Ones who came and went like the tide, weaving knowledge and history around fantastical tales. Sometimes, when the work was complete, there were chariot races, featuring the best Togodubnos's forces had to offer, and demonstrations with blade and spear, the greatest of the dun's fighters putting their hard-earned names on the line as they skewered targets or bested all-comers.

This last was what entranced Cullen of the Atrebates, for those granite-hard war-givers were now paragons in his eyes. He watched their every move. Studied how they carried themselves, which armour they chose, what food they ate and how they maintained their weapons. Because it was as though he had been born anew. No chasing goats on lonely hillsides for him, nor even the drudge of fetching wood for the char pits. From sunrise to sundown, his was a life of learning. Shield-work, swordcraft, long battle spears, short throwing spears, daggers, cudgels and wrestling. Repetition was key to achieving the strength and accuracy demanded by his tutors, and so every day, rain or shine, out he went onto the flatter terrain beyond the town limits, where he would join the other hopefuls beneath the toothy palisades, all eyeing the same goal.

He deserved none of it. The fact gnawed at him relentlessly. The orphaned boy who had killed Branna the Slayer. The intended sacrifice who had defied Arthmael the Learned and earned the favour of a god. But all that was a web of fiction that could not have been woven any better if the most talented poet had played fast and loose with it. Branna had slipped. Arthmael had been wrongfooted by a frightened child with a shard of broken bone up his sleeve. Nothing had been by design. Nothing had been the product of skill. And in the cold stares of his compatriots, Cullen could see reality starkly reflected. Most were careful to mask any outward hostility, of course, because his was a place gifted by the high king, deserving or not. But they simmered all the same. The resentment obvious as they lined up with wooden sticks to mimic sword thrusts, or grappled in the fighting circle made of sand. The blows were just that little bit harder for him. The throws given just that touch more force. The helping hands to pick him up, conspicuously few.

'They are jealous,' Becan had said on one starless night in the early weeks, when the thatch trembled as Cailleach, the howling one, rode the wind.

Their new home was a roundhouse on the outer edge of Verlamion's royal enclosure. It was a huge building, much like his family's, the one in which Branna had met his untimely end, though this was not a dwelling made comfortable by the trappings of grandmothers and aunts. It had long been given over for use by the many and various waifs and strays that a great lord attracts. Pedlars and vagrants, lay-soothsayers, traders from across the Narrow Sea, and trappers from the snowy north, bearing sublime pelts from savage lands. All had to be housed for their fleeting visits to the capital of the Catuvellauni, and this place, amongst a handful of others, was where they would find themselves.

'They know I'm a fraud,' Cullen had muttered across the guttering fire. He kept his voice low, for strangers snored in the sleeping spaces between the great oaken uprights.

Across from him were Becan and Drest, the latter carving symbols into the crushed chalk floor with the point of his stick. Becan grunted. 'You're all frauds, goat-fiddler. None of you could beat *me* in a fight. That is why you are here. To learn.'

'They hate me.'

'Why do you care?'

'A warrior fights for honour, Master Farrad says. If I have none, how can I face an enemy?'

'Honour?' Becan had scoffed. 'Your king brought you here because a god told him to. What is more honourable than that?'

And that was why Cullen persisted, despite the simmering resentment of his compatriots. He embraced the sentiment as the drills became more gruelling, focusing his efforts on his friend's words, silently replaying them in his mind whenever a moment threatened to overwhelm him.

'What if I have dropped my shield?' he ventured now, as Farrad Skull Splitter loped back to his original place at the end of the line of apprentices.

'Then you deserve to be gutted!' Farrad called back, spittle frothing white at the corner of his mouth. He was a beast in man's clothing, Cullen thought. Hunched and pulpy-faced, long run to fat, and ugly as a hog in mud. Some sharpened implement had long ago gravened a deep groove diagonally down his forehead, the same wound that had accounted for his left eye. Yet the practice-master still cursed and threatened his way through the day as if ankle-deep in the blood of battle. 'But, should Taranis favour you yet again, and your innards have not become out-ards,' he brought the alder club down in a thrusting motion that left little to the imagination, 'go low with the blade.

Your opponent will almost certainly aim flat or high. Chest or head.' He limped forward, whipping up the heavy weapon as though it were nothing but a willow wand. 'Let him come on, make contact beyond the spear point, knocking the shaft up and away.' He performed the motions with surprising speed, face set in a grim mask as he imagined the violence. With a lunge, he stepped in, cleaving the air with the club's smooth edge. 'Slide the blade down the length of the shaft and chop the unfortunate bastard's fingers off!' He laughed, a sound like a shaken bag of pebbles. 'Again, you brainless doe-turds! Take your places!'

Cullen lifted the stick in his right hand. It might not have been able to sever a blade of grass, but it was perfect for mimicking the strokes of a sword. With his left foot forward, and his shoulders angled to present the narrowest possible target, he braced behind the shield to receive a blow.

'The sword has nobility, doe-turds!' Farrad was snarling away to his right. 'The dance of the blade is pure art! It has a place alongside man's greatest achievements. The knowledge of the worlds above and below, of healing, of the lights in the night sky and of the working of metal. Swordplay is there, amongst them all!'

Cullen and his much taller opponent circled warily.

'Any fool can poke a man with a long stick,' Farrad bellowed, warming to his theme. 'There's no finesse in it. No skill. Hear this, you stinking doe-turds!'

The youth at the other end of the spear was, technically, a man, having just reached the age of choosing, but he was skinny and sallow, with grey, sagging eyelids that made him look like a walking cadaver. His name was Andoc, and he was paired with Cullen more often than not. Fuelled by a seemingly bottomless well of anger, his enmity was as clear as it was raw. Though the weapons were blunted or entirely fashioned from wood, he managed to make every jab sting and every parry jar, so that Cullen sweated and hissed through the exercises as though his very life depended on it, often coming away with a numb arm and a tidy collection of bruises.

'A club will dash the brains,' Farrad called in the background. 'An axe blow will split a man down the middle. But the club does not guarantee a kill, and the axe will have you blowing out of your bony arse after three swings. The real warrior's friend is the narrow blade. Swords and daggers. Fast, manoeuvrable, deadly at the first time of asking. But only if you know what you're doing!' Cullen was vaguely aware of him cutting the air with the club, his arm scything in straight lines, quartering the space before him, and quartering again. 'To perfect the strokes is to keep you alive. A giant with a man's beard and a long broadsword could cleave a man in half with brute force, but he will always be defeated by one with balance and skill. Knowledge is key. And practice. The nine strokes!'

Cullen and Andoc moved as they had a hundred times before, poised, like cats ready to pounce. Behind Andoc's shoulder the fortification of Verlamion bristled like the spines of a gigantic hedgehog, drawing Cullen's eye so that he was forced to blink hard to wrest back his focus.

'Move your feet!' Farrad boomed. 'Strike hard! Fast!'

'I am trying!' Cullen retorted through gritted teeth.

'Well, I'm certain that is of great comfort to your mother,' Farrad snarled, 'as she watches from the next life. Get your head clear, Storm Lover.'

'Storm?'

'That's what they're calling you. Didn't you know?'

'He is no named man,' Andoc sneered. It was an expression permanently chiselled on his face, whether he meant it or not, for a puckered scar blighted the corner of his mouth, giving him a perpetual look of disdain. But for Cullen there was real, palpable ire that set his drooping eyes ablaze.

Farrad roared with laughter. 'I know precisely what he is, Andoc Streak-of-Piss! A craven collector of goat shit, with an inflated opinion of himself!' He snorted loudly, bringing up another thick wad of mucus, which he spat onto the trampled grass in a great spray. 'But that does not stop tongues wagging of his exploits. Now, get to cutting him down, you cursed bag of bones!'

Andoc attacked. Despite his reedy frame, he had the better reach and the spear's range. He had taken the tests at fifteen, Cullen had learned, which was a reasonable age for a first tilt, but had failed to meet the standard and returned to Farrad with his tail between his legs and a significant chip on his shoulder. Still, he was better than Cullen, more desperate to prove his mettle, and his lunge was low and vicious.

Cullen shoved his shield down, the empty point of the pretend spear smacking dully into the wood, and back he danced, just managing to keep himself upright. Another lunge, another block, another ungainly retreat. He had the wooden sword up, primed for the stroke, but he was too far away. Andoc hissed like a snake as he bade his time, edging left and then right for an opening, feinting with flicks of his wrist to force Cullen's shield into a wrong position. His hooded eyes slid to Cullen's ankles, but his stance did not change, and Cullen kept the shield up, just in time for a high strike that was delivered with venom. The point thudded on the upper part of the willow boards, sliding off the rim as Cullen's forearm buckled and turned. The spear clipped his collarbone, narrowly missed his face, and then the point was past him, suddenly impotent. Cullen came in with a desperate lunge, tracing the length of the ash all the way to its bearer, and he was hacking madly, blindly, at Andoc's own shield, which was now obscuring the taller fighter's face.

'For the love of Epona, hold yourselves still!' Farrad's guttural growl cut through their fury as sharply as any dagger.

They broke away, gasping, arms searing with pain. Cullen dragged his sword arm over his brow, trying in vain to shift the sweat from his eyes but succeeding in blinding himself further. Mercifully, it appeared Andoc fared no better, the tall apprentice bending double as he struggled to regain some composure.

'There is no consideration here,' Farrad complained, dragging himself over to wave his club between them. 'No anticipation. You swing and slash. No thought, no composure, no finesse!' He glared balefully from one to the other. 'By the ancients, are you fighting or rutting?'

'My father,' Andoc opined through rasping breaths, 'told me strength was all. Crush your enemy's defences. Knock down his shield and gut him like a fish.'

'And where is your father now, Andoc Streak-of-Piss? I'll tell you, shall I?' Farrad Skull Splitter walked closer still. He twirled the club skilfully between his fat-knuckled fingers, scratching the bristles of his silver beard with the other hand. 'For I was not a stone's throw from where he stood, screaming at that Cornovii shield-wall. While he battered like a bullock at a fence, his foe considered. His foe anticipated.' He prodded Andoc's hollow chest, making the tall lad take a step back. 'His foe spotted the gap, as your father's blade was raised for the killing blow. Before he knew it, your father had forgotten the battle, and was hastily gathering up his intestines from the mud.'

Andoc's taut expression flickered like a guttering flame. Farrad spat derisively, then turned to the watching group.

'Everything, boys!' He levelled the scarred lump of alder at them as though in threat. 'All your focus. All your rage and your hatred. Gather it. Forge it into a spear point in your mind. Not for strength, but for intelligence.'

'My father was a great man,' Andoc said sullenly.

Farrad nodded. 'Aye. And now he's a great dead man. Want that for yourself? Fight like he did.' He turned away from Andoc, leaving him glaring white-hot hatred at Cullen. 'Do you not see, boys? Fights are not won by the strong, but by the clever.'

'You said hit hard,' some brave soul ventured, 'and fast.' A murmur of agreement from the others.

'That I did. But strike hardest, strike fastest, after you've been patient enough to spy an opening. To wrong-foot the man across, weigh him up and gauge his footing.' He slapped the club against his thick palm. 'Do the preparation work. Then strike fast. Hard. Crush the bastard's skull if you like, but make sure he hasn't pierced your belly while you're busy doing it, or it'll all be for nought.' He rounded on the watchers, whose turn to impress him it would soon be. 'You may have reached your choosing time, where your life path is set out. You may fast be approaching that moment, and intent on taking the warrior's oaths. It matters not. No king or chief will give you a war-name if you have not first passed the tests. Some of you took them as striplings. You failed, or you would not have been foisted on me. Others will take them soon. You're all the same to me. All failures until you prove otherwise. So listen and watch and learn.' He turned on his heels to glare at Cullen and Andoc. 'Again, your stance, if you please.'

CHAPTER ELEVEN

'Rome!' Atebodwos exclaimed as the barge cut the surface of the muddy, yellowish water. He was a little, birdlike man, all angles, sinews and twitches, with darting eyes and a quick smile of mottled amber. 'Drink it in!'

Berikos looked up at the Tiber's looming bank, lined at intervals with statues of bronze and marble. He wormed a finger under the neckline of his tunic, which was suddenly too tight. 'It is as big as they say.'

Atebodwos grinned. 'Whatever *they* say, I guarantee it is bigger. Better.'

Berikos nodded mutely. The little man hailed from the southeast of Gaul, amongst the mountains that separated it from the heartlands of the Romans, and when he had first met them at the bustling port of Narbo, it seemed unfathomable that such a person would have embraced the ways of his conquerors so wholeheartedly. But now he saw why. Rome was truly the centre of all.

The ship on which Berikos had made his dash from Britannia had been called the *Wind-Dancer*, and she had proven as swift as she was sleek, conveying them to the wealthy port of Burdigala, a bustling maritime hub, built on the trade in tin and lead. They had taken to the road, then, leaving behind a good quantity of Berikos's salvaged fortune in the hands of a happy crew, and made the short journey to Narbo on the coast of the glittering sea that would take them direct to the empire's epicentre. From Ostia, the sprawling port at the mouth of the River Tiber, they had taken a barge upriver, Atebodwos smoothing the way with well-chosen words and yet more coin, and soon the largest city in the world had risen out of the horizon like the very homeland of the gods, its spires and temples filling the skyline, dazzling under a clear lapis sky.

Now they were on the final leg of what would be the glorious redemption of King Berikos. The oppressive heat prickled his skin, but so did the intangible sense of opportunity. In Rome, he thought, anything was possible.

The barge reached a sharp bend in the river, where wharves and bridges greeted them beneath centuries-old walls, forbidding gates barring entry to the city. This section of the waterway was overshadowed by three hills that rose within the city limits, all of which were clustered with buildings in a multitude of colour, and all constructed in stone and tile. Berikos stared up at those rooftops, above which an eagle circled, wingtips splayed like fingers. It was a world away from the Isle of the Mighty. So starkly different that it felt like a dream. Berikos glanced at his warriors, each one seemingly as awestruck as he, and their astonishment only increased as they rounded the bend to plunge into the shadow of a huge structure, fronted by a portico of four columns. It was raised on a high podium, the vast and ostentatious doors reached by a soaring flight of steps.

Berikos tugged Atebodwos's sleeve. 'What is that?'

Atebodwos leaned against the side of the barge to spew a stream of unintelligible words at a group of fishermen at the water's edge. One of them, with black, wavy hair and skin the colour of nutmeg, answered him with a cheery wave.

'An associate of mine,' he explained as he twisted back. 'Egyptian.' He pointed up at the colonnaded building. 'He says that is the Temple of Portunus, god of keys, doors and livestock.'

'You speak Egyptian?'

'I speak,' Atebodwos answered with an impish smirk, 'whatever you'd like me to speak.'

'You can take me to the Forum?'

The Gaul affected a disappointed pout. 'You employ me as interpreter, not guide.'

'Be a guide, then, and I will reconsider your remuneration.'

The yellow grin returned. 'I know these streets like the lines of my palm.'

—

Cullen was a slave to repetition as the weeks tumbled by. To the throw and thrust of the spear. The sweeping cuts of the sword and the dance-like postures with the shield. All took their toll on shoulders and flanks, built ridges on his fingers, and put callouses over his palms. But with each back-breaking session under Farrad's grim tutelage he gained that little bit more surety. Each night he fell, aching, into a slumber as deep as death, and understood dawn would bring new strength. His hurting muscles were visible now, shifting like serpents beneath his skin, and his rough grip was firmer around hilt and haft. His movements under attack were becoming less stunted and more a matter of instinct, the memory of Farrad's ceaseless exercises ingrained within his every fibre.

Grief stayed along with hope. It came in waves hugging the shore of his soul. Surging, crashing pain that flooded and filled every crack and crevice in his churning mind, then slinking back, subsiding, dragging, to leave a numbness, a lingering residue of what had been so intolerably acute. And then again, just as he began to recover, another swell, its pain and fury redoubling, coming further, lingering longer, pulling more of him away when finally it would subside.

It was a bitter tide from which he could not escape, though he tried his utmost, wandering out into the deeper woods to seek solitude. He would remember his family under the shelter of the trees, hear their voices in the chimes that hung from high boughs, and smell them in the scents of honeysuckle, dill and waxflower. He would work, too. Swing his wooden sword at the shadows and hurl his blunt spear at ever narrower targets, as if he could exorcise the old horrors through exhaustion, purging them on the flow of sweat.

It was while rehearsing the nine strokes one grey morning that the magpie reappeared. Cullen had been at the movements for some time, clothed only in shoes and braca, his torso slick and hair plastered to his forehead. A stream babbled and frothed nearby, mostly hidden by brambles, its silvered surface flashing at the corner of his eye. He was mostly unaware of it, so immersed was he in the routine, until, as he lunged and retreated in one smooth motion, the blur of black and white streaked across the silver shards. He looked up, blood freezing in his veins. The bird had alighted on a low branch, not much more than a spear's length away. It cocked its head, as if studying his form. He waved the stick, but it merely mocked him with a croaking cackle, and hopped, in a brash haze of feathers, further along the perch.

'Why do you practise alone?' a woman asked.

Cullen rounded on the voice, stick raised, only to meet a pair of pale, narrow eyes he knew well. Where she had come from, he could not fathom, but the air seemed somehow colder. 'It helps me focus,' he replied hastily, thinking on his feet.

She made a soft tutting sound with her tongue. The bright thread in her ears shimmered as she spoke. 'Careful your lies do not insult the nymphs, little red crest.'

He had lowered the mock sword, but he drew himself up at the implied criticism. 'I do not fear the small spirits.'

Moranna of the Silver exposed her sharpened teeth in a slow smile. 'The Romans see their deities above. In the sky. Frolicking amongst the clouds.'

'As do we, lady. Is not Taranis the harbinger of thunder?'

'So he is,' she replied, fingering her necklace of dowels that still lay over the cloak of many colours. Her eyes drifted away, taking in the oak and ash all around them, seeing the wood, and somehow seeing beyond it. 'But most of our gods dwell about us, not above. Ours are the spirits of the trees, and the nymphs of the rivers, and of the soil on which we stand.' She extended a hand. 'Do not the veins on a leaf align with the lines on our palms? All life is intertwined, is it not?'

He gave a sullen shrug. 'If you say so.'

'Then should it not follow that the smallest deity must be afforded the same respect as the greatest?'

'What do you want, lady?'

'Caratacos is here,' she said, then flashed a wry smile. 'But you already know that.'

He felt his cheeks burn. The old hatred boiled up within. Of course he knew. The banner of the Catuvellauni, twin snakes turned white for Caratacos himself, had swept into the hilltop dun at first light. A hundred horsemen, a dozen chariots, one fearsome lord of war at the head. Cullen had slunk out through the terraced ramparts like a slowworm under a buzzard's shadow, despising his own meekness but unable to resist the urge to flee.

She saw it now, the memory and the shame. Read it on his face, for she shook her head gently. 'Patience, red crest. Your time will come.'

'When?' he asked thickly, for she seemed to know the vow he had made. The secret vow of murder he had pledged that dark night. Somehow, she knew.

The daggers in her thin mouth emerged again. 'He has fought in more campaigns than he could count.' She spoke softly but firmly. 'In pitched battles, moonlit raids and bitter little actions in the deepest snow. He has shed the blood of champions in the driving rain, seen his own blood stain sunny hillocks and wild woods. He has been fighting since he could lift a blade or throw a spear. Felled more foes and buried more friends than he can even recall. He has known nothing but violence.' She chuckled, full of scorn. 'You are not ready.' He made to argue but Moranna reached out, brushing his lips with a cold fingertip. 'Do not speak what is on your heart. Just know that your time is not yet at hand. Your life's path stretches out before you. Walk it.'

'The warrior's path?' He stepped back in irritation. 'How? How can I walk it when I swing sticks at trees? By the ancients, lady, I throw blunt spears at straw targets!'

'All paths have turns. Yours is no different. I have seen it. You must take them.'

'Turns? I do not...'

'Take them, red crest.'

The magpie screeched from somewhere in the brush. He wheeled about, the sword-cum-club aloft and ready, intending to smash the troublesome bird to a feathered pulp. It erupted from the undergrowth, all noise and panic, and rose through the high canopy until it was nothing but a speck against the clouds. He spat a curse at the creature, made to ask another question of Moranna, but she was nowhere to be seen.

He stalked back through the trees. No longer in the mood for the precise motions of the nine strokes, he slashed petulantly at bare branches, cut down brown ferns and dismembered anything else with the temerity to line his route, until the stick snapped, pale splinters exploding across the dark leaf mulch. Moranna's evasiveness, her apparently certain statements, always obscured behind a screen of nebulous prattle, had grated on him once too often. He should leave Verlamion, he decided. Leave or make his move. Sneak up on Caratacos, perhaps, and jab his skinning knife up through the big man's ribs. Something, anything, needed to happen. This festering, day after day, was not what he anticipated when he had shed his own blood and uttered his sworn oath.

He was considering how exactly he would get to Caratacos when another figure stepped into view. A man this time, at the edge of the forest, where larger gaps in the trees meant broader swathes of sunlight. That, in turn, rendered him significantly more than mere outline. Cullen suddenly wished he had not broken the weapon, however rudimentary it may have been. He scanned the undergrowth, searching for something to wield and finding nothing but decaying leaves and twigs. At the periphery of his vision, he saw another shape. This one was further off, its silhouette vaguer, but he knew it was too big to be Moranna. The man in Cullen's way had an accomplice. This was no chance encounter.

'Be careful out here in the wild,' Andoc called. He walked slowly now, each pace crackling as he picked his way over log and bramble, coming deeper into the wood, closer to Cullen. He whistled a lilting tune, utterly at odds with his stance, which was unnaturally rigid, as if his muscles were coiled, poised for something sudden, like a wildcat readying to pounce. Without warning, he quickened, closing the distance, angling his approach to cut off the obvious route back to Verlamion.

'What do you want?' Cullen said, though the sudden ice in his veins was answer enough.

Andoc came on. Raising hands that were, mercifully, empty. Even so, he was visibly tense. He made the air between them seem tense too, as if he exuded an invisible but palpable danger.

And then he attacked.

It was more leap than lunge, the long legs bending low and exploding upwards, and then the lean body was in the air, over the last of the thorny thickets, and coming down upon Cullen like some winged beast, the expectation of violence lighting his eyes with unsettlingly fire.

Cullen braced, half caught Andoc, and then he was down in the wet ferns, on his back, thrashing and raging under the larger boy's bulk. He managed to twist as he writhed, wrenching a shoulder clear, and then an arm, so that he could slam a fist into Andoc's bony ribcage. His attacker yelped, snarled, slashed with his own fists, and rolled away.

They scrambled to their feet at the same moment, hauling in air and taking stock. Cullen's nose was bleeding, his left cheek throbbing hot, but his fists were up this time, ready and waiting, while he explored his mouth with his tongue, counting teeth and tasting blood. He spat a crimson gobbet towards Andoc, called him on, beckoning for his enemy to chance his arm again. But it was over. As quickly as it had begun. Quicker, even. The second assailant, whoever it had been, had vanished in the watery light.

'This is your life now, Atrebates!' Andoc shouted as he melted into the bushes, gone to join his hidden ally. 'Taranis will not protect you forever!'

—

Cullen avoided Verlamion's sloped interior. There was more than enough cover in the teeming streets to keep him from running into Caratacos's followers. Anyone, at least, who might take notice of a knock-kneed boy with a swollen eye and a fat lip. But still he shied away from the town proper, staying on the low-lying outskirts beyond the earthworks, nearest the forest, that comprised drained crop fields and a patchwork of heron-haunted wetlands regularly flooded by the river. Near one such marsh, fringed by coarse grass that stretched higher than his own head, he paused to peer into the water's edge, gaining a tremulous view of his wounds. He dabbed at them with his fingers, wincing and cursing under his breath, smearing away the blood with his sweaty arm and dabbing ineffectually at the stained braca with a clump of moss.

The image that appeared in the reflection, standing immediately behind him, almost made him jump straight into the murky water, for his first thought was that Andoc had followed, eager to finish what he started. It was the hair that gave him pause. Long and unkempt, tightly curled. Slowly, as if trying not to startle a wild animal, he twisted on the balls of his feet, easing himself upright as he moved.

'You handled yourself well,' said Aoife the Dread.

Cullen steadied himself, still quelled by the very sight of her. The tall, strong frame and the pale skin and the ostentatious hair. The weapons and the torcs and the rings. The certain knowledge that she could snap him like a desiccated twig if she so chose. 'I took a beating,' he managed to say with all the gruffness he could muster, while swallowing down the urge to vomit in sheer terror.

The lines around her green eyes crinkled as she smiled. 'You took the first blow. After that, you can only survive. I was impressed, for what it's worth.'

That was when he realised who the second person had been. The one in the shadows when Andoc had attacked. But why had she been there? And why had she simply watched? He set his jaw. Annoyed at the revelation but far too cowed to challenge her. 'It won't happen again.'

'Life was never easy,' she said matter-of-factly. The deep, vertical scar bisecting her chin shimmied as she spoke in that strangely exotic accent. 'Especially for those of us consigned to walk land that is not of our blood.'

'It is nothing,' he said brusquely, still annoyed that she had stood by and watched.

'My ancestors, the Eblani, rest in the mud of the Isle of Destiny,' she went on as if he had not spoken, 'over the Clear Sea, which my people call the Muir Menn. I fight for this kingdom, but it is not of me. The trees do not grow out of the bones of my kin. Yours, I understand, are a little closer.'

'Not close enough.'

'Quite. It is a burden not all can bear. Not all *should* bear. You, though, have the light of determination in your eyes. In the set of your chin. You will persist.'

'I do not know.'

'Then it is fortunate,' Aoife said, hooking a thumb at her belt beside the hilt of a dagger that was inlaid with a cobweb of intricate metalwork forming a continuous frieze of oak-sprig motifs, 'that Moranna of the Silver has more faith in your character than you do.' Seeing his confusion, she chuckled. 'Andoc will not leave it here.'

He nodded firmly. 'I'll be ready next time.'

'Next time you will be a warrior,' replied Aoife the Dread, and as the words left her mouth, Cullen saw his life path disappear round a bend.

The florid face of the man in charge of Togodubnos's armoury had crumpled into a deep grimace when Cullen arrived, as though his asking for weapons were something extraordinarily rude. But the irascible armourer had harrumphed his way into the shadows of the storeroom, emerging after a few minutes with an armful of kit to go with his mouthful of muttering.

When he went outside it was to the clatter of metal and wood as the other warriors strapped, slung, and buckled their own equipment.

As had been the custom since time's birth, the fighting party was divided into four groups of nine for the day's action, for nine was divisible by three, and three was the most sacred of all numbers. Cullen was placed in the least experienced squad, and their shields, spears and swords were accordingly plain, devoid of the battle symbols carried to full-scale war and the smaller totems that were the preserve of named warriors, but they would work well enough, which was all that was required. Cullen himself had made what changes he could to make it appear as if his place was deserved. He had pulled the wavy copper-brown hair together at the sides of his head, tying it in bunches, mimicking the way the fully-fledged warriors used braids. He felt stupid. Suspected the named men and women who strengthened the other nines were laughing behind his back, but at least they had not taken offence.

It had been a week since Caratacos's white-snaked banners had marched into the east, leaving only the red of his brother, the high king, and Cullen had felt their departure as a suffocating man feels a blast of cool air. Even so, he had counted down the hours as he awaited Aoife the Dread's promised summons, frustrated as each sundown marked the passage of another day and the snuffing of another opportunity. But then Farrad had come to the training ground one morning, and the lame old killer had sidled over to his charges, clublike hands laced over corpulent belly, and nonchalantly separated Cullen, Andoc and another lad from the rest. He had cursed his pupils' callowness, and snarled at their indolence and questioned their competence. And then he had invited them to fight for King Togodubnos, and he had failed to stifle his own blooming grin as the trio had swelled with pride.

'This ugly thing is not good enough to cut bread,' Andoc was complaining now as he strode up from the armoury, shaking the straight iron blade before him.

'A sword must be sharp, not attractive,' Farrad Skull Splitter growled in response. His three apprentices formed a supporting nine with six bluff but green fighters drawn from the dun's tradesmen, and he had come to offer some final words of wisdom to his nervous protégés.

'The warriors,' Andoc opined as he slammed the sword into its sheath, 'the named. They do not make do with rusty cast-offs. They—'

'Oh, they are dripping in fine clothes,' Farrad said. 'Exquisite baubles. Weapons forged by the best smiths in the land. But those are the trappings of greatness, not its essence. What gives a man his name is that which resides in here.' He poked Andoc in the chest, hard enough for him to stumble back. 'What unites the lark and the nightingale? The humble thrush, even?'

'Song,' Cullen ventured, receiving a look of scorn from Andoc. His heart had sunk when his saggy-eyed foe had been selected to join the raiding party, but he knew he could not let the simmering antipathy distract him from the life path that he had chosen.

'Song, indeed,' Farrad intoned sagely. 'Yet they are drab birds, in the main. Then will you think upon the grand raptors, their teeth-aching screech. Not a pretty tune between them. Or those brightly coloured hedge birds that sing as though their throats have been slashed.' He looked from Andoc to Cullen to the rest. 'Forget the trappings, boys. Your weapons will do their job if you remember to do yours.'

Aoife the Dread, in overall command, put thumb and forefinger to her mouth and blasted a shrill whistle that had ears pricking like so many hunting dogs. They were on the move.

With Farrad's words chiming in his ears, Cullen went to fight for the dignity of the Catuvellauni. He hated himself for it, but he could not deny the exhilaration that coursed like tide waters through his veins.

—

They were not so much warriors as hunters. The quarry was a gang of thieves, who had snatched six head of cattle from a steading almost two days' walk to the west of Verlamion. It was not clear whether it had been a formally sponsored raid on behalf of king or chief, or perhaps nothing greater than a desperate act by hungry folk, recently displaced in the wake of Catuvellauni expansion. In truth, it did not matter. Cattle were precious. The most valuable thing a man could own after gold and jewels, and Togodubnos had decided to take offence.

So they surged briskly into the west. A day and a half to reach the steading, finding a couple of charred outbuildings and a dozen shaken and angry witnesses, who gave descriptions of woad markings and weaponry that told of men able to inflict considerable damage to anyone in pursuit. Aoife's working assumption was that it was a formal thrust by the Dobunni or Cornovii, for those two nations hugged the Catuvellauni western border. A deliberate act, then, in order to test the mettle of the sons of Cunobelin, who laid claim to being the mightiest men in all the Isle of the Mighty.

A swift and brutal example, Aoife told her charges, must be made, and after two more days of scouring the ground, touching the ash of spent fires and gauging the depth and wear of every print of hoof and foot in every track they encountered, they came to a small village on the edge of a wooded vale. And just inside Dobunni territory.

They crept close, slinking like stoats at a shrew-hole, and sending forth scouts with the sharpest eyes and swiftest feet. The settlement was not unlike the one of Cullen's childhood, protected by a circular, ditched perimeter with a wattle screen on the inner face and big, sturdy gates blocking the only causeway in and out. Indeed, it was the kind of place they had passed a dozen times on their journey. The difference now was that the stolen cattle, according to the scouts, were grazing, penned, within.

Aoife bade them split into their nines and bury themselves in the balding branches of the vale and wait, silent, for the sun to sink and the shadows to lengthen. They shivered as dusk crept in, for no flame could be permitted, and they kept their voices to the lowest of whispers, punctuated only by the screech of a barn owl and distant bark of dog or fox.

But then, in the night's deepest, stillest recess, Aoife gave the signal, and chaos erupted.

They snarled as they ran, over a clearing where the grass was slick and a group of startled badgers shuffled furiously into the darkness, eyes gleaming in the moonlight like so many shooting stars, and then the nines were leaping the ditch and the leader of each was armed with a club or axe with which they turned the fence to kindling. The people inside the village, presuming themselves safe behind the latticed wattle, roused as one at the sudden, blood-chilling din, but their bleary stumbling led them straight onto the first spear points and their yawns transformed to screams.

Cullen was swept along on the tide of men and iron that flooded the village centre. He hurled his spear aimlessly, losing his head in the first rush of excitement, and drew his sword, but it remained dry as he moved, negotiating the vague forms of friend and foe as they criss-crossed in the dark. One body came out from a side alley, causing him to whirl to his right and loft the blade, but he saw the small shape of a child skitter sideways, as startled as he, and could not bring himself to strike.

Confusion reigned. Men and women shouted challenges and warnings and threats and pleas as metal clashed with metal, with wood, with flesh. Dogs barked, babies cried, children sobbed, the stolen cattle lowed and brayed and snorted. Somewhere a fire started, flames quickly lapping at the eaves of a roundhouse and up into the thatch. Aoife the Dread was in the thickest part of the melee, for Cullen could hear her snarls, but for the most part all he saw was whites of eyes and teeth, bared in the dark, wild and desperate.

It was a horror to Cullen's eyes. The sounds and the smells reminded him of Calleva. Of his own village. And with that comparison came the heart-rending fear and the yearning to be anywhere but here. He could not run, could not hide, so he dithered, wafting the sword and shield aimlessly, desperate to try and look busy without the need to engage.

From one of the buildings a party of men and women mustered themselves into a knot of armed defenders and came out to force the Catuvellauni back, but they were disorganised, outnumbered, and rapidly overwhelmed. Cullen watched them fall, one by one, but his bowels had turned to water and he hovered at the periphery, hoping simply to survive. Out the corner of his eye he saw a door skin rip clean away, and a big, bearded man burst out from a roundhouse, bellowing like an enraged bullock. His hands gripped the long haft of a woodsman's axe, moonlight skittering along its edge. With a great roar, he held the weapon high, circling it like a banner, beckoning fate to come to him, and so fate came, in the shape of one of Cullen's comrades, a straw-haired youth with cheeks blighted by puss-headed spots. The boy screamed as he lunged, and the bearded man brought down the axe, swatting the oncoming sword contemptuously away, shearing blade from hilt, iron from bronze, as though the whole thing were made of linen. Then up came the axe in a scything arc, punching the shield aside before thumping sickeningly home, and the spotty lad was on his knees, desperately gathering up his intestines with his own hands, whimpering for his mother as he tried in vain to stuff them back into his gaping midriff.

The bearded man grunted as he wrenched the axe free. His wild eyes turned on Cullen, who shrank back. He knew his duty, remembered his training, heard Farrad's barked instructions echo between his ears. Nevertheless, his steps reversed, legs heedless to any will but their own. Terror had him in a granite grip. He struggled against it, tried to prise its cold fingers from about his limbs, but it would not let go. The big man came on, babbling some incoherent curse, spittle frothing at the corners of his mouth, and when the moon lit him for a moment, Cullen could see the blood that spattered his chest and face. He saw in his mind's eye his own innards slithering over his shoes. The image did just enough to wrest back control of himself.

Up went the huge axe. Even in the din, Cullen heard the hiss as it came down, slicing the air above him. His shield took the force, and paid the price, reduced to a tangled mess of pale splinters dangling from a pointless handle. Cullen tossed the shredded carcass away and put both hands to his sword hilt, holding it up diagonally in preparation for the next blow. But the axe was low now, by the big man's ankles, and instead of hefting it for another downward strike he swept it up and out, aiming for Cullen's groin. Cullen staggered out of range, swiping impotently at his assailant's gurning face but finding only clear air, and then the axe was coming round again, hurtling from on high to cleave him in half. He parried it, his sword bouncing aside, jarring his hands so that he almost let go. But he did not let go, and he recovered his posture before the bigger man could bring up the weapon that was so cumbersomely weighted at its head. This time he found his mark, jabbing with the sword point once, twice, to pierce flesh just beneath his enemy's collarbone. The bearded man bellowed, fury mingling with fresh pain, but he managed to haul the axe upwards vertically, snapping the sword just above the hilt, and, finding a surge of new strength born out of animal desperation, he grimaced, slamming the long haft down.

Cullen discarded the impotent hilt and threw himself back, but it was all too late. The flat slab of iron, curved and impossibly sharp, careened towards his face. Then he felt hot moisture pour into his eye. No pain. Just a heavy throbbing, right through his body, from scalp to feet, and he tasted the new blood on his tongue as it cascaded over his lips, and he was on his back, looking up at the stars. He saw faeries; scores of them. Little orange sparks, fluttering and whirling and always rising, tumbling ever upwards, leading his soul away from the stricken body. On to the next.

A growl invaded his reverie. It was guttural and savage, as though a cornered lynx had joined the fray. Into his line of vision, across the twinkling blackness, came a pair of legs. Cullen's eyes adjusted as he took in the rest of the man. Plaid braca, a long mail shirt, a helmet sprouting a horse-hair crest. The faeries flitted and danced about the broad frame as he pulled his sword a hand's breadth from its scabbard.

'You will feed Bear Claw!' the mouth beneath the plumed helm bellowed, and Cullen instantly knew him to be one of Aoife's named warriors, Ulla Jagged Cliff, and he saw now that the faeries were embers from the gathering blaze, and in that moment he also understood that he was still alive.

Cullen sat up. He spat blood. Only one eye worked, so it was through that that he watched Ulla draw the full length of double-edged iron, the twin fullers etched with the images of rearing bears. He swept the huge blade in a couple of arcs that audibly hissed. With his other hand, he threw Cullen a spear. It was heavy, fashioned for a full-grown man and unwieldy in his grip, but he managed to catch it – just. As the howling axeman lunged, Cullen jammed the butt-end into the dirt and lowered the shaft, angling the tip so that it buried itself within the tangle of beard. The raging man stopped in his tracks, then reeled away to the side. Blood pulsed down his front, saturated his beard, pattered the ground, and he roared again, beginning to stagger, eyes bulging with battle-frenzy. Still, he hoisted the great axe.

He died in a handful of moves as Ulla finished the work. It was an awesome sight. A battle-giver in his pomp. But sharpest of all were his reflexes. The sword darted like adder bites before the axe could complete a single arc, reducing its owner to bloody scraps. As Cullen dropped the spear and heaved himself to his feet, he almost felt a perverse sense of regret in witnessing so effortless a demise for one so courageous. It seemed wrong somehow. Then he touched bloody fingers to his eye, probing the flesh that gaped above the brow. Pain seared his skull and more blood pulsed over his cheek. He decided to save the guilt for later.

—

They saw out the remainder of the night in the village. After laying out the dead on a great pyre on the edge of the vale, Aoife told the survivors to keep their stricken cacophony to a low keening or be prepared to follow their kin to the next realm. Most chose to stay, hiding their grief behind firmly drawn door skins. They gathered around the first fire, that which had taken hold during the fight. Its flames were feeding on the collapsed remains of the afflicted house, but not looking likely to spread, so they plundered food and drink from the village's winter stores and they chatted and sung late into the night.

Dawn brought the true nature of their work into stark relief. Some of the houses were nothing but shells, their remains charred and jagged, lined with the black shapes of crows, and wreathed in a miasma of stale smoke that soured the air. The bodies on the pyre reappeared like monsters from the underworld, beckoning the new sun with black clawing hands.

'What if these were not the thieves?' Cullen asked Aoife the Dread when she and Ulla came to check on his group. He sat apart from the others, picking at the flaky blood that had dried around his eye and ear and down his neck. One of the nine had tended his injury as best they could, slipping a thread through the flapping flesh with a needle made from the impossibly fine bone of some long-deceased fish or bird. The axe had chopped a deep swathe through Cullen's right eyebrow and nicked the upper lid, but, mercifully, he had begun to regain his sight once the congealed blood had been cleansed. Now the wound was ragged and crusty, but at least the gaping maw had been closed.

Aoife glanced across to where the cattle were corralled. 'The signs are ours,' she said, meaning the branding marks that showed pale on each cow's rump. But he realised that it did not matter. It was as much about the example they had set. Word would travel. She looked down at him. 'You did well.'

Cullen stared back, bemused. 'I did not, lady.' His parched throat cracked as he spoke. He glanced towards Ulla Jagged Cliff, but could not meet the man's gaze. 'You saved me, lord.'

Ulla grinned, his face becoming even rougher with the exposure of big, crooked teeth. 'Your first fight. First real fight. You drew blood, you spilled your own, you did not flee and you did not perish. A good outcome.' He slapped Cullen's shoulder, sending a lance of pain through his skull. 'And you will have a tidy scar. The women will flit about you like moths.'

'Here,' Aoife said, tossing something into Cullen's lap. 'Your share of what we have taken.' He gathered it, disbelieving, gauging the substantial weight as he turned it in his fingers like a rare jewel. It was an armlet, cast in brass, to judge by the surface patina, with circular terminals shaped into discs, into which a zigzagging pattern had been set in red and yellow enamel. It was old and tarnished, and just about the most exquisite thing he had ever laid eyes upon. Aoife nodded, satisfied. 'For your work.'

Cullen slipped it onto his left arm, just above the elbow. It was too big, too heavy, and he cared not a bit.

The leaders of the warband went out into the village to distribute more rewards. Rings — for fingers or to be woven into hair – were numerous, fine pins and glass beads too. A silver brooch, taken from the waxy corpse of a village elder, was awarded to Ulla, while coins, some with the marks of Cunobelin, others with those of Berikos, and a couple with the heads of Roman emperors, were given to those who had done the greatest deeds. And all the while Cullen wondered why he had received anything at all. He had fought, in a manner of speaking. Defended himself, in truth, when retreat was not an option. But that hardly denoted courage.

Later, as they tied the cattle, one to the next, in readiness to leave, Andoc came to him. 'You soiled your braca,' he said in a low, rasping voice, dripping with scorn. 'I saw.'

They were at the rear of the gathering column, the poorest warriors in the least important nine, and out of the earshot of anyone who mattered. Cullen stared up at the malevolent face that topped Andoc's willowy frame. He tapped the armlet with the hand that was free, now that his shield was no more. 'This says different.'

Andoc spat. 'It says nothing.' He lifted one long finger, encircled by a gleaming metal band. 'We all shared the spoils.'

In a way, it was a relief that someone – anyone – had seen through the illusion of heroism Cullen had somehow garnered, even if that someone happened to be his persecutor-in-chief. Still, it would not do to admit to the truth of Andoc's claim. He let his hand caress the pommel of his sheathed sword. 'Would you like to try and prove my cowardice?'

Andoc spat again. 'I will, Atrebates. Have no fear on that score.'

–

They drove the cattle hard, given the pressing need to return to friendly territory. Still, it took days to traverse the forested downland, and more than a few nervous glances were thrown back into the west, yet no chasing party filled the horizon, nor were the yelps of hunting dogs heard on the increasingly biting wind. Then, on the third day, as a soft drizzle turned the road to a mire, they passed a pair of standing stones, each as tall as a man. A short while later there was a natural dip in the landscape, followed by another made by hand, and they knew they were in the kingdom of the Catuvellauni.

'You said I did well, but you know I did not,' Cullen said to Aoife the Dread as they paused at the bank of a fast-flowing river. It was spanned by a wooden bridge that looked ancient and rotten, but, given the livestock they now escorted, was the only serviceable crossing point for miles. They were waiting, taking water and food, as a hand-picked team of men waded out to gauge the robustness of the decrepit piles, battered as they were by centuries of frothing current.

Aoife ran a pale hand through her red tresses. 'You fought. Many would have run.'

'No one else ran,' Cullen said, and he knew he was overstepping with his tone, but he had spent the entire journey considering what had transpired, picking apart his role in the assault and comparing it with that of his peers. 'The man with the axe defeated me, lady. I am alive only because of Ulla.'

She had been studying the party who were waist deep in the river. Now her cool gaze fell on him. 'I am not fond of this impudence.'

Dragging his own eyes to the ground, he said quickly, 'Forgive me.'

She looked back to the bridge, but it was clear by the way she chewed her bottom lip that she was mulling something over in her mind. 'The fight was hot,' she said eventually. 'You were almost scorched, but you came through.' She smiled, showing neat, white teeth, a gesture as dazzling as it was unexpected. 'Now you have your first scar and your first trophy. Be proud. The threads of our lives are woven by such events. Embrace them.'

Cullen might have retreated there, except, 'Threads?' he echoed. When she arched a single reddish eyebrow, he added, 'You said threads are woven, lady.'

'What of it?'

'It is a phrase I have heard before.'

'Common enough,' she answered tersely, irritation bubbling up like the water around the rotting piles.

'Moranna of the Silver.' The name was all he uttered, but it had the desired effect, for she skewered him with her green eyes, and for an instant he thought she might hurl him into the water. 'Forgive me, lady,' he said hastily, 'but is she known to you?'

Aoife made a face suggesting the question was stupid. 'She is the king's Wise One.'

He was trying her patience. He half expected a backhand in answer. But the matter had gnawed at him for too long. 'And has she spoken of me to you?'

After a painfully tense moment, she sighed. 'Moranna believes you to be touched by Taranis himself. King Togodubnos believes it. Caratacos too.' She gave a chuckle of genuine mirth. 'Even Arthmael the Learned, grudgingly.'

'He would have me killed.'

'If he had nothing to fear, you would be dead already.'

'So you believe?'

She shrugged. 'I respect the beliefs of those I have named.'

He stared down at the rushing river, looking at the water but seeing Moranna's face, Becan's, Arthmael's and the king's. 'What is happening?'

'The lady Moranna,' Aoife replied, 'encouraged me to come to the wood, outside Verlamion.'

He remembered her sudden appearance after Andoc's ambush, seemingly wandering the forest for no apparent reason. 'By the ancients,' he breathed, beginning to feel like a leveret with its foot in a snare.

'Moranna is your friend. She cleared your path. She sees your destiny.'

'Paths,' Cullen retorted hotly, 'turns, roads.' He knew he should keep a respectful tone, but diffidence was rapidly giving way to resentment. He smelled conspiracy, and it was ripe and rank. 'I want to hear no more of destinies.'

Her face became taut. She spoke coolly. 'I fear you will be disappointed, then, orphan of the Atrebates.'

He bowed his head, knowing he had pushed her too far. Kneading his good eye with the ball of a palm, he said, 'Moranna sent you to the forest, knowing I would be there. She sent Andoc too.'

'Like as not,' Aoife conceded.

'Aware that he would take the chance to attack me.' He was quieter now, the events playing out as images on the surface of the river. 'Knowing that you would bear witness.' He glanced up at her. 'What if he had bested me? Killed me?'

'She knew he would not. She insists Taranis has plans for you. That irritating gnat, Becan, insists too. I listen to them. But I cannot train *every* child lusting for glory. Least of all a young captive who did not even take his own tribe's tests. I needed to see your nerve, your backbone. Moranna arranged for me to be convinced.'

'What now?' he asked sullenly, still annoyed that he had been manipulated by the Wise One.

But Aoife was already walking away.

—

That night, they made camp at the foot of a gorse-patched hill, beneath skies layered with bilious grey cloud that all but choked the moonlight. They made a huge furnace of long branches, the greenery shaved off at the edge of axe and sword, and when it was lit the flames were large enough for them all to gather around. In the pulsating warmth that crackled in the deep darkness they spoke of the old days, when Cunobelin had been at the height of his powers, and his delegates had convened summits with the preening officials of Rome. Ulla Jagged Cliff sang a low, mournful song that recounted glorious deaths in long-ago battles, and Aoife regaled them with tales of Innisfail, the Isle of Destiny. Cullen imagined it all as he gazed into the flames, sinking into his own mind as he let her smooth, lilting brogue carry him across the Clear Sea. She told them of the Sons of Tuirenn and their adventures aboard the magical ship, *Wave-Sweeper*, and of the Fomorii, those malevolent half-gods who dwelt beneath the sea, led by their fearsome champion, Balor of the Evil Eye. She spoke, too, of the Children of Danu, the first gods, the Ever-Living Ones, who came to the middle-realm before all other life, and who watered the deserts and calmed the volcanoes and planted trees in the arid abyss so that the earth would be fertile for the coming of mankind. Those oldest tales told not only of Innisfail, but of the Isle of the Mighty, of the birth of Cullen's own people, of the coming of his tribe's gods. Stories his own mother had told.

As the tales moved on, climbing through the years since creation, Ulla began to sketch an image in the dirt with a charred stick. Cullen had no knowledge of such things, but Aoife explained that the crude ovals, one large, one small, represented the islands on which they lived, that had been the first home of the Ever-Living Ones. The smaller, she said, was the Isle of Destiny, her birthplace, and the larger was the ground on which they now stood, the Isle of the Mighty.

Ulla partitioned the larger shape, dividing the land between the kings and queens of the present. Aoife spoke as he drew, naming the greatest lords of the far north. The Caledonii, Venicones and Damnonii. Below them, the most powerful of the mountain peoples were the Parisi, with their formidable fortress of Eborakon, and the Brigantes, ruled by the beautiful Queen Cartimandua. To the east of the island, Ulla traced the borders of the Eceni, the Trinovantes and the Cantiaci, while to the west, hard against the Clear Sea, were the Deceangli, the Gangani, the Demetae, and, of course, the Isle of Mona, where the Wise had their famed institutions of learning. To the south of those kingdoms, forming the north bank of the vast river where the goddess Sabrina dwelt, were the lands of the Silures, the only tribe, in Aoife's opinion, to rival the Catuvellauni for sheer ferocity in the battle-frenzy.

'They extend their territory by the season,' she said, meaning the Silures. The flames danced across her face, bathing her in light and shadow by turns. 'They will need to be pushed back before long.'

'The Ordovices too,' Ulla said.

Aoife nodded. 'And the Brigantes ever press from the north.' She sighed, as if recalling simpler days. 'The Sun Hound maintained the clan alliances because that was Rome's demand. Vast imperial trade, in return for peace and stability. Now Cunobelin is gone, and so is his hard-won peace.'

'Will there be war?' someone asked.

'Togodubnos and Caratacos,' she answered, 'mean to restore order from the chaos, but the old alliances were brokered by Rome. The sons of Cunobelin are not well disposed to the empire.'

'War is the only road to peace,' Ulla remarked, not unhappily.

'And the bitter Adminios,' Aoife added, 'has fallen upon Rome's mercy, requesting help against his brothers. Togodubnos fears Berikos may harbour the same intent.'

The mention of the deposed chief of his own tribe was like a needle on Cullen's skin. 'King Berikos would not betray our people.' He regretted the outburst immediately, for he could see every eye slide to him in the gloom, many of them hostile. He added, 'Your pardon, lady.'

'And who are our people?' she asked him, apparently amused. 'Berikos was king of only one nation, was he not?'

'And that nation has ceased to exist,' Andoc's voice chimed in from the gloom.

'Adminios and Berikos,' Aoife said. 'Two voices on the Senate floor.'

'Loud voices,' Ulla replied grimly. 'Begging for the legions to swarm upon our shores.'

Aoife touched a bronze charm at her neck, warding off evil, then spat into the flames. 'And a new emperor enthroned, eager to make his mark.'

Ulla Jagged Cliff tossed his smouldering stick into the fire, watching it catch alight, red and yellow tongues rearing along its length. He spat too. 'Let them come.'

CHAPTER TWELVE

The ribbons were a vibrant shade of yellow. Cassia cut them down to strips, the length of her forearm. She tied them to her wrists, taking care to cover the little white scars, and wove them into her hair. When she was done, she observed herself in an elaborately patterned bronze mirror that Critheanach claimed had once been owned by a queen of the Smertae tribe, those most savage of people who dwelt in the extreme north, where the land was covered in snow and their bodies were swathed in seal pelts, and the violent seas contained monsters beyond Cassia's wildest imagination.

'I look like a bumblebee,' she said of her reflection, the yellow garish against her charcoal black curls.

'Our very own Muirgan,' exclaimed Critheanach from somewhere behind, amongst the shadows thrown by torches from their high sconces.

In the centre of the cave, a large cauldron dangled from iron fire-dogs. Cassia perched before it on a low stool, making the most of the flamelight emanating from beneath. She angled it now, to take a view of her mistress, while still adjusting the ribbons. 'Muirgan was princess of the evil Fomorii.'

'The ancients were not evil, my child,' Critheanach chided. She was arranging her own costume, a rustling ensemble of leaves, dried petals and stalks, intended to honour the plant spirits to which she owed her expertise. 'They suffered the same vices as we. Some of the Fomorians were driven by malice, it is true, but Muirgan was a rook-haired beauty. When the Feans, those great warriors from the rugged hills of the Caledonii, looked upon her, they were instantly smitten.' The old woman winked. 'So it will be with you, this night.'

This night, thought Cassia, was something she could do without. The festival of Calan Gaeaf marked the end of harvest and the beginning of the year's dark half. It was the time for reflection and for remembering the dead. A time when cattle would be brought down from open pasture and when livestock would be slaughtered, their meat preserved to keep the people through the bleak weeks to come. And Cassia did not enjoy it one bit, for Calan Gaeaf was one of those times when the realms of the Britons lost their hard edges, so that the boundaries between this world and the Otherworld would grow thin. Spirits could come more easily, according to Critheanach. Faeries, both good and malign, would cross to this, the waking realm, to make all kinds of mischief. For an outsider, the whole experience put her on edge. A feeling not assuaged by the fact that Critheanach had moved to the pyramid of skulls positioned near the cave mouth, the pinnacle item of which she now rubbed with a cloth laced with cedar oil. Cassia could not suppress a shudder. 'Must you do that?'

'Life and death follow not a straight line,' Critheanach lisped testily, for this was not the first time she had had cause to defend the heads' presence in her home. 'Think of it not as a spear, but rather,' she traced a circle in the air, with cloth and skull, 'a shield. When a soul dies here, in the waking world of man, it is reborn in the Otherworld, and when its time is done in that land of wonder and mystery?'

'It is reborn here,' Cassia intoned the lesson she had heard many times, 'in the form of animal or human, depending on the favour of the gods.'

Critheanach smiled smugly, evidently pleased her student appeared finally to be listening. 'We must, therefore, look after the lives that pass through the realms, for the gods are watching, always. Our own soul's journey depends upon it. And where does the soul reside?'

'In the head.'

Now Critheanach positively beamed. She held up the skull she had been oiling, its white surface glowing like a small sun in the firelight. 'These were great souls. The greatest. To be revered. We keep their skulls, embalm them and keep them clean and fragrant, as a matter of reverence.'

Cassia blew out her cheeks, her dark eyes flitting back to focus on the image of herself. The cloak and tunic she had selected were yellow to match the ribbons, while her cheeks had been painted in tight green swirls. 'Bumblebee or wasp.'

'You are supposed to resemble lady's bedstraw,' Critheanach said, exasperated. The flower's stems and frothy yellow petals were an essential component in many of the medicines they spent so many hours creating. 'It is a matter of veneration.'

Cassia pouted at the mirror, aware her mistress was watching her reflection. 'I do not see why I am required to attend the festival at all. I am not even a Briton.'

'You have made your life here,' Critheanach said, leaving the skull pile and walking closer.

'Not my choice.'

Critheanach's leafy arms rustled as she planted them on her hips. 'Go back to Rome then.'

Cassia lowered the mirror and stood, turning. 'I just might.' They held each other's gaze for a few moments. Then she smiled. 'Only if you come too.'

Critheanach reached out a fingertip to her protégé's chin. 'Come to the feast, my girl. If not for the honour of the gods or the dead, then perhaps for an old woman who is so very fond of you?'

—

'By the ancients, hurry it up!' Cullen hissed through teeth grinding so hard that he thought they might shatter.

The woman did not look up as she tapped the clay disc rapidly against the slender length of translucent bone that pierced the surface of his skin. 'It is not a thing to be rushed, red crest.'

Moranna of the Silver had spent the morning mixing a concoction consisting mainly of woad, all the while chanting blessings over the ink, the crow-bone needle and the hammer she now wielded with impossible dexterity. Woad flowered yellow at bloom, but, once dried and powdered, the leaves produced a bluish green shade that was deep and rich. Most used the stuff only as body paint, daubing themselves temporarily for battle or a particular ceremony, but some made the marks permanent, if the Wise Ones advised it, and Cullen had been positively commanded.

'I have chosen the wheel,' Moranna said in her languorous timbre, squinting intently at his right forearm, out of which leaked woad-tainted beads of blood that mingled with sweat and tumbled in dark rivulets into the waters of the stream in which they squatted, 'for it is the mark of Taranis. It will please him.'

They were on Verlamion's outer slope, below the earthworks and above the forest. The stream was shallow, bubbling just over their bare feet, but numbingly cold. Not Cullen's first choice of venue for the rite, but Moranna had insisted that it would please the gods, just as she had insisted on the ritual itself. She showed her filed teeth as she worked, left hand bracing and angling the needle, the other rapping speedily and precisely on its butt end, so that together they were a woodpecker blur. Through their movement Cullen could just about discern the emerging design. A chariot wheel was steadily taking shape. Its circumference, adorned with tiny dots to denote the rivets, was already etched beneath his skin, while seven of the eventual eight spokes connected that outer circle to a star-shaped central hub.

'I would have preferred a lightning bolt,' Cullen grumbled as he hitched up the legs of his slipping braca.

She tapped a touch harder, making him hiss and flinch. 'The choice is not the wearer's, but the maker's. And I choose a wheel.'

'You choose much, it seems,' he said sourly.

She neither looked up nor faltered with disc and needle. 'Have you something to say?'

'You are using me.' With difficulty he tore his eyes from the blue wheel, which was, he inwardly conceded, utterly exquisite, and glanced at the man who had slumped onto his rump at the water's edge. 'You and your son.'

Becan had dropped his sticks and produced a bag that he pointedly turned his focus to. 'You know, Aoife's people, over there in the Isle of Destiny, call this the feast of Samhain.'

'By the ancients, Becan, I'll stick this needle where—'

'Now now,' Moranna cut in, the tapping finally losing rhythm, 'speak to me, red crest.'

Cullen threw Becan a caustic glare. His friend continued to pick through the bag, which appeared to contain a salad of dark mushrooms and jagged goosefoot leaves. Thus deflected, he looked back to Moranna, who was already redoubling her efforts with the crow bone. 'You came to me in the forest.' He nodded in the general direction of the woodland stretching away into the distance. 'Out there. No explanation. Told me I should follow whichever turn my life path takes.'

'What of it?'

'Moments later, Andoc arrives...'

'Streak of piss,' Becan threw in with a snort.

'The same,' Cullen said. 'How did he know I was there?'

Moranna said absently, 'Perhaps he was out taking the air.'

'I fight him off. Think no more on it. Then I discover Aoife the Dread has witnessed the whole thing. Were you all simply out walking the woods at dawn? Does that not seem curious to you?'

'Who is to say what is curious and what is not?'

'The world is strange,' Becan added, 'and full of wonders, goat-fiddler.'

'True,' Cullen conceded. 'Or perhaps the turns in my life path have been laid out by human hand.'

'Finished,' Moranna said of the design. She stood, tossing the needle and hammer to the bank and hitching the hem of her cloak clear of the water. 'These may be human hands, red crest, but they are guided by Taranis, your benefactor. Careful not to insult him.'

'Lady, please,' Cullen began, standing to face her, his arm still smarting as it seeped, dyed blood running down to course between his knuckles, 'I deserve none of this. I—'

'You will be a warrior,' she snapped, 'I have seen it. Dreamed it. Aoife the Dread needed to see you fight, in order for her to accept you as an apprentice. Taranis's will must be done.' She gestured at his forearm. 'Now you bear his mark too. Another step on the road to fulfilling your destiny.'

'More steps than I'll ever take,' Becan said as he retrieved the crutches and hauled himself up. 'But I'll race you to the bottom of a barrel, no trouble. Come, goat-fiddler. Let us join the people!'

The feast itself went on from midday to dusk, and then into the frost-coated night. Fires blazed all around Verlamion's centre, while cows and sheep turned slowly on vast spits positioned at all the major junctions, the aroma of their roasting meat heady on the crisp air. Always, a bizarre assortment of men and children ran amongst the revellers. Some naked, others painted in chalk or woad, and many clad in suits constructed of bleached bones, their skin beneath dyed black, so that they appeared in the flame-glow like cavorting skeletons, there to appease the spirits who walked amongst them on this night when the boundary between the worlds was gossamer thin.

Youths, to judge by their skinny frames, raced, jostled and danced. Their faces gone, replaced with grotesque masks, some made of stitched cloth, others the leering, dead-eyed skulls of goats and wolves. They played horns, harps, whistles and drums, and always they chanted, welcoming the gods, pleading for their sympathy in the dark months ahead.

Near the greatest of the roundhouses, that which held the throne of Togodubnos, there were a dozen makeshift hearths above which haunches of venison sizzled and spat, attended by men turning the spits and teams of women who liberally tossed seasoning upon the dripping flesh. To the side had been erected a great dais, upon which the king sat, clothed in splendour and flanked by wives, tribal elders, dignitaries and representatives of Mona, the Order of the Wise.

'Moranna is there, see?' Becan said as they made their way through the festivities.

Cullen glimpsed the dais as he ducked under a swinging flag, its banner that of a leaping doe. Moranna of the Silver was surveying the feast, standing serenely amongst the gaggle of cloaked and feathered Wise Ones who attended the king. 'I see her.'

'He'll be wanting her sight. Not with her eyes, goat-fiddler,' Becan added when he saw Cullen's nonplussed expression. He reached out and rapped his friend's head with his knuckles. 'With this.'

'What does he want her to see?'

'The future. There is talk that your old king made good his escape.'

'He will not ask the emperor for assistance,' Cullen argued stubbornly, though he sensed his instinctive loyalty had been rendered obsolete, now that the role of King of the Atrebates had been subsumed into the Catuvellauni sphere.

'That was what they said of little brother Adminios,' Becan replied as he procured them a couple of pots of fragrant juniper beer, 'yet he plots and schemes.'

A girl came by, handing out blocks of sweet treats, made of nuts and flour, bound together with honey and flavoured with the juice of the marshmallow. They were presented as shards and hard as rock, but, as Cullen crunched his way through a chunk, he thought it a gift from the gods. He ate as they moved on, rounding a corner to encounter a white-cloaked female, impressively tall, made positively statuesque atop a table festooned with food scraps and upended ale pots. She regaled a crowd, mostly warriors, with tales of heroism from the days before time. Her pale face had been caked in chalk so that it melded with the cloth of her hood, leaving only a pair of dark eyes above a pair of ruby lips.

'One of the last gods to live on this earth with their most ancient powers,' the poet called out, her voice querulous and exotically accented, 'was he, known as Manannan Mac Lir, the turbulent lord of the deep oceans.'

Cullen stared up at her, transfixed, as they edged up to the rear of the crowd. The speaker was like a ghost, half lit by the many sources of tremulous light, willowy and tall and ethereal.

'His ire was great,' she was saying, staring sightlessly over the heads of an audience rapt, 'and his breath could summon ferocious tempests.' With pale hands she sketched circles in the air, illustrating angry waves. 'After the fall of the oldest gods, Manannan Mac Lir made a home on Innis Falga, that misty isle buffeted by the Clear Sea, between the Island of Destiny and the Isle of the Mighty.'

'Wrecked countless ships with his vicious whisper,' Becan muttered.

Cullen looked down at him, irritated to have the spell broken. 'You've heard this before?'

'You have not?' Becan said in a manner that suggested Cullen was simultaneously ignorant and fortunate. His eyes swivelled to the chalk-faced orator. 'She will tell of the bones of the dead that make up the island's reefs, and of those poor drowned souls who swim for eternity with the sea-maids. It is a good enough tale, but I'd rather hear "The Sword of Light". Now *that* is a story worthy of the telling. You know "The Sword of Light", yes? Goat-fiddler?'

But Cullen was not listening. He had forgotten the poet too. He was staring.

—

Cassia pretended not to notice the slack-jawed youth, though it was difficult when his gaze felt like it was burning a hole in the side of her head.

'I told you it would work,' Critheanach hissed, close enough that her breath was hot in Cassia's ear. 'The costume,' she added when Cassia glanced at her, perplexed. 'They cannot but look, the young bucks.'

Indeed, as the poet continued her tale, Cassia cast her eyes about the spaces between knots of revellers, each quivering with a timorous mix of shadow and light. She realised that the red-haired man – or boy, it was hard to tell – was not the only one struggling to conceal his interest. Others stole glances from over the rims of ale pots, or pretended to chat with friends, all the while betrayed by their darting gazes.

And yet something about him piqued her curiosity. He with the yellow-and-green braca, and the yellow tunic that was stained with what looked like blood on the right sleeve. Not that his clothes were much to behold, but there was something about that lopsided expression that intrigued her. Something in the way the angry, puckered wound above and through his right eyebrow tugged at the side of his face, pulling him into a private smirk he seemed oblivious to.

'I am Cullen,' he was saying, for he had drifted somehow into her space, crossing the ground between them without apparently trying. He was a full head taller, making her crane her neck to look up, and she realised she was holding his gaze, perhaps returning it as dreamily as he.

She offered the first increments of a small bow, the last vestige of an old habit, before correcting herself, feeling warmth climb her neck. 'I am pleased for you,' she said, forcing haughtiness into her tone to mask the mounting embarrassment.

He coloured, the florid blood in his cheeks appearing almost brown in the night. Up close, she saw that his nose was puffy on the left side, as was the adjacent cheek, and his upper lip still bore the marks of some mostly healed blow. 'I am sorry, I—'

'Don't be.' Cassia stopped him with a little wave, feeling suddenly bad for the affected self-importance. 'It is nice to talk with someone not crying for his mother.' Worse still. Her turn to blush. 'That is to say, I am a healer.'

'You are Roman, I think,' he said awkwardly, clearly struggling not to trip over his own tongue.

She nodded. 'And you are Catuvellauni, I think.'

He looked mortified. 'Atrebates. I am of the Atrebates.'

The pulse felt heavy in her neck. The fate of that tribe was common knowledge. Celebrated, in fact, in the streets of Verlamion. 'Now I must apologise.'

'No need, truly,' he said, which was a lie if ever she heard one. He coughed. It sounded like he was gargling pebbles. 'You speak our tongue.'

'I have been here a long time.'

'Slave?'

'Once,' she said. 'No longer. My name is Cassia. Now I work with my mistress, Critheanach. We heal the sick, the injured.'

'By the ancients,' he said, wafting fingers before the cleft in his eyebrow, 'if only I had known you before today.'

She laughed, surprising herself. 'Now you are stuck like that.'

He thumbed in the direction of the pale Wise One, still up on her makeshift podium. 'She was telling the tale of the twisted piskies earlier. If I'd known it was about me I'd have kept my head down.'

'I don't know. Is it not an honour to be the hero of a story, whatever its subject?'

His smile only accentuated the crookedness of his face. 'Perhaps I should offer to act out the scenes.'

She laughed again – easily, comfortably. 'I think you have found your calling, Cullen of the Atrebates.'

'Just in time for my life choice!' he exclaimed. 'For that I thank you, Cassia of Rome.' He twisted, grabbing two cups of beer from a serving platter that whisked past, its bearer weaving through bodies with practised agility. He handed one to Cassia. 'Here.'

—

The wound had done it. Given him the courage to approach. That, and the wheel that Moranna had needled into his skin with dye and pulverised charcoal. Together they had changed him. The injury might have ruined his boyish features, but, he conceded, it was not as if he had been particularly comely in the first place. Now, though, he looked like a warrior. Or, at least, like someone who had been in a proper fight. The wheel, if Moranna was right, was the physical manifestation of the favour of a god. If that failed to instil a bit of backbone in a person, then, he reckoned, nothing ever would.

Still, he had amazed himself when his legs took him into the girl's presence. She was a dream. Olive skin and hair as black as raven feathers, the tresses spiralled like the most intricate torcs. She had a wide, plump mouth, the lips darker than those of native girls, with a nose that was straight and prominent. And her accent. It was honey in his ears. Harp-song and faerie whispers and forest breeze. Cool water on a fresh burn.

Now, to his continued disbelief, she was smiling, taking the proffered drink. 'For me?' she said in mock surprise. She bit her bottom lip. It made the words melt in his throat so that he could only nod dumbly. Now she licked froth off those lips and he thought he would drop dead on the spot. She said, 'And my people paint you as savages.'

'Oh, we are savages,' he replied, albeit thickly, for she made the air snag in his throat. Made words shrivel. Turned his lifeblood to smoke. 'Just not all of the time.'

Her smile was sardonic, higher on one side than the other, the teeth straight and white and dazzling. Her eyes were hazel, shot through with a million sparks of gold and red, and he found himself studying them, as if the answers to life's great mysteries were hidden within. 'If you are not joining the poets, Cullen of the Atrebates, then what life path do you intend to walk?'

He squared his shoulders and puffed out his chest. 'Warrior.' Immediately he felt stupid, like some conceited whelp, posing at manliness. Grasping for credibility, he added, 'I am training with Farrad Skull Splitter and Aoife the Dread.'

She nodded, apparently impressed, though the knowing half-smile had returned. 'Then I will call your name if ever I need help.'

'Do, please,' he said, too hastily to achieve the nonchalance he had been trying for. Ruffled, heat rising again, he threw his eyes at the ground.

Behind Cassia, amongst the press of people, an old crone hailed her. Cassia threw an impatient glance over her shoulder, then reached out, touching the top of his hand. 'Critheanach grows bored. I must go.'

Cullen frowned, looking past her. 'Why is she dressed like a bush?'

Cassia laughed, the gold in her eyes shimmering. Her bright teeth were a contrast to those dark lips, at which he could not help but stare. Then she was gone, slipping into the crowd from whence she had come, leaving Cullen dry-mouthed and gawking in the midst of Becan's resounding cackles.

—

The darkness came on inexorably. It lingered in the mornings, pushing each new dawn further into retreat, and every evening it gnawed like a mouse at a wheatsheaf, stealing little by little, the nights creeping in like a blight edging through crops.

Cullen lived as a member of the Catuvellauni. He practised his warcraft. Rehearsed the movements of the shield and the nine strokes of the sword. He hurled spears at the straw butts set up in the fields below the town, and he pitted his skills against

Farrad's other charges, so that they might accustom themselves to something akin to an authentic enemy. But no call came, no raids were planned or thieves to be brought to heel, for the cold air made life sluggish and the flurries of rain and sleet turned the roads to slop, and it was universally recognised that these were the weeks best seen off with an extended spell at the hearth. So Cullen tried to stay warm, he refined his skills, built his strength, and inwardly seethed because he had joined the tribe he despised.

After Calan Gaeaf, as the world began to freeze, Cullen reached his choosing time, a seminal moment in any youngster's life. The moment, indeed, when the first steps along their final life path were taken. But those who might have tended that path, pulled the weeds and kicked away the stones, were all dead and on to the next. Moranna of the Silver had shown undue interest, of course, but that was out of reverence for Taranis, not because she had any love for the boy marked out by blood and lightning. Thus, Cullen of the Atrebates chose his place in a tribe he hated one mist-smothered morning in the company of his warrior brethren. It was hardly an earth-shaking choice, for he made his oaths before others of a like mind; some who had already made their choice and others who soon would. Yet it was a good feeling. Something meaningful. He remembered how it felt to have hope. It might, he told himself, even get him closer to Caratacos.

Surprise, delight and terror greeted him in equal measure upon learning that he was to join Ulla Jagged Cliff's band. Not yet a full-fledged war-giver, his age and choice meant that he must nevertheless move from the ranks of Farrad's apprentices. After the fight against the cattle-thieves, Ulla, it seemed, had chosen both he and Andoc for his nine. Thus, they gathered in an elm grove as the first weak light lanced the distant hill-line. The puddles that had started life as wheel ruts and footprints had expanded to boggy pools that now glinted with a thin skin of ice, and tentacles of white vapour coiled at their ankles. Aoife the Dread joined them, as chief of the warbands, with Becan and Drest observing from the edges. Moranna conducted the ceremony, dismissing their shivering disgruntlement with the claim that sacred places such as this were not made by man.

'They are discovered,' she had said, 'and therefore we must use them how and when the gods instruct.'

'Could they not have instructed us to wait for a warmer day?' Becan had asked.

'If you are not careful,' she had countered acerbically, 'they may instruct me to have your blood drained to make poultices.'

Complaints therefore addressed, she had gone about waving various plants at a bemused Cullen as she incanted ancient words and enacted ancient steps. She sketched out symbols in the ground with a sharpened stick topped with a pink crystal, and asked Cullen questions that would test his knowledge, ambition and loyalty. He said what needed to be said, silently begging his mother's forgiveness for the betrayal, and declared his intention to lead a warrior's life. Moranna pawed at him, beseeching Taranis to put strength in his muscles and wisdom in his brain, then she pulled at his hand, lifting his arm, and spat on the image of the life-wheel, tracing a shape in the frothy spittle with a fingernail while she declared that he was a favourite of the mighty deity and should enjoy whatever privileges might come by association.

They cheered him when it was done, slapped his back and dragged him out of the grove so that they might foist horns of strong mead on him without risking the wrath of the gods. Then, to seal the choice, they went hunting.

—

The nine, under Ulla's command, headed north amid a day crisp and brightening, though the moon lingered, a white disc observing all. Cullen and Andoc were the greenest spears and looked to the others for reassurance as they followed the trail of the ferocious wild boar that lurked within the dark and dense forests.

'Ride to catch deer,' said one of the seasoned campaigners, in answer to a gripe from Andoc about sore legs. He was bare-chested, as thin as a spear-shaft and a head taller than the rest, with arms that seemed disproportionally lengthy, almost apelike. 'Walk to catch boar.' He had a dark complexion, with a prominent nose, plaited brown hair and bushy whiskers twisted to sharp points with beeswax. He chewed mint always, so that his teeth were tinged green. 'Only a fool risks having his mount disembowelled.'

'Pay heed to Kurd Long Limb,' another of the named men growled. His battle name went before him. Garn Grey Boulder, whose build was all muscle and blubber, the broad face framed by an unkempt shock of silver hair and moustaches plaited with wire. He carried no shield because he had only one hand, the other a stump bound in leather and armed with iron points. 'Ever seen those tusks up close?' He rattled the heavy necklace of badger teeth that dangled over the fastening of his long cloak. 'Make these look like nail clippings.'

'I'll have him down,' one of the newer recruits claimed. A young fellow, just a little older than Cullen, whose name was Dan. He hailed from the mountainous lands near Mona, where he had committed some crime which led him to join the armies of the Catuvellauni. It was his skill with the bow, now slung over his shoulder, that had secured his place in the nine. Plenty of folk could take a doe with the weapon, and properly fletched the arrows were undoubtedly deadly, but the bow was a tool to put food in the belly. It did not carry the same prowess or dignity as the spear, and rarely graced a warband's ranks. Yet in the hands of a true expert, the flight of a properly loosed arrow was a thing of pure beauty and, to Cullen's eyes, stark terror. Dan could nock and loose an arrow in the time it took for a heart to beat, and his mark would be stuck through by the very next pulse. Cullen had seen him split a withy at sixty paces and take stag at seventy-five.

'A woman's weapon,' Garn rumbled.

One of the full warriors, White Tal, gave a soft chuckle. 'Dangerous, my friend, nevertheless.'

Garn snorted. 'So is a loom if you stub your toe on it. A warrior – one with honour on his name – meets his enemy up close. Where he can smell the man's breath and look into his eyes, measure himself against his foe.'

Dan, who was short, squat and built like a barrel, jerked his shoulders to indicate the quiver at his back. 'I make my shafts with Guelder Rose and Wayfarer. The stems are long, straight and rigid. If a man saw me take aim, I'd have one through his eyeball before he could blink.'

'And he'll never know it was you!' Garn countered. 'Where is the honour in that?'

Dan laughed. 'Give me a clear sight and I'll give you a dead pig.'

White Tal said, 'That is not the way.' He was lean-faced and cleanly shaven, wore plain braca, a loose mail shirt and a simple helmet without adornment. What marked him out, and lent him his name, was the perfect whiteness of his long hair and eyebrows, so that he seemed to Cullen to be an ice-born deity, sent to walk the waking realm. He touched an amulet at his neck, closing his pale-blue eyes. 'To kill the forest warrior without respect is to offend the gods.'

The nine, save Garn, carried spears and shields as they followed the highway out of Verlamion. It was not one of the great paved thoroughfares that bisected Calleva or Camulodunon, but a wide stretch nonetheless, underlaid by a blanket of birch branches and surfaced with oak planks that had been expertly adzed to ensure a uniform smoothness. The route cut through a dense alder wood that tradition claimed was the home of a particularly mischievous tribe of sprites. That being the case, they travelled quickly, in no mood to dawdle, ever watchful of the forest's dark recesses and high boughs.

A warrior named Rues was their lead tracker. He was short and wiry, bare-chested and face-painted. His scalp was limewashed pale yellow and so savagely spiked that it looked as if each hair had been hammered into the skin like so many pins. Eventually he led them silently, single file, off the road and through more trees: hazel, oak and beech. Cullen was at the back, furtive and listening intently. The only sound was the furious wingbeats of a score of linnets as they erupted from a spiny thicket, a blur of browns and whites and reds. Cullen imagined with amusement the racket the crutch-swinging Becan and the blind Drest would have made, and was thankful they had stayed behind.

There was an expanse of dead wood carpeting the forest floor, crunching unnaturally loudly beneath their feet. Stands of decaying bracken bowed, as if in supplication, before stoic oaks, broad of trunk and as old as the hills. Occasionally there were grassy clearings, shorn to stubble by goat and deer, and thin, impermanent streams criss-crossing everything, created by rain and destined to vanish with the turning of the seasons.

Rues pulled up suddenly as they reached the needled mesh of a row of deep holly bushes, throwing a range of frantic hand gestures over his shoulder. They spread out in response; knees bent to the crouch. The spiked head tilted, as if he sniffed the breeze. Now Rues looked behind, raking the eight pairs of eyes with his own. He mouthed slowly. *Two – beyond the holly*.

Cullen licked lips that seemed abruptly arid. He craned his neck to turn an ear to the barricade of dark bushes. There it was. A low, guttural snaffling. His heart quickened. He squeezed his fingers tighter about the spear shaft.

Then they were moving. Four left, four right, Rues staying put.

Cullen went left. They would go all the way around the dark froth of holly, creeping up on the beasts lurking on the far side. His eyes watered a little with the freshness of the breeze. He noticed thin wisps of cloud scudding above, as if in a race, first to the horizon wins.

A clearing opened up. A patchwork of eaten grass and mangled moss and churned mud. The victims of the boar that stood proudly in the centre, ruler of all he surveyed.

Wild boars tended to be solitary animals, stalking their territory alone, except for during the mating season when they would lumber back to the family groups of sows and their young, and fight for the right to mate. It was the season now, which was why Rues could find him so easily — a larger group of females tended to root amongst a run of coppiced hazels close by — but it was also why the beast would be ill-tempered, up for a fight, and at the very height of his powers.

For a moment the boar froze, its little black eyes glimmering behind tusks as long as a man's arm. It snorted once, twice, looked as though it might charge, then turned to run.

The four warriors emerged from the bushes on the far side. Ulla, Dan, Tal and the man-mountain that was Garn. Immediately the startled animal realised it had been surrounded, eyes darting, seeking escape. It shook its huge bulk, the stiff bristles clothing its muscular shoulders shedding rain droplets in a great arc. It scraped at the stubbly grass with a powerful trotter. Then up tilted its slavering snout, and it gave a sharp roar that made Cullen's blood run chill. This was why the wild boar was revered as the fiercest foe of them all. It would run if startled, but once it was cornered, it would fight to its last breath. And so it did.

It charged, dipping its great head, and targeting a man on the far side from Cullen. But that man was Ulla Jagged Cliff, whose angular face was rent with exhilaration, eyes blazing with the fire of bloodlust. He screamed, as loud as the boar, and hurled his spear. He had drawn Bear Claw while the whistling shaft was still airborne, advancing on his quarry even as the spear's wickedly sharpened tip thudded home. The boar bellowed, the long shaft dangling from its flank. The stripe on its spine, formed of a long mane of paler bristles, was spattered with red. It wheeled about, seeking escape, searching for someone to eviscerate, pure rage animating its every action and sound.

Blood spouted from its hind quarter, dappling the ground, mixing with the trampled mud. Ulla was still advancing, Bear Claw at the ready, and the others closed the circle with their long spears so that the desperate beast had nowhere to go.

The beady eyes fixed on Cullen, gleaming bright, intense and intelligent. For the briefest moment it felt as though something crossed between them. An exchange between warriors. At least one of them would die, and they both knew it. Then the boar squealed and kicked into a mad dash, making straight for him, gobbets of mud flinging in all directions, the iron-tipped shaft swaying and bouncing cumbersomely out to the side.

Cullen lowered his own spear, dropped his shoulder and braced behind the shield. He knew he should keep his eyes on the furious creature, but the lids clamped shut unbidden. He tried to fill his lungs but there was no time.

—

The wheel turned.

More than that; it spun, endlessly, viciously. A blur of greens and browns and dark smudges that made Cullen's stomach churn. He swallowed down the urge to vomit. His head chimed like a cauldron tumbling over rocks. His back, he realised, was damp. He was lying flat, the spinning wheel high above. Was this the passageway to the next, the manifestation of the life wheel that he carried on his forearm? Was he in the dreaming realm, awaiting his soul's next host? A lord, perhaps? Undeserved. Probably a hawker, he supposed, or a lonesome hedge-dweller out on some misbegotten moor. No, he thought. The gods had a sense of humour. He would return to the waking realm as a wild boar.

'You clipped him,' the voice said. It was a man's voice, one he thought he recognised, away somewhere to the left. Muffled, though, as if uttered through a blanket. 'The aim was poor.' A chuckle. No, a sneer, the words laced with scorn. 'Hardly a surprise, seeing as your eyes were closed.'

Cullen placed the voice. At the same time he saw chinks of light break the spokes of the wheel and he knew it was nothing but the high canopy. His head ached. Pulses of pain ebbed and flowed across his skull, ear to ear, forcing him to grind his teeth and breathe in gasps. He slapped mud-slick palms over his face to stifle another bout of nausea, and, to his relief, the world steadied a touch. The greens and browns were leaves and branches, of course, punctuated by the shapes of birds. He wondered if that bloody magpie was amongst them.

'Not dead then,' he murmured.

'Not yet,' Andoc said, his words sharpening as the ringing in Cullen's head faded. 'Boar knocked the bones out of you. Sent you right over the top.' He whistled softly. 'Quite impressive, for a harvest festival tumbler. For a warrior?' He left the sentence hanging.

Cullen pushed himself up. The spinning returned, the pain in his head intensified. He paused, breathed deep, waited for it to subside enough to move. Then a quick audit of limbs told him he was merely bruised and shaken. But any relief was fleeting. The churned, scarred and blood-spattered clearing was empty. His spear lay close, but Andoc's foot rested heavy on the shaft. Cold dread climbed up from his guts into his chest, every rib a rung on the ladder of panic that led to his rapidly quickening heart. 'Where are the others?'

Andoc was standing over him. He shrugged. 'You let the pig through. They've given chase.' His smile was slow and measured as he slipped the knife from his waist. 'Now it is just you and I.'

'Why?' Cullen shuffled back as he spoke, digging his heels into the filth, tearing up the wet grass with white-knuckled fists. 'How have I wronged you?'

To his surprise, Andoc pointed the blade upwards at his own sallow face. 'My family were slain by your raiders when I was but a babe. They left me with this.'

Cullen saw that he was running the tip of the knife down the puckered flesh at the corner of his mouth. '*My* raiders? Atrebates?'

'Atrebates.' Andoc's reply was hoarse, constricted, as if the sheer force of contempt had made the word grow brambles in his throat.

Cullen almost laughed, so taken aback was he. 'And mine were slaughtered by yours!'

But Andoc was not listening, and in a surreal moment of empathy, Cullen found he could not blame the looming figure who now advanced with frightening purpose, heavy-lidded, sagging eyes unusually bright behind that blade. Vengeance drove his hate. If nothing else, Cullen could understand that.

'You kill me,' Cullen said, trying and failing to keep the panic from his tone, 'and the others will kill you.'

'They won't know.' Andoc licked his lips, savouring the moment. 'And if they do, I am protected from the likes of them.'

'Protected?'

It was then that the second boar attacked.

It came in a rush, the holly hedge to Cullen's right rustling, parting, shredding asunder, leaves spraying in all directions, mud flinging, birds taking sudden, maddened flight.

From the boar came a high-pitched wail; half squeal, half shriek, all violence. It was as big as the first, hairy and striped and viciously tusked, and it went for Andoc, who twisted, backed away, staggering, slipping, stumbling, crying out in horror. He had the knife in his grip, brandished it, and he might as well have pulled out his prick, much good it would do.

Cullen's head hurt. It pounded, felt as though it would cave in. Blood rushed at his ears as his sight blurred and refocused, blurred and refocused. He reared up, onto his knees, and shoved Andoc, who fell hard, sprawling on his face. The boar charged between the two of them, glancing both but smashing neither. Cullen fell back, rolled. Grass sprayed as the beast wheeled sharply about, rounding on them in a snorting, braying storm of noise and mud and spittle, and it bolted forth, tusks levelled and ready to gut whatever they might meet. Cullen was on his knees again, barely able to see for the grinding pain behind his eyes. In his hands was the long haft of the spear with which he had so ignominiously failed to kill the first boar. He had no idea which end was which, but he thrust it out regardless, and as he did so, he toppled forward, no longer in control of his own body, the light fading from the world.

CHAPTER THIRTEEN

Not for the first time, Cullen woke in a stupor. He might have been forgiven for presuming it was the Otherworld, that he had been transported to some ethereal chamber, there to await his next life. Except that he had already learned that lesson.

So he ignored the ache that still thrummed in his head, and forced open his eyes, greeted by the dingy interior of what seemed to be a house made of stone, fire smouldering in the centre, cauldron dangling above from a set of beautifully wrought fire-dogs.

He knew it was the waking realm, the plain of humankind, of flesh and blood, joy and love and grief. He was certain because of his aches, which were numerous, and because of the stench, which was pungent, and because he could see the hoary light that invaded by way of a large, irregular opening. But, by the ancients, the huge pile of skulls made him wonder.

'Quite the hero,' Cassia said.

The voice was unforgettable, indelibly marked upon his mind, not to mention the accent, which was only shared by Roman traders, and they were generally few and far between. 'Where am I?'

'Verlamion.' She came to sit on a stool by the fire, stirring whatever was in the cauldron with a huge wooden ladle. 'In a cave on the outskirts. The home of my mistress, Critheanach.'

An image flashed across Cullen's mind of an old woman covered head-to-toe in green paint and leaves. 'The Wise One?'

'Not as wise as she would like.'

'Watch your tongue, you,' snapped the old woman herself, from somewhere unseen, her voice cracking and heavily warped.

'She did not complete her studies at Mona,' Cassia said waspishly, 'so she cannot claim to be a member of their order.'

'One does not have to be *Wise*,' Critheanach declared in that strangely sibilant manner, stalking into the light, 'to be wise, as well you know, girl.' She was holding a bundle of material, which she stuffed under an armpit, the better to free a hand in order to stab a crooked finger at Cassia. 'Besides, those bastards up at Mona are mad as a bag o' martins, most of them. And so far up their own arses that—'

Cassia winked at him. 'It is a wound that has not scabbed, even after these many years.'

Critheanach's white brows knitted together. 'Not so many years as you'd think, girl, I'll have you know.' She rounded on Cullen. 'You getting dressed then, little hero?'

For the first time, Cullen became aware of himself. He was lying amongst heavy animal pelts, layers of them, in the sleeping space at the cave's outer edge. He slipped a hand beneath the covers, realising with shock that he wore not a stitch. He sat up with a start, tugging the pelts to his chin, heat rising in his cheeks. 'Where are my clothes?'

'You were filthy as a pig in shit when you came to us,' Critheanach said. She was skinny and pale, all straight lines and sharp angles. She tossed the bundle at him. 'Braca, shoes, tunic. Clean and dry and smelling o' daisies.' A wry smile. 'Do not be so coy, little hero.'

Cullen gathered up the clothes, keeping a hand firmly on the pelts.

'Turn about,' Cassia said to her mistress.

The old woman pouted. 'Nothing I've not seen before.'

Cassia made a show of shifting on the stool so that her back was turned to him. 'Critheanach.'

Critheanach folded her arms with a dramatic harrumph, but she turned away all the same, grabbing a cloth and tending to her macabre collection of blanched skulls. Cullen pulled the braca up his legs, awkwardly under the pelts, but, once he had disentangled himself, he was able to stand. Not that his body enjoyed the sensation. 'By the ancients, my head.'

'It hit you hard,' Cassia said as she turned to face him.

'Felt like Cernunnos's antlers.'

Critheanach scoffed. 'Just a big, hairy pig, t'was all. And the proud creature died for it.'

He patted himself down, assessing each ache to see what wounds had been inflicted. There were plenty of marks, pink and brown and black, some fading to yellow, but none too terrible. 'Why am I here?'

'I told you,' Cassia answered, 'we heal. Moranna of the Silver sent you to us.'

'How long?'

Cassia glanced at Critheanach, who shrugged. 'Days.'

Something jarred in his mind. 'Wait,' he cut in before she could elaborate. 'Hero?' He looked at Critheanach. 'You called me little hero.'

'You killed that boar,' the old woman said, 'and saved another's life. Saved your own while you were at it.'

'He told us there were two,' Cullen said, the hunt tumbling back into his head, playing again, blow by blow. 'Rues Seeker. He warned us.'

'And not a feckless one of you paid him any heed,' crowed Critheanach. 'The thrill of the hunt addled your wits. I am shocked to my marrow, truly.' She snorted loudly, amused at herself, then waved her skull-cloth at Cassia. 'Off you scuttle, girl. Better inform those iron-swinging fools that the magnificent swine-slaughterer has ended his slumber.'

-

There followed a time of recuperation. The days were cold, frequently rain-drenched, and perfect for extended stints under thatch, which almost always smelled of fish, the weather being ideal for smoking trout and eel. Folk visited often, telling Cullen of the events that had followed the boar's charge. Of how he had skewered the beast in the heart, in what was, by all accounts, a strike worthy of Caratacos himself.

'Beloved of Taranis,' Becan had said earnestly, more than once. 'Did I not tell you? You shall be great, goat-fiddler! Greater than Aoife and Ulla and all the rest!'

'I speared a boar.'

'Your life is charmed!'

'I have been cursed by Arthmael.'

Becan had shaken his head as though ridding himself of a troublesome fly. 'Moranna has seen it. Seen your glory. Think of the girls we will attract, goat-fiddler! Think of the opportunity!'

Besides his legless friend's tiresome crowing, the days were good to Cullen. Having departed the home of the nearly-Wise Critheanach, he had returned, still aching and with a slight limp, to his own lodgings, which were less welcoming, but, at least, had fewer skull-shrines to negotiate. He offered help when his neighbours required, be it lifting beams or rethatching rooves or catching escaped piglets, though the many offers of spears and resulting guffaws swiftly wore thin. Sometimes he walked out in the woods, thinking always of his mother and sisters, and, as his strength returned, he would explore the outlying tracks at a run, building himself back to the boy – the man – he had been before the fateful hunt.

Verlamion itself, spiked and formidable on its hill, had gradually transformed from the heart of his enemy to a genuine sanctuary. At night the dun glowed, and he would take to the low fields and look up at his new home. Sometimes Becan would accompany him, complaining of the distance, and occasionally, surprisingly, Cassia would come too, telling tales of far-flung lands he could barely comprehend. He would visit her when he could, though her time was more readily taken up than his own, for her work with Critheanach never ceased, the population of Verlamion coming to them with all kinds of winter ailments, seeking brews and tinctures and poultices at every hour of the day and night. Often, he would arrive at their cave to discover they had travelled beyond the great ramparts, having been summoned to steadings on the northern frontier of Togodubnos's lands, for the raiding season was in its final throes. The stories she brought back were fit to turn his stomach. Wounds to be stitched, flesh to be cauterised, limbs to be amputated. Cullen was to be a warrior, but Cassia, he came to realise with more than a little chagrin, had seen more gore than he ever would.

'My father was a physician,' she had told him as they strolled back from the traders' quarter one bright, frost-kissed day, 'in the valetudinarium at Gesoriacum, on the north coast of Gallia Belgica.'

'Valu...?' he echoed, feeling stupid.

'Tu-di-nar-i-um,' she sounded out each syllable, wearing an expression of amusement. 'It is a big building, where my people tend to the sick.'

They had reached a large roundhouse near Critheanach's cave. He pointed at it. 'Like that?'

She shook her head. 'A *very* big building. Stone walls, tiled roof.'

'Tiled?'

'Clay. Fashioned flat, into thin slabs.' She overlapped one hand with the other. 'Set like this.'

'What is wrong with thatch?'

She smiled, showing those brilliant teeth, but it was a gesture of warmth rather than mockery. 'Nothing at all.' Her hands moved so that she traced a rectangle in the air between them. 'It had four sections, the valetudinarium, each as large as a chief's hall, to accommodate our patients. We could house perhaps four hundred men. Five hundred at a pinch.'

'Why?' Cullen said, unable to hide his bafflement.

'After a battle, there are many wounded.'

'The wounded recover or they die.'

'Spoken like a true Briton,' she chided. 'Rome fights many battles, large ones. Our armies are a multitude.'

Cullen walked on, trying to muster a look of disinterest. Inwardly his mind turned cartwheels, imagining the legions he had heard so much about. Aoife had spoken of them, Becan too, and Drest had even seen Roman soldiers in his youth. Yet any force that required a dedicated place of healing, accommodating five hundred souls at once, was barely conceivable. If five hundred were wounded badly enough not to walk from battle, how many had marched onto the field for the first blooding?

He turned to ask, 'You assisted your father?'

'Every day. I was only small,' she tapped a finger at her temple, 'but I remembered it all. The tools he used. The techniques.'

'That,' crowed Critheanach, leaning against the entrance to their home, 'is what makes her so useful to me. Roman knowledge, mark you. None o' that bilge from Mona.'

'It is not bilge,' Cassia hissed reproachfully, eyes darting furtively to check who might be listening. 'And you do not insult their order without first mastering the art of the whisper.' She turned back to Cullen as the old woman muttered a stream of unintelligible things under her breath. 'I began to assist Critheanach in the preparation of potions and matters of surgery. I learn. Sometimes I teach.' She gave a self-effacing smile. 'Mostly I learn. The druids – the Wise Ones, as you call them – are rich in knowledge.'

Cullen glanced over her shoulder at the woman at the cave. 'I thought she was not fond of the Wise.'

'She is bitter,' Cassia said, raising her voice enough to carry, 'because they expelled her from the sacred isle.'

'Why?' Cullen asked, wincing at Critheanach's spiteful expression.

She shrugged. 'She won't say. But she learned plenty during her time there. Remedy or poison, your druids have the plant for the task. We Romans have more experience of the battlefield than the whole world combined. Together, she and I make a strong alliance.'

'Your father's daughter,' he said, and he meant it kindly, but the ghost of something rippled over Cassia's face. He knew sorrow when he saw it, knew too that he had misstepped, and condemned any further words to perish in his throat.

She looked away. Down. Blinking, swallowing. Fighting back tears, perhaps? 'We were journeying to another Gaulish port,' she said eventually, having drawn a fortifying breath, 'further down the coast from Gesoriacum. I forget which. My father had been summoned to the garrison there. Our ship strayed close to your coast.' She laughed bleakly, brokenly. 'Too close.' Her voice became strangled, fading to a murmur as her dark eyes glazed. 'The white cliffs were above us before we knew they were there. Like giants.'

'The white cliffs of the Cantiaci.'

'We call it Cantium,' she said. 'Our ship foundered. We were wrecked. None survived but me. That was ten years ago.'

A pang of sympathy struck deep in his guts. He knew how it felt to lose the ones you loved. He had a sudden urge to reach out, to touch her arm, to hold her, even. He clasped his hands at the small of his back, lacing the fingers so that he might keep them in check. 'I am sorry.'

Now she looked up at him. 'I know you have suffered, too.' She sighed, long and deep, ridding the moment like blown cobwebs. 'The Cantiaci paid homage to Great Cunobelin in those days. I was offered as tribute. Lived as one of the high king's household slaves.'

'When did he free you?'

Cassia paused then. More than that, she held her breath, as if stung by an unseen barb. She met his gaze, mouth a tight line. 'He didn't.'

'You said—'

'I know what I said,' she blurted, and the colour was rising in her cheeks.

'She's my little slave!' Critheanach called, revelling in a little retaliation. 'The Sun Hound gifted Cassia to *his* son, and his son sold her to me.' She clapped her hands happily. 'A solid investment, if a tad on the sharp-tongued side. Sometimes wish I hadn't bothered teaching her our language.'

Cullen looked from one to the other. 'Why did you lie? Before, at the festival.'

Cassia shrugged, making a study of her own feet. 'Shame.'

This time he did reach out. He could hardly believe it himself, but there it was. His arm, extending, as if by its own volition, to brush her elbow. The slightest touch, barely worthy of the name, but to Cullen he might as well have whisked her into his arms and crushed her mouth upon his own. Not least because she did not pull away.

'Come now, girl,' Critheanach called, grinning. 'Leave the blushin' warrior alone before he besmirches his braca.'

She backed away. Not abruptly, nor with disdain. He kept his hand where it was, so that the fingers slid along her retreating forearm, grazing the top of her knuckles, dropping off her fingertips.

He wanted to grab her. To haul her back, gaze at her some more, drink her in like a parched man denied water too long. But that required more courage than even one beloved of Taranis could muster. Besides, the cackling crone, Critheanach, was leering at him. Instead, he called, 'Three days and nights!'

She turned, nonplussed, her slanted smile more slanted than ever. 'Until?'

'My brethren. Three days and nights.' It was a babble. A vomit of words, just to keep her talking, and he cursed himself for a piss-minded fool.

But she grinned all the same. 'That sounds wonderful, Cullen, truly.'

He cursed aloud this time, then slapped his own forehead, feeling hot with embarrassment. 'What I mean to say is that I join my brethren. My nine. Ulla's hawks. I feel well enough, thanks to you both.'

'In three days and nights, was it?' Critheanach squawked.

He nodded, realising too late that she mocked him. If he could have blushed a deeper hue, he would have.

Cassia had reached the cave mouth. She ushered the old woman inside with something more than a gentle push, then looked back. 'I feel safe knowing that you protect this great fortress, Cullen of the Atrebates.' And she went inside.

It turned colder as Cullen resumed his duties.

Down on the plains beneath Verlamion, Farrad still sidled between his charges in his own cloud of vapour, brandishing the unsettlingly notched and scored club as his snarls echoed up to the dark stripes of earthworks. The men under his tutelage were different now, of course. No longer apprentices, for they had fought for real. Some had bled, a few had killed. Some, like Cullen, had reached the age of manhood, and all were stronger, harder versions of those callow youths that had first come to learn their craft. But Farrad was an effective teacher, and Ulla had commanded that his nine hone their skills while they waited for spring.

Cullen was greeted with grunts of appreciation in the main. Those who had been on the boar hunt were well aware of the tale. Others had heard it spun a hundred times since. Andoc, sullen as ever, kept his own counsel. Only he and Cullen knew what had really transpired. What had nearly transpired.

So it was that, under sour grey skies, he slipped back into the familiar battle rehearsal that was the warrior's life. Shield positions, spear thrusts and throws, sword postures, parries and cuts. Farrad paced, bawled, cursed and mocked. He cajoled more out of them with every cycle of lone practice and paired duel, and, as the days wore on, he intensified Cullen's work, bringing him up to the necessary level demanded of the others.

Ulla's nine, who he dubbed the hawks, took their turns on patrol, or on the battlements, or out in the villages. The ground crunched, littered with curled and brown leaves, as they traced paved roads and ancient byways alike, keeping the peace and enforcing Togodubnos's laws. They checked the boundaries of his kingdom, visiting border ditches and counting marker stones, and often they would gather tithes from far-flung hamlets. The powerful would pay in coin, the rest in whatever counted as valuable. Wool, leather, corn, preserved meat, salt, glass beads or metalwork. Cullen played his part, did his duty, and settled into his new role.

One morning, when the nine had stayed in a riverside hamlet a day's march south of Verlamion, and the eastern horizon was streaked with lacklustre, dirty sunlight, a summons came from Aoife the Dread. It was not unusual, for she commanded Ulla in all things, but his party happened to be preparing for a deep foray into the Belgic lands that hugged the far south coast. The chief there, a new vassal of Togodubnos since Berikos's fall, had not paid his tribute, and Ulla was readying to ask him why. Still, with only half their provisions gathered and none of their pack ponies tacked, they were obliged to turn about, retracing their steps until they reached a small orchard of golden-brown apples, an hour outside the great dun on the hill.

It was Aoife herself who greeted them as they hungrily stripped the branches. She appeared like a war goddess, sword at her hip, fur-trimmed boots on her feet and a thick fur cloak that was fastened by a silver brooch taking the form of an owl in profile. Her face, framed by that mad tangle of red curls, was white as fresh snow and implacable as ever, as she swept imperiously through the trees to swap pleasantries with Ulla. They spoke briefly, an exchange Cullen could not hear, then the two of them beckoned for the rest to approach.

'That man,' Aoife said, the sudden sharpness in her tone dragging all eyes to her. 'Bring him.'

It took a few moments for Cullen to realise she meant him. He looked to both sides, feeling suddenly like a shrew in the gaze of a falcon. Noting, too, the grim line of named men loitering beyond the orchard. Part of him considered bolting for the hills. He swallowed, thickly, and stepped forward.

Aoife, at once beautiful and terrible, fixed him with her hard eyes. The vertical scar in her chin was filled with shadow, contrasting with her skin's pallor. 'Kneel,' she commanded, waiting as he obeyed. 'You have chosen your life path?'

The ground was slick and cold on his knee, damp seeping through his braca. 'I have, lady.'

'And?'

'I would be a warrior, in the service of the king.'

'King of where?'

He ventured a look up. She was like some winter queen, come down from the icy wastes of the far north to pass judgement on lesser mortals. 'Of the Catuvellauni, lady.'

A pause, as if considering the truth of his claim. 'You have not taken the tests.'

'No, lady.'

'But you have fought when your life was at stake, for the honour of the tribe. You have killed too.' Her eyes slid up. 'Where is Andoc?'

A voice at the back. 'Here, lady.'

'Did this man save your life?'

'By the ancients,' Cullen hissed into his own lap, for who better to ask as witness than the man who would have gladly murdered him, had a wild boar not intervened? He braced for the damning tirade.

'He did, lady,' Andoc said simply.

Cullen's head shot up, staring at Aoife, who was, in turn, looking at Ulla. 'This will do.'

And that was how he became a warrior. They took him from the orchard and up into Verlamion itself, where a forge already burned bright, awaiting his arrival. The smith, a balding, flat-nosed man with scar-thickened fingers and forearms like hams, bade them enter with all the solemnity of a Wise One at the midsummer rites.

Ulla's men, their numbers bulked by Aoife's personal guard, formed a protective ring around the building. They chanted in low, deep drones, speaking of warriors long returned to the ground and praising the skill of the smith-god, Gobannos. At a curt prompt from Aoife, Cullen entered the darkness within, the air a hot blast that stung his eyes and snatched his breath. At the centre, the freshly stoked fire glowed incandescent within a circle of stones, as if a dragon lurked in the shadows. When his eyes adjusted, he could see that Ulla and Aoife had joined him. Moranna of the Silver was already there, draped in a many-coloured cape. A lavish headdress of huge, splayed feathers adorned her head, while the thread glinted like frosted cobwebs at her ears.

The smith's wife, donning a long, leather apron, held out a plate and demanded Cullen spit upon it. As he did so, the Wise One, her face an unflinching mask, incanted words he did not grasp. She brandished a small knife, with which she took a lock of his hair and strands of his mother's cloak. She mixed them with the saliva on the plate, then scraped the frothy concoction into the fire with her long fingernails, the flames spitting and hissing in reply.

Moranna met Cullen's mesmerised gaze. 'By the will of the god, Taranis, and the pleasure of Togodubnos, sire of the Sun Hound and High King of all the Isle of the Mighty, you have been chosen to join the host commanded by this woman.' She glanced briefly at Aoife, though the acknowledgement was unnecessary. 'You will carry this weapon, imbued with Taranis's power, and with your own essence, and that of your ancestors.'

The smith crouched beside the small fire, holding an iron bar in long-handled tongs. The bar itself was formed of scores of thinner layers, each heated and hammered onto the next. Cullen knew that laborious process well enough, for he had seen it done a hundred times by Solidu at Camulodunon. Never, though, had he imagined it would be done in his honour, and he found himself enthralled as the iron was put to the heat.

The smith's wife, protected from errant sparks by her thick apron, went to sit opposite her man, working constantly at a set of large bellows, breathing life into the forge's glowing heart. The darkness of the workshop allowed for better reading of the heated iron, and the smith turned it occasionally with his tongs to gauge the richly glowing hue. When he judged it the perfect colour, out it came in a welter of dancing embers, to be placed atop an oaken log. Firmly gripping one end, the smith worked it deftly with his hammer, shaping and refining the glowing bar into the tang that would later form the spine of the handle, lurid sparks showering the sand that had been scattered all around.

When the iron had cooled, it was flipped so that the opposite end could be heated, and the steps were repeated with a fascinating mixture of firmness and skill, until a long, flat blade began to take form.

'She'll do,' Ulla grunted in the darkness.

'The butterfly emerges from its chrysalis,' Aoife said huskily, reverence softening her tone.

Cullen could only nod mutely, words snuffed out like cloud-smothered stars. From brute iron, a thing of beauty was born. And it would be his.

—

They left the smith to finish his craft, walking in sombre procession behind Moranna, who barely drew breath amid her relentless chanting. There was a huge ditch to the east of Verlamion, its width twice the distance of a respectable sling throw, and so deep that at least six men could stand on each other's shoulders and still not see over the top. She led them across by a narrow causeway, constructed from the upcast of a nearby quarry, its bare-chested labourers dropping tools and bowing heads as a mark of respect. On the far side of the ditch, beyond a small group of coppiced hazels, they came to a mound of earth, grass-covered and badger-holed, its summit decorated with patterns of smooth stones, each painted with symbols of beast and tree, moon and sun. It was a place of burial, Cullen knew. One of the sacred places of mystery, left to them by a society long consumed by time's shadows.

Moranna indicated that he should stand at a certain place at the foot of the mound, and he saw that the stones there were marked with the life wheel, the same design as she had inscribed into his skin. She had a pot of blue paint, and she smeared three lines upon his face with her forefinger. One for each cheek and another between his eyes, running down the length of his nose.

'I place on you,' she said, 'the three prongs of the noble triad. Tell me them.'

'To do no evil,' Cullen answered, 'to honour the gods, and to practise bravery.'

'Will you drive these three stakes into your heart and build your life upon them, as a warrior must?'

'I swear it.'

She backed away, spreading her palms to the onlookers, who stamped their feet and thumped the butt-ends of their spears into the ground.

'Life with glory!' someone called out.

'Death with honour!' came the joyous reply.

It was done. Cullen let out his breath, feeling a swell of pride and of relief. Up above, the bare hazel branches resonated with the carolling of an unseen bird.

—

'I'll call her Slasher,' Cullen said, cutting the air viciously to embellish the assertion.

Becan's nose wrinkled as he looked at the new-forged sword. 'Because you like the sound a horse makes when it pisses?'

Cullen sheathed the weapon, privately delighting in the way the freshly oiled iron slid almost soundlessly into its scabbard.

He ran his fingers over the pommel for the thousandth time, revelling in the detail of the workmanship. The hilt had been shaped into the form of a warrior, with splayed legs and arms to provide a guard. The pommel itself became the man's head, complete with wide eyes, detailed hair, and a turned-down moustache. 'What would you suggest?' he asked peevishly, white vapour roiling from his mouth as he spoke.

Winter was coming. They could feel it closing in, its long, cold fingers wrapping around the skies and houses and trees. Each morning the puddles were iced and the hilltops were frost-touched and smoke filled the air as fires were stoked to start the day.

'I suggest you wait until you use it,' Becan said. 'The sword will name itself when the time is right.'

'I'll probably get killed first,' Cullen said morosely.

'Enough with your bellyaching, goat-fiddler. Moranna believes in you, and Togodubnos believes in her.'

'What about the others?' Cullen looked to the rest of the group, who checked their own weapons as they fastened cloaks tight against the cold. His nine had been tasked with visiting a newly marked steading, and they were preparing to move out.

Becan followed his gaze. 'Be the man Moranna says you will become, and Ulla Jagged Cliff will be eating out of your hand.' He jabbed Cullen with one of his sticks. 'Have no fear, goat-fiddler! Yours is the world! But remember to share the spoils with your friends, eh?'

The nine walked for the better part of two hours, into a horizon of low-slung cloud, the feeble sun at their backs. Cullen knew the terrain well enough, for the planned village, intended for the cousin of one of the king's nobles, lay a short distance to the north of Critheanach's cave, and he was able to point out a couple of choice routes across otherwise boggy patches.

As they kicked their way through a drift of large purple leaves in a trackway so narrow that they were obliged to move in single file, Cullen found himself immediately in front of Andoc. It was the first time they had come into direct contact since the hunt, for his willowy antagonist had assiduously avoided him.

'Andoc,' Cullen heard himself say, unable to leave the opportunity vacant. 'The ceremony, I—'

Andoc stopped, rounding on him. 'I do not like you, Atrebates. I never have and I never will. But a life saved is a life owed, and I repay my debts. Besides, I was hardly going to lie to a Wise One, before Taranis himself.'

Cullen nodded above the rustling footfalls of the others. 'Understood. You have my thanks, all the same.'

Andoc turned back. 'And you mine.'

They found the proposed settlement at the foot of a low hill that was thick with sedge and gorse. They traipsed down a single, dew-slick track to the low ground, which was littered with timber and piled reeds, all set within a circular ditch that would, in the fullness of time, be fenced to keep livestock in and trespassers out. Ulla Jagged Cliff, huge and craggy as ever, strode at the head of their short procession, hailing the village elder and asking after the fortunes of the families planted in this new area. The rest trudged over the earthen causeway spanning the ditch, heading for the collection of temporary huts that had been thrown up in advance of the more permanent roundhouses already beginning to take shape.

Cullen unslung his shield as he came to a halt outside the huts. He had dried meat and a hunk of gritty bread in his bag, and he fished them out, eagerly cramming scraps into his mouth. The others gathered in the space too, drinking from leather flasks and chatting while their leader discussed matters with the elder.

In the centre of the ditched ring, a gang of men, stripped to their waists, laboured in the construction of three new roundhouses, thick posts and taut rope forming a skeletal outline of what eventually would be. Nearby, off to the side, a man sat on a stool, one leg thrust out in front. That extended foot was bare, the ankle heavily bandaged. Two figures flanked him, speaking, hands on hips. With a jolt, Cullen saw that one of them was Cassia.

She turned at the same moment and her face lit up. She waved enthusiastically. Despite the embarrassment caused by his comrades' stares, he found himself walking over to her.

'What brings you here?' he asked.

'This fool,' Critheanach answered brusquely, wagging a finger at the poor wretch on the stool, 'thought he'd sample the local mead while he lashed the roof beams together.'

'I always said your people were bad builders,' Cassia said.

'Bad?' Cullen affected a look of offended horror. He pointed to the roundhouses taking shape. 'Look at those things of beauty. What more do you need?'

'You sink posts into the ground, pack them with flint, join them with sticks, cake the whole thing in shit, and consider it a palace.'

Cullen turned a circle on his heels, admiring the view. 'Beautiful spot, this. Perhaps I will build a house here one day. Out of sticks and shit.'

'Perhaps you'll get some goats,' Cassia retorted archly, 'and then your life will be complete.'

'I might,' Cullen laughed, 'I just might.'

She left the injured man in the capable but scathing hands of Critheanach, and walked with Cullen around the settlement's perimeter, while Ulla continued his summit, and the fighters took their ease.

Cassia looked him up and down. 'You are walking the warrior's path again.' An obvious enough comment, given the body-shield and spear he carried. Not to mention the new-forged blade that had been imbued with powers beyond his comprehension. But he saw more reflected in her attentive gaze. There was the thickening at his neck and shoulders, and the eyebrow, gouged and mangled, and the new crookedness to his nose. Then there was the dark blue wheel that permanently stained the skin of his right arm, and the circlet of brass clinging to his left.

'That I am.'

'I am glad to see you fully recovered.' She glanced at the lounging warriors, who had spotted a trickling brook, and were now happily bathing their feet. 'Why nine?'

'Three is the most sacred number, the ideal number. The number of the Wise and of the gods.'

'The noble triad,' Cassia added in an exaggeratedly sage voice, 'as Critheanach never fails to remind me.'

'Critheanach is right,' Cullen laughed, 'but three is too few to form a fighting unit.' He shrugged. 'Nine is divisible by three.'

'So it could have been twelve?' she observed.

'I suppose,' he began, 'but—' The impish glint in her eye cut him off abruptly.

They walked on, skirting deep pits that would eventually be used for grain storage. Further out, in the fields beyond the ditched perimeter, men and women sowed the bare soil with the rye that might, come next summer, find its way onto the homes they would soon be thatching.

'How do you find it?' Cassia asked. 'The life, I mean.'

'Truly?' he asked. 'Terrifying.'

She laughed. 'How so?'

Cullen glanced over at the nine. A group bristling with leather and metal, scars and spikes and shields and mail and brawn. 'Ulla, our commander, has fame. Real fame. Some of the others have earned their names in battle.'

'Garn Grey Boulder I know. Crith makes an ointment for his stump.' She indicated a slim man who was studiously inspecting a huge axe-blade, polishing it every so often with the hem of his green-and-black cloak. 'And is that Five Thorns lying on his side?'

'It is indeed.'

'Some esteemed company, then.'

'I can hold my own,' he said hotly, immediately feeling foolish.

She raised one of her thick, dark eyebrows. 'I'm sure.'

'That is to say,' he stammered, the heat rising unchecked through his cheeks now, adding to his embarrassment, 'that I have earned my place. The nine is composed of named men and...' He trailed off, feeling as though he was digging himself an ever-deepening hole.

'Those of less experience?' she prompted. When he nodded, she asked, 'Aoife the Dread commands Ulla?'

'Others command the cavalry and chariots, but all the nines are hers, below the king and his chiefs.'

'They find the dirty work,' Cassia replied wryly, 'and she sees it done.'

'Aye. Though Togodubnos himself is fierce, so they say.'

'You've not seen him fight?'

'Only his brother,' Cullen replied, and was immediately struck by an irreparable sense of injustice that formed a knot in his chest. The mere thought of Caratacos fed upon him like a thousand leeches, reducing him somehow.

Perhaps she read the distress on his face, for she said, 'There have been many patrols of late. More than usual for this season.'

'Rumours of war,' said Cullen, thankful for the shift in subject. 'With the Coritani and the Eceni. Even the Cantiaci, many of whom remain loyal to the traitor, Adminios.'

'Traitor?' she asked pointedly. 'Has your own king not fallen at the feet of the emperor?'

'There is no proof of that,' he said tersely.

'But plenty of rumour.'

He wanted to argue, but he had heard the same tales, brought back by merchants from the Gaulish ports. He rubbed a hand over his eyes, the thought of impending doom a sudden weight.

They had stopped walking. They were standing now beside the perimeter near the earthen bridge, looking back at the builders. Cullen asked, 'Will your people invade?'

'Where there is a will, my people find a way.' She stepped a little closer, her tone becoming strained, earnest. 'Do not fight them, Cullen. The legions cannot be stopped.'

'They've been stopped before,' he said obstinately.

Again, the roll of the eyes. 'Casivellaunus, I know. No poet may visit without retelling the tale.'

'It is a great tale,' Cullen countered, unable to keep the petulance from his tone.

She looked at him as if he were simple. 'Would you believe me if I said Julius Caesar was half-hearted? That his invasion was not a tenth of what Rome is capable of?' She placed a hand on his. 'That if this new emperor, Claudius, has a mind to take Britannia, he will come as a raging storm, flooding these lands with soldiers, the like of which you cannot begin to imagine?'

Cullen pretended to consider her plea. Then said, 'No.'

She spun away in exasperation. 'You Britons are so pig-headed.'

He grinned, following, tugging at her wrist to bring her round. 'That's why you love us.'

'Oh, do I?'

They halted, facing one another, no more than an arm's length apart. Cullen's voice was thick as old wax. 'I think you do.'

She looked up at him, craning her head. Her eyes searched his face. Her breath was warm on his neck. Her olive skin was unblemished, and he had to ball his fists to keep himself from reaching for her cheek. She smelled of honey and lavender. He felt a flush of heat, as though his very body was made from glowing coals.

She pulled away, blinking, as if jarring herself out of a trance. 'I've been meaning to give you this.'

From her cloak she took a string, to which was attached a wooden disc. She held it out for him to take. 'Carved from hawthorn.'

He held it in his palm. The wood was a dark reddish brown, polished to a high sheen. The edge of the disc was impossibly smooth, but the centre had been worked by an expert hand so that it bore an intricate image. He still stared at it as he spoke. 'The three-tailed horse.'

'The sign of the Atrebates,' she said softly. 'It is heartwood.'
He glanced up. 'Heartwood?'

'As a tree grows, the core becomes hard. It supports the rest. It is the spine. The heart. It is the most sacred part.'

'The Atrebates,' he said wistfully, turning the three-tailed horse over and over.

'A gift,' Cassia said, 'to mark your life choice. Move forward with your new tribe by remembering your old.'

'It is too much,' Cullen managed to murmur. 'I cannot—'

'You can,' she cut him off, 'and you will.' For a moment she bit her lower lip, apparently giving her next words consideration. 'I have few friends here, Cullen. I am foreign. A spy and an enemy, so folk whisper. You have always been kind.' She gestured towards the pendant in his hand. 'We have both lost the ones we love. We both make new lives in a strange land. Wear it, Cullen. Think of your people.' She offered a small shrug. 'Think of me.'

He looped the string about his neck. The heartwood felt reassuringly solid against his chest. 'Thank you, Cassia, truly.' The words sounded unnatural to his ears. Thick as broth. Is that what desire sounded like? He wondered, with rising panic, whether she could detect it herself. What he felt was undue, he knew. Out of proportion to the length of their acquaintance, and not likely to be reciprocated. And yet the air between them felt like it had changed in texture. It seemed to have a new frisson, like the haze above a flame. He felt his fingers flex, readying themselves to reach out for her. She did not move.

'Gather up!' Ulla Jagged Cliff bellowed. 'Cullen Goat-Swiver! Get over here before I stick that new blade so far up your arse it'll pick your nose!'

CHAPTER FOURTEEN

'Troublesome,' the short man called as he descended the pristine marble stairway.

'Oh?' Berikos answered, standing at the foot of the broad steps.

The short man flashed a disarming grin that was as white as his toga. 'The two of you. Troublesome Britons bringing their troubles to my doorstep.' He bowed when he reached them, then tutted as though they were errant children as he winked at Berikos's companion. 'Big brother wants you back, Adminios. High King Togodubnos demands the return of traitors.'

'Traitors?' Berikos echoed, emphasising the plural.

Another flashing grin. 'Oh, he knows you are here too, King Berikos, and he is not best pleased. He would rather like it if we sent the both of you home for a smack on the wrist.'

Adminios, erstwhile ruler of the Cantiaci on behalf of Great Cunobelin, younger brother to the new rulers of the Catuvellauni and guest of the Roman emperor, gestured to the man in the toga. 'Chief advisor to Claudius himself.'

The man in the toga beamed, crow's-feet pushing out from the corners of dark, intelligent eyes. 'Tiberius Claudius Narcissus, at your service.'

Adminios said, 'I present King Berikos of the Atrebates. Exiled, now, thanks to my brothers. Thank the gods he was able to find me.'

Berikos returned Narcissus's bow and smile, suppressing his disgust at having to treat with a former slave. Narcissus was the famed freedman who had risen all the way to the top of the empire, a shrewd operator and formidable powerbroker. He was to be treated with deference. That did not mean Berikos would not inwardly hold his nose. 'And what will you do?'

Narcissus sucked at his teeth, latticed his fingers. 'A very good question.'

'They will not send us back, so do not fret,' Adminios said brusquely. He was tall and dark, like Caratacos, but not as powerfully built. His face was long, his features as sharp as his words, and his nose was severely crooked. 'No petty chief makes demands of Rome.'

Narcissus inclined his head. 'This is true. So what will be our response, I wonder?'

Adminios looked like he might spit, but caught himself at the last moment. 'Response?' he said sourly. 'When first I came to Rome, Emperor Caligula swore to wrest the Isle of the Mighty from my brothers' grip. In the end, with his legions massed at the water's edge, he bade them collect seashells.'

'A new emperor reigns,' Narcissus said in a well-honed conciliatory tone. 'The old is forgotten.'

Berikos glanced around nervously. They were in the Forum. The very centre of elections and processions, of triumphs and speeches, of judgement and legislation. Great buildings lined the edge of the broad plaza. Temples and courts and the Curia, the meeting place of the Senate. Statues in bronze and marble looked down from high plinths and from the sweeping steps on all sides. It was Rome's beating heart. The furthest he could ever be from his enemies in Britannia. And yet still he glimpsed malevolent shadows in every alleyway. Still he saw knives behind every back. 'Will he come to our aid?' he asked in a low voice.

'Claudius is hungry for military glory,' Narcissus said. 'That much requires no saying. But that alone is not reason to embark on such an ambitious undertaking.'

'The emperor does not sit easy on his throne,' Adminios interjected, dropping his voice to a conspiratorial tone. 'Many question his fitness to rule. The mob is not yet satisfied.'

'Careful now,' Narcissus warned smoothly. He checked for eavesdroppers briefly, making a show of carelessly adjusting the toga. Then said, 'What you say is true. But what you propose is an audacious thing. The risks are vast.'

Berikos did not like where this was going. He gritted his teeth, sending shards of pain from the rotten molar into his jaw and neck. His cheek twitched in response. 'The tribal alliances have fractured. Resistance will be muted. Now is the time to strike. Send the legions.'

Narcissus held up his hands. 'It is not as simple as that. We have marched the road to Britannia before.'

'The Isle of the Mi—' Berikos retorted quickly, catching himself as he heard his own desperation. He forced a steadying breath. 'Britannia, as you know it. There is strife. The treachery of the sons of Cunobelin knows no bounds. Their thirst for land cannot be slaked.' He touched a hand to Adminios's elbow. 'You see the proof of their greed.'

Adminios nodded firmly. 'Other nations will fall in time. Other kings will rise up or lose their thrones.'

'You will have support for the venture,' Berikos went on earnestly, loathing himself for having to beg this overreaching little toad. 'Many chiefs will flock to your eagles.'

Narcissus affected a grimace, as if his reluctance were physically painful. 'We remember the lesson of Casivellaunus.'

'There was cohesion in the time of Casivellaunus,' Berikos said. 'No longer. Now they are ripe for the picking.'

Narcissus's eyes shone as he calculated. He glanced at Adminios. 'How many legions would it take?'

'Not many. Three or four.'

'Enough to shake the log,' Berikos added. 'The beetles will scatter.'

Narcissus clicked his tongue. 'Many of the emperor's advisors counsel him against such an undertaking. Through our existing treaties, client kings, trade, the Britons pay more in customs and duties than we could ever raise in taxation, should we conquer their lands on a more,' he wafted a hand as if he could pluck the word from the air, '*permanent* basis.'

'But that does not stifle the questions over Claudius's ability,' Adminios said.

'Nor,' Berikos added, 'does it quell the unruly mob.'

Narcissus steepled bejewelled fingers beneath his cleanly shaven chin, the corners of his mouth upturning slowly. 'No, my friend, it does not.'

Winter came, bitter and frost-dusted. Mornings saw Verlamion's earthworks loom white, the vapour from the sentries' breath pulsing above the palisades like low cloud. The wells and dewponds froze over every night, the howls of hungry wolves drifted ominously on the whipping wind.

Respite from the grinding cold came with the solstice. As the low sun illuminated bare branches, bringing brilliance and texture to the hitherto unseen, the people of Verlamion could celebrate the time of rebirth and renewal, as signified by the gradual return of the light. It was the year's pivot point, about which the seasons turned, swinging back towards the still-distant times promising warmth and plenty. Yet the days remained short and bitter for now, and the nights long and more bitter still, and so what better way to fill those forbidding hours than with warmth and laughter and song? Poets wove their tales of years gone by and their Wise brethren, the dreamers, whispered of years to come. Drums beat low and harp strings tinkled and the sound was magical in the high thatch of Togodubnos's great hall as his guests feasted on mutton, duck and venison.

Cullen lived with his warrior-brothers. He set to the sword-work that was his duty, watched for enemies in the short days and long nights, wrapping his numb fingers in rags and hunkering tight in his mother's beaver-skin cloak. He yearned to see Cassia again, but she was away during the dark days, when sickness was most rife and food most scarce. The people of the vast Catuvellauni confederation needed healers now more than ever, and she and Critheanach were in high demand. Thus, Cullen busied himself with his work, and at night he joined Becan and Drest in the high king's hall, filling their bellies as they listened to the songs of the word-weavers.

Togodubnos's favourite poet spoke much of Great Cunobelin, the Sun Hound, and his wily ways. How he had defeated his foes with both strength and guile, using the threat of Rome to hold his alliances together. The tales spoke of his sons, too. The young boys who had displayed superhuman powers, even as children, with sword and shield, in the saddle or upon the chariot. Those prodigious talents, those godlike princes, who had forged a new path for the greatest tribe in all the Isle of the Mighty. Who had subdued their own enemies and eschewed the old ties with foreign tyrants. The songs embellished their victories and tactfully omitted any mention of their younger brother, or the toll in lives that had been the cost of their ambition.

Visitors came to Verlamion in those chill days. Other Wise Ones, schooled at the sacred island of Mona, sent out to the corners of the Isle of the Mighty to do the work of the gods in this middle earth. To bring cheer in the dark and to share the knowledge of the Wise. They brought their own tales. New ones, delivered in sing-song verse to eager ears of young and old. They told of heroes long dead. Of brave mariners, battling giants of the grey deep. Of beautiful princesses, kidnapped by the fae of the wild places and rescued by daring heroes wielding magical weapons. Of animals in the deep woods and trolls of the deeper caves. Of the ancient ones and how they came to be.

Togodubnos made offerings to each of the storytellers, for to receive a story, well told, was to receive a precious gift. Pelts and leathers, good shoes and examples of fine metalwork all found their way into the saddlebags of the Wise. Italian wine left the dun too, with beautiful drinking vessels, bottles of olive oil, glassware, bowls from Gaul and glittering jewellery. A price, Cullen could freely admit, that was well worth the paying.

After solstice, teams of men were sent to mend the roads, capitalising on the scarcer traffic of the dark months. Further afield patrols were the domain of cavalry, distances being an ankle-deep slog for men on foot, and the nines were given the duty of playing escort to the workmen, watching for bandits or wolves.

'The year's getting old,' Garn Grey Boulder grunted one evening as they collected hazel twigs for kindling. 'Soon be time for war.'

Ulla had sent them to the edge of a stream, where the hazels grew thick and entwined. They had had a dusting of snow, which gathered in little drifts around the trunks. Cullen, a bunch of sticks nestled in the crook of his arm, instinctively glanced up at the slew of iron-grey clouds. 'Who will we fight?'

Garn scratched his silver stubble with the studded stump that had replaced his left hand. 'There is always someone. Come spring, you will see.' He touched the stump to the badger teeth at his neck. 'Gods protect me, but I dreamed it.'

White Tal, hair and whiskers almost glowing in the hoary dusk, had dropped his twigs and was staring with concern at Garn. 'You dream again?'

'We all dream,' Andoc muttered dismissively.

Dan sniggered. 'I dream of Shana, the baker's daughter!'

The spiked head of Rues emerged from behind a thicket. 'Garn's dreams hold portent. What exactly came to you?'

'The wild hunt,' Garn said.

Rues chewed his upper lip. 'The soul-raving?'

Garn nodded. 'Ghostly hunters and demon hounds. I saw them, right enough. It means war.'

White Tal kicked at the snow, making it spray in all directions. 'Blood will stain the land.' The heavy wingbeats of a trio of swans pulsed overhead. He glanced up. 'The gods confirm their warning.'

'Cassia thinks Rome will come,' Cullen said, unnerved.

Garn's broad face split in an amber-toothed grin. 'Gods, but I hope she is right.'

'You hope?' Andoc repeated the word incredulously. 'Are they not unbeatable?'

Garn rumbled a low laugh, the studs clinking as he tapped the pommel of his sword. 'Even the fiercest bear can be killed if you know how.'

That night they retreated to an abandoned woodsman's hut on the bank of the stream and sat, thawing, by a small fire. They shared trout, seasoned and smoked on a frame of sticks at the apex of the roof, just inside the thatch. The flames danced as they ate, the wavering glow filling the hollows in each man's face with tremulous shadow.

Before dawn, when the land was the shade of a wolf's pelt, they made a sacrifice to the gods to dispel the disquiet Garn's blood-dream had brought to the group. In the hut they had found a pick and a spade and worked by the light of the moon to dig a shallow pit by the water's edge. White Tal regaled them with stories of soul-ravings, complete with details of the calamities they always presaged, and Ulla, grimly, put his sword through the neck of one of his hounds; a real hound for a ghostly one.

As the sun rose and the air bit at their faces and the sky became layered in purples, pinks and yellows, they filled the pit with spoil. Then they returned home, to discover that news had come. By traveller, by trader and by spy, by road and by ship. It came as a torrent and was twice as frightening. Garn's dream had indeed been portentous. His bear, the fiercest of all, had come out of hibernation.

—

'We join with the horde at Cunobelin's Dun!' Aoife the Dread called down to the men as she reined in at the side of the road. She was mounted on a dappled grey mare that snorted and wheeled and shook its head, though Aoife appeared utterly at ease. Cullen stared up at her from the long line of marching warriors. She looked every inch the goddess of war, her long red hair flowing about her fur-swathed shoulders like a flaming waterfall. Cullen did not think he had ever seen anything more impressive.

Andoc, behind Cullen, asked under his breath, 'Will Sego command the foot?'

Ulla, at the head of the hawks, did not turn as he replied. 'Sego is Caratacos's most valued warlord. The greatest of his nines.'

'Aoife is the high king's battle chief,' Andoc said.

'She is younger than Sego,' said Ulla, 'with fewer honours to her name.'

'I'd rather follow her orders than his,' Andoc muttered.

Ulla grunted, something between amusement and scorn. 'Feel free to tell him that yourself.'

The king had waited until the snow had melted, making plans at Verlamion, passing messages between himself and his brother until the sun had strengthened and the roads hardened. And then he had raised his serpent banner and gathered his forces for the march eastwards. Now they crossed countryside showing the first signs of the new season, shoots pushing up through the mud, the roads better than they had been for many weeks. Where the ground had been thick with ridged beech leaves, the breeze now swept the way clear, pushing them up into drifts of yellows and browns that gathered in ditches and beneath hedgerows. Sheep and cattle were back on the higher climbs, the preserve of grizzled goats during the coldest days, and the scudding clouds were bilious and white instead of winter's uniform blanket of grey.

Word had ripped through the Isle of the Mighty like wildfire through drought-parched heath. From the white cliffs of the Cantiaci under which the first traders had anchored to impart their news, the rumours had spread west into the lands of

Cullen's tribe, on and on, as far as the Durotriges and distant Dumnonii. At the same instant it had come north, over the great sea-river, Tamesas, through the combined territory of Trinovantes and Catuvellauni, to Togodubnos at Verlamion and his blue-eyed brother at Camulodunon.

Even now, as the Sun Hound's heirs moved to put together their heads and plan a response, Cullen knew the whisper of coming tribulation would be carried, as if on the wings of falcons, up into the flat marshlands of the Eceni, and over the mountain ranges to reach the ears of Coritani, Cornovii, Ordovices and Brigantes. All would be gathering around fires, consulting gods and ancestors and the Wise. All looking for a prophetic word. All fearful of the coming storm.

Because Rome was on the move. Legions had been spotted massing at the Gaulish ports. Vast ships with great banks of oars were anchored in the harbours facing the Narrow Sea. Some thought invasion imminent. Others claimed it was nothing but a show of strength, a shadow threat, to bend the tribes to the emperor's will. None knew for certain.

It was on the long march that Cullen encountered the high king, the first time he had seen him at close quarters since the pony drift, which seemed a lifetime ago now.

'The young goatherd,' Togodubnos called out. 'Bane of wolves!' He was standing on the platform of a chariot that was harnessed by pole and yoke to two bay ponies. The sides of the vehicle were painted in red and gold, and the wheels had huge spikes fixed to the hubs, spinning in a lethal blur. 'A fighter now, as Moranna foretold!' He proffered the smile Cullen remembered so well. Unexpected in its kindness. Beneath the rim of his helmet, his green eyes gleamed like emeralds. 'How does Aoife treat you?'

Cullen stepped out of line, letting the column trudge past. He bowed as low as his scabbard would allow. 'Well, lord. I am grateful for her patronage; and for yours.'

'Moranna of the Silver is persuasive,' Togodubnos said. 'Hold here,' he said to his driver, who crouched on the step in front.

Then to Cullen, 'Perhaps I have gone soft. Perhaps not.' The corner of his plaited moustache lifted. 'Time will tell.'

Time, Cullen thought, was not something any of them could take for granted. That was why the king's own army of Verlamion was rushing to meet with Caratacos's force at their father's old seat. 'Are we invaded, lord?' he ventured. 'Is it true?'

The king blew out his florid cheeks. 'The Roman eagle prepares to take flight. She would nest here, if we let her.'

'We will not surrender, then?'

'When a man has his foot on your neck,' Togodubnos said, 'you have already lost. We must act before the foot comes down.' Looking up at the passing column, spears pointing skyward like a thick forest of ash and iron, he drew a huge breath, and bellowed, 'I would rather see us all dead than enslaved!' The noise was so sudden that the ponies whinnied and fidgeted, their gorgeously enamelled harness fittings jangling madly. 'To my father's dun!' he shouted again, receiving cries of support from amongst the warriors. 'We will join together the tribes, bring down the eagle before it lands and pluck it like a chicken!'

They cheered and they thumped spears against shields. The high king's chariot wheeled about and raced along the endless line of nobles, named warriors, village levies and the multitude of hangers-on. And on the horizon, the fortress of Camulodunon gradually emerged.

—

'Come, boy, share a drink with an old man.'

It was Drest who hailed Cullen as a long train of jolting wagons rolled into town. He and Becan shared a seat at the rear of one of the vehicles that was otherwise stacked with sheep skins and scraped deer hides. Becan was muttering to the blind man, describing what went on. The barrels of ale and mead being brought up the teeming middleway, the extra food too, the general hubbub of a dun that was adjusting to a sudden influx of people.

Cullen had been chatting with Dan, weighing the merits of different types of sling stone, but he thumped his comrade's shoulder and almost ran to the wagon upon hearing Drest's voice. 'How was the journey?' he called up with a grin.

'Bumpy,' Becan complained. 'My arse is numb and my throat parched.' He grabbed his crutches as Cullen unhooked the wagon's rear gate. The driver had already brought up some steps for them to descend. 'The king should have stayed at Verlamion.'

'He would rather be nearer the coast,' Drest said as Cullen helped him descend, 'should Roman ships appear on the horizon, which they will not. Not yet. It is still too cold.'

Cullen looked at them both, feeling unexpectedly comforted by their presence. 'It is good to see you.'

Drest's empty eye sockets shifted to him. 'And what would *I* see?'

Becan cast his own eyes over Cullen. 'A warrior. Moranna spoke true.'

Cullen smiled ruefully, expecting a barbed addendum to follow quick on the heels of the compliment. It was disconcerting to realise Becan had no wry agenda, and he was mildly taken aback. Yet he supposed he had indeed changed. He was, after all, a member of an established nine. Ulla's hawks, no less. He carried a slim, beautifully balanced war spear in his right hand, the leaf-shaped tip polished to a high sheen. At his right hip hung the sword Aoife had ordered made, while his leather-bound shield lay with Dan, the twin red serpents of Togodubnos entwined about the stout iron boss, the image of a small raptor in flight painted in one corner to mark him out as Ulla's man. But it was more than mere weaponry, he knew. The scars he had collected, not least the deep damage above his eye, and the new brawn he had developed, all diminished the boy he had been and added to the man he was fast becoming.

Drest's long hands reached out, squeezing his shoulders. 'Muscle where once there had been only gristle. Good, good.

We are proud of you, boy. You have risen above your station. Above your grief. Under whom do you serve?'

'Ulla.'

'Jagged Cliff. Good. He treats you well?'

'He is a fair lord.'

Becan said, 'Cassia sends her regards, goat-fiddler.'

'Oh?' Cullen responded a little too hastily. He realised Becan had glimpsed the heartwood carving that hung at his neck. Self-conscious, he slipped it inside his tunic.

Becan grinned. 'She and that crone have gone east.'

'East?'

Becan nodded. 'The king has parties on the coast, watching the horizon. If the Romans land, our people will need healers. And Cassia can interpret, should negotiation of some kind be required.'

'They won't come till spring,' Drest scoffed. 'Now, let us find some food, and you can tell us of your new life, Cullen of the Atrebates.'

The city heaved.

Lords and their retainers strutted in the streets, weapon-toting hard men, named men, mingled with farmers brought in by the royal call to arms. Washerwomen chattered at the stream-edges, excitable children scurried between the buildings like so many mice. The sellers in the middleway did a roaring trade as more and more people poured into Camulodunon's streets. It was the two Catuvellauni armies at first, and they were large enough, bolstered as they were by units and equipment from the conquered Trinovantes and Atrebates. But Cullen quickly realised that this was no happy meeting of brother-kings. No joyous reunion like that which he had witnessed back in the summer. Now was a time of uncertainty, of concern for the future; not simply for the Catuvellauni, but for every family, clan, tribe or nation across the breadth of the Isle of the Mighty.

There was, therefore, to be a council of war. A great forum, where every spokesperson of every tribe in attendance would be given leave to speak his or her mind. Togodubnos's riders had been dispatched on their swiftest steeds to convey the summons. There was no love lost for the sons of Cunobelin, and plenty snubbed the promise of safe passage, but plenty more had heard the rumours themselves, and they feared Rome a great deal more than they feared the Catuvellauni. Thus, what began as a trickle soon became a flood. Banners came like the prows of ships. Dragons and snakes, boars and bears, wolves and stars and lightning bolts. The twin serpents, entwined like lovers, flew high above Camulodunon's gates, and at strategically selected intervals throughout the vast dun, rippling in the vagary of wind atop tree trunks relieved of their branches, leaving none in doubt as to whose territory this was.

Ulla's nine were lodged in temporary shelters that had been thrown up in the woods beyond the city limits, the homes within the rampart having been allocated to those delegates who had travelled the furthest, or whose influence carried most weight. Thus began a week of watching and waiting as the pendants came in from the remotest reaches of the island. Cullen had the occasional duty to carry out with the hawks, but most of his time was spent with Becan and Drest, who, unsurprisingly, found themselves respectable lodgings as soon as they invoked Moranna's authority. He would find them most evenings in various beer dens and mead halls, there to loiter and take in the spectacle of a swelling city. They counted the different sigils, the various weapons, the strange furs on display and the even stranger dialects. Cullen pointed, Becan described, and Drest usually had an explanation. 'Setantii, of the northwest,' he would say, upon hearing of a striking kind of face-paint. Or, 'Brigantes, whose queen is the formidable Cartimandua,' when an identifying mark had been seen on a shield. When a banner of a green snake bobbed past them, its hooded acolytes following in eerie silence along the middleway, he had looked up, as if his sightless eyes had learned once more to see. 'Is it circled, the snake? As though the head devours the tail?'

Cullen had confirmed that it was, watching the procession with a sense of building unease, for the silent march seemed so at odds with all the other arrivals.

'The serpent of rebirth,' Drest said. 'Of the waking realm and the dreaming realm that form life's perpetual loop.'

'Mona,' Becan had elaborated. 'They're a delegation from the sacred isle.'

And that was when Cullen truly understood the gravity of what was coming to pass. He had been annoyed when first the march to Camulodunon was announced. He had barely seen Cassia, for her work took her to all corners of the newly expanded confederacy, and now it was he who had been torn away, compelled to join the convergence of the Catuvellauni nation as they wrestled with a response to Rome's threatened ambition. Annoyed, in truth, had been an understatement. And yet things were happening. The wheels of fortune were turning in a manner not seen since the days of Julius Caesar. It was terrifying, but it was undeniably exciting. And so Cullen had kept his iron sharp and his scabbard oiled and now he waited in this sprawling settlement as the greatest congregation in living memory began to take shape.

It was a surreal time. There should have been celebrations at so momentous a gathering. Nights of feasting and revelry. But the rumours were dire enough to smother what joy there might have been, and the necessary meals, though plentiful enough, were muted. There was fighting, of course. News of impending war made such traditions more crucial than ever. Spear throwing, sword-work, horsemanship and chariot racing all had their place at such a time, and all drew immense crowds. Yet the atmosphere remained tense, as though a bank of poison mist sat heavy on the air.

The night of the great council was crisp and cloudless. There was a grand feast in and around the king's hall. The Wise prowled amongst the host, reciting protective charms in the tongues of this world and the next. The poets amongst their number spun their tuneful stories to the spellbinding play of harps, recounting the deeds of the ancient heroes who had fought the ocean monsters, the Fomorii, and of Vercingetorix, the Gaulish champion who had defied Rome. The parallels hung like smoke. They competed for the most raucous cheers, the loudest table-thumps, the deepest rumble of stamping feet. When it was done, they stood as one to toast the health of the gods, and then they gathered on the middleway and progressed from the dun by the light of pitch-smothered torches, down into a valley designated sacred by the Wise Ones.

All the great men and women were present as they filed into a large clearing that was edged by boulders painted with magical marks in red and black. Those rocks had been inset with iron sconces, into which the torches were thrust, throwing flickering light over delegates wrapped in their best furs, adorned with flashes of copper, bracelets of bronze, winking ingots of silver and gold. The power of the Isle of the Mighty coalesced in one place. An event not seen since the days of Casivellaunus. Chiefs of hilltop earthworks and mountain fortresses rubbed shoulders with those of river valleys and marshy labyrinths, coastal villages and isolated inland clans. They stood in tight pockets, guarded by retainers, though no blades were to be brought into the sacred circle. At the centre of the meeting place there was a table of stone, the kind first set by the old folk who had no mastery of iron, its purpose lost in the haze of centuries. In front of that table stalked Moranna of the Silver, cowled in her cloak of many colours, a long, crystal-capped staff in hand. Behind her, a man clambered onto the stones, turning to face the assembly: Togodubnos himself, resplendent in a neck-torc so large and so fine that none could deny its wearer's importance. He wore a circlet of gold about his head, like the ones sported by charioteers, but far grander, a gleaming red jewel set into the front like a fiery eye. He was wrapped in fine, thick furs that were decorated with silver brooches, and his red hair had been brushed smooth, left long and worked through with feathers and ribbon. There he stood, jewel-encrusted hands planted on a bronze-buckled waist, surveying the sea of faces down his scarred nose. None could be left to wonder where the night's true power resided.

'Friends!' he called out, and the talk faded to a low hum. His eyes roamed wide as he spoke, words echoing off the stones. 'The Roman emperor means to land his fleet on our shores. Means to invade our kingdoms, slay our men, ravish our women and enslave our children!'

A wave of disquiet swept through the sacred circle. Togodubnos let it surge and subside, nodding slowly, knowingly, at anger flaring particularly hot from certain sections. It served his purpose to fan the flames of fury and let them spread.

'I know the enemy has sent forth envoys to your halls,' he went on, 'looking to seek alliances. Do not believe their lies! They would fracture our unity. Divide us in order to conquer us!'

Cullen, Becan and Drest had filtered into the back of the crowd, drifting with the press of bodies to stand between the rearmost stones so that most of what they saw was the backs of heads. But Togodubnos could not have been missed if they had tried, so high was his podium and so magnificent his presence.

'Envoys?' Cullen whispered.

'Of course,' Drest replied. 'This kind of council is precisely what they will seek to undermine. Their people will have been on this island for months now, sowing division, making pacts. It appears many chiefs have answered the king's call, but how many have not? How many have long since reached a settlement with Rome?'

Cullen instinctively cast his eyes across the knots of huddled folk, the lords and Wise Ones of each community, weighing words and gauging their future stance. There were indeed many tribes represented, but there were just as many conspicuous by absence. 'What kind of settlement?'

'They will promise not to intervene,' Drest answered, 'in return for their neighbour's land and wealth. Their fisheries and their cattle.'

The shouting had dissipated as folk waited for Togodubnos to continue. He let forth another barrage of ire, complaining of the Roman menace and the avarice of empire, painting a stark picture of the collective threat they faced. He spoke of an imagined military force, one that was combined of all the tribes, all the nations under the true gods.

Clearly his intent was to inspire, but from where Cullen was standing, what emerged in response was a ripple of bitterness. Like smoke seeping through mouldering thatch, it came as muttered disgruntlement, whispered accusations, grunted rancour. At Catuvellauni expansion. At the temerity of Togodubnos in naming himself over-king, when it had never truly been his father's mantle to pass on. At the presumption that he might summon other, more experienced, kings to this council. At the arrogant assumption that they might consider an alliance with the son of Cunobelin any less perilous than one with Emperor Claudius. Cullen was beginning to realise that Togodubnos's task was not as easy as he had assumed.

The king was looking down to his right, where a number of aides waited. 'What do we know?'

One of them bowed low. 'They are massing on the Gaulish coast, lord king. At Gesoriacum.'

A nobleman amongst the crowd, draped in a gorgeous robe of glittering thread and scarlet garnets, called out, 'Four legions for now, but that is simply the vanguard, like as not.' He turned to address the people. 'The Romans do not work in ones and twos.'

Another swell of cheers and jeers, vying for supremacy. Some calling out in support of the point, their own retainers stamping the ground as if more noise equalled greater legitimacy. Others derided the assertion as crafty fear-mongering or wilful ignorance. Cullen noticed all were careful not to denounce the claims for outright lies; not in Togodubnos's own dun.

'Friends!' the king bellowed above it all, holding up his palms in supplication. 'Friends! Let us not argue. I invited you here so that we, the peoples of the Isle of the Mighty, might put aside our differences. That we may come together for the greater good.'

'Isle of the Mighty?' someone called out scathingly. Cullen glimpsed the speaker near the front, a squat, fur-clad, bearded man with a bald pate. 'I understood it was the Isle of the Catuvellauni now!'

More jeering and catcalls. Moranna's sing-song voice rose over them. 'The council sees Boduoc of the Dobunni.' Cullen saw that she had levelled the crystal staff at the bald man, who bowed in acceptance of the floor.

All fell silent.

Boduoc performed an about-turn, making eye contact with as many folk as he could. 'Friends, he calls us! When only weeks ago did his raiders come to my land and burn one of my villages! Families homeless, fatherless!'

Cullen looked sideways at Becan. 'I was there.'

'It is true?' Becan asked.

Cullen nodded. 'They stole our cattle.'

'Boduoc will have forgotten that little fact,' Drest said wryly.

Togodubnos was shaking his head. 'I am sorry for the wrongs we have done one another. None of us is free of guilt. But we must forget those things in a time such as this.'

'Forget?' Boduoc spat. 'You think me a fool, *lord king*? The Dobunni do not forget, and we do not forgive!'

Uproar met his words. Chaos. Pockets of warriors bristled, even without their swords, like dogs with hackles up, snarling and snapping at one another in defence of their masters.

'The wolf is at your door, you fools!' a new voice roared.

The din faded, to be replaced by a collective intake of breath. Then an awkward hush where outrage should have been. Cullen knew instantly why, for he recognised the voice as he would recognise an arrow in his chest. The tall man strode to stand beneath the platform, his steps crunching in the near silence. He turned to stare at the crowd, his back to the king. His scarred face was a mask of malevolence in the shifting shadows, split by a tar-black moustache and framed by long hair, braided into ropes, that were splayed about broad shoulders. Swirling images marked his neck with dye, ruined on the left side by a deep, jagged scar. He was repugnant and beautiful all at once, and he cast his bright gaze across the sacred circle as if he were a fox who had stumbled upon a nest of chicks.

Moranna of the Silver swung her staff towards him. 'The council sees Lord Caratacos of the Catuvellauni.'

'There is but one course,' the high king's younger brother said, his voice dipping to an ominous growl, 'and that is to slaughter each and every legionary who dares step foot on this island.' His hard gaze shifted to Boduoc. 'Our strength and your weakness has no bearing on this council.'

Boduoc visibly bridled. 'How dare—'

'How dare,' Caratacos interjected harshly, 'a coward such as he speak in this hallowed place?'

'I am chief of the Dobunni,' Boduoc blustered, 'and I demand—'

'You demand only scorn,' Caratacos cut him off again, 'and that is all you shall receive. Not a season turns without insurrection in Dobunni lands. You cannot hold together your own tribe, so do not address me as an equal.'

'Enough!' It was Togodubnos, standing above them both, his own face rigid with anger now. 'Brother, enough.' He looked between them both, then out to the rest. 'I am not here to speak of past conflicts. Only of the conflict that faces us all. By summer there will be legions on our land. We have not the fleet to fight them at sea, so they will come. And we must be ready.'

'Ready?' Boduoc asked disbelievingly. 'How can we be ready for Rome? No one is ever ready. They fight and they are crushed. It was ever thus.'

'Wrong!' Caratacos snarled. 'Rome came before. She invaded. She fought. And she was defeated! We will fight her again!'

That drew a fresh round of cheering, but another chieftain – a senior man from the mountainous far west, according to Becan – lifted his voice to reverberate amongst the great stones. 'What benefit is it to us if you win?'

Togodubnos thumped his chest. 'We!' he laboured the word. 'We will win! Together!'

'We, now, is it?' the westerner asked, cynicism dripping from his question. 'When this past year I thought it was the sons of Cunobelin,' he looked to the crowd, 'against the rest.'

'Put from your minds, that which has gone before,' Togodubnos wearily beseeched the dissenters, who appeared to be growing bolder, despite the white-hot glower of Caratacos. 'I beg of you. There are more pressing matters now.'

Scoffing noises, even mocking laughter, rippled up from the onlookers. 'Join with you and be trampled by Rome,' a voice with the accent of the Cornovii, according to Drest, climbed above the rest, 'or join with Rome and be trampled by you. I know which path seems less fraught.'

Togodubnos shook his head. 'There will be no alliances with Rome. They spin a web of lies to deceive you.' He spread wide his arms, encompassing all. 'They intend to destroy this misty isle. To ruin all that we have built over countless generations. We can run or we can fight, my friends.' He shrugged. 'And there *is* nowhere to run to. It will end with the legions pushing us into the sea.'

'Buffoonery!' An old man stepped to the front, beneath the platform. His snow-white whiskers turned from Cullen's sight as his face tilted up to address the king. His head and neck were covered in a pale grey-blue headpiece featuring the fanged skull of a creature Cullen could not identify, and he spoke the common tongue, though his accent was so thick it could not have been of Belgic descent. 'You worry like nanny goats, oh offspring of the Sun Hound.'

Moranna swung the staff his way. 'The council sees Dalrax Whale Bone, of the Caledonii.'

Drest leaned close to Cullen's ear. 'Rulers of the savage north.'

'What is that thing on his head?'

Becan said, 'A seal.'

Dalrax moved to face the people. He had a ring fixed through his nose and more rings on his wrists, upper arms and neck. 'Britannia,' he sounded out the strange word as if it had been made up by a toddler, 'is not an enterprise worthy of undertaking.' He looked back at Togodubnos. 'Have you been across the Narrow Sea?'

'No,' the high king said.

'They think us barbarians. Animals. If they had wanted to conquer this land, they would have done so already. They do not require conquest, only trade. It is folly, this talk of fighting.'

'Then why have you come?' Togodubnos asked sourly.

Dalrax grinned, exposing brown, mottled teeth worn to nubs. 'My fool died last winter. I needed entertainment.' This elicited more raucous shouts, competing voices of support and denunciation, and the Caledonii chieftain tilted back that seal's maw and brayed amid the din. When Moranna had waved her crystal-topped staff like a war-banner, quelling the clamour sufficiently, he held up his own hands for the people to pay heed. 'In truth, I am here to listen to this new lord with my own ears. And, naturally, to trade with his people. Why? Because trade is king under the sun. Our lands are rich. Tin and gold and precious stones. The pearl fisheries of the Carvetii. The fine fleeces of the Regnenses. The horses and chariots of the Atrebates.'

'These,' Caratacos interrupted with barely concealed hostility, 'are perfect reasons for conquest, you doddering fool.'

'They are perfect reasons for the continuation of trade,' Dalrax answered, unshrinking. 'As it has always been. You think it costs nothing to raise an army? Equip it? Feed it? Cross an ocean with it? And when they capture land, they must pay again to maintain their garrisons and suppress our own armies. Conquest is expensive, my young lordling.' He showed Caratacos his back and looked up at Togodubnos. 'Trade is profitable. Why would Rome ruin what they have?'

'They are coming,' a woman's voice came in answer, making Dalrax give up the floor.

'The council sees Cartimandua of the Brigantes,' Moranna's sing-song voice announced.

'The great queen herself,' Drest whispered, though it was hardly necessary, for even Cullen had heard of the woman at the reins of the powerful tribe whose lands covered a sprawling wilderness of valleys, rivers, hills and peaks. Visitors to his mother's hearth had often brought tales from that northern nation, in part because they were the natural counterweight to the rapacious Catuvellauni, and in part because they were ruled by one so young and so beautiful.

'My truth-sayer has foretold it,' Cartimandua said. She was indeed beautiful, thought Cullen, standing now on tiptoes to get a better glimpse. Lithely built and golden haired, she wore a black cloak over a red tunic, her shoulders puffed up by bunches of dried flowers and huge feathers. She drew eyes to her. Stole focus. She was neither tall nor broad, but the way she used her bright gaze seemed to give others no choice but to return it. 'My dreamers have dreamed it. The eagle of Rome flies west. She will make her nest here. We cannot win.' The queen shook her head at Togodubnos. 'If we treat now, bend the knee, they will be merciful.'

'Bend the knee?' Caratacos spat.

She gave no indication of having heard him, keeping her eyes firmly on his brother. 'If we fight, there is no hope for mercy.'

'Gods,' Becan muttered. 'He is trapped between those who would fight, those who would surrender and those who do not believe war will even come.'

'Which one is true?' Cullen said, receiving silence as reply.

'Worrying as to what mercy you'll be shown,' Togodubnos was saying, 'is not the best way to begin a war.'

Cartimandua furnished the assembly with a dazzling smile. 'Then do not begin one.'

'By the ancients!' Caratacos exploded, fists tightly bunched as he stalked past the queen to engage the nearest of the onlookers. 'By thunder! By all the gods! What has happened to the people of this land? Where have our spines gone? Rome is coming. She is sending her legions. They will be as grains of sand on a beach.' He stamped hard on the compacted earth. 'But this is our land.' He beat a fist at his densely muscled chest. 'Our land! We must fight them!'

'There is no *we*,' someone barked back.

Moranna cleared her throat. 'The council sees Volisios of the Coritani.'

A tall, thin, stooped man stepped out. He was clean-shaven and plainly dressed, but the number of burly guards who kept watch over him spoke volumes. 'There is no common foe. No shared adversary.'

Togodubnos drew breath. 'The Romans—'

'Are just another enemy in a long line,' Volisios went on unabated, 'and they are by no means at the front.' He stretched out a long arm to point at a party of delegates. 'The Cornovii are *my* foe.' The arm swung about like the boom of a boat to first identify Cartimandua, and then other rulers nearby. 'The Brigantes and the Parisi and the Eceni. These are the men and women who steal our cattle and burn our steadings. I would sooner ally with the emperor than fight him, if he would put down my true enemies.'

'True enemies?' Togodubnos retorted indignantly. 'Have your Wise Ones forgotten the tales of the first Caesar? How he slaughtered the Gauls in their fields? Scorched their earth until the land was nothing but ash and bone. The Belgae, from whom many of us descend, were wiped from this earth by his vengeance.'

'Because they fought against him,' Cartimandua said.

Togodubnos stepped to the edge of the platform. He was shaking his head, his jaw twitching as he ground his teeth. The hitherto sense of cool diplomacy seemed to have dissipated on the evening air. 'Rome is a remorseless blight,' he said. 'Our people are crops in her path.' He looked up, skewering certain members of the crowd with those green eyes, now glimmering hard as emeralds in his broad face. 'She poisons every stalk, every leaf, until there is only decay and death. I say we come together.' He stabbed a forefinger into his palm. 'Here. Now. We are the scions of the Isle of the Mighty!' He was shouting now, his face florid, the veins showing at his neck and temples. 'I say we stand firm! Stand together! Let the legions come onto our swords. Let them fall beneath the wheels of our chariots and march onto our spear points. There are no greater warriors in all the waking realm than we here. Yes, my friends, they will come.' He drew a long, lingering breath, staring at every corner of the sacred space. 'And their blood will nourish our soil! Their bones will feed the worms! Join me! Join me! If we come together, fight together, bleed together, none can stop us!'

When he fell silent, the air seemed to shimmer, as if the remnant of his rage, his passion, lingered between the ancient stones. The other kings and queens, the lords and chiefs and nobles, the warriors with fame and those without, simply stared up at him. Then he seemed to slump, as if the effort had rent his every fibre. He nodded to himself, to his brother and to Moranna, and jumped off the platform. Offering a perfunctory bow to the delegates, he stalked into the night.

Cullen watched him go like all the rest. 'I suppose it is over,' he said to no one in particular.

'The council,' Becan replied, 'or his ambition?'

Cullen looked at his friend. 'They will never join with him, will they?'

Becan pulled a noncommittal face. 'Some will, most won't. They came because they do not want to make an enemy of him, but their decisions are long made.'

'What will he do?'

'What do you think, boy?' It was Drest, blinking but unseeing as the sacred circle steadily emptied. 'He will fight.'

CHAPTER FIFTEEN

'A summons,' Ulla Jagged Cliff spoke, though Cullen could barely see him, so oppressive was the dark.

They walked quickly, though it was greasy underfoot, made treacherous by the dampness of the leaves and the steepness of the slope. Cullen followed the others, all bleary-eyed and drowsy, roused unceremoniously from sleep by their leader and the messenger who flanked him. They had filed along alleyways, across empty yards, and through the gates set in the southern arc of Camulodunon's earthworks, to plunge into undulating woodland.

'Who summons us in this manner?' Rues Seeker complained as they slowed amongst a tangled patch of goosegrass. 'We, the hawks of Ulla?'

'My apologies,' replied Togodubnos, King of the Catuvellauni and High King of all the Isle of the Mighty. 'But there are many foreigners in the dun. Too many for secrecy.' He was dressed plainly, his cloak the colour of cream, fastened with a simple pin. The goosegrass climbed halfway up his braca, straggly stems clinging to the chequered wool, and he was unarmed, save a modest dagger sheathed at the hip. Yet his ordinary appearance diminished him not a bit. It was in the eyes, Cullen thought. Bright with amusement. And the insouciant manner that seemed to put even the spikiest hard-head at ease.

He threw them an uncomplicated smile, as if the hawks were old friends and this was a Calan Haf feast rather than an elicit meeting in the depths of the night. There were other men near the king. Bigger men, brawnier, more warlike to judge by stance or scar or weapon. Yet there was no mistaking to whom they paid deference. No missing where the charisma belonged or whence the power emanated.

Ulla knelt. His men followed suit.

Togodubnos bade them stand. 'I have a task for you, Ulla Jagged Cliff. You will go west, crossing our lands and those of the Dobunni.'

Cullen felt his eyes roam over the faces that were full of torch-thrown shadow. Moranna was there, taking her usual place at Togodubnos's right hand. Aoife the Dread stood close, a flame-haired vision in leather and fur. A party of heavily armed fighting men loitered further back, unsubtly fondling sword hilts and axe hafts, not so much alert to trouble as hoping for it. Cullen glimpsed them only as lurking silhouettes, but two men resolved fully from the murk, as though the shock of encountering them forced his eyes to penetrate the dark.

Caratacos, sinewy forearms folded casually over his barrel chest, leaned against a tree as he watched his brother. His companion, whispering something close, was tall and skinny. He was bizarrely attired, with a dark grey bull's hide draped over his stooping spine and a white headpiece of speckled feathers. Below those feathers, highlighted in the flame-light, star shapes glowed on his cheeks, the legacy of long-healed branding.

Just as Cullen saw the thin man, so he returned the stare. Arthmael's eyes widened in recognition, flared bright with fury for a moment, but he recovered quickly, turning back to hiss more earnestly in his lord's ear. Caratacos seemed to smile.

Ulla's severe features had tautened as he listened to the king. 'The Dobunni hate us, lord.'

'I am aware of that,' Togodubnos said.

'Nine will go,' Moranna said now, 'as is befitting a quest of the gods. It must be nine. You will cross into the kingdom of the Silures, who rule on the far side of Sabrina's River.'

'To what end, lady?' Ulla asked.

'The council did not have the effect we desired,' she answered in that off-kilter voice Cullen had come to know so well. 'Many tribes will honour the prior treaties with Rome.'

'Prior treaties?'

'They have made agreements with her agents,' Moranna said. 'In the event of an invasion they are bound to keep their blades sheathed.'

'Traitors,' Caratacos snarled from beneath his tree. All heads swivelled to regard him, though he stayed put, wearing a grimace of disgust. Behind him and Arthmael, an impossibly huge warrior materialised from the dark, as if Caratacos brought with him his own thundercloud.

Togodubnos turned to reply, 'Traitor to what, brother? To whom? I call myself high king, for I am strongest. But each king is leader of his own nation. He may treat with whomsoever he pleases.'

'But *Rome*,' Ulla said, with a hostility that made clear he agreed with Caratacos.

'Rome offers a future to those willing to work with her,' Togodubnos said. 'Obliteration for the rest. I meant what I said in the sacred circle. I intend to assemble a great horde to resist an invasion, but it is proving more difficult than I had hoped. I must work harder to make alliances. We have our confederacy, and a handful of others. The Eceni are strong. Their chariots would give us a keen edge.'

'And are they with us?' Ulla asked.

'They waver,' Togodubnos said. 'I would bring them to my way of thinking.'

'King Antedios,' Moranna of the Silver interjected, 'is elderly.'

Aoife said, 'He was not at council.'

Moranna glanced at her. 'He ails.'

'Then how can we bring him to our side?'

'The princess of the Eceni,' Togodubnos answered her, 'and blood-heir to their throne, has been taken.'

'Taken?' Ulla echoed sharply.

'By the Silures,' the king said. 'She was leading a delegation. Making trade agreements between the tribes.'

'And they decided to keep her?' Ulla said in astonishment.

'That,' said Moranna, 'is what appears to have come to pass.'

Ulla thought for a moment, then nodded. 'And you, lord king, mean to fetch her back.'

'One girl,' Togodubnos said, 'for an alliance with the Eceni against Rome.' He looked round at the glowering man beneath the tree. 'Some have advocated against it.'

'The Silures hate Rome more than we, brother,' Caratacos growled. 'To enrage them now would risk losing a vital ally.'

'Silures lands are many miles from the Narrow Sea,' Togodubnos said. 'Lestinos will not lose his throne to Emperor Claudius. Not yet, at least. He may prefer to sit on his hilltop and watch the Catuvellauni brought low. The Eceni, however, have as much to lose as we. Their lands are hard against the coast. In Rome's path. Then again, they are strong, and they would provide a great many spears.' He looked at Aoife, then at Ulla. 'If they can be wooed. I asked the lady Aoife for her best nine.'

Ulla dipped his head. 'My hawks are honoured to serve, lord king.'

'Sego is the greatest warrior we have,' Caratacos intervened. He indicated the storm front in human form who loomed behind. He was a colossus, dwarfing all the rest, with a chest like a bullock's shoulders and a face that was a jumble of creases and valleys, fringing a full beard of unkempt bristles. His scalp was as bald as an egg, and in place of hair there were stars and moons, an axe, a life-wheel and several snakes. Some of the symbols had the faded look of permanence. The dye mixed with soot and tapped into the skin with sharpened bone splinters. Perhaps as many as fifty winters had worn Sego's complexion, but blue eyes, piercing and icy, incongruent in their bright vitality, betrayed a latent power. As though at any time he might spring into action. Cullen felt himself quell under the man's gaze and he stared at his feet.

'Aoife is my war-giver,' Togodubnos answered.

Caratacos frowned. 'Sego is senior to her.'

'And I,' Togodubnos retorted stiffly, 'am senior to you.'

Caratacos sniffed, shrugged, looked away.

Togodubnos addressed Ulla again. 'Cross the great river and bring the princess home, Ulla Jagged Cliff. It must be done to save our people. All our people.'

—

They were ready just before dawn, having collected horses and weapons quietly and unobserved, assembling at the dividing ditch between two meadows of tall, dew-glistened grass.

They headed west, buffeted by an obstinate northerly wind. Cullen had never been entirely adept in the saddle, but riding was a skill as ubiquitous to the Atrebates as walking or breathing, and he managed to keep the mare on the right paths, though he was secretly thankful for her forgiving temperament.

The days were cold but crisp, even bright at times, and their furs and cloaks spent much of the hours of light tethered to the rear of saddles, bunched up and tied so as not to snag a hoof or trail in the mud. Most of the scenery featured tree-trunks and branches, any distant horizon choked off by the dense forests through which the roads cut. They stopped for respite at villages every few miles, for this was still Catuvellauni land, and they were welcomed, fed and watered after making their allegiances known.

At one wood-hidden hamlet they were treated to a display of horseback spear throwing by the sons of the local chief in the hope, Cullen presumed, of reports of their prowess reaching the ear of the king. They duly watched and applauded as the wicker butts thudded, short spears protruding from the targets like hedgehog spines.

'The mystic mare, Eiocha, was white,' Five Thorns told them as one of the boys galloped past on a pony the colour of milk. 'Made of sea foam, she was.'

Dan, who was tearing chunks of roasted venison with his teeth, shook his head. 'Made of shells, I was always told.'

Five Thorns regarded him across the well-stocked table that had been set out under a gnarled bough adorned with colourful ribbons and a child's rope swing. 'White shells?'

'I've seen white shells,' Dan said defensively.

Five Thorns wrinkled his nose, as if the idea smelled as rotten as it sounded. 'Sea foam.'

Ulla – craggy and imposing at the head of the table – glowered deep, his long, severe face crumpling as he sighed, 'Proceed, by thunder.'

'She was imbued,' Five Thorns continued, 'with the most ancient magic. But she fell pregnant—'

'How,' Garn asked, 'if she's made of foam?'

'You want to tell it?' Five Thorns retorted.

Silence.

'I did not think so. Eiocha carried the god, Cernunnos.'

'I thought it was Cernunnos impregnated her,' Garn said.

'That was after.'

'After what?'

Five Thorns clicked his tongue in irritation. 'The birth,' he went on, clearly deciding to ignore the one-handed man's questions, 'was so agonising that she tore strips of bark from a nearby oak tree.'

'One of my wives did the same,' Garn said. 'Well, she tore off the door skin and took clumps of thatch out of the roof.'

'When the pains were done,' said Five Thorns, 'she cast the bark into the ocean. That was how the giants of the deep were created.'

'From the bark?'

Five Thorns shrugged. 'Magical bark.'

'Like a sorcerer's dog,' Dan said, receiving a mixture of chuckles and condemnation for his efforts.

'But, mark you,' Five Thorns went on, 'upon seeing the ocean now so teeming with life, Cernunnos became very lonely. Very jealous. So he made Eiocha pregnant again. Not with one child,' he added archly, spreading his palms, 'but many. Those children became the gods Maponos, Taranis and Teutatis. And the goddess Epona.'

'May they protect us,' Ulla intoned, his words immediately echoed by the others.

Five Thorns took a swig of his ale and let his gaze flit between them. 'The new gods were bored and wanted to be worshipped, so from the same oak tree, they removed more bark.'

'Can't have been much tree left,' Garn muttered.

Five Thorns glanced at him sourly. 'They took that bark – yes, the magic bark – and formed the first man and woman. Soon, Cernunnos had created an entire forest of creatures. Eiocha saw what she had helped spawn, and she was pleased. Contented, she returned to her true home, the sea.'

'May *she* protect us,' Rues said. 'Sink the Roman fleet as soon as it leaves Gaul.'

They all lifted their cups, slammed fists against chests and begged the goddess to return to the Isle of the Mighty. Because soon, they knew, another great force was coming, and that one might just be unstoppable.

—

Dark hills emerged in the distance as they walked, as if one of Five Thorns' great ocean creatures had beached itself on the western horizon. Leaving the robust roads laid out by Cunobelin, Rues, whose role it was to guide them, traversed land that seemed to alternate between suffocating forest and open plain. After three days and nights, he took them south and west, tracking the shape of the rolling chalkland named by local farmers as the Chilterns, which, though jumbled with escarpments, valleys and thick woodland, was criss-crossed with trackways as ancient as the barrows dotting the landscape.

They kept to the Chilterns' northern fringe, unwilling to risk their mounts in the range's high, rugged heart. Still, the climbs became slower and steeper, still the valleys deepened, but the horses provided by Togodubnos had been as doughty as promised. That did not assuage White Tal, whose natural unease in these wild places was a constant companion.

'Gods, but I'd take my chances against Sego Blood-Swill,' he had muttered darkly as they splashed along a stream that spanned the saddle between two rising hills, the buzzard-haunted crests smothered in stands of ash and beech. 'If I could leave here and never return.'

'If ever you face Sego,' Ulla replied harshly, 'you can be sure you will not return.'

White Tal eyed the wooded hilltops, squinting against the bright sun, his face a mask of worry. 'They harbour strange people, those places. Little men, who dig for gems. They have the power to enslave the mind, our Wise One used to say. Knocker-folk, he called them.'

Garn, up ahead with Rues, regarded the swell of forest on either side. 'If a knocker tries to enslave my mind,' he lifted his curtailed arm, the metal studs winking where his hand once was, 'I shall introduce him to my stump.'

White Tal shot him a look of genuine concern. 'He'll whisper riddles, Grey Boulder. Befuddle your reason.'

Ulla snorted. 'It does not require magic for that!'

The forests grew sparser as they left the forbidding crests behind, though the land remained an undulating sea of grassy hillocks, stretching out to meet the violet sky in the far distance. They were near Dobunni territory now, the hills hereabouts disputed between the kingdoms and held, day to day, by petty chieftains who exchanged insults and cattle raids, season on season. One such nobleman, Ulla told them, kept his hall in a hilltop fortress not far from their route. He was loyal to the

Catuvellauni, and they stayed the night at his hearth, watering the horses and restocking provisions. The next day they paid a visit to the sacred cutting of the great white horse, etched into the chalk of a nearby hillside. They all knew of it, for its existence had been a mainstay of every fireside story since childhood, its very presence, massive and exquisitely wrought, proof of the early gods placing an indelible mark on the land. That being so, Cullen had not been prepared for the sheer scale, the undeniable majesty, of the image. As the dawn sun gleamed against the exposed chalk of flanks and limbs, head and tail, he imagined a giant, a god or goddess, cleaving the soil from the hill, as if branding the Isle of the Mighty, claiming it for their own, bestowing upon it a significance none could explain but all profoundly sensed. From his saddle he gazed across at the beast that stretched along the opposite ridge, a deep, verdant vale lying between, and put fingertips to the three-tailed horse that clung to his own neck. 'Surely the gods who made that image,' he said, 'will not abandon their people now?'

No one answered.

The sun was at its zenith as they passed into the kingdom of the Dobunni. It began with low-lying grasslands, great meadows dotted with wildflowers and irrigated by a latticework of rivers that seemed abundant with fish. It was good country, green and fertile, and Cullen could see why the tribe were so keen to protect their sovereignty, and why the major nobles squabbled over every scrap of land within its borders.

They rode on, slowly, happily, under a sky that was dazzling and cloudless. As seemed inevitable to Cullen, more hills shadowed the far west, and Rues explained that these were the hills of Cuda, the local mother goddess. But here, along a gravel track that ran alongside a man-made border ditch, the slopes were gentle and bleak, often empty, save for grass and gorse, and patched with outcrops of yellow limestone, devoid of the dense forests and tangled ravines of the Chilterns.

The harder work began in the evening, as the sun dropped low before them, sinking beneath the horizon into which they climbed. Woodland clogged the land as the track inclined, making the world darker than it should have been, and eerier than they would have wished.

'Over there,' Rues Seeker called over his shoulder, 'is a great ridge. Golden in colour and sheer in places.'

He was indicating right, to the north and east, and Cullen turned his head that way, though he could see nothing from here but massed ranks of trees that promised only darkness beneath their entwined canopy. 'Can we see the river from there?'

'We could,' Rues replied, 'if we made the climb, but that would take too long.' He nodded straight ahead. 'The road sees us down a gentler way, and we'll observe the water without the effort.'

He meant Sabrina's Sea. That vast, tidal river, named for the powerful water goddess, that cut deep into the island in one direction, and flowed wide as a sea in the other. It was the greatest of all the waterways in the Isle of the Mighty. The widest, the fiercest, protected by more deities than any other. A kingdom of the Otherworld right in the middle of this one. Cullen was desperate to see it. Simply to lay eyes on the rushing, glittering depths would be a profound experience, he suspected, for a lad from Calleva. Yet there was trepidation too, for the nearer they strove to that distant coast, the further they were from safety.

'Wits sharp,' Ulla, up near Rues, commanded in his gruff tone. 'King Boduoc will have the skins flayed from our bones if we are caught.'

Garn Grey Boulder spat into the ditch. 'Boduoc would do well to antagonise Togodubnos no further.'

Ulla twisted in his saddle to look at his named man. 'We did fire one of his villages.'

Garn spat again. 'After he stole our cattle. He was the instigator of that feud.'

'And we have pushed him into the arms of Rome.'

'If he wishes to make an enemy of the Sun Hound's sons,' Garn said, 'then more fool him.'

Ulla nodded, evidently accepting the truth of it. 'The invincible warrior brothers,' he said with a white-toothed grin. 'Aoife's favourite tale of her homeland.'

'And what a tale!' White Tal exclaimed, ever pleased to regale them with the times of heroes. 'The most fearsome of their number, Cúchulainn, crossed the Clear Sea in his youth. To this very land.'

'As Aoife herself once crossed,' added Kurd Long Limb.

'But his journey took him to the far north,' said White Tal, 'where the mountains are ravaged by the sea, and the tribes are more savage than wolves.'

'Than bears!' encouraged Kurd, who, as ever, smelled strongly of the mint he voraciously chewed.

'There he was taught the spear-dance,' White Tal went on, 'at the school upon the Island of Shadows, which was the haunt of the goddess Scathach.'

'She was woman before she was goddess, Tal,' Ulla said. 'Gorgeous, so they say. Tall and strong and flame-haired.'

'Are you certain her name was not Aoife the Dread?' Garn barked, rewarding himself with a great bray of laughter.

To Cullen's surprise, Ulla twisted back again, and this time his severe face had cracked with a wry smile. 'All the best warriors are female. By thunder, they are.'

'By the ancients,' Garn exclaimed, 'is it possible Ulla Jagged Cliff blushes?'

Ulla did not dignify that with an answer, and he let Rues guide them through an avenue of close-knit trees, so intertwined that their combined canopy formed a living tunnel. On the far side they came to a series of murky ponds. Tall stands of dew-draped greenery fringed the stagnant black pools, bowing as if in deference to whatever was concealed beneath the weed-clothed surface. As they picked a careful path, Dan, immediately behind Cullen, asked, 'How were the women back at – where was it?'

Cullen turned, saddle creaking under his rump. 'Calleva. Just outside.'

'Calleva,' Dan sounded it out slowly. 'You tended goats, yes?'

Cullen nodded. Dan had repeated the word as if it were some exotic location, like one of the spirit havens in the old stories. He realised that that was how he also remembered it. So much had come to pass since leaving that shell of a city, sacked by the acolytes of the twin serpents, under which he too had come to march. The memories seemed like they belonged to someone else now, faded and nebulous.

'I bet he tended a few goats' arses,' Kurd chuckled. 'Up in the hills, all alone.'

'There were girls,' Cullen said, and his mind ran inexorably to his village. To his lost life.

'That Roman bitch now, isn't it?' Andoc said at the very rear of their little column.

Cullen did not bother to turn this time. 'What about her?'

'We've all seen you stare at her, moon-eyed,' Andoc continued in a voice hard with condemnation. 'Barely able to walk straight after she leaves. I wonder, for whom will you fight, when Rome comes?'

Now Cullen tugged gently on his reins. The placid mare drew up, dipping her muzzle immediately to graze. He shifted his rump so his torso could turn fully. 'You spoke for me at my initiation,' he said to Andoc. 'For that, I will let this go.' He pointed a finger, keeping his words smooth but his gaze as spiked as Garn's stump. 'Do not mention Cassia again in my presence. Honour will not allow me to see it pass a second time.'

Andoc held his stare, those hooded, sunken eyes dark with dislike. Between them, Kurd watched the exchange with his usual phlegmatic expression. He craned his neck and spat a jet of green juice over his shoulder, the spittle sluicing the grass.

'Turdlings, turdlings, please,' Garn cut in. 'You are disturbing my peace. Do not make me come back there. I would not wish our nine to become seven before we even spy Silures lands.'

Ulla had wrenched his mount about. 'We need all our iron for this task.' His face was grim now, returned to the implacable cliff for which it was named. 'See to your work.'

Andoc muttered, 'I heard the Silures are drunkards.'

'Do not fool yourself,' Ulla retorted scornfully.

'They gulp at fire water before battle,' Five Thorns said, 'to give them courage. It makes them mad men. Brings on the battle-frenzy.'

Garn shuddered. 'A fearful sight.'

Andoc squared his skinny shoulders, puffed up his chest. 'I am not afeard.'

'Gods,' Garn said, 'but if you do not near shit yourself in a fight then something's amiss in that pasty skull of yours.'

'You're saying I should be scared?' Andoc blurted, baffled. 'What about Lord Caratacos?'

'You think he doesn't feel fear?' Ulla answered. 'Fear's what keeps him alive. It keeps him cautious, keeps him watchful. The only warriors with no fear in their hearts are those whose hearts no longer beat.'

'Lord!'

They all looked to Rues, at the front, for he had hissed the word at Ulla, who, in turn, waved the rest to silence. They followed Rues's rapid hand gestures, frantically indicating a threat of some kind. They righted themselves, gathered reins, looked to the front and to the sides and the rear, senses suddenly keen, alert to peril in the shadows.

Cullen saw Ulla slide Bear Claw free. Dan unslung the bow from his shoulder, fished an arrow from its quiver. Garn was fingering the badger's teeth draped about his neck. Five Thorns dislodged the axe he called Cleaver from its saddle loop, hefting it in his large fist as if gauging its weight for the first time.

'Smell that?' Kurd said, sword in hand.

Cullen did. It was a strong, musky odour that seemed to emanate from the trees. 'Fox piss?'

'Worse,' said Five Thorns with a wrinkling nose. 'Polecat.'

'There,' Rues hissed, pointing. Fifty paces up ahead, a shape moved silently along the smooth, grey branch of a young wych elm, its coat of yellow and reddish-brown stark against the rich purple-black of the squat leaves. It looked to Cullen to be the size of a large dog, though its movements seemed too stealthy and lithe, not to mention the fact that it was halfway up a tree. Rues turned to Ulla. 'Lynx.'

The creature watched them for a moment, its bright, near luminescent stare like a pair of backlit crystals, then dropped effortlessly to the ground, landing on all fours and innately assessing the terrain without seeming to move its eyes.

Cullen was captivated. He had never seen the like, not even on the most isolated hilltop when his goats had been as ducks to an eagle. He stared, feeling his skin prickle. The lynx padded soundlessly through a patch of tall grass. It was lean yet muscular, tall ears twitching, turning to cup the air in the direction of every noise, near and far. For a moment it froze, sniffing the breeze, deciding on a course, then through a gap between overlapping gorse bushes it vanished. A gap that was not even there, like a door to the Otherworld, unseen to men.

As it slunk away, merging with the thicket, becoming one with it, vanishing altogether, Cullen let out a ragged breath, honoured to have seen the elusive beast with his own eyes. The others turned, thanked the gods for their irrefutable favour, for an omen so unambiguous it took no Wise One to interpret.

'We'll rest a moment,' Ulla commanded, audibly relieved as the tension dissipated.

Cullen sheathed his sword, slid from the saddle, and went to piss in a bush. That was when the branches on the far side of the ditch began to shake.

The lead man, thick woollen smock stretched tight over an ample midriff that draped like a fleshy apron over his crotch, clutched a light throwing spear, sweeping aside the foliage with the long, dark shaft. He looked up with watery, red-rimmed eyes from beneath the peak of an antiquated-looking helmet that was pot-shaped, dented and without adornment. Behind him, half a dozen more men emerged, all carrying rectangular shields, curved at the corners and spangled with the yellow stars of the Dobunni. They stepped over the ditch and fanned out, cutting off the track behind Andoc, Cullen and Dan, who were the rearmost markers. Their spears, mostly the heavy kind, made for close-up work, were promptly levelled.

Cullen, hurriedly stuffing away his member, pulled free his sword, for he found himself nearest to the man in the dented pot. He felt sweat bead immediately at his forehead and prayed to the ancestors that his palm would not become slick.

The fat man in the helmet sucked at his teeth, scanned the track as far down as Ulla, then let his glistening gaze return. 'What's this?'

Cullen swallowed hard. He lowered the sword slightly, pointing it at the track. The last thing he needed was to rile a gang of warriors into doing what they did best. 'Peace delegation,' he managed to blurt, though it was difficult while tentacles of ice seemed to be creeping steadily up his legs, enveloping his torso and crushing the air inside his lungs. 'From High King Togodubnos.'

'That so?' The fat man sniffed the air, grimacing as if he smelled dung. 'Thing is, Cironion is a day's walk,' he swung the spear round to point at the trees, 'that way. Whoever guides you needs a swift knock on the head.' He grinned, revealing gums that were sore and sparsely populated. 'Never mind, we can take you up to King Boduoc, no trouble.'

'No,' Cullen heard himself say. He felt trapped, an animal in a snare, unable to run but unwilling to surrender. His mind raced with what he guessed Ulla would want him to say.

The brow shot up beneath the helmet's rim, skin bunching into a solid roll. 'No?'

Cullen shook his head. 'We can find our own way.'

'Now what kind of hosts would we be if we failed to escort honoured guests through our lands?'

'I said we will make our own way to Cironion.'

'Thing is,' the Dobunni leader scratched at his stubble, 'we've had some trouble with the black shields of late.'

'Do we look like black shields to you?'

'Looks all too often deceive, wouldn't you say?' Now the brows came together in a tight furrow. 'Who commands here?'

Every fibre of Cullen's being urged him to look towards Ulla, but that would draw the fat man's scrutiny, and Ulla's was a famous name. With that fame came connotations mainly associated with violence. A peaceful visit would be a difficult notion to sell. Cullen said, 'I do.'

The fat man's throat wobbled as he gave a derisive laugh. 'How many winters since last you sucked your mother's teat, lad? Not many, I'd wager.'

Strands of dread spread through Cullen's chest, coming together, twisting and writhing until they formed a tight knot at his breastbone. He forced the words out of his throat as he finally raised the blade. 'I'm warning you.'

'Are you now?' The fat man dug a finger at the helmet strap, hooking out some irritant, the skin under his chin bulging. He glanced down at Cullen's sword. 'Fine piece, that. Know how to use it, do you?'

'I know I'll stick the next man to take a forward step.' It was an assertion he was not entirely convinced of. What was certain was that his hand was trying to tremble, and his forearm was beginning to scream with the ache of gripping the damnable length of iron.

The fat man held his own spear up, as if placating a jumpy foal. 'Calm your ire, boy.' He stepped closer. 'We mean no harm.'

'That why your man's crouching in the bushes?' Cullen asked, stepping forward himself.

The fat man's eyes widened to big wet orbs. 'Now wait there a moment.'

Cullen stabbed him in the belly. It was an unthinking movement, as if his body acted of its own accord, abject terror sprouting wings at his feet, giving strength to his arm. He lunged, twisting his hip, putting everything behind the thrust, and the fat man garbled something as he dropped his spear and tried to unsheathe the sword, severing half his fingers in the process. Cullen yanked his own blade away. It was difficult, flesh and guts sucking back, and when his hand jerked free he was sprayed with gore.

Dan's arrow was still nocked, and his horse trampled forth, knocking Cullen aside as he stretched the bowstring. He loosed into the nearest thicket of dense scrub, the one Cullen had eyed before his lunge, and out came a young man with a starry shield and a throwing spear still cocked at his shoulder. Now, though, there was an arrow jutting from his chest, and blood spilled hot from his flapping mouth. The spear clattered into the ditch, the shield followed, and so did the young man.

Perhaps it was the surprise of the attack, or perhaps it was because their leader had been run through without issuing an order, but the spearmen behind Andoc dithered. They shouted and snarled, jabbed with their weapons, but they seemed reluctant to come on, and all the while Ulla, Kurd, Rues, Tal and Garn were kicking at their mounts, surging back up the track.

Finally understanding that events had overtaken them, the Dobunni spearmen formed a rudimentary wall with their large body-shields, the spears angled up from the sides. It might have staved off horses on any other day, but Dan's bow was creaking under tension again, and then a face at the centre of the Dobunni line snapped back, a puff of red mist drizzling his comrades, and then his shield had gone and a gap had opened, and into that gap, a whirl of snarls and savagery, charged Garn Grey Boulder. The enemy line swallowed him.

For the briefest moment Cullen felt sure Garn would be butchered, so he blinked away the blood and went on the attack, ramming into the rear of the clustered Dobunni. Andoc was at his side, hacking with his own blade, screaming a garbled oath that was lost in the chaos, and the other hawks quickly joined them to whittle away that block of shields like quarriers excavating for limestone. But the converged bodies erupted, staggering back, and up came Garn Grey Boulder, champion of old Cunobelin, named man of the Catuvellauni. With his shield he swatted men away like flies from a horse's tail, and with his stunted arm he smashed throat and face and skull, the iron studs making jelly where once was flesh and bone.

The Dobunni fled. Some of the star-painted shields clattered onto the track, discarded in panic, and a couple of the men tossed their spears at Garn, who ducked beneath their flight and spat curses at their throwers and tilted back his head in a booming guffaw.

Cullen breathed. That was all he could do. The sudden outbreak of violence, and its equally sudden curtailment, had exhausted him beyond understanding. He pushed the tip of his sword into the nearest piece of soft earth and leaned on the hilt for support. He absently counted the bodies. The fat man who had died on Cullen's iron, the hidden spearman with the arrow in the throat, and four others, all Dobunni.

Garn, standing over one of the prone men, was pounding his own chest with the blood-streaked stump of his arm, the string of badger teeth rattling discordantly. 'Gods of war, turn your faces upon us!' He looked up at the sky, grimacing like an Otherworld fiend. 'Warriors come to you this day, straight as the spear. They fought and they died. Welcome them at the feasting fires of their people. Let them tell of their deeds as they sup with those who have gone before. Give their souls respite before they move on to the next!'

Ulla Jagged Cliff, wiping his blade on a patch of long grass, called, 'On to the next!'

'On to the next!' they echoed to a man.

As soon as Cullen uttered the words he saw Garn in his eyeline. The silver-haired monster was panting and grinning, but the fire in his gaze had dimmed, the battle-frenzy ebbing now that the work was done. The big man raised his shield. 'You.'

'Me?'

'Yours was the first blow.' Garn offered a short bow. 'Your iron shed the first blood. The honour of the victory is yours.'

'But I—' Cullen began to dissemble, doubts nagging, suspecting the deaths might have been avoided entirely, had he kept a cool head.

Ulla's crushing hand fell startlingly on his shoulder. 'You saw the one hidden. It was good work. Your fame grows.' His big sword, Bear Claw, flashed as he slid it back into its decorated scabbard. Cullen's eye was drawn by the line of congealed blood where iron met hilt. 'Your name is greater today than it was yesterday.'

'Dan of the arrow!' Kurd Long Limb slid long arms under the first of the bodies, dragging it into the ditch. He grinned up at Dan, who, alone, was still in the saddle. 'His own renown expands. You did well.'

'Ha!' Garn brayed. 'By the ancients! By the dead! By Belinos and Teutates and every god between here and Mona!' He picked a route through the debris of corpse, spear and shield until he had reached Dan. 'I was wrong about that bow. There is much honour to be found in its carrying.' He winked. 'By those expert enough in its use.'

Dan visibly blushed. 'Thank you.'

'And you, Andoc,' White Tal said to the willowy figure who had retrieved his horse and was checking the bridle. 'A fight well joined.'

'All of you,' Ulla said. 'Your names are worthy in this company.' He pointed down the track. 'Now let us rid the road of these bodies and make haste for the river.'

CHAPTER SIXTEEN

An eagle tipped its wing to the wind, circling high above them as they descended a gently sloping field of sprouting green barley. The bottom end terminated in a sparse hedge, dilapidated fences partially plugging the gaps, and stands of downy birch dominating the space beyond. When they were past the fences, which was hardly a trial, even with the horses, it was a matter of twenty or thirty more paces and they were through the trees, finding themselves on the edge of a bare ridge, the lack of foliage affording views for miles to the north.

'There lies the kingdom of the Silures,' Ulla said.

More fields stretched away below them, a patchwork of shades that spoke of wheat, barley and flax, all interspersed with stands of ash and birch, and the darker lines of dividing ditches. In the distance there were yet more fields, many dotted with sheep, running to the shaded swells of hilltops further off. But that was all on the far side of the water. All in another kingdom; another nation entirely. Between the immediate field system and the ones supporting livestock, there was a broad stripe, glittering like a silver ribbon, that cut the land in half. The Sea of Sabrina, marking the extent of King Boduoc's lands, and the beginning of those belonging to King Lestinos.

There was a ferry crossing to the west, so Rues confidently claimed, and they veered left through the crops, the river always in sight. They saw not a soul, save a scarecrow, crudely fashioned from sticks and rags, and that seemed a little strange, until the rain clouds rolled over the hills on the Silures side, darkening the land like dye spreading across white cloth. Their massed shadow spread quickly, dimming the shimmer of the wide waterway below them, and then the rain began to patter, softly at first, beading in the manes of the mounts, and then harder, as if sent by Lestinos himself to deter their progress.

'Have you a name for that blade?' Kurd asked Cullen as the horses grunted and snorted in the rapidly softening mud.

'Slasher?' Cullen offered, half wincing as he was reminded of Becan's earlier reaction.

'A toad's shit of a name,' Kurd said.

Some of the others had kicked up to within earshot. 'How about Biter?' Dan suggested.

'Stinger?' White Tal said.

'Bleeder,' said Garn.

'The sword did not bleed,' Kurd replied before Cullen had so much as absorbed the suggestions. 'It was the *cause* of the bleed.'

'Then it should be called Blood-Letter,' Garn said happily, clearly pleased to be discussing such matters.

'How about,' Cullen drew in a breath, 'Blade of Taranis?'

A moment's pause, then a great wave of laughter.

'You have the god's favour,' Ulla chided, 'but you are not his right hand.'

They crossed a brook by way of stout planks set upon massive stones, the water clear and slow beneath them, the depth of a man's waist. They could see the dark shapes of fish flitting at the edges, where roots and reeds tangled for ascendancy, and in the very middle was a tiny island of smooth pebbles, its summit poking just above the surface that pulsated under the incessant rainfall.

'Where are they?' Ulla asked of himself as his horse completed the crossing. 'Those who made the offerings to the water sprites?' He looked in all directions, holding a hand to his eyes as a guard against the rain.

'Too quiet,' grunted Garn.

There was a kingfisher further along the slick bank, where the brook twisted in sinewy fashion, disappearing into the trees.

It should have been a good omen, but Rues Seeker was sniffing the air like a hound, tilting up his face to the rain, which was beginning to streak down in heavy, slanting sheets.

'Not another lynx?' Andoc asked.

Rues pulled a puzzled expression, scratched amongst the rain-beaded spines of his bleached hair. 'House.'

'How do you know?'

'Houses smell different.'

Andoc screwed up his thin mouth in a look of amused scorn. 'To what?'

'Everything.' Rues counted them off on his fingers. 'Piles of wood. Corpse pyres. Heathland wildfire.' He looked at Andoc levelly, 'And that,' he sniffed hard, 'is a house.'

On the very last word did Andoc look past Rues's shoulder to notice the funnel of black smoke climbing to mingle with the ominous clouds. It was joined by a swirling mass of birds, big and black, cawing and swooping and tumbling.

White Tal spoke quietly as he fingered his sword pommel. 'Follow the crows and bad deeds you will discover.'

—

The rain was oppressive and miserable; he could feel water seeping into the tops of his boots where the braca were tucked, but his mother's cloak was practically impervious, and the air was far from cold. The problem was that it hung an opaque screen over the steading he now approached.

Rues and Five Thorns led the group in. They went on foot, the horses left to shelter under dense branches, reins looped about sturdy trunks. The place had a perimeter fence, which yawned open, and an outer yard which they crossed without challenge. A shallow ditch and staked bank protected the inner sanctum, and that barrier's gates, complete with mounted ram skulls, were open too. Within the ditch, hut circles huddled around a shared patch of open ground and associated grain stores and outbuildings, most of them aflame. The rain hissed and the fire spat, but otherwise the place was empty and silent.

Ulla drew Bear Claw, and the rest followed. All except Dan, whose bow gave a low creak as he eased back on the string. They fanned out, edged in, alert to sudden movement. The rain pulsed, damping the fires, but that only kicked up more smoke, which added to the overcast gloom. Cullen held his blade in one hand and dagger in the other, braced and nervous, squinting into each building he passed. A lone dog, bedraggled in the rain, scurried out from an unfired storehouse and was almost decapitated for his curiosity.

Cullen went to the building, screwing up his eyes to investigate the gloomy interior. Inside there was the heavy wooden beam and spike of an ard, with which a field may be broken up for sowing. There were tools, too. Chisels, hammers, small saws and large axes, scattered haphazardly around the toppled benches upon which they had once been arranged. Reaping hooks and sickles lay at the room's edges, beneath the posthooks that had housed them.

Someone outside hailed them. Cullen went into the rain to see Five Thorns peering over a wicker fence, beckoning with his big axe. When he reached the fence himself, all he noted were nonplussed expressions.

'Empty,' Garn said of the pen.

Rues pursed his lips, leaning over as Five Thorns had done. 'It wasn't.' He looked up, finding Ulla. 'Cloven hooves. Five or six.'

'Oxen,' Ulla said, turning so that he could scan the scene in all directions, though the view was severely hampered by the rain and smoke.

From that greyish miasma emerged Andoc. 'Shields!' he called, pointing back over his shoulder. 'Over there. Black ones.' He drew up, panting hard, hands on knees. 'And two heads, impaled.'

Ulla and Garn exchanged a look, then the former turned to Rues. 'Track them.'

Rues's bright eyes slid up to the portentous crows, still swirling in a black pall a short distance beyond the village limits. 'I won't need to.'

They left the village, crossing a cornfield behind Rues who examined the ground every few steps, then checked the sky.

Cullen told of the tools that had been ransacked but not stolen, and the named men amongst the group agreed that the raid's purpose had not been petty plunder.

'They had bigger prizes in mind,' Kurd said as they rode.

'Who did?' asked Andoc.

'Silures,' Garn said. 'They paint their shields with tar.'

'And the prints we follow,' Rues said, 'are foot as well as hoof.'

Cullen realised that it was not only the livestock that had been taken. 'Slaves.'

'The women and children,' Ulla said.

'The men,' Garn added ominously, 'we will soon find.'

Sure enough, a shallow ditch that had once been furred with sedge and gorse was now piled with corpses, splayed at odd angles, twisted and grimacing. This was where the crows had congregated, and their squawks of protest rent the air as they took flight, leaving eyes and lips pecked to tattered shreds.

The nine dismounted. They went to check for survivors, though anyone could see it was a futile task. One man had lost an arm, perhaps defending himself in the face of a blade, while another's mouth gaped, a look of pure astonishment, his hands braced on either side of a gashed belly. There were children too. Just the boys. Throats slashed and brains dashed.

There was a felled tree nearby. Cullen went to it, propped a boot on the slippery bark and examined his rain-beaded braca, making sure they were as tightly tucked in as possible.

Ulla just stood and stared at the body-filled ditch, jaw quivering as he ground his teeth, knuckles white as he gripped his sword pommel. 'Which way?' he murmured.

Rues pointed north. 'The river lies just beyond that rise.'

'They're going home,' Garn said. 'Good riddance.'

'Do we not follow?' Andoc asked.

'At a distance,' Ulla agreed. 'Let us see what can be done.'

'A fool's errand.'

The voice was nasal, sibilant, and utterly out of place. It was answered by the immediate zing of drawn iron. Cullen, still inspecting his boot, almost fell over the log, for the speaker had appeared at the corner of his eye, perched on a part of the trunk that was sheltered from the rain by thick overhanging branches.

Cullen righted himself, brandished his own sword, and brought up the tip to nestle beneath the stranger's chin. 'Name yourself or step quick to the next life,' he snarled, and he hoped he did not colour, for the ferocity of his words was fuelled by the mortification of having let the man come so close.

The man leaned back slightly, nervous of the blade, but ventured a smile, revealing a sparse arrangement of browning teeth. 'Hush, my rust-haired friend. Hush, I say, I mean you no harm.' He raised a hand slowly, in which he held the half-eaten limb of some cooked animal. 'Lest you fear this bone. In which instance,' a glance down at the sword, 'I would suggest you have picked the wrong life path.'

'Let him up,' Ulla commanded, presumably reading no danger in the exchange. Not a surprise, Cullen conceded, for the man was old. More than sixty winters, he reckoned, with wild, grey weepy eyes, thinning grey hair and a greasy, pale-grey moustache. He duly retracted the sword's tip.

Ulla said, 'Who are you?'

The old man declined to stand, for he was dry on his perch. Instead he raised his palms. They trembled a little, betraying his age. 'Nynniaw is my name.' He spoke the common tongue with a distinct accent that was familiar to Cullen. Twitching one hand, in which he still held the meat, he said, 'And who is it that disturbs my meal?'

'Ulla Jagged Cliff.'

Andoc wrinkled his nose. 'He stinks like a polecat's arse.'

'And you, my spidery friend,' Nynniaw's reedy neck convulsed as his head whipped about to round on Andoc, 'smell like a lavender field in high summer, I do not doubt.'

Andoc loured. 'You'll show some respect, weasel, or—'

'Nay, says I, and nay again!' the old man's tone hardened, and he waved the meat like a weapon. 'For the Wise sit above petty chieftains and their creatures, as well you know.'

Andoc physically backed away, as if the wagging animal bone had transformed into a wand. He mouthed what might have been an apology, but the words appeared to snag halfway up his long throat. He looked at his comrades, at Ulla, at the ground.

'But below royalty,' Ulla said levelly, 'and I answer to the high king himself.'

'High?' Nynniaw canted his head, studying Ulla and finding amusement. 'He is only the highest amongst the Belgic nations. Of the fertile south and east. The mountain folk of the north and west do not recognise him as their overlord, says I.'

'But they recognise him as strongest.'

Nynniaw gave a bird-peck of a bow. 'Aye, you have me there.' He grinned. 'I speak for Mona, and you for your *high* king. Perhaps we will agree at our equality.' He took a bite of the meat, tearing it messily from the thin bone. 'And as an equal, I advise you not to chase the black shields. A fool's errand, says I.'

'They destroyed the village back there,' Ulla replied. 'Took slaves.'

Nynniaw slurped at a drip of fat, wiped glistening juices from his moustache with the sleeve of his threadbare tunic. 'Your village? Your women?' He laughed, though it was not a harsh sound. 'Ulla Jagged Cliff brags of his devotion to the offspring of the Sun Hound, but he risks his life avenging the honour of Boduoc?'

A tightening rippled across Ulla's already hard face. 'There are children amongst the corpses.'

'War is war, says I,' the Wise One countered.

'The Silures and the Dobunni are not at war, so far as I know.'

'Then you do not know as much as you ought. The Silures cross Sabrina's water because they can. They raid, pillage. Boduoc is weak. He has enemies within and enemies without. Even now, half the kingdom has been claimed by his cousin.' Nynniaw glanced skyward at the circling birds. 'The Silures come to pick at his bones, like our guests up there.'

'Is Boduoc your lord?'

'I answer to no man.'

'A wanderer, then?'

Nynniaw exposed those brown teeth. 'Cartimandua, Queen of the North Mountains, has my heart.' He tossed the cleanly picked bone over his shoulder. 'But I walk these roads, these hills, every springtime. The tribe from whence I sprang was called the Dumnonii, from the farthest corner of this island.' He pointed south and west. 'Where the endless seas smash the lonely rocks. I left my people when I was but a small boy.'

'Sent to Mona,' Ulla said.

Nynniaw nodded. 'There to learn the sacred ways. Now I serve Cartimandua and her Brigantes. But I visit my people when I can. That is, when the roads are not haunted by black-shielded demons or clogged with the recent dead.'

Garn gave an incredulous grunt as he looked round at the ditch, the crows venturing a return even as they spoke. 'How did you survive?'

'I hid, of course.'

Five Thorns pointed at the twisted cadavers. 'Did they not hide?'

'Not very well, says I.' Nynniaw stood, stretching, eliciting a couple of joint cracks for his efforts. 'Now, then. I must walk on.' He looked at Ulla sternly. 'And you must turn about before your own futures are filled with blackened shields.'

'We intend to cross the water,' Ulla replied.

Nynniaw gave a sceptical snort. 'Cross? Cross, says he? Then you are addled, friend, and no mistake. The Silures are not as you Belgic folk, nor we ancient tribes. Their forefathers came from overseas, in times long forgotten. They are a different breed. Dangerous, unpredictable. You Belgae have no edges any more. Your dealings with Rome have sanded you down, smoothed the grain. Turned you soft, says I.'

'Your concerns are noted, Nynniaw. Respected, as the words of the Wise must always be. But we will manage. Now tell me, where can we find the ferryman?'

—

Gesoriacum swarmed.

It had not been a small town to begin with. A fortified dun of the Gaulish Boii tribe, the Romans had transformed it after Caesar's conquest, building wharves and jetties, huge storehouses and gigantic timber cranes, so that now it was the premier port of this part of their burgeoning empire, and the natural staging post for any invasion of the Isle of the Mighty. Now, though, it positively teemed, for the legions of the most powerful army on earth had descended upon it.

Berikos shielded his eyes against the sun as he tracked a flock of starlings, swirling and swelling. They formed shapes that morphed as they moved, breaking apart, then coming together as if ordained by the gods themselves. Eventually they dived behind the vast stone lighthouse that was the most prominent of Gesoriacum's impressive panoply of structures.

'Gaius Caligula had it built,' Adminios whispered at his ear, 'to commemorate his conquest of Britannia.'

'A conquest that did not happen,' Berikos said, tearing his gaze away from the building. 'Let us dwell instead on the task at hand, yes?'

The camp abutted the town itself, using its wall as one flank. From there it had spread as far as the eye could see. Semi-permanent wooden structures had been thrown up to house some of the great and the good of the nascent invasion force, while thousands upon thousands of white tents were being erected in precise rows, cohort by cohort, legion by legion, so that a great city was gradually appearing from the soil.

Atebodwos, the little interpreter, appeared between the two lords. 'Shall we?'

Adminios touched the older man's elbow. 'Our new friends will get our thrones back. Let us go and show them how.'

Berikos dismissed his retainers, took a steadying breath and followed Adminios and Atebodwos into the camp headquarters. It was one of the few timber buildings, placed right at the very centre of the camp, a fat spider in a sprawling web. Candles lit the interior, and sumptuous carpets covered the floor. Half a dozen men in the uniform of the legions stood around a wide, circular table strewn with maps. Amongst them, both seated, he recognised Narcissus, the former slave, and Aulus Plautius, the overall commander of the expedition.

Berikos bowed to the latter. 'General.'

'Lord Berikos,' Plautius said. He was powerfully built beneath his cloak of white fur. His face was broad and ruddy, his hair brown and his eyes bright. A white scar ran diagonally through his upper lip, which he gnawed as he returned his focus to the map pinned beneath his thick fingers. In Latin, he said, 'Come and lend us your thoughts.'

Berikos and Adminios approached, standing over the map as the other officers moved to give them space. Immediately Berikos recognised the beautifully sketched features and contours, the little circles denoting major settlements and the meandering lines that plotted river courses. 'The Isle of the Mighty,' he said in barely a whisper, though Atebodwos translated.

Some of the officers muttered to one another in amusement, silenced by a snap of Plautius's fingers. The general cleared his throat. 'We will send four legions to conquer Britannia.'

Berikos glanced up at Adminios, who said, 'Each consisting of more than five thousand men.'

The former king of the Atrebates felt his eyes widen so severely that he feared they might pop out of his head. 'From where do these multitudes come?'

Atebodwos immediately spewed a stream of Latin.

'Second Augusta,' one of the lesser Romans replied, 'Fourteenth Gemina and Twentieth Valeria. All spared from the Rhine area where no trouble is expected.' He gave a smug smile as the interpreter went to work. 'The natives there have come to understand the way of things.'

'And the fourth?' Berikos asked, ignoring the barb, for he had assurances that his own power would be perfectly safe.

'Ninth Hispania,' the same man said, 'have come with General Plautius from Pannonia.'

Plautius nodded. 'They have much experience in the use of boats. Amphibious attacks, disembarkation of troops and resupply. Vital for our enterprise.' He sat back, taking a peeled orange segment from a little plate and popping it into his mouth. 'There are many auxiliary troops too. Cavalry, archers, bridge builders.'

'Batavians, I hear,' Adminios said. He nudged Berikos. 'Specialists in river crossings.'

'Thus, we will have more than forty thousand troops dedicated to our scheme,' Narcissus said smoothly. 'Quite irresistible, I'm sure you'll agree.'

Berikos could only nod mutely. There were simply no words.

'A large force,' Plautius conceded. He looked up hard at the two Britons. 'But how will we deploy?'

A murmur of discontent ran through the assembly. Narcissus raised a hand for silence. 'This, gentlemen, is lord Adminios, rightful chief of the Cantiaci. He knows this savage isle as he knows the lines of his palm. Pay heed.'

Adminios pored over the map, squinting as he traced the features, moving a forefinger ever eastwards towards the line of the Cantiaci coast. He traced the corner of the isle with his nail, sweeping round the extreme edge of the land and down to the southern coast, where his hand stopped. 'I know you had considered this stretch as a landing point.'

'Go on,' Plautius said.

'Do not.' Adminios ran his finger up through the landmass that compromised the southern portion of Cantiaci territory. 'Saltwater marsh, swamp, filth. You will not be able to advance through it.' He stabbed at a point to the east. 'This side, the anchorage is no better, but if you find some ingenious way of disembarking here, you will immediately be forced to negotiate thick forest. My people call it the Lonely Wood, on account of the fact that it is impenetrable.'

Berikos leaned in, stabbing his own finger at a spot slightly higher on the map that was marked by zigzagging lines. 'This range runs for many miles.' He slid his finger along the zigzags, the green stone capping his gold ring, carved into the shape of a frog, tracking their progress. 'One could march across them, for they are hardly more than hillocks and a track cuts along their length. But a marching column would be vulnerable.'

Adminios nodded. 'The woods are deep and dark, and my brothers know their business.'

'Then the north?' Plautius prompted.

'Here,' Adminios agreed, tracing a line from the extreme east coast to the broad stripes of two rivers. The first was unmarked, and it curled from the sea down into Cantiaci lands. The second, further north and much more prominent, was labelled *Tamesis*. 'You will need to take Camulodunon as swiftly as possible. In order to do that, you must cross both of these rivers. This first we call the Vaga.' He waited as one of the officers noted down the name, then put his finger back on a point on the east coast. 'The route inland from here is considerably more favourable. And this island,' he indicated where a chunk of land was separated from the mainland by a narrow channel, 'can serve as a natural harbour.'

Plautius rubbed his stubbled chin. 'We will move in three waves, a day or two apart.'

'Three?' Berikos echoed incredulously. 'You would split your—'

'How many seaborne invasions have you planned, lord king?' Plautius cut him off acerbically. 'Three divisions, for three operational tasks. One.' He indicated the little island Adminios had identified. It was a rectangle of land, with a long sand-spit jutting from its southern coast. 'The channel, here, connects the Oceanus Britannicus and the estuary to the north. It is both broad and navigable. The advance group will land here, on the sandy peninsula.' He looked now to one of his commanders. 'You will establish a fort and bridgehead. Secure the island. Purge it clean if necessary.'

'Bright Island,' Adminios warned, 'is so called for its beacon.'

'We will land at night,' Plautius said, unruffled, 'before they ever know we are there. The second phase will arrive a matter of a few days later, when the bridgehead has been established.'

'They will attack while we await reinforcements,' one of the officers said.

'Then they will have to cross the channel first,' replied Plautius, picking up another orange segment. 'And in the face of our fleet at anchor. When we are ready to strike, you will cross the channel and thrust inland.' He prodded a dot on the map, through which a very fine line crossed. 'There is an oppidum on this smaller river.'

'A dun,' Adminios said to Berikos. He looked at the Romans. 'Durouernon. Capital of the Cantiaci. My capital.'

'It is defended?'

'There is a hillfort nearby, but the oppidum is not formidable. It has three ditches and a serviceable rampart, but it is a place built upon trade.' At that Adminios shot a dagger-like stare at Narcissus.

The emperor's advisor grinned. 'Something we are keen to re-establish as soon as we take control. Propriety will return, Adminios, thanks to you.' He let his gaze slide to Berikos too. 'And to the Atrebates, have no fear.'

'The oppidum controls the river and the road,' Plautius said. 'It is the spider in a web of communications, and, therefore, crucial to our operation. You will take it and pause while the third division makes landfall. This final group will bring more auxiliaries, supplies and heavy weaponry.' He looked from Berikos to Adminios in turn. 'What numbers can the chief of the Britons muster?'

'Tens of thousands,' Berikos said. 'But the tribes are restless. Cynical of Catuvellauni ambition. Suspicious of the sons of Cunobelin.'

'And those grievances are like cracks in a wall,' agreed Adminios.

'Berikos, here,' Narcissus said, 'has worked tirelessly with our emissaries to apply pressure. Since arriving in Rome, he has sent messages to allies in Britannia. Made assurances and received pledges. The cracks are beginning to widen. The wall will crumble.'

'All to the good,' General Plautius said, putting the orange piece onto his tongue. 'Then let us go forth.'

—

'Simple enough,' Garn Grey Boulder growled as he stood atop the high cliff, staring down at the muddy expanse below.

Bluff words, spoken gruffly by a warrior in possession of a famous name, and yet the tremor in his voice would have been audible to the deaf. In truth, the crossing looked perilous, for the river was a broad swathe of brown, rushing water, the better part of a mile across, where tides eddied and frothed, and boats bucked like unbroken colts.

'Simple,' Kurd Long Limb echoed, just as unconvincingly.

Yet they all knew simplicity – or otherwise – hardly mattered. They had come this far, and none would countenance turning back now.

They left the horses with a meek labourer in a modest farm and followed a treacherous path down the sheer face that was layered in rich red and white stone, there to mount the wooden wharf that seemed like the very end of the world.

Below their feet, lapped by the water, were three tall poles, each topped by a human skull. All had been picked or boiled clean and all had a tell-tale puncture hole at the temple.

'Sacrifices,' White Tal murmured, fiddling immediately with whatever charm he could grab first.

'By the Silures?' Cullen asked.

Ulla shook his head. 'Dobunni. See how they face north? They protect against the Silures.'

Garn spat. 'Much good they did.'

Further along the shoreline, amid the debris of rope and old nets, women and children busied themselves with the business of the day, brandishing wicked filleting knives as they worked on a recent catch, clothes reddened and hands silvered, the smell of fish guts prominent on the wind. From amongst them strode a man of middling age who waded the shallows with a rolling limp, coming to meet the warriors on the wharf. Named Lux, he was the captain of the ferry. There was not much to see of him between a woollen cap and a hedge-like beard, but his eyes were small and his cheeks polished to a high sheen by the elements. His vessel was made of oak planks, stitched together with yew withies and caulked with moss. It was flat-bottomed, four generous strides wide and fifteen long, and Ulla's men fitted comfortably on the benches, the four grizzled paddlemen standing in pairs, fore and aft.

'The warband have slaughtered Dobunni,' Ulla told him on hearing that the ferry had earlier transported the black shields back to Silures territory.

'Tell us something new,' Lux, taking one of the front paddles, muttered into the whipping wind as the vessel slipped away from its moorings and out past the weed-draped crags of a stone circle, protruding from the water like crooked teeth.

'Yet they keep the crossing open?' Ulla replied, disbelieving.

Lux gave the circle – and therefore whichever water nymphs he honoured – a solemn nod as they bobbed beyond its last marker. 'It does no good to shut it. They need the ferry for trade.' He glanced pointedly back at the knot of folk on the shore, a hive of industry unperturbed by recent events. 'Need our fish.'

'And are you not in danger?'

Lux shook his head. 'The Silures are hill dwellers. They keep livestock, grow grain, but they understand they must raid away from the coast. Besides,' he added, touching the half-moon amulet strung about his neck, 'the lords of Mona provide protection. Not spears, you understand. Spells. Threats. No man wishes to anger the Wise. Not even Lestinos.'

There was a muddy peninsula on the opposite bank, at the confluence of this river and another, and it was there that a corresponding wharf could be seen protruding into the water. 'The second river comes down from the mountains in the north,' Lux told them. 'Good drinking, but do not swim in it. The water will freeze your balls off.'

'When we reach land,' Ulla said, 'we make for the fortress of Lestinos. You know it?'

One corner of Lux's hairy face rose in a sardonic smile. 'Do the Wise worship the gods?'

—

Dunlin and shelduck waded in the deep mud as the nine left the wharf behind. Gulls swooped, cackling, as redshank foraged for insects at the reed-rustling edges of glassy pools. The booming calls of secretive bitterns reverberated about the rushes. White Tal prayed to the gods of hills and woods. Five Thorns sang a mournful tune. Andoc complained of blisters.

It was getting dark. The hillfort of the Silures was a day's walk away, according to Lux, who had made little secret of his belief that the Catuvellauni warriors were insane. They made camp at the edge of the second river that formed the peninsula, and waited out the night, staring down at the black waters that were punctuated by withies, set at intervals to mark the depth for navigators and fishermen. At dawn they crossed by a rickety wooden bridge onto the mainland and struck out westwards, tracing the course of the road that led into the heart of Silures territory, but keeping an arrow's shot off the main footworn track. The terrain was forgiving for the most part, babbling streams wending through rocky patches, breaking into sticky marshland and ancient forest, the occasional rise and occasional fall.

Just after midday the landscape began to alter, the patchwork of bog and field opening out into more fertile ground, divided into small fields that nurtured green corn. It was these crops that must feed the Silures, and that knowledge fuelled a growing unease, for it marked their passage into the heartland of King Lestinos. As if to accentuate the point, a high ridge gradually came into view, looming on their right, dominating the north, dark and forbidding. It was up there, amongst those forest-clothed hills, that they would soon have to walk. And it was there that the enemy lurked.

From here, on the low ground, the dun was invisible, nestled as it was atop the high ridge, beyond so many thousands of trees, but woodsmoke trailed into the sky, daubing bilious funnels against the clouds, and there were enough that their providence could hardly be mistaken. A significant settlement lay up on the hill. It would be heavily fortified, they knew. The encircling land scarred by deep earthworks and formidable palisades.

'Go at dusk,' Ulla said to Rues when they rested near a mossy clearing marked by broad-branched yew and carefully placed stacks of pebbles. It was a good place to shelter, for three sides were packed densely with hedges of overgrown brambles. The fourth side dropped away in a steep slope, ending in a natural depression, the height of a man, before rising again to meet a crop of spelt.

Garn had pulled a face like a war-hound chewing a hornet. 'What about the rest of us?'

'You want to charge headlong up the slope and attack their rampart?'

'We've come all this way,' the big man said petulantly, hovering on the edge of the clearing, but reluctant to enter, for an image depicting stacked heads had been carved into one of the yews, leaving no doubt that this was a sacred nemeton of the Wise.

Ulla smiled, thumped Garn's oak-bough shoulder, but shook his head. 'Rues will cast an eye.'

'Sniff the wind,' Cullen said.

Ulla chuckled. 'And you'll go with him.'

'Me?'

A noncommittal shrug. 'He wants you.'

'The Dobunni patrol,' Rues explained, already checking his weapons, eager to get moving. 'You spotted the man hiding. That'll do me.'

—

They climbed after the sun had slipped out of view, the moon huge and orange in its stead. At first Rues had ventured west, while there was still a sliver of light on the horizon, hoping to gauge the extent of the fortress and perhaps spy any outlying defences or patrols. They found nothing but way-markers in the shape of painted boulders and a couple of trees hung with animal-bone charms. There was a brook, too, about three hundred paces to the east of the high ridge. Fast but shallow, its silver surface frothing as it crashed over rocks and round twisting bends that it had carved from the bedrock since the days of the first gods. Cullen peered into its crystalline depths, wondering if his mother could see him through that cleft between this world and the other. He was startled by a shake of the shoulder.

'The fortress outworks will not extend this far,' Rues said, turning back. 'Let us look at the scarp itself.'

Up they went, slowly, quietly, and often sideways, leaning into the steep hillside like a pair of crookbacks, resorting to levering themselves by the trunks of trees that jutted at bizarre angles from the root-meshed soil. It was almost pitch-black beneath a canopy smothering the sky, but Rues's short hair, spiked with slaked lime and water, carried a wan glow that Cullen used as a beacon.

Bluebells carpeted the forest floor, swathes of rich colour caught in glimmers under the snatches of moonlight, and they vied for space with the white stars of stitchwort and the fat leaves of bogart posy. It was all a scrabbling confusion in the dark, but they had waited until the sun could not glint upon their weapons, and the sentries would have difficulty differentiating their wraithlike approach from foraging deer. They had watched the daylight ebb, huddled in a crevice in a rocky outcrop away from the low track, thankful for the cessation in the rain, given the impossibility of a fire. Foxes had barked. An owl, white as snow, had crashed through the layers of a great beech to skewer some unfortunate rodent in its talons. All else had been quiet. Ulla had counted down the hours, watched the moon emerge and given the command for Rues and Cullen to move out. Here they were, edging up the scarp, scrambling and cursing softly, breaths kept shallow, hearts in mouths.

From the foot of the ridge, Cullen reckoned, a competent slinger would not reach halfway with his best throw. Now they were a third of the way up, eyes straining into the dark to catch a glimpse of the outlying works of the Silures fortress. Even without sight of the defences, it was clear that to attack from this direction would be a brute of a task, a weighty endeavour for a full army and risible folly for nine tired men. They would have to work their way round to the higher ground to the north, he decided. The main gates would be there, and so, too, would the bulk of defenders, but at least there was no great slope to negotiate.

He was thinking all this when he saw the glow through the trees. It came and went as he moved, branches obscuring the warm light, causing it to wink like a great eye in the gloom, a lurking beast, prowling the dark. At the very same time he caught the heady aroma of woodsmoke. Something else too.

The tang of herbs, overlaying the rich, fatty scent of roasting meat. Someone, hidden further up that hill, was cooking.

Naturally, Rues had already seen it. When Cullen looked across, the man they called Seeker was gesticulating madly from the shelter of a deep tree-throw, his fingers working like pale spider legs, weaving a message that screamed in the silence.

Cullen sketched a reply, begging Taranis to give him the right signals. Rues immediately edged out of the root-torn depression, confirming the god's assistance. As far as Cullen could ascertain, he had identified the source of the smell, which, to judge by the predatory skulk he now employed, was not far away.

The sentry was sitting by himself, cross-legged, at the base of another throw, just like the one Rues had hidden in. At first only his head could be seen above the pit's edge, bathed in a tremulous glow, but more of him was revealed as Cullen crept closer. The tree that had excavated the throw lay nearby, the rook's-nest concentration of roots exposed to the air in a soil-caked block. Cullen moved in a wide arc, finding the far end of the collapsed tree, a tangle of spiked branches, splintered and compressed by the fall, and he started inwards from there, following its length, hunching low to the broad, lichen-spotted barricade that was the trunk.

Rues had gone. Consumed by the night. Cullen swore the man moved like the lynx they had encountered. He could walk through a rainstorm and not get wet.

Further off, up the slope, more spots of flamelight punctured the blackness. More warriors. More danger. In the pit, the sentry was staring into a small fire. Above those flames, a squirrel, skinned and sizzling, had been rigged upon a twig frame. The sentry prodded it with the tip of a finger, testing its readiness. He hummed a low tune, shoulders hunched within a heavy-looking cloak that was trimmed with milk-white material. A helmet, chased similarly in white, lay on the ground at his side. His moustache and beard were plaited together at the chin, running in a thick, black rope to his sternum, and that was where the blade of Rues's sword emerged, pushing the plait up and away as the keen iron nestled against the man's skin. The sentry struggled, bucked, snatched a breath. Rues's hand clamped down firmly over his mouth. Cullen pulled his skinning knife and dropped into the hole.

—

'We are to give thanks.'

The kneeling man spoke through gritted teeth, face a mask of anger rather than pain, though no doubt the woollen strip, knotting his wrists at his back, chafed like a hot brand.

'For?' Ulla's gravel-voice rumbled in the dark.

'The harvest,' the Silures managed to eke from his smattering of common tongue. He had been abducted from his post, the little fire left to smoulder. The fur cloak, which, it transpired, had been woven with dozens of tiny bones, was draped over a pile of sticks in the hope that his absence would not soon be noticed. They had dragged him, Rues and Cullen, down the slope to the rocky outcrop where the others waited, and now, having retreated the better part of another mile from the ridge, they gathered around him in the deep dark.

'Harvest?' echoed Dan, absently inspecting an arrow's fledging. 'Now?'

Ulla shook his head, eyes not leaving their captive. 'Not that kind of harvest.'

'Slaves,' Garn said.

The Silures nodded. 'They'll be sold at the markets over the Clear Sea.' He knelt beneath a flowering rowan, clustered with blossom that shone silver under the moon. One of his eyes was puffy and half-closed, the result of an ill-advised sneer in Garn's direction, but he was unharmed apart from that. 'Or north, in the icy lands where there are giant fish and white bears.'

Ulla was crouching an arm's length from the man bound with strips torn from his own braca. 'When is this thanksgiving?'

The captive glared through that swollen eye, but he knew better than to prevaricate. 'Sun-up.'

Ulla looked round at the others. 'A chance.'

White Tal's wan face darkened with lines. 'How many blades will they have?'

'At least fifty,' Five Thorns said. 'Double that?'

'Madness,' Andoc muttered. His sunken eyes shifting between the named men, evidently searching for a look of support. 'We cannot possibly—'

'We won't attack the ceremony,' Rues said.

'Madness indeed,' Ulla said. He stood, stretching, and gazed down at the sentry. 'Will the thanksgiving take them out of the fort?'

A moment's hesitation, hailed by hands sliding to hilts, then, 'Yes.' He jerked his chin in the general direction of the east, where a thread of dim light was beginning to stretch along the far hills. 'Castrogi Brook. It is ancient. Magic. A door to the next.'

'We saw it,' Cullen said, recalling the watercourse that had carved its groove deep into the earth.

'Not far,' Rues added. He looked pointedly at Ulla. 'But far enough.'

'Will they take her?' Ulla asked, meaning the Eceni princess. The kneeling man shook his head sullenly.

'As a foreigner, she would not be welcome.'

'They'll keep her in the fort,' Ulla muttered to himself, mind working.

'Under guard,' the prisoner muttered.

'And if we free her?' Andoc opined. 'What then? They will come for us like a wolf pack and tear us to shreds.'

'Wolves,' Cullen echoed. The word had chimed in his head, dragging up memories from his old life. When he realised all eyes had alighted upon him, he felt himself quell, but he could see Ulla's severe expression expected him to elucidate. 'That is to say, a wolf pack can be dealt with if a man knows how.'

'And you know how?' Andoc blurted incredulously.

Ulla looked at the prisoner. 'And you say she is at the tanning stone?'

'Beside the vats. It is carved and decorated. There are buildings nearby. She is held there.'

'Which building?'

The Silures sniffed. 'I do not know.'

Ulla made a soft clicking sound with his tongue. Garn Grey Boulder advanced like a huge bear, kicking away the helmet, which, like the cloak, was decorated in tiny, clean bones, drawing his sword in one massive hand and taking hold of the prisoner in the other. 'On to the next for you.'

The Silures tried to wriggle free, but he stood no chance, dangling instead in the big man's irresistible grip, a fox cub in a hound's maw. 'No,' he blurted, his plaited beard coming loose of its ties as he frantically shook his head. 'I have children, wives, I...'

Ulla's hand was up, staying Garn's blade. 'Perhaps I am getting old.'

Garn looked baffled, then crestfallen. 'You cannot be...'

'Tie him to a tree,' Ulla commanded.

'But...'

'Strip him, take his things, bind him.' The hard face regarded the softly jabbering captive. 'Your people will find you eventually.'

'Or the wolves,' Garn growled, hauling the man onto legs that seemed devoid of bones.

'Or the wolves,' Ulla conceded. 'Pray to Cernunnos that his forest will be your ally.' He glanced at Cullen. 'Speak to me, lad. Tell me how a man may outwit the pack.'

CHAPTER SEVENTEEN

Dawn burnished the world from the high ridge down to Sabrina's Sea. In the fertile fields between, nine Catuvellauni, Ulla's hawks, cracked joints, prayed to ancestors and begged gods for strength and guile. Then they struck out for the high fortress of Lestinos, King of the Silures.

The way would be mostly clear, they knew, for Rues and Cullen had spent the night's final hours at watch, bearing silent witness to the flame-lit procession that trailed down from the forested heights to observe an ancient rite beside the sacred waters of the Castrogi Brook. Now the nine crept north, aware that time and opportunity were scarce, and began their ascent of the wooded scarp.

Dan felled the first lookout. The man – dressed in skins and draped in necklaces of tiny bones – had one of the black shields they had heard so much about, but it was unemployed at the foot of a tree and the arrow thumped into the centre of his chest, stealing the air so that his cry was just a soundless gape. They moved past him, even as his legs scrabbled in the leaf litter, and the next position came quickly into sight.

They were angling their approach to the south of the fort, because, according to their erstwhile prisoner, there were two gates. The main entrance was situated to the north, where the road came down from the heart of Silures territory. A small path branched off that road, leading away to the west and the brook beyond. As such, the north gate was the one through which the majority of the population had gone, by which they would doubtless return, and carried a permanent, heavy spear-presence. The second gate, cut into the rampart on this side of the dun, where the slope was steepest and the forest at its least penetrable, was barely used at all. Rather, its presence was required only as a means of swift counterattack in the event of an assault, and that was why, as the sun gradually lent a dull light to the canopy, the defensive positions that emerged up ahead were few and far between.

A second man died. Like the sentry they had taken in the night, he was bedded into a depression in the slope, only his top half visible. The arrow, aimed at his head, clipped a shoulder, wheeling him physically about to plummet face-first into the soil. The consequent yelp of horror and pain was muffled by the dirt and followed up by a crunch as Garn's sword was buried in the side of his head.

The nine spread out, dropping into two more ditches to dispatch those within, and then they were coming together on the summit, the trees thinning to nothing, incline easing, summit opening before them.

Here the land had been cleared, leaving open grass, no tree or building in sight, so that slingers and bowmen on the wooden palisade could turn the ground into a killing field. That palisade, set fifty or so paces back from the treeline, was constructed out of stakes, double the height of a man, and shaved to lethal points. They lined the top of a high bank, which, in turn, threw its shadow across a deep ditch. An assault at any other time would be an invitation to step into the next life. Now, though, with attention turned to the brook and the giving of thanks for an abundant slave harvest, the sharpened teeth of the high rampart were conspicuous for how few bodies were moving beyond.

Cullen knelt where forest met clearing, dew soaking his kneecap. He told himself he felt no fear. That he had made of his heart a lump of pig iron, cold and hard. But telling oneself a thing and living it were two different matters. He could hardly ignore the mad rushing of his blood, or the tremble in his hands or the fact that he was about to piss himself. Kurd Long Limb was poised, silent, to his immediate left, shield on his back, iron in one hand, finger and thumb of the other busy twisting the waxed points of his moustache. Andoc waited at his right, lean body curved into a crouch behind his own shield, sword naked, sun gleaming along its length.

Together they stared up at the sentries on the gate, which loomed above a bridge of planks spanning the ditch. There were only three of them, the metal of their armour and trinkets winking like shards of glass. Skulls of every kind lined the rampart all the way in both directions, a macabre string of oversized pearls. Black rags trembled gently from poles atop the gate, while two black shields had been nailed to the doors, warning outsiders of what lay beyond.

Out from the trees strode Five Thorns, breaking into a run, of sorts, as soon as he was sure he would not be pelted with sling stones. He possessed no Silurian words, and his common tongue would mark him out as foreign all too swiftly, so instead he affected a dragging gait, feigning vague injury, and waved his hands manically as he loped like a wounded stag towards the gate. The guards up on the rampart leaned between the stakes, peering down at him with first suspicion, then rising alarm, as he bellowed something unintelligible. His head remained dipped to obscure his face, and the bone-adorned helm they had taken from the kidnapped sentry was slanted further down his forehead than was customary, but between that recognisable piece of armour, and the bone-trimmed cloak, the effect appeared to be enough.

The gate groaned open. Five Thorns lumbered across the timber bridge, still babbling. Two of the three guards came down off the rampart to receive him.

Cullen braced. He wanted to go, to dash out from the treeline, but they would have the gate barred before he had covered half the distance. So he muttered to Taranis, begging a warrior's patience. He touched a finger to the horse amulet at his neck. Kissed the wheel emblem etched into the skin of his forearm.

One of the guards crumpled over a long blade. Five Thorns held onto its hilt, twisting viciously, jerking it savagely free, letting his victim fall heavily onto his face. The second guard's shout of alarm was drowned by Five Thorns' screamed challenge, and the pair went to the sword-dance with howls of rage.

Now Cullen went, because they could no longer shut the gate without moving the corpse, and because Ulla was already running, screaming, shield high in case of arrows or stones. It was chaos. It was noise. But that noise was coming from the attackers, for the rampart remained almost empty, and with every passing stride it became clear that Ulla's gamble had paid off. With all thought bent upon the brook, the garrison was nominal.

Cullen ran. He glanced over his shoulder to be sure there were no hidden spears coming out of the woods, a sweeping, iron ambush that would see nine lives step into the next. What he saw was open, empty ground.

A sling stone whined, scything the air an arm's length above his head. He raised the shield, belatedly, cursing his own sluggishness, and wincing for the next shot, but he was at the bridge now, rattling across the planks, the range too close for anything effective. And then he was through the gateway, still half open, Five Thorns and the second guard engaged in the sword-song that is the warrior's music.

The nine gathered, panting, whispering thanks to the gods each had invoked. Dan put an arrow into the guts of the slinger. Another in the spine of the guard who was fighting Five Thorns, receiving a brisk nod for his assistance. Then all was quiet.

A stream of commands spewed from Ulla's mouth, and they were moving into the dun, which, Cullen saw, was a cramped affair. Necessarily a fraction of the size of Verlamion or Calleva, given the confines of the hill's crest, the Silures appearing to have made every effort to squeeze as many buildings inside the fort as possible. Amongst the first of those, folk were scattering like startled geese. One or two of those bore the swarthy complexion common to the local tribe, but many more were fairer. Slaves, it would seem, preparing homes for the return of their households, and these, it was hoped, might prove less keen to cause a fuss at the sight of intruders. Still, they vanished into hanging linen, drying skins and the hovering coils of smoke from countless cooking fires, and many might well be making haste to the exit on the opposite side of the dun and the road down to the Castrogi Brook. The nine had to work quickly, and Cullen thanked Taranis for his assistance, because they knew where to go.

Kurd and Andoc held the south gate, Dan and White Tal moved deeper into the town to cover its northern section, while the rest followed Ulla as he took a sharp right turn towards the earthen walls at the fort's eastern extremity. It was a mean sort of place to Cullen's eyes. Small and miserable compared to the sprawling duns of the Belgic tribes. Roundhouses and pens nestled close, the alleys between them muddy and narrow, clogged with goat and fowl, the odd rooting pig, a perpetual veil of smoke loitering stubbornly.

They splashed through puddles and slid across patches of dung, always wary of sudden threat lurking beyond bend or lintel. But the populace had truly gone for the time being. The granaries and builders' yards were empty. The premises of spinners and weavers, potters and hurdle makers, leather workers, bronzesmiths and blacksmiths, all seemed deathly quiet. They moved unchallenged to the standing stone that the captured sentry had described, and the trio of generous structures behind it. The area, set back from the smaller, more homely shelters, was dotted with large vats full of liquid, the atmosphere contaminated with a pungent odour that only grew more potent as they approached.

The rock itself, about as tall and broad as a large man, was pale, smooth and carved with reliefs of stags, sea monsters and uncurling ferns. It had been draped with vines, from which hung a myriad of cleaned bones, large and small, the empty eyes of countless skulls staring back at them. Garn, just as hard and implacable as the stone, took up position beside it, immediately joined by Ulla. Five Thorns, still wearing the bone-embellished helm, slipped between two of the vats and made for the first of the big buildings, while Rues took the second.

Cullen, making for the last, bypassed the vats, which appeared to be brim-full with a solution comprised mainly of oak galls for tanning hides. Nearby lay a large midden, piled high with offcuts and debris from the skinning process, the dominating smell in a neighbourhood rich with odours. It stank of putrefying flesh, sodden ash, ripe piss and discarded galls, and he was forced to hold his breath as he rounded it.

The storehouse was a structure of wide planks set upright in a continuous trench, so that the walls were solid timber. It had wicker hurdles for doors, and Cullen pushed them away, bracing behind an extended sword. His eyes strained to adjust, desperate to identify danger in the sudden murk. It came in the form of an axe, short-hafted, stout-headed and dazzling as a shooting star as it sliced the fleeting beam of light. That beam, flooding over Cullen's shoulders as he shoved through the doors, saved his life, for he glimpsed that bright arc of metal with time enough only to check his forward motion and sway rearwards like an addled drunk. The axe-blade's edge zinged across his field of vision and was gone as he toppled, flailing, landing – squelching – on his back in something soft.

He stared at the sky. It was blue and white, turning rapid circles, black-spotted with crows. Red-spotted too. Blood. His own. He was vaguely aware of approaching feet and acutely aware of an encroaching, overpowering stench. Panicked, he heaved himself up to see the axeman approach. Then, baffled, he watched the axeman fall, softly grunting, right next to him, face-first in the stinking midden.

A girl stood where his attacker had been. She was dressed like a man, in tunic and braca, and in one hand she gripped a brutish-looking club. The other, pale and delicate, she extended to Cullen, who took it gratefully, heaving himself to his feet. Dazed, he felt his face. There was plenty of blood, but then head wounds bled like crimson fountains, so he groped until he found the nick in his brow. The axe had caught him, taken a sliver for its trouble, but nothing more. He wiped at it with his sleeve and looked at the girl, who was probably around his own age, tall and long-limbed.

'Who are you?' she asked in the common tongue, the brogue belonging to one of the Belgic tribes, not far removed from his own. She gave him an appraising look, as if inspecting a calf at market.

'Cullen of the Atrebates,' he said, feeling suddenly clumsy under her gaze. 'Cullen will do.' He cleared his throat thickly. 'I'm here to rescue you.'

'I am Betha of the Eceni. Betha will do.' The corner of her mouth twitched in an expression of amusement. 'And I cannot thank you enough.'

He was glad of the blood that would hopefully mask his blushes. 'Thank you,' he glanced down at the prone man, now drowning in shit, 'for that.'

She grinned, showing small, neat teeth behind thin lips. 'You are welcome.' Her complexion was milk-white, hair vixen-red, and nose prominent beneath eyes that were the colour of mint. She wore exceptionally thin wire bracelets on both wrists and a sunbeam pendant at her neck. She made a show of sniffing the air. 'But I fear you will need a bath.'

Suddenly aware of the midden's stench, he stepped back involuntarily and almost tripped on the prone Silures, only avoiding the indignity by grasping the club Betha held out. He realised it was a chair leg, broken off.

'We must take our leave,' he said hurriedly, composure marginally – if not entirely – regained.

'We?'

'Ulla Jagged Cliff and his nine.'

Her auburn brows came together. 'Jagged Cliff is of the Catuvellauni.'

'He is.'

'You serve him, Cullen of the Atrebates?' she asked, labouring the final word.

Cullen nodded stiffly. 'He is my lord.'

Evidently stowing her confusion for the more pressing need, Betha turned away. 'What are we waiting for?'

—

White Tal had found a stable.

'Can you ride?' Cullen asked as they moved quickly to the standing stone where the hawks had arranged to gather. Nine ponies waited there, skittish and nervous, corralled by Dan, Tal and Garn by way of bridles, ropes and growls.

Her derisive snort was answer enough. As she clambered onto the bare-backed beast, she enquired, 'Can you?'

Ulla kicked his pony towards them, offering a brief bow and exchanging a smattering of words verifying that she was indeed the person they had come to locate.

Betha stabbed a pale finger westward. 'They've gone down to the river, but they'll be back when the sun's highest. You'll have come from the south?'

Temporarily dumbstruck by her forthrightness, Ulla simply nodded.

'Follow me,' commanded the Eceni. 'The scarp is too steep for the horses, but I know a track that will take us to the low ground.'

And just like that, she was off, thrashing her pony's rump with the flat of her hand, leaving her liberators trailing in her wake.

Cullen caught Kurd Long Limb's eye. The older man grinned. 'A princess, truly.'

Cullen could not help but laugh as he watched the red haze of her long hair disappear round a bend. She was a remarkable creature. Delicate as glass, strong as iron. He wondered if this was what Aoife had been like before she had become the Dread.

He wondered, too, what this brave girl would become, if they could get her over Sabrina's Sea in one piece.

—

Betha had known what she was about. The track she had followed was an old forester's route, not immediately obvious and obscured by bramble and fern, but solid enough under hoof, snaking down through the trees to the foot of the slope and opening out into the meadows beneath the high wooded ridge.

They rode relentlessly, thankful that the ponies seemed hardy, their backs well-muscled and evidently accustomed to lacking a saddle. The thunder of their hooves, the splash as they crossed streams, the clatter as they negotiated rocky patches, it was music to Cullen's ears. They were away and flying, heading south and east, the wide estuary beckoning, their only concern the presence – or otherwise – of Lux's ferry.

Betha and Ulla led the way. Andoc and Cullen, the junior men, formed the rear. Gulls called high above, circling and swooping, erroneously expecting scraps of food to accompany the procession. Cullen embraced the face-numbing breeze as he galloped, resigned to the tickling beads of blood that still seeped from the axe-nick and ignoring the raucous birds. Until one cry was louder, shriller than the others. Nor did it come from above. It was not an unpleasant day. The sky was blue in the main and the clouds were light, yet, on hearing that shriek, a chill knifed its way down Cullen's spine all the same. For they had been caught.

—

The shrieking men were riders. Their mounts were bigger than the hawks' stolen ponies, better fed and fleeter of foot, and the distance between hunter and quarry diminished all too quickly. There were a dozen, forming a loose line across the fields, and they came out of the northwest, from the direction of the hillfort, tracking Ulla's party like so many hounds. Their horses were clothed in white bones and the shields strapped to their backs were blackened with pitch, and their fluttering pennants were black rags. Some wore coats of mail, others pieces of plate iron or bronze that glinted in the sun, but most were naked from the waist up, smeared in paints of white and black, and clothed, like their horses, in bones. Their shouts carried on the wind. Triumphal, like barking dogs closing on a scent. Challenges to single combat or all-out brawl.

Ulla bade his group veer south when they passed a hornbeam with a canted trunk that had developed in a distinctive spiral. The route took them over a shallow, water-filled ditch and into a patch of impossibly profuse scrub, overgrown and tangled with thorns. The scrub was almost impenetrable, its spiny tentacles nearly as thick as a man's wrist, but bisected by a narrow animal trail that was rapidly expanded, pulverised by their crashing hooves. On the far side was the nemeton at which they had paused before. The yew grove, marked by mossy stone-stacks and dead-eyed carvings of severed heads.

This time they entered the sacred space without consideration for the gods' sensibilities, the alternative being swift death. They drew up in a crash of hoofbeats, earthen clods flung up in all directions, and dismounted, looking to Ulla, who immediately sent Dan back to the entrance. Five Thorns took his axe to the opposite side, where he began to lop branches from the yews.

Out on the track, the black riders had reached the ditch and the trickling rill at its base. They pulled up, hooves flailing, stopping short of the narrow gulley, though whether that was out of respect for the nemeton or fear of arrows, it was impossible to tell. They drew back, sensibly wary, when Dan presented his bow, waving it high like a battle-standard.

Cullen followed his friend through the tunnel in the brambles that now functioned as a natural breastwork. He had taken the sling stones from his pouch and now crouched at the mouth of the passage, lining up the stones on the grass. Big river pebbles all, smooth and round, carefully selected. He knelt before them, reverently, asking the gods who dwelt in this nemeton to imbue them with killing power. They were unassuming objects, like grey eggs amongst the dewy blades, but Cullen had felled more than one predator with such a weapon. His mind swam back to those vanished times of lonely hills and still woods.

The riders withdrew further, holding their ground just out of bowshot. They glowered, snarled oaths, but declined to venture any closer. A couple disappeared, perhaps seeking a route round the back, but Ulla had selected this ground because of the near-impenetrable terrain of branch, trench and bramble that stretched a long way in both directions. The Silures had the numbers. He was gambling that they would opt for a direct assault.

Behind Cullen, back beyond the thicket, Ulla's voice rang out, putting his men to work. He could hear Betha too, arguing her usefulness, and it was no surprise when she came into view at the far end of the bramble tunnel, clutching the makeshift club with which she had demolished her guard.

The riders lingered out beyond the ditch. A score of bone-clad ghouls, pitiless, expectant.

'What are they waiting for?' Dan muttered as he fingered the fletching on one of his prized arrows. 'They could ride us down if they wanted. We cannot outrun them.' He held the weapon up. 'I am running low.'

'If they come straight at us, they'll lose men,' Cullen said. 'They're thinking.' He shrugged. 'Maybe they'll starve us out.'

Dan patted his belly. 'That won't take long.'

The beginnings of a bleak smile moved the corners of Cullen's mouth, but the gesture reversed almost instantly. His body felt suddenly cold. A dark line was moving through the trees beyond the ditch. The scrape and rustle of branches seemed as loud as blasting carnyxes. Cullen braced himself. Swallowed down a surge of stinging bile. Caught a glimpse of white through the breaks in the undergrowth. Bones. Boiled to a pristine glow. The occasional patch of plaid cloth too. Metal. Wheels. Pale skin darkened by woad. Men, women, weapons.

They came into the open. A warband of chariots. Eyes bright, teeth bared. They turned, almost as one, to stare into the trees from whence they had emerged, and from those dark shadows trundled another chariot, larger than the rest, drawn by two white ponies and escorted by riders bearing javelins and black shields. The Silures bowed before the chariot, honouring the man perched in the rear, gently swaying with its movement.

'Lestinos?' said Cullen.

'Who else?' said Dan.

The man on the chariot was ancient. Swaddled like a babe in furs, he was veiny and brittle-looking, as though his skin was made of autumn leaves. His hair was thinning and long, threaded with the tiny bones of toes and fingers, while around his neck hung more bones, larger ones, which appeared to have images of human heads whittled along their pale lengths.

Footsteps padded through the grass behind Cullen. He twisted to see Ulla, Betha and the rest stride up through the bramble tunnel.

'Gods flay me for my arrogance,' Ulla hissed, almost to himself.

Cullen followed his chief's gaze. It took him back to the biggest chariot and its grim escort. Amongst the faces he saw the man they had captured on the hillfort's slope. The man Garn had intended to kill and who Ulla had spared. In that moment he understood Ulla's self-reproach, and how the Silures had come upon them so swiftly. The warning might have reached the thanksgiving ceremony even before they had located Betha.

'I'll put one in him,' Dan said darkly, recognising the same face.

'Save it,' Ulla's voice came from behind and above. 'He is not important.' He seemed to sigh. 'Cernunnos was truly his ally.'

A tense silence followed the words, the implication stark. If the lords of the Otherworld had favoured that single Silures, did it not follow that they would favour the rest?

'The gods are capricious,' White Tal said, addressing the tacit concern that hung like a pall between them.

The spear-riders waited as the king's chariot pulled ahead. It bumped and jerked over a layer of tufty turf and came up close to the rill. Behind it, a single warrior dismounted from another vehicle, walking with long strides in the wake of his chief. The warrior was clearly huge, even framed against the large vehicle. To the side of the king trotted a horse of brown and white. Cullen's eyes were drawn to that beast, though at first he could not ascertain why. He watched it come, only realising what was amiss as it came closer. It was small and mean, and so skinny its every rib might have been visible had it not worn the ribs of another horse, long dead. Indeed, the little bay was clothed in an array of bones. Far more than all the others. Each piece a brilliant white, cleaned to perfection, and reassembled using straps and thongs and pins, the parts articulated expertly, joints shifting with the movement of the living creature beneath. It was a suit made from an entire skeleton, save the spine, which had been omitted to make room for a four-pommelled saddle. On that high perch, swaying along with the skeleton-horse's natural gait, rode an entirely naked woman, with raven-black hair that fell across her back and breasts. Her ash-ringed eyes raked over the Catuvellauni, resting finally on Ulla with a look that could skewer rock.

Time seemed to slow. Catuvellauni and Silures eyed one another across a ditch narrow enough for a man to simply hop. The former could not run any further, the latter reluctant to risk a frontal attack.

From the bone-chariot, the king shifted his rump. 'To whom do I speak?' he called, his voice crackling like dried twigs under foot.

Ulla cleared his throat. 'I am Ulla, of the Catuvellauni.'

The woman on the bone-horse twisted in her saddle to face Lestinos, her long hair shifting slightly to reveal the shadow of a nipple behind the tresses. 'The Jagged Cliff.'

'I recognise your fame,' Lestinos acknowledged with the faintest of nods, 'and I wish I could welcome so esteemed a warrior to my lands, but, alas, you trespass this fine day.'

'That was not our intent, lord king,' Ulla replied, invoking a clear, stentorian tone that seemed to echo around the nemeton, disturbing magic older than the very land into which it had been cleaved.

'Lies!' the woman screeched, so unexpectedly that it startled her own mount, sending the snorting beast into a sideways skitter.

Lestinos held up a withered hand in placation. When she had become still, he addressed Ulla again. 'Forgive my Wise One. Erien of Mona offers only the coldest welcome to those who would trespass.'

'Perhaps I might offer her my cloak,' Ulla said archly.

The dark-haired woman hissed at him like an incensed cat. Lestinos ignored her. 'That said, Ulla War-Giver, it is customary to seek permission before you cross a man's kingdom.' His eyes took in the others. His face was thin but sharp, the accumulation of years acting like a whetstone on his features. 'Especially when accompanied by a party so clearly ill-equipped for peace.'

'My humble apologies, lord king,' Ulla replied. 'I would seek permission now.'

Lestinos's face cracked in a slow smile featuring more gums than teeth. He spoke over his shoulder. 'What think you, Tellos?'

From round the chariot sidled the giant. As big as Caratacos's champion, Sego, or perhaps even bigger. Wrapped in dusty furs, he appeared like a ragged bear, except for the helmet of bronze that crowned his massive head, topped by a bronze eagle with hinged wings that only increased his height. There was a pale scar along his chin, a long line of puckered flesh that looked like the footprints of a lizard in sand. His hair, long and brown at his shoulders, was shot through with objects, though Cullen could not discern their nature.

'I think,' said Tellos in a voice like summer thunder, 'that I need some new ears.'

And Cullen realised what had been strung in the clumpy braids of the big man's hair. Severed ears, big and small, ragged and blackened. Trophies, celebrating violence.

Lestinos giggled; a childlike, querulous sound. He stood, shedding the pelts to expose an almost bare torso that was painted in ash markings and wrapped with strips of cloth beneath the navel. He touched the fabric, then the charms hanging at his breast. One was a hunk of black stone, polished to a mirror gleam, the other a wood carving of a leering face, eyes hollow, tongue lolling. 'You have made a grave mistake, Ulla Jagged Cliff, so let us not trade empty words. I know you have the Eceni bitch. Give her back, or my champion will have your ears, and I will have your bones, boiled bare and nailed to my gates.' He glanced down at the woman on the bone-horse. 'Or Erien will have you, and that will go worse.'

Ulla's harsh face creased in a look of dramatic regret. 'Alas, I cannot do that. My king commands—'

'King?' Lestinos's high voice became shriller still, a score of festering grudges leaking out behind the bitter word. 'The Sun Hound has gone to the next. His whelps are not worthy of loyalty, nor reverence.'

Erien kicked her mount forward, eyes blazing down at Ulla as if she tried to melt him with the heat of her enmity. 'Togodubnos has a loud bark,' she called out, her tone, surprisingly husky, incongruous coming from so delicate a frame, 'but his bite is weak. Caratacos has a bite, we understand, but not a shred of wit. And Adminios has the brains, but no honour. They are usurpers, only. The gods have abandoned them.' She closed her eyes, revealing another pair, painted upon her lids, that glared down, wide and soulless. 'I have seen it. Seen their destruction.'

'If the Catuvellauni,' Lestinos said, 'are fool enough to hand the whelps power, so be it. But I will not be their vassal.'

'I came for the girl,' said Ulla, 'and I mean to leave with her. That is my only concern.'

Lestinos spoke. 'The only way you are leaving here, Ulla Jagged Cliff, is by travelling to the next life.'

Erien kicked again so that she was at the edge of the rill. 'I will cut the life from you, so that you stagger to the next, calling for your mother.' She had spoken softly this time, as if telling a fairy-tale to a child. A flicker of movement at her hips, and the bone-horse sidled along the ditch line. She half-yawned, stretching as she reached a particular spot, for all the world as though she were out for a spring jaunt, but now the sun was directly behind and above her, so that her enemies were forced to squint up at her silhouette. A sly move, Cullen thought, by a woman who knew the business of unsettling an adversary. 'My dogs will lap at your blood and my slaves will chew your eyes.'

'You would risk war with the Catuvellauni?' Ulla asked of Lestinos, pointedly disregarding the Wise One.

'The world is a drab thing when you are as old as me,' Lestinos said, a wistful island amid a sea of glares and threats. 'Dull and grey. I would gladly burn it all, just to give it colour, one last time.' He licked thin lips, seemed to sigh, then signalled for his driver to turn the white ponies about. 'Another thing you learn when you reach my age, Ulla Jagged Cliff, is that time is not your ally. There will be no tarrying, no opportunity to reconsider.' The animals whickered and snorted as they eased away. The black riders turned too. Lestinos twisted to peer back at Ulla. 'Give me the girl,' he called, 'or Tellos will tear her from you. Your bones will adorn my wagon. We will sup from your empty skull.'

CHAPTER EIGHTEEN

'Hawks,' Ulla snapped, bringing them to him as a huntsman might summon his hounds. Except this day he, his nine and a princess of a rival tribe were the quarry. 'We will defend the nemeton.'

'How?' Andoc, face twisted into a grimace of worry, had already unsheathed his sword, and he gripped it hard now, white knuckles betraying his fear. 'They bring too many spears.'

Ulla's pale eyes slid to Cullen's. 'Speak to your blade-brothers as you spoke to me.'

Cullen tried and failed to meet the collective gaze of Garn, Kurd and the rest. Great men of renown, worthy of their battle-names. He managed to swallow dryly. 'We always knew they might run us to ground.' He looked back through the gap between the dense brambles, catching sight of the clearing they obscured. 'This place can be held.'

Andoc did not deign to look at him, instead keeping his baleful stare firmly fixed upon their leader. 'This scrap of gristle speaks for you, lord? Makes decisions for you?'

A ghost of annoyance rippled across Ulla's features, fleeting but unmistakable. 'Do you question my ability to command?'

'I do not,' Andoc answered, head visibly retracting on that long neck, like the turtles that had occasionally graced the markets of Calleva. 'Never would I.' Now he looked at Cullen. 'But I question his.'

'As your chief,' Ulla growled, 'I tell you to listen and take heed.'

Andoc sniffed haughtily, prudently holding his peace. Cullen said, 'I did not take my tribe's tests. I did not learn warcraft in the halls of our great men.' He glanced, with difficulty, from one face to the next. Tal, Dan, Five Thorns. All sun-burnished faces, tough as leather, hard as stone. All better men than he. 'My father went to the next life when I was a babe. I remained in my mother's house, helping her with my sisters, swept the floors, ground the grain, tended our animals.' He licked parched lips, wrestled to overcome bonds of timidity that threatened to lock each word in his throat, never to emerge. 'I am not fit to lead you. I am barely fit to hold a sword. But I believe we have a chance, by the grace of the gods.'

'A chance?' Five Thorns said, flicking the killing edge of his great axe with a broad, filthy thumbnail.

Cullen faced the west, where the shadow-forms of the Silures cavalry and charioteers shifted ominously in the gloom. Lestinos had left fewer than thirty, more than a score. Ample numbers for the hunt. The black shields would be regrouping at this very moment, calling orders and encouragement to one another, preparing for the final assault. 'Think not of them as an army, to be faced and fought, man to man. Think of them as a pack of wolves.'

Garn's bushy brows came together as one. 'What are you saying, boy?'

'I am saying that wolves can be beaten. They can be frightened off. They can be killed.'

As the Silures warriors slowly emerged, dismounting, and forming a ragged spear-line amongst the branches at the tree-edge, Cullen told them what he had told Ulla. The others listened, prayed to the gods, high and low, prayed to Cernunnos, who ruled the forests and whose acolytes dwelt amongst the stacked stones of this very grove, and to their own ancestors, whose blood coursed through their veins and whose strength and courage resided within each of them.

White Tal glanced up, shielding his eyes against the bright disc of the sun. 'The chariot wheel of Belinos is ablaze.'

'Do you think,' Five Thorns asked, following his distant squint, 'he rides for war?'

'He rides for the brave,' Ulla answered firmly. 'For us.'

Garn intoned, 'May he ride with us.'

'Life with glory,' Kurd said. 'Death with honour.'

'Life with glory, death with honour!' every other voice echoed.

Betha of the Eceni came to stand in their midst. She hefted the club to her shoulder, a look of grim determination hardening her soft features. 'Death with honour.' She looked to every face in turn. 'Thank you, men of the Catuvellauni. If I live out this day, your labours will not be forgotten.'

Ulla regarded them in turn. 'We have set our trap. Let them tumble in.'

They growled ascent, clasped hands, butted heads, spoke warm words, invoked ancient powers.

To Andoc and Cullen, he said, 'You are brothers. Not of blood, nor tribe, but of battle, of iron. Ulla's hawks, together.'

'Lord, I—' Andoc began.

Ulla's huge palm came up to curtail his complaint. 'Your bond will be made this day. A man cannot choose his family. He is born into it, and sometimes, when the gods deign, a second family is thrust upon him, forged in a furnace of blood and suffering. Do not resist this truth, either of you.'

Cullen looked up at Andoc. His rival's face tightened, unwilling to argue but unable to acquiesce. He bowed, retreated, following Garn, Kurd, Tal, Five Thorns and Rues into the brambles and the nemeton's inner sanctum.

Ulla held out his hand to Cullen, who clasped it as hard as he could, if just to prevent his own fingers from snapping in the warrior's grip. The big man pulled him in so that they butted heads. He did the same with Dan. 'Courage of Belinos to you both.' He grinned at Cullen. 'Perhaps Taranis will favour us too, Cullen Lightning-Bringer.'

The black shields attacked.

It was slow at first, a black swathe, walking into the light of the open ground. Bleached bones, painted faces, bared teeth. At the front, the huge form of Tellos bellowed like an enraged boar, the severed ears of defeated foes suddenly so conspicuous.

Ulla had gone, retreated through the brambles, dragging Betha with him. Only Dan and Cullen remained to face the might of King Lestinos's spearmen, and Cullen looked to his sling, the sight of it transporting him to a simpler time. He tugged the leather cords, testing them, snapping flat the pouch suspended between. The tension felt strong, reassuring. At the end of one cord was a loop, and at the end of the other, a knot. He examined them quickly, looking for frailties. Finding none, he stooped to put one of the stones in the pouch.

They were coming now, the black shields, trampling the grass of the open ground, screaming the usual challenges, devouring space before the shallow ditch. Amongst them strode a thickset man clutching a tall pole, its crosspiece hung with severed heads, tied at the hair, the yellowing, flaky faces slack and sightlessly staring.

A twang at Cullen's ear as Dan loosed an arrow. It thudded into the standard-bearer's chest, plucking him off his feet, sending the heads rolling in all directions and eliciting howls of rage from his comrades. The Silures broke into a run.

Cullen slipped the cord loop over the middle finger of his right hand, at the same time jamming the knot between thumb and forefinger, making an oval ring of the weapon, its lowest point cradling the stone. He picked a target, a short, bearded man wearing a circlet of finger bones about his curly pate.

Someone threw a spear. Cullen flinched, but it fell short, smacking into the turf between him and the ditch.

Cullen twisted at the waist so that his left shoulder pointed at the bearded warrior, shifted his feet, left advanced before the right, and whipped his wrist and forearm in a savage circle, swinging the sling in a great arc, building power and speed with each revolution, feeling the air pulse at the side of his head.

It was all a matter of timing. Of gauging distance, adjusting for terrain, wind, and the target's height. Something Cullen had done since he was a scrawny child. Something that came as second nature. And men were slower than wolves; taller, easier to hit.

He released the knot, the cord snapping out at the extent of the arc like the tongue of a lizard, and the stone sung as it scythed the air. The bearded man vanished. Then Cullen saw the soles of his bare feet, twitching in the grass. He crouched again, chose another pebble, kissed it and placed it in the sling, and all the while the black shields were coming.

Tellos was the figurehead, at the very front, brandishing a short-hafted axe in one fist and a sword in the other. His face was taut with malevolence under that grandiose helmet, atop which the eagle's wings flapped in time with his gait. Cullen sent a stone his way, aiming just below the intricate bronze bird, but if he so much as clipped the huge Silures, it did not show.

Dan was loosing like a man possessed, mercilessly snatching the skeleton warriors out of the advancing line, but his arrows were diminishing fast. Cullen fought to keep up, flinging his rocks to smash metal and bone and flesh. The exultant chorus of bellows was fraying, watered down by screams of anguish, and that sent a wave of hope through his limbs, quickening his arm as it whirled and snapped and whirled again.

The Silures were losing cohesion, faltering, but there were too many of them, and they were too close to turn back now, too close to stop.

Cullen sent a stone low, shattering a kneecap. Another went high, burying itself in the forehead of a female fighter whose mouth and chin were obscured by the lower jaw of a badger, giving her the appearance of great white fangs. The top half of her head splintered, flipping back like the crown of an eggshell, and a spray of red and white misted the air as she dropped.

Cullen stared, stunned by his own deed.

Dan pawed at his elbow, shouting something that he did not heed.

'Now!' the archer cried again. 'Go!'

This time the words lanced his reverie. Grisly astonishment melted away, transforming to action. Because the Silures were leaping the rill.

He abandoned his precious cache and followed Dan into the tunnel that cut through the thick mass of brambles, snagging his braca on thorns as he dashed along its length, picturing the iron boss of a pitch-daubed shield smashing into his spine. No such blow came, but he could hear them howling at his back, and he knew they must be funnelling into the thicket even as he emerged into the grove on the far side.

They ran across the clearing, between the stacks of mossy river stones, turning as they reached the far side, hard against the edge of the depression where the land fell steeply away. Drawing swords, they faced the first of the oncoming black shields, chief of which was Tellos himself. Cullen's mouth was dry as ash, his bowels water. Never had he felt more out of place – more like a naïve child – than at this moment. He tried desperately to recall Farrad's teachings, but still knew he was hefting his blade like a clumsy woodsman's axe. He heard Farrad's mocking gravel-laugh, then realised the laughter came from Tellos, who was a mountain of sheer brawn up close. For a moment Cullen stared up at him, immobile as the stone stacks, and found himself absently wondering what Tellos's battle-name would be. Ear-Snatcher? Head-Taker? He realised he would never know, but he hoped, at least, there was honour in death at so fearsome a man's hands.

Then another named man came into view. And another, and a third. Ulla Jagged Cliff, Garn Grey Boulder, Kurd Long Limb. And they were hacking and slashing at Tellos, who reeled away from Cullen to parry their blows, and it was as if a great bear had been set upon by so many war hounds.

Cullen fought. He had little choice, for more of the black shields had burst into the nemeton in their leader's wake, but there was no conscious decision to be made. Up came his sword in one hand, his knife in the other, and he was blocking, slashing, stabbing with the rest, utterly desperate, utterly unthinking, only the roar of his own blood surging in his ears like a rain-swollen river. He kicked one enemy away, shouldered a woman to the ground, slammed his sword hilt into a tar-black shield and thrust his knife through the empty socket of a leering sheep's skull, puncturing the living eyeball beyond. He stooped quickly to collect up a discarded enemy spear, jabbing it to keep the Silures at range. All the while, he was backing away, keeping close to the others. Andoc was near, White Tal, Five Thorns and Rues Seeker. Ulla, Garn and Kurd disengaged from Tellos, who breathed heavily, bled from a dozen slash-wounds, but still fought like a crazed beast. The monstrous Fomorii, crawled up from the ocean depths. There were no shields, so there could be no fighting wall, but the nine came together in a line of blood spatters and bristling iron, retreating slowly, step by step. At their backs the ground was a tangled mesh of leaves and branches, felled by Five Thorns and piled thick at the edge of the grove. Beyond that, Betha of the Eceni, club upright in both hands, stood like a cornered animal, eyes wide and wild, lips paired back, teeth grinding.

The line shortened as the Catuvellauni scampered across the branches. They had to go in single file, one after the next, careful to watch the placement of their feet, and all the while the black shields pressed in. Andoc went first, then Rues, then another and another. It was Cullen's turn, and he ran for it, praying that Taranis would keep his steps firmly on the single broad log that spanned the deep hole. Behind him he could hear the yells of the Silures as they leapt to the pursuit.

And with that, they began to fall. Crashed, in fact, with a chaotic, deafening, horrified din through the loose covering of branches to the pit below. The first few plunged through the loose, leafy carpet suspended over the hole, and the next, bunched so closely, tumbled over the freshly revealed lip like so many sleepwalkers, and momentum carried over those behind. It was a violent, shocking and utterly beautiful thing to behold.

A trap sprung.

Cullen turned when he reached the far side, springing with a great leap off the log. As he watched the calamity unfold, he felt hope surge through his chest, pulsing ice and flame all at once to scale his neck and tingle at his face. The wolf pit was swallowing the pack, and he could not help but remember the hills about Calleva, where his goats would graze, and his days were filled with watchfulness. He would scan the sky for raptors on the wing and search the dawn for sly foxes and plunging owls. But the darkest nights were a place of horrors. They were the times reserved for the wolves, and those grey monsters would prowl in their skulking groups, slipping, wraith-like, through shadows cast by gnarled trees, eyes glittering like gems, and there was no chance a lone boy with a knife and a sling could hope to fight them off. Which was why he set traps. Lots of them. Good ones.

He would dig them himself in those carefree days, before burning houses and slaughtered kin. Before disfigured faces and crazed Wise Ones and flame-sacrifices and the intervention of gods. He would find soft patches of soil along known wolf-tracks and sink his pits deep, baiting them and concealing them with branches. The wolves, deadly and vicious as they were, had not the cunning of the fox. They could barely resist the smell of rotting meat, and once that thrilling scent had snagged in their muzzles they would track their prize to the pit, single-minded and unremitting, there to tumble in a welter of limbs and fur and yelps and snarls, imprisoned in those dark depths, scrabbling helplessly at the loose soil, until the dawn would bring Cullen and Cullen would bring death.

Here he was again. Wolves in a trap. This time, though, he had not had to dig the hole. It had been there, waiting in his memory since the first time they had taken rest in the ancient grove. All this pit had required was disguise.

A strong hand grasped his shoulder. Ulla, grinning. 'Good lad,' the warrior said, eyeing the mayhem with evident satisfaction. 'I confess I had my doubts.'

'About me?'

He shrugged. 'Moranna forced the king's hand. I'm a cynic.'

'And now?'

Ulla grinned again. 'You'll do.'

Cullen's heart soared. He had the Silures spear and he went to the edge of the exposed hole, and he stabbed down, killing the nearest man with one firm thrust. The black shields were in disarray, scrabbling at the slope, but it was too steep to climb. They could wrestle their way to the sides, through the tatters of the collapsed roof to the shallower slopes, and in time, he felt sure, that thought would occur. But for now, panic had them in its grip, and they knew only forwards or backwards. A few brave souls jumped for the tree trunk that, alone, bridged the gap, but any managing to grip the bark soon lost fingers to Catuvellaunian iron.

Someone called out in shrill alarm. It was a high-pitched, blood-freezing babble in the common tongue, and the words snatched Cullen's attention from his human wolves. On the far side, the Silures side, he caught sight of Dan, stumbling rearwards, slashing his bow stave in a frantic arc as though swatting at a swarm of angry bees. But there were no insects bearing down on him. Only Tellos.

'By the ancients,' Ulla breathed at Cullen's flank, seeing the stranded archer for himself. Then his sword was up and he was bounding over the log, indifferent to the grasping hands of his enemies beneath. 'Protect the girl!'

Cullen ignored the command, following in his lord's wake. He did not know why. Did not think. He was running. Just running.

Tellos lunged. His great axe came up in an arc from the waist. Dan recoiled, screwing shut his eyes, and he brought up his bow, which was no more of a shield than a green sapling might have been, and the huge blade met with his face, mangling the mouth, smashing teeth and lifting the archer clean off his feet.

Then Ulla was amongst them, between them, snarling savage curses at the ear-draped Silures who grinned as a malevolent ghoul might grin, and brought up the reddened axe once more. He had two others with him, behind him. Bone-clad and jeering, but they hovered out of arm's reach, unwilling to face the Jagged Cliff or the death-pit he had miraculously, frighteningly conjured from the depths of a sacred grove. So the two fought, circling, coming together in a smash of skull-ringing metal, spitting at one another as their grimacing faces came together, feigning scornful laughter as they parted in a hard shove.

Dan lay to the side, curled up, a giant foetus. His twitching legs kicked one of the stacks so that stones toppled and rolled.

Ulla lunged, quick as an adder, the tip of his sword taking a chunk out of Tellos's forehead. Blood spurted, free and fast. Tellos grunted in grim acknowledgement. His eyes were wild, bright as gems. As if the scarlet smeared all over his face was a sinister, cunning mask behind which he was planning his revenge. And indeed he was, for he seemed to slip on a patch of his own blood, turning an ankle with a deep groan of pain, but when Ulla darted in for the kill, the Silures champion managed to wrench his big frame to the side with shocking agility, sliding beyond the oncoming blade and swinging the great axe in a scything blow that took Ulla square in the chest.

It all happened so quickly that Cullen barely had a chance to digest what he had witnessed. Dan prone, Ulla collapsed on his back, the long haft of an axe protruding from his torso like a ploughshare in soil. Tellos standing over them both. Bloody and triumphal.

It had gone wrong. So very wrong. But then Cullen was moving, running, charging at the huge, bearded, ear-adorned killer, tears hot in his eyes, throat burning as he screamed, and Tellos was turning, recognising him, shouting a challenge for him to take his place in the next life. But Cullen had the spear. Tellos, for all his stature, all his prowess, could not match the range of the tapered, iron-tipped shaft of ash that careened towards him. For a moment he seemed to recognise the danger, for his dark eyes widened and his big shoulders braced, but then he smiled, because his two sheepish acolytes were finally coming up, their nerve regained at the sight of Ulla's defeat, and they were raising shields and drawing swords and Cullen knew that he was about to die.

Andoc overtook him. The tall, willow-framed man, who hated even to share the same air as Cullen, bellowed for him to hold his courage, slamming into the brace of shields with a yowl of defiance and rage fit to startle the gods themselves. The three barrelled away, collapsing together, and for a brief, sublime moment, the way was clear. Cullen drove the spear hard at Tellos, upwards at an angle, so that the leaf-shaped point slipped into the shaggy hedge of a beard and crunched into flesh and sinew and bone. Blood flowed, down the spear, down the giant's chest, over his necklace of severed ears and out of his mouth. He looked surprised as he fell to his knees and his eyes rolled, white and bright, like the eyes of a spooked horse. Almost admiring, as if he were impressed that someone had finally done it. He babbled a stream of nonsense as he died, bloody bubbles popping over crimson-slick lips.

Probably he fell, but Cullen did not see it. He had gone to assist Andoc, drawing his sword again, punching its tip into the base of one of the Silures who tangled on the ground with his grudging comrade. The other was knocked unconscious by Andoc's headbutt, and then the skinny man was up, nodding thanks, and Rues was with them, Kurd too, and between them they dragged the broken forms of Dan and Ulla back to the toppled tree trunk and over to the far side of the pit.

The fight was over now. The stragglers on the Silures side had coalesced around Tellos's corpse, slack-jawed and scared. A flock without their shepherd. The warriors in the hole had no more stomach for it either, cowed as they were beneath the poised blades of Ulla's hawks. And those wielding the razor-edged iron were in no mood for mercy, for on the far side of the makeshift pit, their namesake lay dying.

Ulla Jagged Cliff, named man and illustrious war-giver of the Catuvellauni, stared up at the blue sky, fighting for breaths that were shallow, rasping and flecked with pink spittle. The axe had made a ruin of his ribs and everything beneath. His crag of a face, creased even in serene times, was a mass of gorges and valleys, cleaved by pain. He spluttered, pitiful and wet, wafting a bloody hand to be heard.

'Cullen,' he managed to utter through lips bubbling red, the sound grating, feeble. 'Andoc.'

The pair exchanged a glance, went to crouch on either side, each taking a hand to let him know they were there, unsure if his dimming eyes were already peering into the dreaming realm.

Ulla looked up, between them, wincing. 'Tell me,' he ground out the words, as if each were lodged in his throat, 'the three prongs... of the noble triad.'

'To do no evil,' Cullen answered.

'To honour the gods,' Andoc said.

They shared a look, nodding, and saying together, 'And to practise bravery.'

Ulla smiled sightlessly, spoke with great effort. 'Remember these things. Courage and honour. That is why a warrior does what he does. How he earns his name.' He paused, riding a wave of pain. 'This is the hero's forge,' he said eventually, tapping his slick fingertips on the trampled grass, 'in which nines are bonded and great names made. You have made your names together this day, as brothers. Put aside your differences, for you are warriors of the Catuvellauni, now and for the ages.' He released Cullen's hand and flailed in the direction of the collapsed stacks. 'Let me touch the stones. It will soothe my journey.'

Cullen shook his head. 'I will carry you home, lord.'

'I am heavy.'

'I am strong.'

Ulla's face convulsed as he coughed up a dark gout of blood which spewed over his chin and neck. Andoc scrambled to gather up some of the fallen river stones, piling them against Ulla's body like mossy buttresses. One he handed to Cullen, who placed it in the dying man's hands.

'It is a place of raw magic, this,' Ulla said, whispering now.

'These stones,' White Tal said solemnly, 'were placed here by the old people, with the knowledge of the old gods. If you stand amongst them at dawn on the winter solstice, you would see the sun rise over Sabrina's Sea.'

Ulla's eyelids fluttered weakly. 'A good place to step into the next life, wouldn't you say?' He let his head loll to the side, eyeing Cullen. 'We have won because of you, goatherd of the Atrebates.' His hard face cracked as he forced a smile despite the pain. 'You have repaid my faith. Your ancestors would be proud, as I am proud.'

'Lord, I—'

'You will be a great man,' Ulla croaked softly, as if Cullen had not spoken. 'Your name will carry fame.' He heaved in a crackling lungful of air, the effort almost too great for his broken body. 'A storm gathers over the sea. You must lead our people to safety. Moranna saw it.' He coughed, bloody and ragged. 'Now I see it.'

The wreckage of his chest became still.

Cullen sat back, numb. It felt as though he had toppled into ice cold water, never to thaw. Above the pit, a magpie strutted along the fallen trunk.

The fight had gone out of the black shields, for they had no intention of risking a spear to the head, and the Catuvellauni were unharried as they reclaimed their mounts and rode into the east. It was a subdued party for all that. Ulla was dead, Dan grievously wounded, but the Eceni girl had been liberated and that had been their task, no matter the toll.

The two casualties had been lashed over the backs of their mounts, making the journey slow, but they could not leave Ulla to the vengeance of Lestinos. When the elderly king discovered his defeat, the gods only knew what fate would befall their leader's sacred remains. They took him, then, to the ferry over Sabrina's Sea, and only when they had reached the Dobunni shore did they take one of Lux's spare crafts and set the Jagged Cliff's corpse within. As the light dimmed, they made a fire of the vessel and its mortal cargo, and pushed it downstream.

'On to the next,' Garn rumbled as they watched the flame-lit boat drift out on the tide, bound inexorably for the grey deep of the Clear Sea.

The others repeated the phrase they all knew so well, never having expected to utter it in the wake of this particular corpse.

—

'They looked scared at the end,' Betha said, swaying with the roll of her mount.

On reaching the south bank of the Sabrina, they had returned to the isolated farm for their horses, relieved to discover them well-fed and ready to ride. The night was clear and not too cold, the roads shining under a bright moon, so they pressed on, striving deep into Dobunni territory, keen to put distance between them and the Silures.

'Wolves, without their leader,' Cullen remarked, riding alongside the Eceni princess. The fact that the hawks, too, were leaderless was not lost on him. Garn had naturally taken on Ulla's role, but the loss felt spear-tip sharp.

'Lestinos lives,' White Tal said. His mount led Dan's, on which the injured bowman had once again been tied. The one mercy coming from the feverish stupor now enveloping him was that he barely seemed aware of his surroundings.

'Erien too,' Betha added.

'But not Tellos,' Cullen said. 'Not their named man. Their war-giver.'

'Soon as he fell,' Kurd agreed, 'the others had not the bones for a scrap. They wanted only to scurry back up their hill and cower from Ulla's hawks.'

'You covered the hole with branches,' Betha said to Cullen. Her neat teeth and lily-white skin seemed to shine under the moon. 'Clever.'

Embarrassed, he shrugged. 'It occurred to me when we passed through a few nights ago. Ulla expected the Silures to pursue. He asked for ways to obstruct them. We had more than one choice, but in the end, the pit was nearest when they caught us.'

'Your idea?'

'I tended the goats at home. Laid many traps. If you slaughter the chief wolf, the pack falls apart.'

'Cullen Wolf Scourge,' Rues Seeker spoke in the silvered dark.

'Wolf Scourge,' several voices echoed the sentiment, their deep, hard tones like honey to Cullen's ears.

Ashamed of the rising pride, he looked across at Betha again. 'Why would Lestinos risk war for—?'

Her auburn eyebrows arched. 'For me?'

'For any reason,' he blurted, glad the night would conceal his blushes.

'The grubby old weasel is dying. A canker here...' She pointed to her midriff, nose wrinkling. 'It stinks.'

Cullen remembered the wrappings at the old man's waist. He remembered, too, the king's reckless desire. 'Burn the world.'

'He seeks excitement,' she said. 'Thinks he'll kick a few nests before the end. See if any hornets come out.'

'The hornet being High King Togodubnos,' White Tal said ruefully.

Betha nodded. 'And my father, King Antedios.'

'That's why he took you?' Cullen asked. 'To enrage your father?'

'To enrage the Eceni nation. And it would have worked. Erien was intending to cut my throat. Lestinos was to drink my blood.'

'The Wise claim it reverses a man's winters,' Tal elaborated. 'Returns youthfulness to his bones.'

'Puts iron in his member,' Betha said with disgust.

At first light they stopped at a stream, a ribbon of molten tin in the new dawn, letting the animals dip their heads to the gurgling waters. When Cullen returned from checking Dan, he found Betha kneeling at the edge, slurping thirstily from cupped hands.

'What were you doing in Silures lands?' he asked quietly, crouching beside her. 'We were told you were agreeing trade, on behalf of your father.'

'You do not believe that?' she asked, not looking up.

'The hill people do not seem the trading sort. They are raiders. Why would your king risk his flesh and blood for such a mission?'

Now she looked round, green eyes lustrous. 'There was no errand.' She jutted out her jaw in a look of defiance only marginally undermined by the bead of water trembling at her chin. 'I was alone. Trying to reach the Demetae.'

Cullen's mind fumbled as he dredged teachings long ago silted. 'The kingdom beyond Lestinos's borders, hard against the Clear Sea. Their people are more savage than the bone-collectors.'

'Not all of them,' she retorted sharply. Then she smiled, a gesture bright and unforced. 'Their queen has a nephew. Hallax.'

And in that instant Cullen understood that this Hallax, nobleman of the Demetae tribe, owned Betha's heart. The next realisation came to him as though it had been obscured by the first; suddenly, starkly revealed. He opened his mouth to speak but she hastily cut him off.

'Do not worry, Cullen of the Atrebates,' she hissed, 'I will come willingly.' She glanced about at the others. 'No more blood will be shed on my behalf. It was foolish of me, and I will not make the mistake twice.'

'Why did you run? Does your father not believe this Hallax to be a worthy match?'

She snorted scorn as she stood. 'I am promised to another. A man named Prasutagus.'

'And you are,' Cullen fumbled for the appropriate response, 'unhappy with the prospect?'

She screwed up her face as if the stream had poisoned her. 'Prasutagus is a sniveller. A belly-crawler. A worm.'

'You do not like him, then?'

Betha punched him lightly. 'Do not jest. Prasutagus would be king after my father.'

'Does he have the support of your council of elders? I mean no disrespect, lady, but a life-bond with a king's daughter is no promise of inheritance.'

'It makes his claim considerably stronger,' she said bitterly. 'But you are right. There is no certainty.' She spat into the stream. 'As I say, he is a belly-crawler.'

'And to whom does he crawl?'

Betha looked hard up at him. 'Rome.'

They passed through farmsteads and hamlets, took provisions where they could, ate enough and tended to the dressings holding together Dan's ruined face. Enraged inhabitants soon stifled their ire to a simmering disgruntlement, stilling tongues when they saw their grim guests, and the encounters remained peaceful enough. They rode until the moon was at its zenith, sheltering in deep woodland from vengeful Dobunni search parties, and sat in a circle around a gnarled apple tree, taking turns to whisper soothing encouragement to the injured man who lay sweating and groaning.

The night was cold and damp, kindling too moist and green to be of use on its own, so Five Thorns felled the apple at thigh height, delimbing the stump, and drove Cleaver into the flat top with quick, precise chops that quartered the trunk almost to its base. They tore strips from Dan's discarded bandages, stuffing them into the slots, then made a nest of the kindling at the top of the stump. Lighting it with flints, Kurd blew gently until the nest smoked, and then they watched, mesmerised, as embers tumbled gradually into the deep base, igniting the dressings and, eventually, the trunk itself from within. It would burn for hours, steady and slow. Around it, murmured chatter drifted into the dark.

'Will Togodubnos resist Rome?' Betha asked, her breaths afforded a glaucous glow by the smouldering light.

Garn was eating one of the apples that had scattered like oversized hailstones under the ministrations of the axe. He nodded, wincing at its tartness, beads of juice tracing a route through his white stubble to dapple the badger teeth hanging at his broad neck. 'If they invade.'

'They will invade,' she said firmly, poking the dirt between her feet with a forked twig. 'They are making alliances daily. Preparing the ground.'

'Then yes. Will King Antedios?'

'I do not know.'

And Betha, thought Cullen, had been rescued by Togodubnos in order to secure an alliance with her father. He cast about his gaze, searching the other faces, wondering if they, too, had realised this quest might all prove for nothing.

'If I were queen,' Betha said in that hard voice she employed when talk turned to the Eceni court, 'we would kill every last bastard who stepped foot on this island.'

Not for nothing, Cullen corrected himself with a private smile.

She tossed the twig into the top of the torch. It flared briefly as it was consumed. 'But I am not queen.'

'You remind me, lady, of Aoife the Dread,' Garn said, stealing the very words from Cullen's mouth. Not that he would have had the courage to utter them.

She cocked her head, the red tresses shimmering. 'A compliment, I hope.'

'None higher,' Rues Seeker spoke across the pulsing light. 'She is one of our greatest warriors.'

Kurd snorted. 'The Romans will walk right back into the sea when she leads our charge.'

'A soul-raving,' Tal said, 'made flesh.'

'I hope to stand beside her in that battle line,' the girl murmured distantly, drawing her knees up to her chin.

'What if your people make peace?' Cullen asked tentatively, wary of a barbed reply.

She did not look at him. 'No tribe can live alongside Rome for long. Rome is a weed. She will take a stranglehold in the end. I pray the gods will let my father see sense before it is too late to tear up the roots.'

'Have you shared this with King Antedios?' Cullen asked gently.

'My father is well-meaning enough, but he has been duped in his dotage by the man he would make his son and heir.'

'Prasutagus,' Cullen said, and her earlier assertion of his treachery began to gain clarity.

She nodded, almost weary. 'He knows he is likely to ascend to the throne. War does not bring prosperity. So he bargains with the Romans, offering submission in return for trade, protection and everything else the empire can offer.'

'The best hope of stopping him is to deny him a royal match.' It was Andoc who spoke, surprise in his tone as reality dawned.

'There you have it,' Betha answered, evidently deciding she could trust the rest of the group with the truth. 'I fled.'

'And now we bring you back,' Cullen said grimly, noting with quiet satisfaction how she did not deign to mention Hallax, the private revelation remaining his alone.

'I was almost killed for my hubris,' Betha said. 'Almost brought war to this island without Rome's help. It was foolish.'

'We will warn our own king of Prasutagus's treachery,' Cullen announced, looking for reassurance and pleased to see a smattering of nods.

'He is not the only one,' Garn warned. 'You know this. There are as many tribes ready to submit as to fight.'

'I will return to my father,' Betha said. 'Better to be with my people when the storm comes.'

'Storm,' Andoc said suddenly, head jerking up on that over-long neck. 'I will be Andoc Storm Cloud.'

'Name your own sword,' Garn growled, 'but others will name you.'

'Storm Cloud is good,' Andoc argued, a note of petulance in his voice.

'It is,' Kurd said with an indulgent smile. 'But your brothers choose whether it will be yours.'

'And?'

'I always liked Master Farrad's suggestion,' White Tal said.

'Streak of Piss,' said Kurd.

Tal clicked his fingers. 'That's the one.'

'Staunch.' All eyes went to Cullen, none more surprised than Andoc to hear him offer something sensible. Cullen returned the skinny man's nonplussed gaze. 'You stood over Ulla, fought beside me, in peril of your own life. Andoc the Staunch.'

For a long moment Andoc, who so despised him, held his stare, perhaps gauging whether this would transpire to be some trickery or mocking wordplay. Then his shoulders seemed to hunch slightly, as if a breath had been contained for longer than was comfortable. 'Thank you,' he said. 'It is a good name.'

—

Camulodunon's fearsome earthworks loomed on the eastern horizon, the sky above them speckled with crows and gulls. They were home, Cullen supposed, though he doubted the place would ever be anything to him but a nest of vipers.

Men and women toiled in the fields, scattering manure on the burgeoning blankets of corn or tending to the herds. Further out, fields were dotted with sheep and goats, watched over by lone shepherds, the barks of their dogs drifting on a vagary of wind.

'Why do you serve the Catuvellauni?' Betha asked Cullen as the bridleway along which they had travelled gradually widened into what would soon become the main road into the dun.

The question blindsided him at first, for he had been staring at the distant forms of the shepherds, recalling a life since faded. They were riding side by side and he glanced across at her. 'Opportunity.'

'Oh?'

'It was serve or starve.'

'I heard Caratacos took Calleva bloodily.'

'Not a day I care to dwell upon,' he answered tartly, wishing her natural curiosity would occasionally find repose. He returned to the flock, shifting like a thousand tiny clouds along the side of a green rise. It did no good, for he could feel her gaze linger on him. He turned back, irritation bringing heat to his face. 'I took no warrior tests, had no talent with metal or wood. I tended my family's goats.'

'And then Caratacos came.'

'Then Caratacos came.' He lowered his voice to bring it out of the others' earshot. 'I hate him for what he did. But after Calleva fell, I had nothing. No purpose. The Catuvellauni gave me the chance to make a name.'

'But you feel conflicted?'

'Honestly? I feel treacherous. Wretched. But am I to rot when I could make a life?'

'Far from it,' Betha said, and though her green eyes gleamed, the usual playfulness had been replaced by something else. Something harder, more resolute. 'You are no longer simply Atrebates, nor Catuvellauni. To me, Cullen, you are a Briton.'

'That is what the Romans call us,' he replied scornfully.

'Are they wrong? To them, we are one people.' Her hand had turned white where she gripped the reins so fiercely. 'What if that were our future? One where the tribes can come together. That's what's needed to fight Rome, after all.'

Cullen laughed. 'You are mad.'

'I am ambitious.'

'That too.'

Evidently a memory flitted into her mind, for her features gradually softened. 'My mother always told me I would lead armies one day.' She looked at the sky for a moment. 'I pray I will make her happy.'

'She has gone to the next?' Cullen asked. 'Mine, too.'

'I am sorry.'

'So am I.'

Garn and Kurd were leading, as was their right as the senior warriors, and they signalled for the party to slow as they hailed a band of spearmen who had marched out of Camulodunon. It was soon apparent that the detachment's duty was to take the princess back to the lands of the Eceni. With a sideways glance at Cullen, she drew in a long breath, as if girding herself for whatever lay ahead, then kicked her mount out of the line. He went too, already feeling strangely bereft.

A fidgety bay trotted alongside, bearing an almost comically oversized rider. They looked across at Andoc, who held out a water flask. Cullen took it, swigged enthusiastically, then handed it back when Betha demurred.

'A new friend?' she asked when Andoc had fallen back into line.

'What makes you say that?'

'The way Ulla spoke to you both at –' she hesitated, cringed a little, '– the end.'

At *his* end, she meant, and Cullen nodded. 'My people slaughtered Andoc's kin. His people slaughtered mine. He blames me personally.' Now it was his turn to hesitate, the words sounding incongruous. 'Blamed me.'

She smiled. 'The wheel of life has turned, as it always does. Grudges are more like iron than granite, Cullen. They can be melted down, hammered into something different. The two of you must take your anger for one another and find a new purpose for it.' She looked back at the waiting spearmen. Forty heavily armed fighters, half of which emblazoned with the twin snakes of the Catuvellauni, the rest bearing the back-to-back crescent moons of the Eceni. She gathered up the reins. 'A shared adversity, even with an enemy, makes blood brothers of you both. The same can be said of the tribes.' She leaned closer, saddle creaking, her expression tightening with that familiar earnestness. 'That is what I am trying to say, do you see? Can the same bonds be made between entire nations? Grudges set aside for a greater good?'

'Against Rome?'

'That is what it will take. Nothing less.'

Cullen said, 'I believe you.' And he meant it, looking into those green eyes that blazed with almost otherworldly purpose. 'If ever you unite the tribes, you have my spear.'

Betha flashed a grin as she wheeled away to join her escort. 'Until then, Cullen of the Atrebates. Until then.'

CHAPTER NINETEEN

'Beer! The one with the rye this time, gods curse you!' Becan winked at Cullen as he took the proffered pot, spitting out the long blade of grass that had dangled from the gap in his front teeth. 'That barley muck will have your belly broiling by sun-up.'

It had been a happy reunion, for Drest and Becan had sought him out as soon as news of the hawks' return swept the city. They had dragged him to the alehouse and plied him with strong drink and begged for tales of the journey, specifics of the fight, details – appropriate and otherwise – of Princess Betha. Yet wider celebrations had been muted, partly out of respect and grief for Ulla Jagged Cliff, and partly because all eyes remained fixed on the Narrow Sea and the Roman fleet lurking the other side of that grey expanse.

'They make coins,' Becan said, moving to a bench and setting his crutches on the grass. 'Lots of coins. Togodubnos has had moulds made at Verlamion and Caratacos at Calleva.' He winced. 'Forgive me.'

Cullen waved him away. Life as a warrior had somehow jaded him, worn down his emotions as the tide wears away a beach. The old pangs of loss and rage seemed duller somehow.

'They stamp them with their own names,' said Drest, sitting beside Becan, 'instead of their father's, so that all know who holds the power.'

Those coins, they explained, were loaded daily into massive chests the weight of a man, and taken by cart to every nation under the sun. They would be used to pay for alliances, and for spear points and axe blades, the best archers and the most expert slingers. The coffers of the Catuvellauni would forge an army for all the island that the Romans called Britannia. An army Britannia had never seen before.

And yet it seemed a surreal venture, for word had come readily from the continent that the Roman fleet had dithered, faltered. Its legions had mutinied at Gesoriacum, for fear of the mysterious isle and its savage tribes. Every legionary had heard of the misty forests and magic nemeta that were home to malevolent spirits beyond mortal understanding, and they had all heard tell of the Wise Ones, the druids, who came from the sacred island of Mona and were as one with the dreaming plane as they were with the waking. Perhaps, it was said, the Romans would not come at all. And, though the watchers stood by the coast, waiting patiently with their beacons ready for lighting, the great armies gathered by the Sun Hound's fearsome offspring remained inland, clustered around the towns and hillforts, half an eye on a heady summer devoid of the carnage that had so often been threatened.

'How does he look?' Drest asked.

Becan cocked his head, examining Cullen. 'Like he fell out a tree.'

Cullen put his hands to his face, dabbing the new cuts, probing the fresh bruises. Most would heal, some would join the patchwork of scars he had collected over the last year. 'It was a close-run thing. We were lucky.'

'How fares Dan?' Becan said.

'He lives.' And that was all that could be hoped. His friend had survived the journey home – a surprise, in truth – and he had found himself in the care of the Wise, whose stitches and leeches, poultices and spells were all that stood between the archer and the next life. Yet persist in this realm he did. His mangled face had been sewn into some semblance of humanity, though he had groaned and sweated through the painstaking procedure, and his jaw had been strapped together with leather thongs that were permanently draped in strings of spittle. Gradually they had coaxed him into eating a thin gruel, albeit gingerly, and with a great deal of help, and now his life would be decided by the fates.

'Tellos sounds a rare creature,' Drest said, almost wistfully. 'A beast for the ages.'

'He collected ears,' said Cullen, unable to suppress a small shudder. The memory of the fight made his guts churn. He thought of Betha, too. Her courage and resolve. She would be somewhere to the north now, in the lands of her father. She was due to be joined to Prasutagus around this time. Perhaps the ceremony had already taken place.

A horn sounded somewhere. Its call began softly, distant, then grew louder and shriller, moment by moment, urgency building. They exchanged a look. It was not likely to be good news. People were coming out of their houses, hurrying towards the noise. Becan reached for his crutches, Drest stood, grasping Cullen's elbow. 'What is it?' the old man breathed in his ear.

'I'll find out,' Becan called over a shoulder as he swung forth his stumps, gathering the momentum he needed to move.

Cullen simply stared after his friend. It hardly seemed worth the panic, for the answer was inevitable. He took Drest's hand, patted the autumn-leaf skin. 'It has begun.'

—

The ships lay at anchor just off Britannia's far eastern coast. They basked in the warmth of a clear day, the swell of the sea causing them to rise and fall in unison, a gentle breeze playing at the shrouds and straining rigging.

'By the ancients, but I've nothing left.' Berikos, deposed king of the Atrebates, stood at the side of the shallow-drafted transport as it eased between a pair of high, sleek warships. He knuckled the crusty yellow stain that blighted his cloak and the fine, tunic beneath, the mere sight sent cramps to his guts.

'The Narrow Sea,' said Adminios, son of the old over-king, brother to the new, and enemy of both, 'wrecker of ships, voider of stomachs. It was ever thus.'

Berikos gave an involuntary shudder, the memory of the fleet bucking and flailing on the vicious open water would not be one easily forgotten. 'The Swamp River,' he said, changing the subject when he set his gaze on the entrance to an estuary that gaped like a mouth, breaking the shoreline. It opened into the channel that divided Bright Island from the mainland, and that island was now home to a supply base, whence the legions would launch their assault. Another, far smaller, island sat in the channel, around which muddy waters slewed. It would soon be home to a port, under hurried construction, where the big troop transports would dock. Already, a flotilla of little supply craft was unloading men, animals, timber and provisions.

Adminios moved closer, gripping the rail. 'The river floods the land,' he said, 'hence the name, but the soil is fertile enough beyond the swamps.' He blew air through his crooked nose. 'My kingdom is a paradise.'

'But you were never king, my friend,' Berikos chided, absently sucking at the misbehaving molar, inflamed anew by a sweet almond cake at the captain's table.

'I ruled,' Adminios retorted caustically, 'no more or less than you.'

A pause as both men simmered in their own resentments. Berikos shielded his eyes with a flat hand and traced the undulating coast. A small cluster of roundhouses and a timber wharf made up the original port, such as it was, and beyond that, as the estuary tapered into a wide, twisting river, it cut through a patchwork of field and marsh. He glanced sideways. 'How far inland is the nearest dun?'

'Half a day in the saddle.'

Berikos nodded, recalling the markings on the general's map. 'They will defend it.'

'If they've any sense.'

Berikos thumped the rail. 'Why does he not strike while the enemy is absent?' *He* was Aulus Plautius, commander of the invasion fleet, and Berikos suspected the man to be significantly more timid than he looked. Despite the general's exemplary record and grizzled appearance, he had been slow to disembark the troops and showed little sign of making a thrust into the island's interior, despite there having been no opposition thus far to the landing.

'He awaits the rest,' Adminios said.

Berikos sucked his tooth harder, frustration negating the pain, and watched as a warship cruised past, cutting the water smoothly as its banks of oars rose and fell like the legs of a vast centipede. There was a score of the ocean-going monsters in the channel anchorage, escorting forty or fifty wide troop transports and a myriad of smaller vessels, and many more were due to arrive in the coming hours and days. The fleet was to cross the Oceanus Britannicus in three tranches, a vast operation planned to take at least a week, possibly two. This first wave, of which he and Adminios were a part, consisted of two legions, the majority of the invasion's command structure, and units of auxiliaries, which would be tasked with spearheading the eventual advance. 'We have enough men here to make our move.'

Adminios offered a helpless shrug. 'The second and third waves will bring the remaining legions. We'll have forty-five thousand men in all. More than ten thousand animals. Armour, weaponry and everything else. General Plautius wants everything in place before he commits to a fight. He will engage when he knows he cannot lose.'

That made Berikos return to the Swamp River, studying the glittering band as if he might identify Catuvellauni slinking along its banks. 'Where are they?'

Where indeed? The choice to make the sea-crossing in three waves was in part due to the limitations of the selected beachhead, but no less because they fully expected the landing to be opposed by marauding spearmen, zinging sling stones and thrashing chariots. Yet nothing beyond the occasional horseman had greeted them, present only to observe.

'My brother is no fool,' said Adminios. 'He's been watching the coast. But how long can he afford to maintain an army?'

Berikos acknowledged the truth of it with a tilt of his head, swallowing down the dregs of unease. Word from spies and traders had been that the Britons had lingered on Cantiaci cliffs and beaches for several weeks, poised to fend off the expected attack, but that attack had never arrived, and the warbands, so far from home, had gradually dispersed, looking to their families and farms.

'They've gone,' Adminios continued. 'Back into the interior. Back to their tribes.'

'I cannot believe your brother would allow us to make landfall at all.'

Adminios watched a trio of swans pass overhead, wingbeats competing with the splash of oars. 'He is not a god,' he said with a snort of scorn. 'He cannot feed a hungry army on thin air and promises. Nor can he let their cattle go untended or postpone the harvest. The seasons turn, however inconvenient.'

'Our delay has left him vulnerable,' Berikos murmured, eyeing the dark hump of the land, imagining the conquests that lay ahead. The glory of a recaptured throne. Pyres of enemy dead blotting out the sun. Every hill transformed to an immense hedgehog by spikes capped with severed heads.

'He has overreached,' Adminios agreed. 'Now his force has crumbled just as we make our play.'

Berikos hoped he was right. He gnawed his lower lip, anxiety rising. 'Their conquests have brought a great number of spears.'

'And an even greater number of adversaries.' Adminios turned to him, dark eyes boring into his. 'Have you made the preparations?'

'By the will of the gods,' Berikos said, kissing the frog-ring on his clenched fist, 'all is in place.'

The festival of Calan Haf marked the beginning of summer.

The mid-point between spring equinox and summer solstice, it should have been a time of joy, a celebration of the fertility of the earth and the coming of warm, bountiful weeks. But the Romans had come too. They had landed far to the south and east, beyond the mighty rivers, Tamesas and Vaga. Beyond the downland scarps and the dense marshes. So far away from the great duns that one might have been forgiven for thinking it all a dream. A rumour, made of whispers and fear. But they were there. Skulking at their island bridgehead. It was just a matter of time before they made their move.

And time, it seemed, was something the Romans had in abundance, for they were in no obvious hurry. They built their quays and lookout towers while the full force grew. Ships had come and gone and come again, bringing more and more legionaries until their numbers were greater than any spy could count.

It was a deliberate tactic, Togodubnos had declared. A measured ploy to instil fear in the fractious tribes. *Let them see our power and be awed into bloodless surrender.*

But, according to the high king, the curious lull had provided opportunity too. Togodubnos had set the Cantiaci to scorching the earth around that burgeoning Roman port. He had torn up crops, spoiled grain pits, brought cattle west and north across the great rivers and salted the earth so that the enemy would have to forage far to fill their multitude of bellies, leaving those advance parties vulnerable to spears in the shadows. All the while, the people of the Isle of the Mighty gathered at Camulodunon. Just as it had been for the king's council, contingents had come from every corner of the tribal nations, from the coasts and the wetlands, the woods and the chalk hills, to the clifftop dwellers and the wild mountainfolk. This time, however, they had left the kings and diplomats behind, for the time for talking was over. This time, the gathering was accompanied by war banners, carnyx players, drummers, spearmen, horsemen, charioteers and painted shields. All awaiting the order to fight.

It was a horde for the ages. One not seen since Casivellaunus faced Julius Caesar all those years ago. A combined force, drawn from across the island. The sons of Cunobelin made up the majority, for their all-conquering Catuvellauni had added Trinovantes and Atrebates spears to their ranks. But the folk of the teeming dun found themselves sharing Calan Haf with warriors of the Regnenses, from down on the Narrow Sea coast, and with northerners like the Brigantes, Parisi and Setantii. There were Cornovii from the extreme southwest and Ordovici, Deceangli and Gangani from the western mountains.

The warriors slept in the open, for the weather was fine, and they watched for messengers and passed the time with practice at sword and saddle. The festival, as subdued and surreal as it was, needed to be observed, for the gods demanded appeasement, now more than ever. Thus, the Wise had gathered, and, like the warriors with their multitude of emblems and customs, they brought together the traditions not only of Mona, but of the tribes they represented. Together, they sprinkled things on the roads and mumbled sacred words. They spied the depths of ancient crystal shards and read the entrails of slaughtered lambs and still-born calves. They beat the hedgerows until birds erupted and hares bolted, then studied the direction of flight and sprint, divining the future from those scattered patterns. They made pungent brews of toadstools and leaves, gathered from the edges of mystical groves, and sipped the steaming concoctions until their eyes rolled in their skulls and their spirits journeyed to the dreaming realms of the Otherworld.

And while the Wise applied their secret knowledge, great fires were lit, and great spits turned in that balmy darkness when the veil between this world and the next was momentarily torn. Folk sang and danced and communed with spirits. The Wise drove cattle between the fires as a protection against disease, and they intoned their ancient incantations to curse the invading legions. After the feast, the sacred flames were used to ignite large faggots that were pushed down steep slopes. Lovers danced around those tumbling fireballs, harnessing the flames' magic to secure their love for eternity. All this happened because, despite the Roman landings, Calan Haf was a special, revered moment in time. That was why, as the faggots smouldered and the couples slunk into the shadows and drunken warriors sang to the stars, men who had earned spear-fame were taken to a place on the dun's outskirts, where the canopy of wizened trees melded to compose an arch, and there given heroes' names.

Cullen felt slightly absurd in full battle regalia. He wore new shoes, and his best pair of braca – chequered green and yellow – were freshly clean, tied by leather straps at ankles and knees. His yellow tunic, faded and patched though it was, had been scrubbed by the washerwomen down at Stoney River, and his large shield had been painted by Becan in his absence, so that it now bore the life-wheel of Taranis, the three-tailed horse of the Atrebates and a small rendering of a magpie, along with the high king's red serpents.

'Red crest,' Moranna of the Silver crooned in her slow, dove-coo voice. She had come to stand before him, the staff with its pink crystal in her taloned grip. Her sharp fangs seeming especially macabre in the gloom. 'Little red crest. Tonight I am your mother.' She paused, apparently expecting his confused frown. 'For a hero must be named by his mother, and what other mother have the gods seen fit to provide?'

Cullen nodded. He felt the eyes of a dozen others on him, warriors all, and a swell of emotion threatened to shame him with tears. He gripped the hilt of his sword, suspended from a chain-link belt at his right hip, and brought closer his shield, as if the barrier could protect him from his own treacherous feelings.

Moranna turned away, reaching for one of the onlookers, and when she returned to him she was holding a tall spear. 'As your mother, it is my duty to represent the mother goddess, whose land you have watered with your life's blood. In her stead, I acknowledge your fame, warrior of the Catuvellauni and Atrebates.' She handed him the spear. He took it, tentatively, for something about its dark shaft, decorated along its length with tiny carvings of cats and birds, ignited fragments of memory, like swirling embers he could not quite catch.

'I arm you,' Moranna went on, 'as is the way of our people, with a weapon won in battle. Yours by right.'

Cullen knew at once that this was Branna's spear. Branna the Slayer. The man who had led the warband that wiped out a village near Calleva. He suppressed a shudder. Felt a warm tear tumble down his cheek. For Fi and Cora. For all of them.

'Who names this man?' Moranna was saying, though her words seemed distant.

'I,' responded a low, grinding voice.

Cullen peered into the dark. The huge shape of Garn Grey Boulder loomed above the others like a standing stone.

'I,' came another affirmation. Kurd Long Limb this time.

A third man took a step in. 'I.'

To Cullen's surprise, he saw the speaker was Andoc. The Staunch, as the man would be known by the night's end.

Moranna offered a solemn nod. 'And what name shall be forever twinned with that given at his birth?'

'Wolf Scourge, lady,' Andoc replied.

Moranna turned to him. 'Cullen Wolf Scourge, named man. What do you swear?'

'I swear,' Cullen said, 'by all the gods, that I will bear this name with honour, as a warrior should.'

'Then it is done.'

'It's done?'

Togodubnos beamed broadly, while Cullen fell to his knees, a movement rendered ludicrously clumsy by the sword hilt that jabbed him in the guts and the shield he effectively vanished behind.

'By the ancients, get up.' The high king, still smiling, balled his fists either side of his dense waist while Cullen clambered to his feet. 'Wolf Scourge.' He said the name slowly, sounding out the syllables as if testing its mettle.

The gathering had dispersed when the last of the fame had been acknowledged and the names duly claimed. Cullen had made sure to sponsor Andoc, who had been puffed up like a mating pigeon to receive his recognition, while they had named Dan too, even if the accolade would not be consciously received for weeks to come.

'Moranna told me you were blessed by Taranis,' Togodubnos said. He was clothed in tunic and cloak of creams and browns, a casual ensemble for one so powerful, but the gold at his neck, wrists and fingers told the truth where fabric could not. His eyes caught the light of a distant torch, darkly radiant like polished nuggets of jet. He spread his big palms in acquiescence to Moranna's wisdom. 'Here you are. A warrior of renown.'

'Forgive me, lord, but I heard you were in the east.'

'I have left my brother in command. The enemy has not deigned to strike out from their base. We await their move.' Togodubnos fiddled with the ends of his thick, red moustache. 'I have returned to see what the tribes have offered.'

And make a list of those tribes to have offered nothing, Cullen thought. 'Will we give battle, lord?'

'Of course. When the moment is right. When the terrain and the omens are favourable.' The king's affable expression crumpled a little. 'You were there at the end? With Ulla?'

Cullen swallowed hard. 'He fought like a crazed boar, lord.'

'I never doubted it. And you fought well, I hear. The mighty Grey Boulder does not throw compliments away lightly.'

'I am humbled, lord,' Cullen said truthfully.

'Garn tells me your wits proved the difference. That Ulla himself commended you before he crossed to the next. You deserve your fame.' Togodubnos glanced over Cullen's shoulder, up at the great works hewn in earth and stake and stone that ringed the dun like a barrier built by giants. 'Still, to be named in Camulodunon must be a bittersweet thing.'

'I do not relish the city, lord, it is true,' Cullen said, in what was, he thought, an almost laughable understatement. Avalloc's Shelter, the place where they had tried to burn him alive, was but a short walk from here.

'I prefer Verlamion myself,' the king said, breaking into a sheepish smile, 'though my reasoning rather pales when compared with your own.'

Cullen looked back. 'It is a mighty place. The Romans will not find it an easy conquest.'

'The stronghold of the old Trinovantes kings,' said Togodubnos, 'on whose behalf Caesar invaded so long ago. My great-grandfather, Casivellaunus, led the resistance then.' He chuckled softly. 'Of course, one might say he caused the invasion in the first place.'

Just as you and your brother have caused this latest calamity, Cullen did not say. 'Chief of Tin was his war-name?'

'For he was inflexible when it came to his enemies, so the stories go. He was looking to expand our territory. Invaded the dun, ran the Trinovantes king through.' Togodubnos pointed a bejewelled finger up and to the right, indicating some location Cullen could not hope to recognise in the night. 'Just over there, so they say.'

Cullen knew the stories. 'The dead king's son, Mandubracius, fled to Rome for help.'

'And the great Caesar was only too happy to oblige. Of course, he took his legions back across the grey water eventually.'

'Not before coming to terms with many of the tribes.'

Togodubnos inclined his head. 'Including ours. But trade and protection in the main. Not subservience.'

'Did it not amount to the same thing?'

The king laughed. 'You are sharp-witted, Wolf Scourge. Insolent, but sharp.'

'I meant no disrespect, lord,' Cullen blurted, feeling heat climb his neck. 'Simply that Casivellaunus was pushed back from here, into his own lands.'

'We lost overlordship for a time,' Togodubnos conceded, 'but we won it back, through patience and blood.'

'Now you rule over the Atrebates as well,' Cullen said, and the thought was chased by a pang of bitterness that gathered into a barb on his tongue. 'You are the Caesar of the tribes.'

That drew a sharp look. The king considered Cullen for a lingering moment, as if trying to read what was behind his eyes. Then he brandished that open, gregarious grin. 'Are you ready to fight?'

Cullen almost vomited with relief. 'I am, lord,' he breathed.

'They will leave the landing site soon. They will come for us here. Verlamion is my home, but Camulodunon is the symbol of power.' Togodubnos pulled at his moustache again. His shrewd eyes roamed up to the ramparts and back to Cullen. 'That is why I have come to see you. We need to slow their advance. Kill as many as we can in the swamps and forests before they so much as lay eyes on the great rivers that block their advance. I mean to frustrate them. Make them rash. By the time they reach the Vaga, they will be beleaguered and ragged.'

'Have you work for the hawks, lord?'

'Yes,' the king replied, 'and no.'

'Lord?'

'The hawks as you knew them are finished. Without Ulla, they cease to exist. The named men will join other nines along the Swamp River. It cuts the land,' he went on, clearly seeing confusion in Cullen's face, 'just beyond the Roman camp. They must cross it first if they are to advance. It is fordable, but they will take a day, maybe two, to reach it on foot. I want you to take men, join with the Cantiaci and Dobunni screening the position.'

'Dobunni?' Cullen echoed, his memory of Boduoc, the tribal chief so scornful of Togodubnos, lacing his tone with incredulity.

'They are a broken tribe,' Togodubnos said. 'Many of the clans support my cause, while many would settle with Rome. They do not move with one mind. The clans who choose to defy Boduoc have come to my banner, and I have sent them ahead. The tip of my spear, if you will. Let them prove their loyalty, eh?'

'And I, lord?'

'You will command a warband. The Cantiaci are soft. They love Roman money, Roman trade, Roman clothing. For a time, they loved my brother, Adminios. I do not trust them any more than I trust the Dobunni. You will keep them under a close eye. Assist them in their efforts.' Togodubnos's auburn brows came together, and the iron that so often lay beneath the surface of his character was suddenly, frighteningly at the fore. 'Delay the Romans, Cullen,' he said in a hard voice. His eyes had lost their colour somehow, leaving them pools of deepest black, as if the pupils had consumed the rest. The scar across his nose was brighter in contrast, as if bragging of his deeds. 'I mean to destroy their advance at the Vaga, but in order to make that happen, you must buy me time.'

Cullen could barely hear him for the rush of blood in his ears. Was it pride, trepidation, downright terror? He was not entirely certain. So he bowed low. 'Lord.'

'Good,' Togodubnos said with a king's finality.

'Lord?' he said again, straightening. 'Betha, lord,' he blurted when Togodubnos indicated he should speak. He felt his throat tighten but pressed on regardless. 'That is to say, the princess.'

Suspicion ploughed furrows across the king's forehead. 'The Eceni girl?'

'She was not in Silures lands on behalf of King Antedios. Rather, she had run away.'

The furrows deepened. 'For what reason?'

The leap had been made. The spear thrown. He had promised her, and now he would fulfil that oath, as a warrior should. 'Her proposed match, a man named Prasutagus, means to ally himself with Rome, should the elders name him king after Antedios.'

'Why would she run?'

'She hates Rome. Fears them. Would resist them.'

'And yet the Eceni are on their way.'

'Here?' Cullen asked incredulously.

'And in numbers.' Togodubnos stepped in, making Cullen flinch, but he patted his subject's shoulder in comradely fashion. 'Your mission bore fruit.'

Cullen knew he must be gaping like a landed fish, but he was powerless to do anything else. 'Lord, I do not understand, I...'

Togodubnos's jovial chuckle boomed in his ears. 'You would not be the first, Cullen Wolf Scourge. Nor will you be the last.' He slapped down with that great paw again, shaking every bone in Cullen's body. 'She is beautiful, no?'

'Yes, lord, but...'

'Put her out of your mind,' the king said firmly. One last thump at Cullen's chest and he was already moving away, retainers emerging from the darkness like living shadows. 'You are a war-giver now. One of mine. And we have work to do.'

—

That was it. He was a warrior, beloved of Taranis, patronised by Moranna of the Silver and on speaking terms with the high king of the Isle of the Mighty. It was beyond his wildest expectations. A life further removed from a callow goatherd he could not imagine. Yet his promises were worthless. His words empty. It was in a state of chagrin, then, that he stalked back to his lodgings within the dun, his ire inflamed and his fury bubbling like steaming stew.

The streets were quietening now. Children had gone to their beds, tables were being cleared, fires were ebbing. Fighters would be looking to their rest and their equipment, knowing that many would be moving south in the morning, crossing the Tamesas and Vaga, then all the way into the lands of the Cantiaci, there to become links in the chain that Togodubnos had strung about the encroaching Roman legions. Cullen seethed as he strode past a row of clay-lined dew ponds and on into an avenue of sweet-smelling trees, wondering how hubris had so completely outfoxed him. He drove the butt-end of Branna's spear into the dirt like one of Becan's crutches, putting his frustration into every thrust, which was why he almost tripped over it when Cassia stepped into his path.

'You are here,' he garbled, trying to extricate his legs from the spear and the end of his scabbard.

She laughed, waggling her fingers in front of her face in the way a child would mimic an apparition. 'Or am I a ghost?' The moonshine sparkled on her wide eyes, and her teeth were a crescent against skin already dark without the night's help. 'Have I interrupted something?'

'No... I...' he stammered, feeling as awkward as ever in her presence. 'I am pleased to see you.'

'I am pleased to hear it,' she said with affected coyness. 'But you were in a black mood, any fool could see it. Gods, Cullen, but you almost barged right through me.'

'Never,' Cullen protested.

She touched his arm, calming him as she might an agitated patient. 'What is it?'

He shook his head. 'It does not matter. A question of trust. I am a warrior now and my word should count for something.'

Cassia snapped her feet together, squaring her shoulders and holding an arm across her midriff which he presumed was in lieu of a shield. 'Of course. And I beg forgiveness on behalf of those who caused you this indignity.'

'You're mocking me.'

Her lips came together in an exaggerated pout. 'Maybe just a little.'

'Maybe just a lot,' he countered, trying to sound light-hearted but suspecting it came across as mere pomposity. He could sense himself colouring and was glad of the night. 'I am named now,' he tried to explain. 'Initiated, and—'

She had reached out for his face, the cold fingers dissolving whatever words had been queuing on his tongue. Her hand moved up, gently touching the scar that cleaved deep above his right eye.

He let his own hand rise, sliding from her elbow to her hand. At her wrist he paused, feeling a row of jagged lines. 'You're hurt.'

'They are healed, do not worry.' Her face was taut, as if she were suffering some unseen agony. 'It distracts me.'

'Distracts you?' He realised the lines were the legacy of old cuts. Scars that were uniform in length, each one shallow and parallel to the next. 'You do this to yourself?'

'When I'm alone,' she said, her voice soft and distant, 'the ship comes back to me. The fury of the sea. The groans of the ship as she broke apart. The saltwater in my eyes, my throat.' She took her hand away, clasping the wrist in the opposite palm. 'I am alone a lot.'

'No longer,' Cullen said, his voice catching in his throat. 'No longer.'

She blinked away tears. 'Smell that?'

'The linden tree,' he said thickly.

'The scent heralds the beginning of summer.'

'It is the symbol of friendship.'

'Not just friendship,' she said.

He swallowed. It felt like he'd tried to consume an entire loaf of bread in one gulp.

'Critheanach tells me the old myths. In those tales, there are other initiations.' She was staring up at him, close enough for her breath to be warm on his face. Her hair tumbled about her shoulders as she spoke, like rivulets of black water. 'Other ways people might unlock magic.'

His shield and spear clattered to the ground and his hands were on her waist, drawing her in. Her other arm joined the first so that she took his head in her hands as if he might try to break free, and she was pulling him close, kissing him, crushing him, hungry, desperate, and he knew now that he had never truly been kissed before. He broke away, gasping, gathered her up and she was off the ground, clawing at him, loosening his tunic as he staggered with the weight of them both, and then they were under the linden tree, its heady aroma mingling with that of their breathing and of their bodies.

CHAPTER TWENTY

Two hundred warriors left Camulodunon at dawn.

Thousands stayed behind, for they were to form the core of Togodubnos's lines of defence, to be deployed first on the River Vaga, then, if necessary, on the River Tamesas, for those broad, fast and deep waterways were more formidable barriers than man could devise, their fords forcing any attacker into an effective funnel, nullifying the weight of numbers. If not the king's last hope, the rivers were certainly his best.

The cavalcade clattered along the middleway out of the dun, shields and hilts and spears and chains and bridles and scabbards chiming like discordant instruments as they marched into the southwest, Stoney River at their backs, the new sun transforming it to molten gold. A score of horsemen formed the vanguard, coupled with a dozen drummers, while the rest travelled on foot. A long line, two abreast, like a spiny serpent. At the head was one of Togodubnos's nobles, in a polished helmet with enamelled cheek-guards and a fox's tail fastened at the back. He was straight-backed atop a piebald mare, and his banner led the way, a great staff with yet more fox tails nailed to the crosspiece.

Somewhere in the middle of the column walked Cullen, pride giving strength to each pace. His new shoes chafed a little, and he looked ruefully towards the evening when he would need to tend blistered feet, but he had a nine to command. Not just one, in fact, and he could not help but glance back at the leader of the second group. Andoc. Andoc who despised him, had fought him. Andoc the Staunch as he now was. They exchanged a nod.

Clearing the outermost earthworks, they passed a tall hedgerow humming with life. A gang of jackdaws alighted on its tangled top, their eyes glittering silver rings, quizzical and penetrating. Some of the Wise were there, waving wands made of elder and apple as they blessed those going to war. The very last of them, tall and thin, seemed to limp to the road's edge. Cullen's eyes were drawn to the bare feet, which were each devoid of the littlest toe, and his pride evaporated like high summer mist. The Wise One drew back his deep hood, revealing a face of raw savagery, twisted by pulsating hate. It was a face marked by star-shaped brands and a bald head permanently needled with the faded blue symbols of moons and suns. Cullen almost faltered, almost stumbled out of line, and it was all he could do to keep his fear in check as Arthmael the Learned jabbed his long, knotted wand directly at him. The thin lips were working rapidly, describing some spell, and the wand was trembling with the passion of its wielder, and Arthmael's forked tongue flickered out, tasting the air like a viper tracking prey.

Cullen felt a hand on his back, firm between the shoulder blades, and he half expected a knife to have found its way there, somehow willed by way of dark magic. Andoc's voice was in his ear. Urging him to pick up the pace. Reassuring him that all was well. That a wizened old miscreant could not harm the man who carried Taranis's wheel on his skin, the man who had gained fame and who his peers had named Wolf Scourge. It was Andoc's palm, pushing him on, keeping him to the task at hand.

Then they were away. Away from the town. Away from the Wise Ones. Cullen could breathe again. Could almost feel the heat of Arthmael's hatred recede with every step. It was a relief, but he prayed to Taranis for protection all the same. For he was going to war, and, not for the first time, he had been cursed.

It was hot. The sun a malevolent eye, glaring through desultory wisps of cloud. The fires of Calan Haf had not been a fortnight cold, but the gods seemed eager for summer, Belinos's fiery disc relentless, the ground beneath Cullen's knees dry and hard.

He was watching the glistening progress of the Swamp River as it meandered through the reedy beds and into the band of salt marsh, after which it would empty into the channel that now teemed with vessels of all shapes and sizes. That was several miles off, out of sight, but he could imagine the busy harbour, had seen it with his own eyes on first joining with his Cantiaci hosts, had slept fitfully since. They were as the stars, the Romans. As grains of sand on a beach. Uncountable in their thousands as they swarmed like ants upon the shore. Already Bright Island was part of the empire. Already a bridgehead had been established, garrisoned and fortified on the smaller island nestled within the channel. Already the first of the legions had marched onto the mainland.

Now Cullen knelt in the bushes on a rise above an otherwise tranquil river, his gaze trained firmly on a far-off bend that seemed threatened only by kingfishers and sedge warblers.

Andoc was prostrated amongst the wildflowers beside him, his ear flat to the ground.

'I hear them,' he said. He clambered to his feet. Tall and willowy as ever, but bearing new tissue these days, both muscle and scar. 'They're on the move.'

The nines were a stone's throw further back, their earthy colours blending amongst the leafy limbs of a small copse and the tightly curled fronds of spring bracken. Cullen smiled at them, for they were his to command. The reward for changing his life. Beating his own path, as Moranna had foretold. It was with gnawing dismay, then, that he called the order for them to rise and make themselves ready. Their mettle was to be tested against the most implacable foe to ever walk the earth.

Andoc, his second, had hailed the leader of a group of Cantiaci who were resting a little further down the slope. The man gave them each a brisk nod and squinted at the river. 'It is time?'

'Yes,' Cullen said.

The Cantiaci sucked at his brown moustache and adjusted his helmet, the crest of which had been elongated, tapered and pointed into the bill of a marsh bird, the back and sides patterned to resemble feathers. 'Down to the water. Andraste be with us.'

'Andraste be with us,' Andoc said, the clatter of weaponry overriding all other sounds as the warriors shook themselves into motion.

Cullen opened his mouth to intone the creed but hoofbeats shook his feet and ribs. He turned to see a young lad gallop up the slope, his roan pony plunging straight into the bracken, careless of what might be concealed within. His face was a rictus of concern, grimy with sweaty dust.

'What news?'

The rider slewed to a thundering halt, expertly steering the mount with his thighs as he twisted to point back at the serene-looking water. 'So many, lord,' he called, the words tumbling hoarsely from a parched throat. 'So many, so many.'

'Calm, lad,' Cullen urged, privately chiding himself for the bubble of pride that rose in his chest, for it was the first time he had been addressed thus. 'Breathe. Speak your message.'

'They are a river of metal, lord,' the boy continued, deliberately slowing his words, though it was clearly a struggle, so panicked was he, 'stretching all the way to the sea.'

Cullen glanced at Andoc. To the boy, he asked, 'How many?'

A shrug that spoke of futility. 'As numerous as the leaves on the trees. I've never seen so many men in one place.' He wheeled the pony about to face the river. 'So many.'

'Ride, boy,' Cullen snapped. 'Ride as if death is at your heels. Tell the other chiefs hereabouts.'

The roan sidled about. 'I will, lord.'

Cullen regarded the beast, its flanks still heaving with the effort of the gallop. 'Then take a fresh mount. Ride to Togodubnos. Tell him they have finally broken camp. Tell him to ready the barricades, for there is no chance we can hold them for long.' He reached out and took the head collar, gripping firmly as he met the boy's frightened eyes. 'But tell him, by the ancients, that we intend to try.'

—

The carts bounced and juddered over dried ruts, traces and chains jangling discordantly. The convoy had turned off the road and, to the spittle-flecked orders of a bearded and barrel-chested Dumnonii, fanned out in a clearing where the grass had been overwhelmed by tough sprouts of sedge and jagged lumps of rock.

Cassia dropped from the rear of the vehicle and brushed the dust from her skirts and cloak. She held up a hand for Critheanach to take, easing her down.

The older woman's shrewish face rumpled. 'This'll do, I suppose,' she lisped, as she began unloading piles of cloth, leather tool bags and dozens of pots, large and small, from the wagon. 'Long as the fighters remember where to find us.'

'We'd have told many more if you hadn't wasted our time prattling to Garn.'

Critheanach gave her a dirty look. 'Wanted to be sure the Grey Boulder was in rude health, seeing as he'll soon be in mortal peril.'

'His health,' Cassia said, 'is not the only rude thing on your mind.'

Critheanach flashed a rapacious grin. 'My blood is as red as yours, girl.'

Cassia could not help but laugh. They had encountered some of Ulla's erstwhile hawks a little way upstream, stopping to inform them of the healing space they would be establishing in case of the anticipated Roman advance, but her mistress had dallied like a blushing girl at the massive warrior's honeyed words. Still, they were here now, beside the Swamp River's great beaver pool, a landmark significant enough for the fighters to locate them should the need arise.

Cassia went to help unpack the medical supplies, readying poultices and bandages next to blankets and food. The convoy's stout leader was shouting again, organising their small escort into a rough picket line, while simultaneously snapping at a young lad to take a message to the nearest war-chief, letting him know of their position.

'They say the attack will come soon,' Critheanach was muttering as she unstrung small bags of herbs, gauging the contents with wrinkled nose and the occasional flicking tongue-tip. 'The fighters cannot stem the tide. Not here, anyway.'

Cassia was looking at her mistress, but the words drifted over and around her like dawn mist on seasoned branches. She was remembering the old times. Her father, the perfect existence they had led together at the valetudinarium. In those days he had been her teacher, her confidante. It had all gone in one crashing, freezing, horrifying instant. The roar of the sea lingered in her ears even now. The scars at her wrist tingled.

Critheanach was making an impatient snorting noise. 'What say you, Cassia?' She drew herself up, hands on hips. 'Am I invisible? Where is your mind, girl?'

'What?' Cassia rubbed a hand over her face, as though she could force down the memories.

'Your eyes are glazed as pots.'

'It is nothing.'

Critheanach put down the jar she held and went to Cassia, taking her gently by the shoulders. 'Your old life comes to threaten your new life. I would not call that nothing.'

'You doubt me?' Cassia said brusquely.

Critheanach offered a kind smile, incongruous in that harsh face. 'I worry for you, girl.'

Cassia shrugged her off, taking a few paces towards the river. 'Do not.'

'They're your people,' Critheanach said, following, 'out there. Coming to kill us, like as not.'

'They are not my people any longer,' Cassia retorted hotly, rounding on her.

Critheanach did not flinch. 'Words are simple enough to say, girl, but when one of your own kind comes out of that forest—'

'What?' Cassia snapped. 'When they come, what? What will I do? Take a knife to your throat? Run into the arms of the nearest legionary?'

The older woman held her ground, folding her arms as if awaiting the cessation of a child's tantrum. When she spoke, her voice was soothing. 'Hesitate, girl, because that is the human thing to do.'

'I will not—'

'And hesitation might just get you killed. And that is why I worry.'

Cassia stepped back. Tears pricked her eyes and she blinked them away angrily. 'I am sorry. My mind does wander, you are right. I am Roman, my father was Roman, I—'

Critheanach raised a staying palm. 'You will do as your heart tells you. Do what is right.' Her face cracked in an impish smile. 'Now, tell me. Does your mind dally on thoughts of another man? A younger man? A red-headed goatherd, perchance?'

'He is a warrior now.'

'He makes war in your dreams?' Critheanach winked. 'Or does he make love?'

Cassia felt herself blush, heat pulsing hard in her cheeks so that she was forced to turn away. She was staring over the water again, to the dense forest beyond. Deer grazed at the edge of the trees, their big shapes shifting silently. 'He is out there, somewhere.'

'Does he know you have come?'

She shook her head. 'I thought it would distract him.'

Critheanach grunted amusement. 'I'd imagine it would.'

'What if he dies?'

'Then his soul will await yours in the chambers of the Otherworld.'

'Will we live our next lives together?'

'No question.' Critheanach went back to the supplies, still scattered at the foot of the cart, waiting to be ordered and set at stations around the clearing. 'Now come and help me with this mess, girl. Our skills will soon be required.'

By late afternoon, the river bend had vanished in a cloud of dust, and out of that cloud came men. A lot of men.

Cullen and the other war leaders came down off the rise and moved through the wood, careful and silent as deer until they could see the road. Still, they were the better part of two hundred paces away, and the tangled shadow-world of beech and ash was not a place the Roman scouts wished to negotiate, preferring to wade the stands of bracken that greened the forest edge, sweeping the fronds with their throwing spears like men scything corn. Thus, the men of the Isle of the Mighty lurked in the gloom and studied their new foe. These were not the painted killers to whom Cullen had grown so accustomed. They were like child's toys from this distance, each figure the same as the next, clothed and armed the same and moving in perfect unison. They marched in blocks, six abreast, several rows deep, filling the roadway and spilling onto the grassy verges. Between each block he could see a standard gently rippling with the motion of the march, its images the same red and gold that marked the huge, rectangular shields they carried.

Andoc and the Cantiaci war-chief were with him, gathered about a knotted trunk. The messages had gone out into the countryside. Not only up to the king on the River Vaga, but along the length of the Swamp River too, begging the desperate parties of warriors who camped on its banks to be on their guard. The bulk of fighters were of the Cantiaci of course, for this was their homeland, and they were bolstered by the defiant Dobunni who had come here without the permission of Boduoc. But there were parties of Catuvellauni too, besides Cullen's own men, along with some mounted Coritani and a company of slingers from the western kingdom of the Durotriges, and together they loitered and watched and waited for their time to come.

'We do not have enough,' Andoc muttered, his mind following the same course as Cullen's.

'We do not need thousands,' Cullen answered. 'The king has chosen to make his stand on the Vaga, so that is where his main horde will lay in wait. Our task is to frustrate and delay the reds.'

'We must make alliances with the marshes and forests,' the Cantiaci said, fiddling with a carved hunk of bone suspended by a string from his sword pommel. 'My people have slaughtered sheep in the deep woods. Their blood will assuage the spirits.'

'What about Taranis?' Andoc asked sullenly.

Cullen followed his gaze. One of the marching blocks, led by big men with red crests on their helmets, carried shields painted with lightning bolts, one of the old god's marks. 'He is not with them.'

Andoc sucked his teeth. 'How can you know?'

Cullen patted his right forearm. 'Because I know Taranis is with me.'

It felt as though the forest was alive, for the thrum of Roman feet made the very earth vibrate beneath them. Out on the road swarmed the invaders. They shone, despite the dusty pall. Helmets, daggers, short swords. There were units wearing mail shirts, not so dissimilar to those favoured by some of Cullen's people, while others were encased in full armour, like giant beetles, their torsos and shoulders fastened within a cage of horizontal metal strips that overlapped from top to bottom. Every inch of Roman armour was polished to a high sheen that reflected the sun as they traipsed past, shoulder to shoulder, drumbeats calling the time.

'Heavy-looking spears,' Andoc said.

'Pilum,' Cullen said. 'For throwing. They have a head like this,' he steepled his fingers, 'that will punch through iron.'

Cassia had described them to him, told of the devastation the weapon would wreak. A volley of pila would rip through a massed enemy, regardless of whether they had formed shield-line or not, and the legionaries would march into that mayhem with their body-shields and short, stabbing blades, and souls would rapidly be moving on to the next life. His mind lingered on Cassia, even as he stared at the trudging column, and he wondered where she was now. What she was doing. Her smell was still in his nostrils. The warmth of her body. Holding her again was all he wanted. He was prepared to die in the fight against Rome, but, by the ancients, she was worth living for.

A bellow from a short, stocky Roman brought the march to a sudden halt. The man, armoured in plate metal that had been intricately moulded to resemble the naked torso of a muscular man, carried a staff and wore a helmet with a magnificent crest.

'He's the leader,' Andoc said unnecessarily.

'But what is he about?' the Cantiaci murmured.

Just as the words left his mouth, a large wagon emerged from between two of the marching blocks. Immediately men set to work unloading the cargo, which appeared to be various types of tools and scores of animal skins, stitched together to form huge sheets.

'They make camp?' Andoc said. 'They have not yet reached the fords.'

Cullen touched his arm. 'They're splitting.'

Sure enough, while the tight formations of legionaries waited, silent, like a myriad of standing stones under the sun, three blocks were moving to the front of the column. The first were around fifty in number, mounted on big, muscular horses and clothed in mail.

'Gauls?' the Cantiaci said, frowning.

Cullen noted the long, fair hair that sprouted from beneath the riders' helmets, and the plaited moustaches that were so far removed from the Romans, clean-shaven to a man. 'Maybe.'

Andoc spat. 'Traitors.'

'They're going ahead,' Cullen said, as the second and third blocks moved to the fore. They appeared to be legionaries, made in the same mould as the majority of the column, though one group wore simple mail shirts and the other were encased in the distinctive overlapping bands.

'Why don't they stay together?' Andoc asked. He wiggled his spear. 'It is dangerous out in the woods.'

'The bridge,' Cullen said, and even as the thought came to him he knew he was correct. 'The reds are looking for the bridge.'

The Cantiaci wrinkled his nose. 'How can they know it is near?'

'How can they know,' Andoc added, 'that there is a crossing at all?'

'They have Adminios,' Cullen answered. He sketched the run of the Swamp River in his head. There were fords where the riverbed was made of shingle and the water was shallow enough to cross, but it was far more likely that the king's treacherous brother, who had ruled this territory before his expulsion, had merely told the Romans where to go.

'And they have Berikos,' Andoc reminded him.

Cullen nodded. He could hardly argue the point, though he hoped to the gods that it was not true.

'So the reds know where to cross,' the Cantiaci said grimly. 'What do we do? Destroy the bridge?'

Cullen gradually stood, silently unfurling himself from the foot of the tree, his eyes still fixed on the parties readying to leave the legion. 'Not yet.'

Cassia slurped a thin broth from a wooden cup as the light steadily bled from the day. Steam roiled around her face as she blew gently over the rim, obscuring the line of the river, the sprawling willow and the deer grazing serenely beyond.

'There,' Critheanach was saying somewhere back towards the now empty cart. 'A fine display for those swine-sons to gaze upon.'

Cassia saw that she had unloaded half a dozen human skulls and promptly arranged them into a small pyramid facing the river. 'Is that enough?'

Critheanach made an irritated sucking noise at the side of her mouth. 'Save your sarcasm for when we've sent the invader back across the sea.' She stooped to gather up a rolled blanket, unfurling it to reveal a wooden statue. 'For now, we need as many souls as we can get on our side. You heard the stripling. The enemy advances.'

A fresh-faced lad, too young to have taken the warrior's tests or choose a life path, had thundered in on a skewbald pony, proud as a cob in spring. He had breathlessly announced the sighting of a vast Roman column, trudging slowly behind more rapid advance parties. 'I heard him.' She eyed the statue with distaste. 'Why do you insist upon bringing that thing?'

The old woman cradled the wooden figurine like a newborn babe. 'This *thing*, my girl, possesses more power than you could possibly imagine.'

Cassia regarded it without concealing her disgust. It was a man, carved from dark bogwood, his phallus proud and pointing skyward. He held a spear and stood aboard a boat with a snakehead prow. She had always hated the figure, for its eyes were made of polished hunks of glittering stone, creamy and translucent, and, in the right light, his dead glare made her skin creep. 'Could he not, at least, put on some clothes?'

'Fine,' Critheanach sniffed, plucking the penis free to leave a chasm in the carving's groin. 'If your Roman sensibilities cannot bear to look upon it.'

'It comes off?' said Cassia, appalled.

'He sails a ship to the Otherworld. He has no need of such equipment. He is neither man nor woman, but soul and spirit, in purest form.'

Cassia shook her head in wonder. 'Then I hope he brings us luck.' She walked out of the ring of blankets and equipment they had prepared and fished the ladle from the small cauldron bubbling with broth. As she upended a measure into her cup, she could hear the lowing of a bullock far off to the west, the sound abruptly severed. 'Sacrifice?'

Critheanach cocked an ear, then nodded. 'The Wise – a chosen few, with soothsaying gifts – will feast on its flesh and drink a broth made from the cooked meat.'

Cassia sipped the hot mixture. 'To what end?'

'They'll enter a meditative trance, while others chant over them.' She grunted, evidently unconvinced of the rite's efficacy. She knelt to begin shredding leaves into a stone mortar. 'Probably make a pig's ear of it, knowing that lot.'

Cassia laughed as she brought the broth up to her mouth. But instead of sipping, her hand froze, the cup poised before her lips, steam hot and moist on her chin and cheeks. But she did not notice the sensation. Her eyes had fixed on the grazing deer again. All of them, a dozen or thereabouts, had looked up sharply, all focused in the same direction. Then they bolted, as one, twisting and darting into the shadows with a single mind, like a murmuration of starlings.

The girl walked into view at that moment. She had been obscured by the huge willow trunk, but now she strolled into the open, searching the long grass, a bunch of twigs braced in the crook of one arm. She seemed oblivious. To the scattering deer, to Cassia, to the unseen perils lurking in the east.

Cassia found herself at the river's edge, waving. 'Girl!'

'She's fetching kindling,' Critheanach chided, 'leave the poor mite be.'

'She can fetch all she likes on this side of the water.'

The beaver dam looked like a solid stripe of black now that the sunlight was in retreat. A smudge of shadow breaking the glittering run of the water. Cassia found it somehow sinister as she stepped gingerly from one creaking foothold to the next, Critheanach's exasperated reproach ringing at her back. The girl had, at least, acknowledged her. Waved happily, in fact, dropping the twigs as she did so. She was probably eight or nine, Cassia reckoned. Snub nosed, fair haired and skinny as the willow fronds dangling above. She ran to Cassia, hailing her with a delighted grin, as though they were long-parted sisters. A gesture so warm and welcoming that Cassia almost threw her own arms wide to gather up the waif. But it was also one that was utterly false.

Cassia stepped back, avoiding the intended embrace, making the girl slow to a halt. And in that moment she saw that the narrow, chapped lips were flecked with white poppy seeds, and in one of the girl's hands there was a ball, the size of a small egg, its outer surface golden and crispy. Cassia's mind was tumbling pell-mell down a valley into her past, just as the girl was holding out her hands, asking for more. More of the sweet treats. Globi, as Cassia remembered them. A Roman delicacy, made of cheese, spelt, honey and white poppy seeds. The same delicacy her own father would buy at Gesoriacum's bustling market.

The girl, she realised, was not addressing Cassia, but the soldier who strode, grinning, out of the treeline.

–

The defenders of the Isle of the Mighty had used the final daylight hours in preparation. At the shallower sections of the waterway, they had driven sharpened stakes into the riverbed, those wielding hammers muttering apologies to Cernunnos as otters, fish and fowl had fled downstream. As dusk fell, warbands of combined nines were ranged at intervals along the western bank, for they could not be sure where the Romans would cross, though the growing assumption was that focus would necessarily fall on the bridge.

Thus it was that, as the shadows began to lengthen, Cantiaci, Dobunni, Catuvellauni, Coritani and Durotriges, melted into trees, crouched in meadows of long grass, or hunkered behind boulders. They ate sparingly, sharpened swords and exchanged stories of the heroism of old. A smattering of Wise Ones had come east with them, so that they could intercede with the spirit world and, eventually, tend the warriors' wounds. Together they watched the river as a bilious fog descended on its bubbling surface. Some of them ate dried toadstools or rubbed an ointment of henbane into their skin to smother fear and make crazed killers of men who would rather be working the crops, and every one of them prayed to the gods and to the ancestors, knowing that this night could prove their last.

There were no potions for Cullen of the Atrebates, nor any toadstools for Andoc of the Catuvellauni, for their heads needed to remain cool if Cullen's guess was proven right. They led a combined force of their own nines and the men of the Cantiaci who had been spared by the warrior with the heron-billed helm. Together they had fallen back on the only bridge across the Swamp River, in expectation that this would be the enemy's chosen crossing point.

Cullen had slingers, spearmen and war hounds, arranged in groups and covering both sides of the water. He had released other, smaller parties too, to gather food, supplies and whatever weaponry, however agricultural, they could snaffle. One party, meanwhile, had taken what few mounts were at Cullen's disposal and galloped back to Durouernon, the only substantial dun on the Swamp River, there to locate a brace of oxen. Another section, commanded by Andoc, had gone east, in the face of the Roman advance, scouring the fading wolf-light for isolated enemy scouts.

Cullen placed himself at the very centre of the bridge, as though his presence as a sentinel would somehow dissuade the

Roman vanguard from crossing. There he waited, immersed in the gathering gloom, embracing it. The bridge itself was a wide and robust structure. Two parallel lines of oak posts had been set in the riverbed and banks, woven together by a lattice of withies and connected by a walkway of planks. The fog slipped over and under that walkway, writhing around his legs, and he wondered what spirits rode those curling wisps. Was his mother there, watching, witnessing this boy who had gained a name? 'By the ancients,' he whispered, 'give me courage.'

A Wise One padded barefoot over the planks behind him, his twisting cane clopping the timbers every other stride, black cloak flowing out like wings. It was a man to tell by his chanting voice, though his face gave no clue behind a headpiece made of a feathered ram's skull, the curled horns strangely chilling in the hazy miasma. He spat on his palm and smeared the frothy spittle over Cullen's shield. 'They come,' he said in the common tongue, though his accent betrayed an upbringing across the Narrow Sea, 'and you will draw strength from the water's nymphs.'

'Gaulish?' Cullen asked, surprised.

'Born of the Ueneti,' the ram-faced man said, 'but raised by Mona.'

'And what do you say of the Gauls we face?'

The Wise One grimaced. 'Fast, ferocious,' he glanced at the shield with its darker line of saliva, 'but wary of magic.'

'Curse them for us?'

The Wise One grinned. 'You'll need more than words, my friend.' He raised the cane, levelling it beneath Cullen's chin. 'Show them the gods.'

CHAPTER TWENTY-ONE

On the Swamp River's east bank, hidden amongst the trees that brought night early, a Roman unit awaited its orders, and Cassia waited with them. She had been placed with another captive, a copper-haired woman of similar age to herself, at the foot of a great alder, there to observe the gradual creep of a small wagon as it emerged from a sunken track not quite wide enough for the purpose.

'We were hoping to draw out spearmen,' said the optio who eventually came to inspect his grudging guests. He was a moon-faced man with bloodshot, protuberant eyes and cheeks deeply pockmarked. The huge red crest embellishing his helmet was far too large, making his head seem disproportionately shrunken. He leered at Cassia, then exchanged a glance with the legionary standing guard. 'But you'll do.'

'Oh, she'll do,' the guard muttered.

'Touch me,' Cassia replied in the language of her birth, 'and I'll cut off your balls.'

The optio beamed. 'I see I'll have to tie you down.' He licked his lips. His tongue was a glistening slug in the gloom. 'Spoils of war.'

'I am Roman,' she hissed.

He cocked his head, inspecting her as he might a new foal. 'You look Roman, sound Roman,' he pointed the long, ball-ended staff that gave away his rank in the direction of the river, though it was not visible from here, 'but what were you doing over there?'

'A slave,' Cassia said, taking the little sack that was handed to her by a mail-clad aide. She plucked a hunk of stale bread from within. 'My father and I took ship from Gesoriacum ten years ago. We ran aground. I alone survived the wreck.'

The optio whistled softly. 'Washed up on these barbaric shores.' He shuddered theatrically. 'At the mercy of the painted Britons. I bet they had some sport with you, eh?' He looked at his subordinate. 'Eh, legionary?'

As the pair shared a lascivious cackle, Cassia's eyes were straining against the gathering darkness, trying in vain to evaluate what she saw. Soldiers sat in the open, others moved like half-formed wraiths amongst the trees. Not enough for a full legion, but a good portion of a century, perhaps. There might be sixty here at a pinch. Part of a vanguard, she felt sure, for they lacked the train of a marching army. Where was the grain, the weaponry, the fodder? And yet these were no mere auxiliaries.

'Let me go,' Cassia urged them. 'You have rescued me. I thank you. Now, I want only to re-join my people.'

'In good time,' the optio said. He gazed at his surroundings, grimacing with evident dissatisfaction. 'It is dangerous country. Yet you sauntered across the river. No hint of fear. None of those painted animals close at your heels. I'll have a few questions when the time comes.' He tapped the staff-head against the lorica segmentata encasing his chest, the metal bands clanging like iron pots. 'Gods, but they're making a turd-pile of that.' He was peering through the trees at the vehicle labouring up the inclining track, the cracks of a whip speaking volumes as to the willingness of the oxen. With a harrumph that might have had the crowds cheering in Rome's theatres, he stalked into the treeline to berate the struggling driver.

'They move slow,' the native girl muttered to herself.

Cassia glanced sideways. 'They prefer wide roads,' she spoke under her breath, 'paved with smooth stone.'

The Briton gaped. 'You speak the common tongue.'

'I am Roman.' She gnawed a little of the bread. 'I was captured by your people when I was a child. I have lived with the Catuvellauni these ten years.'

'A slave, then?'

'At first. Now?' She shrugged, thinking of Critheanach. 'I am not sure what I am. But I am no longer a daughter of Rome.' She noted the small shiver trace its way through the girl's fragile frame. It was not yet cold enough for that. 'Do not be afraid.'

The girl bit nails caked in grime. 'Will they kill us?'

'What is your name?'

'Etain.'

Cassia forced a smile. 'No, Etain, they will not kill us.' She prayed to the gods – of Britannia and of Rome – that her confidence would not prove misplaced. 'How many soldiers have you seen this side of the river?'

'Too many to count. They swarm all the tracks.' She heaved a sudden gasp of air, as if the mere thought of the invaders constricted her chest. 'All the lanes, all the fields. A great line of them, all the way back to the sea. I ran away. Thought I had left them far behind, but there they were,' she paused, shuddering, 'in front of me. Even in the woods they appear.'

'You outran the main column,' Cassia asked, 'but found these men and their wagons in the forest?'

Etain nodded, gnawing again at the rapidly reddening stubs of fingernail. 'Their nines are everywhere.'

'They do not arrange themselves in such a way,' Cassia said. 'They divide their fighters into small groups, called contubernia in my language. Each contubernium contains eight men.'

Etain nodded, as if her point were proven. 'Like our nines.'

'Except,' Cassia said, 'a contubernium never fights on its own. They are arranged like that as a matter of organisation. Each group has a mule and a couple of slaves.'

Etain peered into the treeline. 'I did not see any.'

'This is a special party,' Cassia replied, 'moving ahead of the rest.'

'What are you saying?' the guard, noticing for the first time, stepped off his mark, dropping the point of his pilum to hover level with their faces.

'That you are not part of the main invasion force,' answered Cassia. She smiled, instilling the gesture with as much warmth as she could muster. 'That you're a vanguard of some kind. A foraging party, perhaps? Finding villages, requisitioning supplies?'

The legionary smirked. 'Fancy yourself general, do you?'

She drew up her knees, dropped her chin to perch, and peered up through her eyelashes. 'I'm just a woman,' she said, hoping she sounded coquettish and assuming he would see right through the clumsy affectation, 'but I know a legion on the march, and this is not it.'

A creamy smile spread across his face. He bobbed his head, grudgingly conceding the point. 'We have auxiliaries – Gauls in the main – riding ahead on the main road. Flushing the savages out. Other units have spread out along the various tracks, seeking better routes. Wider fords. Bridges.'

'There is no ford here.'

His eyes strayed beyond her to take in the weeping willow. 'Only the dam. We needed to see whether it was defended.'

Hence the girl with a fist full of globi, she thought. Good, then, that it was only she who had been lured across. The fighters on the west bank might yet prove an unexpected welcoming committee. 'If you are not foraging, then why have you come this far from the legion?' She sucked her bottom lip, letting it pop out wetly. 'The Britons are brutes. I fear for you.'

A ripple of something traced its way across his face. He mastered it, but not before it could betray him. He cleared his throat and the pilum was now almost scraping the grass. 'I did not say we were not foraging.'

Cassia twisted a ringlet of black hair about her finger and brandished an ostentatious pout. 'But nor did you say you were.' She made a show of searching the trees. 'I see only men of the legions. Not auxiliaries from far-flung lands. These are real men. Hard men. Fighting men. You have a higher purpose than merely locating food.'

He stole a furtive peek over his shoulder, presumably anticipating the optio's return. 'Look, I should not tell you this.'

She forced her pout to deepen. It hurt her cheeks, but her pride even more. 'I am on your side. The side of civilisation. These filthy creatures,' she glanced pointedly at Etain, 'need to be tamed.'

He grimaced, checked again for approaching officers. 'Special mission, this.' He waved the pilum at the cart, which, at the place where the forest relinquished its grip, had emerged into the hoary grey evening. An attendant busily greased one of the wheels with tallow, while another brought a bag of fodder for the brace of oxen. The wagon contained its driver and eight passengers, all men. 'Escorting that old bastard.'

Even from this distance, she saw that one of the men, perched serenely in the rear as though it were a litter on the Via Appia, had white hair and whiskers. She squinted, trying to make out his face. 'Where is he going?'

The pilum swung in the direction of the fog-blanketed river, encompassing the entire west. 'Into the savage lands.'

She covered her mouth with a hand, offering up a little horrified gasp. 'You cannot be serious.' She watched the cart with renewed interest. Most of the passengers were clearly soldiers. They wore cloaks, hiding whatever armour lay beneath, but their faces were grim and hard. That left two men; one looked young, slight, with deeply tanned skin and heavy stubble. The older man was stockily built, his white hair hanging long over a cloak and tunic of a clearly Roman design, though his beard was plaited in the style of the Britons. 'Who is he?'

The soldier gave a cursory grunt to show that he did not much care. 'Some barbarian chieftain. Claims to have ruled part of Britannia.' He laughed. 'Don't they all, eh? Won't matter now. The only rule will be our rule, thank the gods.'

Cassia's mind was awhirl. 'Adminios?'

'How should I know? Another savage. Pigs in shit, that's all they are. Wallowing in their mud huts, dressed in rags. Disgusting.'

A tug at Cassia's elbow. She looked down, into the wide, fearful eyes of the native girl. 'I saw him once.'

'Who?'

Etain jerked her chin towards the cart. 'Him. The grand council at the winter solstice, a long time ago, when all the waters froze and the kings came to Cunobelin's dun.' She pointed at the passenger. 'I saw him there. That's Berikos.'

—

'Success?' Cullen asked, as the chopping thuds of axes on timber punctuated the evening.

Andoc strode at the head of eight warriors, some of whom bore dark spatters on their chests and forearms. He had traced the line of the riverbank from the north, careful to call out the watchword that would avoid a sudden evisceration in the gloom, and now, at the bridge, he dropped two large sacks on the ground, one of them crashing in a metallic din. 'Their scouts are feeble.'

Cullen grinned, holding out his hand for Andoc to clasp. They butted heads gently. 'You found some, then?'

'A half-dozen,' Andoc said, 'blundering about in the dark. Trying to creep up on us.' He shook his head, baffled. 'Imagine it.'

Cullen glanced at the sack that had jangled. 'Good armour?'

'Who needs armour?' said Andoc, touching a long finger to one of the protective sigils smeared in woad across his chest. He took his spear and shield from one of the others. 'What of the supplies?'

'Returned.' Cullen indicated the bridge behind, and the men splashing beneath.

'All is ready, then,' said Andoc, perusing the work undertaken below. 'Gods preserve us.'

'Life with glory,' Cullen said. 'Death with honour.'

Andoc's eyes burned bright under their deep hoods. 'Life with glory, Cullen Wolf Scourge, and death with honour. Let them come.'

—

They came, the Gauls, as the moon climbed out of the black to gild the treetops. The river, a slash of silver and white, babbled beneath Cullen's feet and the fog seethed and swirled, and the rumble of approaching hooves made the pulse quicken in his veins. The surrounding canopy shook as nesting birds took startled flight, and on both riverbanks a low murmur of unease rose from the warriors secreted amongst the bushes.

Cullen felt his grip tighten on the spear shaft. He adjusted his feet, bracing as if about to stride into a gale. Images flitted out there in the gloom. Horsemen? Spearmen? Ghouls from the deep wood? They became memories in his head. Folk back at Camulodunon. At Verlamion, too, and Calleva. Children playing, unaware of the great jaws closing around them. Labourers, toiling in the fields, young bucks practising for their tests and slaves scurrying to tasks. They would hear of this moment before long. Word would reach them and they would panic. They would wring their hands and beg the gods to intercede. Beacons would flare, futures would be augured, and sacrifices made. And then what? Would the horizons fill with the smoke of burning thatch? Would the rivers become clogged with the dead of this island?

He kissed the wheel indelibly needled upon his forearm, a blue smudge in the dark. 'Taranis, be with us.'

Andoc's lofty frame loomed to his right. 'For Ulla.'

'For Ulla.'

The thrum of hoofbeats increased, vibrating up through his boots and along his spine. He gritted his teeth. Swallowed down the urge to cry out as fear threatened to consume him. Kept his eyes fixed firmly on the gap in the treeline that marked the arrival of the road.

The night erupted. Horses, men, armour. A tidal wave spewing from the impenetrable abyss. He heard himself scream in response, but he knew not the words that came, aware only of the noise and the terror that seemed to swirl through his every fibre. He glimpsed a battle-standard on a bobbing pole, some kind of animal skin, long and flapping, impossible to make out as it sped in the darkness. He saw riders, high above mounts, snarling and roaring, teeth white under the moon, eyes like blazing nuggets, the war-haze fully descended, possessed of their souls. The drone of a horn sounded somewhere, harsh and jarring, heralding his death.

He thought of Calleva. Of the callow boy he had been. The wheel of life had turned, inexorably, and now he was here, on this riverbank in a foreign land. The gods knew Cullen was not of the Catuvellauni. Indeed, he hated the very soil upon which they walked. But he would fight with them, because to taste defeat to the forces of Rome was to invite the annihilation of all he held dear. Yes, he would fight alongside this foe, to push a far greater adversary into the sea from whence it came. Because he was a warrior. He was Cullen of the Atrebates. Cullen Wolf Scourge. Slayer of Branna. Beloved of Taranis. The Romans were coming, and he would fight. Would fight for Togodubnos, who he loved, and for Caratacos, who he hated.

The time was now.

So he stepped forward.

The leading Gaul's fearsome glare descended upon him. He looked powerful, with wide-set shoulders beneath a long coat of mail. His blond moustaches were thickly braided, and his head was encased in a helm of iron, crested with a rearing horse. He came on, big shield in the left hand, spear in the right, steering a snorting grey with deft touches of his thighs, man and beast angling towards the men braced at the bridge's mouth. Behind him, more riders careened from the road, their bellows a song that called on the powers of death to descend on this body of water, for blood to run red over its pebbled banks. The earth shook.

Cullen held his ground, Andoc at his side, and they were screaming, both of them, though neither could hear his own voice above the chaos.

Andoc went high. Cullen low.

Between them the horse fell in a welter of blood and thrashing hooves, and they were stabbing down, battering with their sturdy shield bosses, and the Gaul, a leg stuck under his saddle, was reduced to a twitching pulp, even as his comrades bore down on the scene.

Then the nines were up. Around Cullen and Andoc. In front, behind. Spearmen surged from below the lip of the riverbank. Slingers appeared on the flanks, secreted within the tall reeds and the stands of bramble and sedge and fern, and the whir of their leather thongs joined the other discordant sounds, and they were releasing – again and again – and the darkness crackled with impacting stones and fractured bone and screams of the wounded and dying.

Only moments had elapsed but already the fight had descended to a blurring swirl of iron and limb, blood and bone, played out to the music of man and horse, screeching in rage and agony. Blades flashed in the moonlight, spears rose and fell. Shields thudded as they parried, cracked as they splintered. Helmets bobbed in the shifting fog, the crests of wheels, moons, feathers and stars moving in and out of view, vanishing briefly to return spattered in gore or dented deep. The majority of Gaulish horses reared and whinnied on the edges of the fighting, kept at bay by Cullen's spearmen, their eyes huge as apples, white as snow. The bright rings of snaffle-bits glimmered as their heads were wrenched about by riders slashing down at the press of bodies below, and all the while the screaming melee edged closer to the bridge.

It was a scene of horror to Cullen's eyes. Not for the wounds and the cries, but for the knowledge that this fight was a battle of brothers. Those of Gaul against those of the Isle of the Mighty. But everyone knew that that was how the avaricious empire worked. Greedily consuming territory, subjugating tribe after tribe, nation upon nation, they would subsume the warriors of the vanquished into their ranks as auxiliary units, turning each conquered people against the next. Was this his own destiny? He might have wept, were he not too busy staying alive.

Andoc was down, an unhorsed Gaul standing over him, sword battering the shield with which he desperately covered himself. Cullen ducked a swinging blade, dodged flailing fetlocks caked in mud and blood, and jammed Branna's spear – his spear – into the Gaul's side. The man brayed, tried to twist away, found himself skewered. He hissed an oath, dropping his blade to fumble ineffectually at the impaling shaft, staring at Cullen in shock, almost offended at the temerity. Then his eyes turned glassy, and his fingers slid limply away. Cullen pulled hard but the spear was stuck fast, lodged between ribs. A horse was pushing through the mob, its rider hacking at all comers. Cullen was forced to relinquish the spear, freeing his sword as Andoc managed to roll clear, scrambling to his feet with a howl of fury. The Gaul barged his way through the pack, using the horse's bulk to wade through thrashing bodies, but Cullen stabbed the beast once, twice, three times in the breast, a black torrent steaming as it flowed free. His braca were drenched in blood now, and his face flecked, and he stabbed again, feeling the animal's massive strength ebb, its stride falter. The big head drooped, forelegs crumpling, and it was on its knees. The rider saw Andoc attack from the flank, pulled the green-and-white shield across to take the anticipated blow, and Cullen raked his own reddened sword along the man's exposed neck, lily-white in the gloom. It was a hard cut, deep and savage. Blood spilled over mail-coat and mane, and the Gaul lolled in his saddle, a courageous war-giver turned to a child's puppet in the blink of an eye.

They leapt clear of the falling body, Andoc and Cullen. Gave the horse ample room to twist and slump heavily on its side, hooves scrabbling ineffectually in the newly slick turf. Already, others were closing in on the defenders. Too many to fight off. Too many to count. Cullen screamed until his lungs were hot stones in his chest. Screamed fury, screamed bloodlust, screamed battle-rage. Screamed for the nines to fall back on the bridge.

Cassia found herself moving forward, away from the trees, at the behest of her guard's razor-sharp pilum. They were treating her well, the Romans, for her incongruous presence amongst the captured natives had taken an unnerving effect, but that did not yet mean they trusted her. So, she would remain with Etain and the trickle of other Britons that were beginning to arrive, gathered up by forest patrols or corralled in the wake of fired homesteads. The century commander, a swarthy swaggerer with short, tree-trunk legs and a bull neck, had returned with a squad from somewhere down river, and explained that he was keeping them as hostages for the time being, for leverage might be required at any moment. The whole unit was now mobilising, moving out of the canopy's shelter and towards the sprawling willow, its massive arch of branches forming a dark gateway to the beaver pool beyond.

'Where are you taking us?' Cassia said, staring in the general direction of the north, from whence the sounds of fighting carried to them on the desultory breeze.

'Hear that?' the guard answered, cocking his head as if listening intently. 'Our vanguard crosses the Swamp River.' He grinned wolfishly, making a thrusting motion with his hips. 'We're to sneak up on your painted friends and bend them over.'

She watched the century gradually take shape, noting that they were no longer arranged in their contubernia, nor with slung shields for a long march, but ready for battle. The legionaries formed a column, two abreast, the signifer with his standard towards the fore, though not so near the front that he might be slain in the first moments of an engagement. The centurion was with him, his transverse helmet crest marking him out. Each man clutched a pilum and shield, eyes fixed to the front. There was a nervousness about their gestures and expressions that had been absent until now. A frisson that spoke of men about to face a reckoning. She indicated the wagon, which had drawn up under the tree, adjacent to the column. 'You won't get that across. Not here.'

'We do not need to. Old goat can wait until we've secured the west bank.'

She watched Berikos, the deposed king she had heard so much about. He had dropped down from the wagon, flanked by the hard-looking retainers, and was standing beside the rear wheel, lean and tall. She saw he had a prominent, hooked nose and cornflower blue eyes. A handsome man, long ago, though age had caught up with him. He was busily strapping on a scabbard and hefting a legionary's shield, frowning as he gauged the unfamiliar weight. 'Why is he here?'

The guard grinned. 'That'd be telling.'

His mouth snapped shut as the bulbous-eyed optio broke off from the column and strode towards them. 'Keep a close watch, legionary.' His voice was tauter than before. 'We'll leave a half-dozen men with you. The rest cross the water.'

'Soon be over, sir,' the legionary said, voice clipped and smart.

The optio forced a sneer. 'They charge like branded bullocks, I hear. All muscle, no brain. We'll make short work of whatever we encounter.'

'Beasts of the wild woods, sir,' the legionary said.

'They are not stupid,' Cassia said.

The optio glowered. 'You've lived too long in the pigsty, young lady. We'll forgive you for thinking yourself a sow.'

'They have cavalry,' she persisted, 'infantry and chariot. They are good. You will find they resist to the last.'

'Groups of ten,' her guard said, evidently amused, 'so Centurion Sollonius says. Like the contubernia, except that they fight in their groups. Then scatter, engaging man for man.' He whistled, shaking his head. 'No way to win a battle.'

'Strange bastards,' the optio agreed.

'Nines,' Cassia corrected them, finding their self-assurance oddly irritating. 'They fight as nines.'

'Ten,' the legionary retorted scornfully, 'nine, twenty-three, what does it matter?'

'They like numbers divisible by three,' she said, curious at her own prickly response, 'because they believe the number three has great power. Their gods exist in groups of three. Their most important colours are blue, red and yellow.' Her voice was rising. The more she felt she had to explain the ways of her adopted people, the more the blithe indifference of her countrymen infuriated her. 'Humans are created body, soul, spirit. The world is earth, sea, air. Nature is made of animal, vegetable and mineral.'

Optio and legionary glanced at one another, as if they had encountered a mad woman. The former smirked. 'Strange, as I say. They'll learn.'

'What news?' someone said in heavily accented Latin. All three looked around to see the severe face of Berikos, erstwhile chief of the Atrebates, standing before them. He was a peculiar sight, his beard and hair styled in the manner of the Britons, while his clothes and weapons were firmly of Rome.

'Lord king,' the optio said in an obsequious tone as the elderly man's twitchy companion came to stand at his shoulder. 'The dam, obscured by that willow, leads to a briar patch and then open ground. There appeared to be a baggage train of some description on the far bank, but very few warriors.'

'It is a medical station,' Cassia interjected, dread steadily constricting her chest.

'Was,' the optio said, addressing Berikos's companion, who immediately translated into the common tongue of the Belgic tribes. 'We have secured the area.'

'Was?' Cassia heard herself echo, though her mind had abandoned her, gone to a place of horror, populated by images of Critheanach and the rest, sprawled in the thorns, disembowelled by gladius and pilum.

'The battle, lord king, has been joined to the north,' the optio continued, ignoring her.

'I have ears,' Berikos answered impatiently. His words were a little slurred, and his cheek slightly puffy, as if he had a rag stuffed against the gum on one side. 'When do we march? I must make for the meeting place as a matter of urgency.'

'You want to cross now?' the optio's eyebrows climbed into the rim of his helmet. 'You may find that you are devoid of a head by sun-up. Fret not, lord king.' He waved his staff at the column of waiting soldiers. 'These are not mere auxiliaries, nor green recruits. These men are seasoned campaigners. That is why you have us as your escort.'

Berikos's jaw worked and he winced, hissing through evident pain, 'Then escort me.'

'We must first extinguish the threat. Push the natives all the way back. Our spies whisper Togodubnos makes his stand on that river you call the Vaga. Let them scurry back to their positions. When the way is clear, we will take you south, to the rendezvous. Adminios is with his own escort. He will go north. All is arranged.' He offered a smooth bow. 'Have patience, lord king.'

'Patience?' Berikos spluttered. 'It is imperative that—'

'We are aware of our mission, lord king,' the optio cut him off. 'Make no mistake on that score.' He looked again at the column. 'That is why we have been ordered over the dam. Centurion Sollonius takes us north, against the defenders at the bridge. We will engage the enemy positions in the rear and make an end of the night's work. I'll leave a squad behind to hold the prisoners. I suggest you stay close while the danger remains.'

It was full dark as the column crossed the Swamp River, gingerly for the most part, their heavy armour and shields rendering the task of negotiating the latticed logs a significant challenge.

'I can help him,' Cassia was saying as the last pair of soldiers vanished beyond the willow. She was back with the rest of the prisoners, watched by a trio of stern sentries. Berikos, his interpreter and their half-dozen retainers had returned to the wagon, a short distance away, there to await the summons that would invite them up to the bridge about which battle now raged. But why, she wondered? Why did he want to cross so urgently, in the face of undoubted danger? And where was Adminios in all this? That was why she had offered to assist him with the pain that clearly racked the side of his face. 'He has toothache,' she tried again. 'Bad toothache. I'm a healer. I can make a treatment from the plants hereabouts.' That was a lie, for without Critheanach her ability with native leaves was nothing to brag about.

'He said no,' answered the legionary, giving a robust sniff to signify his disinterest.

'He does not know how effective I can be.' It galled her, but she hitched up the corners of her mouth, forcing what she hoped would be a flirtatious smile, playing to the legionary's predictable response. 'Maybe, after that, I can do something to help you.'

That seemed to rekindle the hungry glimmer in his black eyes. He licked his lips. 'Go.' Swinging round to address the ragtag band of glum-looking Britons, he said, 'You lot, stay put.'

—

'Begone,' Berikos barked at Cassia as she reached the wagon, the little interpreter deftly reeling off the words in her native language. 'I do not share camp whores with common soldiers.'

For a moment she was taken aback. She had not considered it until now, but her status as a prisoner had apparently escaped his notice. Rather, her complexion and fluent Latin had brought him, naturally, to the conclusion that she was one of the legion's hangers-on. Part of the mirror-army of baggage carriers, food sellers, washerwomen and purveyors of pleasure who had trailed after every marching body of men since time immemorial.

'I am a healer, lord king,' she decided to persevere. 'With the Second Legion. I can see you are in pain.'

'It is nothing,' Berikos said, immediately betrayed by the veiny hand that traced its way by instinct to probe the swollen portion of his jaw. He even winced a touch, a gesture quickly stifled, but it was all the encouragement she needed.

'I have knowledge of salves to deaden the gums, lord.' She lifted the bread sack she had been given earlier, shaking it meaningfully. 'Let me mix some for you.'

The blue eyes, almost translucent in the moonlight, flitted to the sack and back to Cassia. He touched his painful face again, then made a small sound with his hooked nose, which she took to be grudging acquiescence. 'Very well.' He dismissed the waiting armed men with a flapped hand. 'Be quick about it.'

Cassia went to the back of the vehicle and placed the bag carefully at the edge of the timber platform. It was empty, save the last piece of bread, so she had to conjure contents from thin air, making quizzical grunts as she rummaged for nothing. And what was she doing, she asked herself with a rising sense of panic? Curiosity had coaxed her here, but now what?

'How are things aligned?' Berikos was saying in his own language. 'Worry not, the bitch is Roman.'

If Cassia's ears had physically pricked up, she would not have been surprised, and it was all she could do not to turn and look directly at the two men. She swallowed dryly, forcing herself to keep working at the bag, thrusting out her elbows and shielding the mime with her body.

'Claims to know a remedy for this cursed tooth,' the deposed king went on. He gave a derisive snort of amusement. 'Services every cohort, I shouldn't wonder.'

'Officer's meat, I'd wager.'

'She is pretty, I'll give you that. Perhaps I'll tup it myself later, when matters here have been put right. For now, I'll take a deadened mouth. By the ancients, I would.' He cleared his throat. 'Plans?'

'I understand Adminios,' the interpreter replied, speaking in the language of the Britons with a tinge of a Gaulish accent, 'has already made contact with those Cantiaci who remained loyal.'

'He drives ahead,' Berikos growled bitterly.

'He went south, through the marshes and salt flats. Terrain he knows well. No big rivers to cross.'

'And the Brigantes?'

'He means to meet their representatives tomorrow.'

'I must make haste, then.'

'Let the legion get you onto the far bank,' the interpreter urged. 'All will be well.'

Cassia heard the rasp of a sword being unsheathed a short way, then thrust home. 'By all the gods,' Berikos said, 'I would cross the dam on my own.'

'Not without that,' the interpreter countered, and Cassia had the distinct impression that they were now staring at her back. But they surely did not mean her, so she glared into the gloomy wagon, straining her eyes to make out the cargo, and all the while the two men talked.

-

Show them the gods. That was what the Wise One had said.

Cullen was in a crouch. Had been for what seemed an age. His thighs probably seared with heat, screamed for him to straighten, but he did not feel them. Did not feel anything.

Heard only his own blood as it thrashed in his skull. Tasted blood too. His own? Another's?

He sensed Andoc at his side. Glimpsed the edge of the taller man's shield and brought his own across to make a nominal wall. The others under his command were streaming along at either side, funnelling between them and the rail of withies. They fell in behind, turned, panting, and took their places, packing the bridge with more and more shields. Those with spears slipped forward, sliding their weapons between the heads of those in front, so that a bristling barricade of man and metal took shape.

'Hold!' Cullen bellowed. 'Hold your ground!' Without looking round, he cried, 'Hounds! Hounds!'

The Gauls had wheeled about, dropping out of the fray to regroup, coalescing behind a big rider with a broad, bare chest and thick red beard. They were battered but undaunted, for this was what they lived for. It was the hunt, writ large. The ultimate test of skill and courage, and they, like their cousins on the bridge, would give not an inch without extracting a rich price in blood. They took charge of themselves in a broad line, rearranged harness or bridle, checked weapons, adjusted helmets. Then the flame-bearded Gaul, atop a magnificent palomino, drew back his arm and flung a heavy javelin high into the night. It vanished against the black sky, lingering amongst the stars, then fell, plummeting to the bridge, punching clean through a round shield, through the naked chest of a Catuvellauni and out the other side, pinning him, face up, on the timber walkway.

The Gauls cheered, kicked at their mounts, and they were galloping as they shifted from line to wedge, Red Beard leading at the tip.

Yelps – pitched high with excitement – overlaid the hoof-thunder, and around the defenders, through the splashing river, scrambling up the slippery bank to burst from the fog, came the dogs of war. Cullen had kept them for this moment, for when he needed to stall the enemy's momentum, and nothing worked like an eager hound with the stench of blood in its nostrils and the sense of violence on the air. They leapt, the dogs, as they bounded onto the east bank. Flung themselves at the oncoming horses without a care, their howls becoming snarls and their snarls turning to screams. The riders slashed at them as their frightened mounts kicked and reared, and the loping grey hounds shrieked as they died. But the impetus of the charge had leaked away, the gallop now a ragged mess of apple-eyed horses, wheeling and whinnying, more concerned with the last of the red-muzzled demons tearing ferociously at their legs. And all the while, Cullen's slingers took position on the west bank. He did not see them, did not need to. But their unmistakable whir filled the air as it had during the birth-pangs of the fight, and the noise of a deadly swarm droned above the yelps of the final dying dogs, and then the clangs of stone-pummelled armour punctuated the night.

Gauls fell. Eyes were smashed to jelly, helmets knocked clean off, brains dashed. One man dropped his javelin as his knuckles were shattered. Another groped at his face, his nose pulverised to a gaping mess of gore. The men on the bridge jeered. They spat. One of them turned about, yanked down his braca and presented the Gauls with his naked rump.

But there were too many. Just too many. Red Beard emerged from the chaos. No javelin now, but a big, cleaving sword raised high, and his mere presence seemed to reinvigorate the stuttering cavalry. They kicked their mounts into action again, shouted cries of rage and melded around their leader, who smacked his own horse's flank with the flat of the blade and sent it into a snorting charge.

The shield-wall on the bridge shunted back, step by step. They could not hope to stave off this overwhelming tide, but to cut and run would be to invite their own slaughter. Cullen called the time, but each rearward step would be carefully taken to avoid stumbling, and gradually, as the horsemen closed the distance with frightening speed, they gave ground.

Cullen had the sack Andoc had brought. Not the one containing captured Roman armour, but the second one. He hurled it at the bridge's mouth so that it spilled open and six severed heads rolled free, scattering in all directions, their matted hair and staring eyes and slack-jaws a macabre welcome for the approaching Gauls.

'Show them the gods,' Cullen said to himself, and he saw that the Wise One had been wise indeed. The charge slowed as the Gauls stared down at the pale heads. Death was no stranger to them, nor even the sight of a decapitated man, but the head was where the soul resided, and from whence great magic could be extracted, and who knew what curse had been placed on this grisly barrier that they were now forced to break?

In the moment of hesitation, Cullen broke away from the shield-wall, dancing round the edge of the tight formation like a cat on hot embers, gesticulating frantically at men on the west bank. From there came a shooting star, streaking across the twinkling black abyss, and it looped down, growing rapidly as it plummeted to the bridge. Not a star, but a torch, its oil-soaked rags flickering red and spewing dirty smoke.

That was the signal. Cullen screamed for all he was worth.

The most advanced Gauls were wrestling their rearing mounts into submission and pressing on, followed by a smattering of their braver comrades, and they dared to cross the sightless heads, clattering onto the bridge. Red Beard emerged in front, the palomino turning whirling circles. He whipped his sword in great arcs above his head to show that no harm had befallen him, and more of his followers kicked forth, shamed into pursuit. They grinned like vengeful spirits, all teeth and fury and bloodlust, as they watched the shield-wall crumble before them, the defenders peeling away to flee for the illusory safety of the west bank.

And then the bridge began to collapse.

CHAPTER TWENTY-TWO

King Berikos, true chief of all the Atrebates and their vassals, lord of the great chalk scarp and the deep southern harbours, was positively itching to cross the Swamp River. He made a show of listening as his interpreter droned caution, but, in truth, he was staring at the Roman bitch's exquisite backside, bent as it was over the wagon's edge, and listening to the furious sounds of bloodshed that seemed to be building inexorably to a shrill crescendo. That did not surprise him in the least, for the Romans did not know the men of this isle like Berikos knew them. Did not know their resolve or their skill at arms or their downright insanity when soaked in the battle-frenzy. It would be a hard fight. A hard conquest. And the Romans would have to learn quickly, shed their arrogance and their hubris. But learn they would, because that was what Romans did. What they always did. Still, tonight would be bloody and no mistake.

He allowed himself a small smirk. Romans would bleed, and that was never a bad thing, but the Catuvellauni would bleed more profusely. Bleed out entirely, if it pleased the gods, so that the cursed tribe's snow-white carcass would be ripe for dismemberment.

'While she treats you, lord?'

Berikos looked up with a start. 'Oh?'

The interpreter gave the faintest of smiles to show sanguinity, failing utterly to conceal his irritation. 'I said I will answer the call of nature, lord, while the girl treats your tooth.'

Berikos wafted a hand. 'Do as you please, Atebodwos, I am not a toddling babe.'

The little man sketched a cursory bow and slipped into the night. Berikos snapped his fingers, summoning the hovering wench, then turned to face north, as if he could picture the scenes of carnage playing out less than a mile downstream. His armed men and the remaining legionaries, charged with guarding the prisoners, were looking that way too, and he absently wondered whether they were keen to enter the fray or relieved to have avoided it. Heroes would be made at the bridge, but scores would stride into the next life. And then, when all was done and the river ran red with the blood of the defenders, Aulus Plautius would take his vast killing machine across Cantiaci territory until he found the traitors Togodubnos and Caratacos on the Vaga. They would be annihilated, which was nothing short of what they deserved. And the history of the Isle of the Mighty would upend.

That was a pleasant notion. What would he do when the whelps of the Sun Hound had been overthrown, he wondered? A feast, without doubt. A celebration for all Britons, as his knew overlords would call them. All Britons, indeed, for there would be no more Atrebates, nor Catuvellauni, or Eceni or Cornovii or Cantiaci. There would be only citizens of Rome. Subjects of the emperor. But an emperor whose palaces were far away. Whose face would only adorn statues and coins but would never be seen in the flesh. No, the real power would lie with men like Berikos and Adminios. Those who had the foresight and intelligence to side with the irresistible tide of progress.

Yes indeed, he thought, allowing himself the smugness he had been denied for so long, a great feast, with dancers and gladiators, and a pair of Catuvellauni kings lashed to wooden frames, the skin flayed from their bodies, inch by terrible inch, for all to see.

The stirring idea inspired him to pat the hilt of his sword. It had been a gift from Narcissus. A gorgeous piece in iron, bronze and enamel, with patterns of horses engraved along the blade and a horn pommel that had been polished to a high sheen.

He felt that cool pommel and wondered at the choices he had made. Yes, he had been driven to this. Defeated, humiliated and expelled by the upstart whelps of an overreaching chief. But now that matters had come to a head, he was gnawed by a nagging sense of perversity. Preparing to stick this beautiful piece of workmanship into the flesh of fellow Britons was not a course of action that sat comfortably, however necessary it might be. So he forced himself to remember Calleva, the day it had fallen. The fear and confusion. The way he had scurried into the countryside like a rat before hounds, with a sack full of gold, a handful of retainers, the clothes on his back and a lifetime's worth of regret. The day still made him sick to his stomach. Caratacos and his chariots, his spearmen and slingers. All jeering and laughing as they reduced Berikos's kingdom to nothing. Now was his time for vengeance. By the ancients, it would be sweet.

'Their fault,' he muttered softly. 'They brought me to this.'

He almost cried out when warm skin snaked over his knuckles, looking up sharply into the Roman girl's beautiful face. Her eyes gleamed large and bright, and he felt her sweet breath on his face. She was moving closer, her hand still on his, a thumb rubbing gently against the back of his hand. He felt his groin stir at her touch.

'Open,' she said, and in the palm of her free hand she presented the beige, paste-like substance she had been mixing. 'Your mouth, lord king. Let me see the offending tooth.'

Berikos nodded dumbly, tilting back his head and letting his jaw drop. 'Lower right,' he managed to garble, 'towards back.'

She stood on tiptoes, leaning so close that he could feel the warmth radiate from her body. He felt the beginnings of a frown tug at his brow. Something about the girl seemed out of kilter. He tried to place it, but then his senses were assailed by her smell. Not just her breath, but her skin and hair. He let the thought go, breathed her in.

'Very swollen,' she said, and he hoped she meant his gum. 'You poor, poor thing.' She had eased his hand away from the sword hilt, so he let it snake gradually up her waist. He was pleased not to feel her shrink from his touch. A night full of promise, he thought, in more ways than one.

The girl applied the salve with her fingertip, rubbing it gently on the tender spot. He flinched, but it would take more than that to make him let go. The mixture was warm and moist, tasted familiar. Almost like bread. She was coming closer still, peering into his gaping mouth, her own plump lips just a finger's width from his.

It came to him. Her words. She had spoken the common tongue.

The pain as she sank her teeth into his long nose was excruciating, overwhelming. It was a searing flare, as if a shower of sparks from a hammer and anvil had sprayed the centre of his face, the heat unrelenting and unquenchable. And she kept coming, kept biting, clamping down so that the sound of crunching bone reverberated around his head. She had a hand on his shoulder, demon-claws digging tight into his tunic, and he stumbled back, mewing in shock, unable to slow himself under their combined weight. Then the pressure of her body was gone. She was gone. He was clutching his face, pawing at it with both hands and all he saw was haze in the dark, for his eyes were filled with tears, and all he felt was his own hot blood as it seeped through his fingers and into his mouth to mix with the salve.

The bread. Mix with the bread. Bread that the bitch had chewed up and spat out.

Rage overwhelmed him in that instant. An incandescent fury that wiped clean all but the need for retaliation. His hand abandoned the nose and went instead for his sword. But there was no horn pommel, no bronze hilt inlaid with intricate enamel work. His fingers groped, found only a void. The open mouth of an empty scabbard. He heard scrabbling in the long grass. His lounging retainers trying to rouse themselves, tripping on their own swords as they tried to ascertain what transpired in the dark. Before him, resolving from the haze, came the Roman bitch. She was clutching the weapon in both hands. He reached out to take it, made to thank her, and only understood that she meant him harm when the beautiful iron with its horse-patterns slid into his belly and out through his spine. He was falling. She was running.

—

The riders Cullen had earlier dispatched deserved their weight in gold. That was what he heard himself scream as he bounded from the collapsing bridge onto the Swamp River's west bank.

The oxen they had been charged with locating were a pair of irritable and massively muscular beasts who seemed to want to pull the moment their handlers gave their head collars an inch of slack. And pull they did. Tied as they were to the great posts underpinning the walkway. Posts that had earlier been whittled to frail imitations of themselves by skilled axemen.

The bridge had swayed like a drunk at first, then tilted sharply to the side, groaning like a sick mule, and as it had shunted back, as if trying in vain to right itself, the stout oaken stanchions had creaked and splintered and failed, and the timber planks had bunched and then scattered and the wattle railings had been reduced to a tangled mess of kindling, suspended for a fraction of a heartbeat over the dark waters. Then the whole structure had disintegrated under the weight of the Gaulish horses, man and beast falling together in a screaming, seething melee.

Cullen was laughing, panting, crying, as he peered down at the watery carnage below. The bulk of the empire's green-shielded auxiliaries were cut off on the opposite bank. They could cross in theory, for the river was no match for a large horse handled expertly. But that failed to account for the hail of sling stones that would greet their painstaking progress, and the warriors who would wade into the currents to drag the beleaguered cavalry from their saddles, and the spears that would stab down as they neared dry land. That was why the majority of the Gauls now reined in on the east side of the river and made do with insults and impotent fury.

Yet danger remained, for some of the enemy had made it across, and he quickly hauled his senses back to the here and now. He barked orders with a parched, stinging throat, rallying his fighters for one final endeavour before they would fall back and melt into the wild countryside. Red Beard had brought with him a score of cavalrymen, and they had regrouped in flailing, thundering fashion as the bridge toppled at their backs, and now they were raising their throwing spears, readying for another charge, knowing that the odds were no longer in their favour.

On came the Gauls in a mad gallop, the river hard on their left flank. Cullen's defenders came together, formed a shield-wall at a half crouch, those still with spears bracing at the front, shields tightly overlapping. It was a combined force, Cullen saw, as he looked from taut face to taut face. A demonstration of savagery and heroism fit for the ages, but it was more than that. It was a coalition. There were the Cantiaci and Catuvellauni, looking to Cullen for leadership, but he had Dobunni here and Durotriges, Dumnonii and Coritani. A shield-wall for all the tribes. They might not stand together on many things, but they were united in opposing a common threat – an existential peril – and he felt a rush of pride as he stamped his left foot down and locked his shield over Andoc's.

The Gauls smashed home. It was they who fought for their lives now that their companions had been cut off, and they reared in the face of the spiked shield-wall, hooves thrashing at the leather-bound boards, hoping to punch holes in the formation's cohesion. Spears jabbed up at them. At the horses' muzzles, eyes, throats. At the riders' legs, hoping to nick a groin so that death would come rapidly in the wake of pumping, undammable blood.

The Gaulish leader inevitably came for Cullen. If the mass of fighters were a pair of serpents, the two of them were the heads, their mutual importance undeniable. Red Beard's skin was wan in the dark, as if the colour had sapped under the strain of battle, and his face seemed to take on an ethereal glow. His long beard was matted, the plaits ragged where they draped over the blood-smeared mail-coat. The horse wore a richly decorated harness set with precious red stones. A handsome creature up close, and Cullen felt a pang of reluctance as he swung his sword into the beast's long face. He missed, the Gaul wrenching the head round by the reins, and then the horse was flank-on to Cullen, its rider looming over him, and it took every ounce of strength to bring the shield across to absorb the blow before it cleaved his skull in two.

Red Beard roared. The sound rumbled through Cullen's body. He braced for a second blow and glimpsed his enemy's gurning face on the other side of the barrier, realising with horror that his shield had fractured just above the boss. The next hit sent him back a step, widened the fissure in the shield, and his jarred arm was suddenly numb. He sensed he could not withstand another strike, so he lunged forward, shoving the broken shield in the palomino's face, twisting and pushing. It was barely a scratch for so impressive a creature, but the horse turned its head away, skittering back a touch, and that was all it took for Red Beard's sword to fall out of range. The tip, coming down in a crashing arc, caught Cullen's scalp, ran down his temple, and immediately he felt heat and moisture flood the side of his face. But it was not enough, and he was driving up and up, his own sword at arm's length, wrist and elbow rigid so that his entire bodyweight pressed in behind the hilt as the razor-sharp point buried itself in Red Beard's side. The Gaul tipped back his head and brayed like a gelded bear, and then a woman came from amongst Cullen's shield-wall and leapt like a fawn onto the wheeling mount. She was a vision from the Otherworld to Cullen. Naked from the waist up, her torso daubed in blue. Her hair was cropped short, black as the night and spiked like nails, and her cheeks were streaked with tears painted in charcoal. She was in the saddle in one movement, behind Red Beard, reaching round his broad frame, and the dagger in her hand sawed savagely at his neck and then both toppled backwards into the churn of hooves and bodies.

The defenders cried out in joy as the Gauls backed away. But Cullen's force had the taste of victory now, and they pressed on, keeping their tight formation but rolling to the left so that they might pin the cavalry between their spears and the river. The Gauls died hard, even as their comrades looked on impotently from the far bank, the occasional hurled javelin a meek gesture in the face of the sling stones that kept them at bay.

Horns rent the night, pulsing through Cullen, setting his teeth on edge. The noise came from behind, desperately close. The named men and women turned to see a block of soldiers marching towards them. Men in plate armour and mail. Men with polished helmets that were crested in huge plumes. Men who carried big shields, painted red, bearing the images of golden lightning bolts.

'Shields!' Cullen bellowed, though it was hardly worth the waste of breath. He braced himself to receive the next onslaught.

The Romans were advancing at a steady pace behind those huge body-shields, and they looked like something from the ancient tales. The Fomorii, risen from the depths of the sea, here to do battle with the heroes of the Waking Realm.

Except those heroes were leaving. The shield-wall was fraying, thinning, and Cullen turned in alarm to see dozens of warriors slip out of formation, running for the wide-open space of the west. He searched for Andoc, but the tall man's mouth simply flapped open like a trout in a net.

One of the men nearest Cullen took a sideward step. Cullen threw down the tattered remains of his shield and reached across the line in time to take hold of his cloak, twisting him savagely about. 'Why?' was all he could think to say.

There was no trace of callowness about the man's hard eyes and scarred face. The sight of him made Cullen freeze. This was not retreat. It was betrayal.

The warrior shook him off, and in that movement the stars spangling his shield glowed yellow in the gloom. They were the stars of the Dobunni. He spat in Cullen's face. 'King Boduoc sends his regards.'

Then they were gone. Not only the Dobunni spearmen but many more besides, and the stout shield-wall had thinned to a pathetically brittle line, and all the while the enemy's massed formation trudged towards them.

'What is that?' Andoc said at his ear. He meant the red banner that fluttered high above the heads of the oncoming column.

'Looks like a ram,' said Cullen, squinting at the banner's golden emblem.

Andoc snorted. 'Fitting, goat's turd, wouldn't you say?'

They laughed. Together, unbridled. Andoc turned, holding out his hand for Cullen to take. Their palms clasped and they butted heads softly. When they parted, a ripple of something uneasy traced across Andoc's face.

'That time,' he said, 'on the boar hunt. When I drew my blade. Arthmael paid me to send you to the next.'

Cullen nodded, scarcely surprised. 'I knew he would not rest with curses.'

'He will work to see you dead.'

Cullen laughed bitterly. 'Hardly matters now.'

Andoc shook his head. 'If you survive this, Arthmael is your sworn enemy. Never forget that.'

'And you?'

'I am your blade-brother. Your blood-brother.'

The Roman front rank gave a howl of challenge. They cocked their arms above their shoulders, like so many serpents poised to strike. Instead of fangs these were the black teeth of heavy javelins.

The pila volley. Cassia had described it in grim detail. Cullen screamed again for shields, even as he realised he no longer held his own. He took his sword in a double-handed grip as he crouched low with the rest and then the pila were up and away, arcing high above.

They slammed home. The sound was horrendous, sickening, like so much iron punching so much meat, for that was precisely what it was. The shields were no match for the javelins, splintering like worm-eaten timber in the face of those heavy points. The warriors fell, plucked from the battle line to stare sightlessly at the stars.

Now the charge.

Throw, draw, smash. That's what Cassia had said. Wreak havoc with the pila, draw the short, stabbing gladii and crash headlong into a shield-wall in disarray.

The hiss of the gladii leaving their scabbards was enough to freeze the blood. A trumpet called out, short and sharp. Orders bellowed from the crested fiends. The pace of the legionaries quickened. Now was the moment. Cullen stood shoulder-to-shoulder with Andoc, ready to receive the might of an empire. But this time it was with a remarkable sense of peace. Because he would die. There was no alternative. No possibility. It was almost a relief.

Vaguely, as if dreaming, he became aware of a new sound. It was a coarse, jarring, whining drone, like a million angry hornets, and at first Cullen could not place it amongst the din. Perhaps, he wondered, the loss of blood had taken a toll on his hearing or his wits. But the noise became louder all the same. Closer, more persistent.

'Belinos!' someone screamed.

'Teutates!' came another.

'Andraste!'

'Taranis!'

The voices were not with him, but behind and to the sides. He blinked. The drone was even louder now and he recognised it as the blare of the carnyx. Several of them, in fact, and he knew, too, that such an instrument was not employed by the forces of Rome.

The legionaries faltered.

Cullen looked round.

The chariot sped between the two bodies of warriors. Its wheels bouncing over ruts, its axle blades a blur, and on its platform stood Andraste herself. Goddess of victory. Bringer of war. And her lithe body was wrapped in furs and her hair was aflame and the spear she hurled took a legionary in the throat and the world erupted in cheers.

Cullen's eyes stung with tears. He was moving forward now, drawn inexorably in the chariot's wake, and he could see that Andraste had transformed into a named woman of the greatest renown. It was Aoife the Dread.

'Life with glory!' a man roared. He was huge. As wide as he was tall. With silver hair, a chain of badger's teeth about his neck and one arm that was an iron-studded stump.

Garn Grey Boulder. He was there. Right there, in front of Cullen, challenging the Romans to come onto his great blade.

With him was Kurd Long Limb, who held his own sword aloft, swirling it as a rallying point for all to see. 'And death with honour!'

There were many now. Scores. Spears and shields and swords and daggers and axes. Rues Seeker, White Tal and many more. Snarling faces, painted bodies, glimmering torcs. The forces of the Isle of the Mighty.

They ran at the Romans. Charged behind snarled oaths and spitting rage. Cullen slammed his sword against a big Roman shield, swayed out of range of the gladius that lashed up at his groin and grabbed for the shield's upper rim, tearing it down so that he could bury his blade in the legionary's face.

Pandemonium. Noise. Blood.

The Romans were good. Their movements well-practised and their discipline frightening. But they were woefully outnumbered, overlapped, overwhelmed. The bridge had gone, and their route back to wherever they had crossed was now blocked. It was the river for them, and as their formation began to fray, the first of their number took to the water, thrashing desperately as their armour slowed them, weighed them, drowned them.

Cullen found himself deep amid the melee. He stabbed one way, slashed another, ducked and spun. He thought he bit an ear, though he could not be certain. A shield boss took him square in the chest. He tasted vomit. Spat it in a man's face and strode on. A Roman, face streaked with blood beneath a severely dented helmet, stepped into his vision. He drove the sword up into the exposed throat, twisting hard as he yanked it free so as not to get it stuck. He glimpsed Aoife somewhere to the left. Saw Kurd's head, high above the rest. Heard Garn's thunderclap challenge. Ducked a hacking blow from a gladius, then was blinded by his opponent's blood as Five Thorns scythed his head clean from his shoulders.

The Roman block – so smart and consistent – collapsed. Those who fought died. Those who fled flailed in the black waters of the Swamp River. On the far side, the Gaulish cavalry turned away, riding back to the road. Cullen fell to his knees. The turf was slick and dark. He breathed hard. His head and chest hurt. His fingers were cut. His whole body was slick with sweat and blood. All around him the men and women of the Isle of the Mighty strode amongst the tattered remnants of the Roman force, ending lives at the end of spear and sword. Armour was taken. Heads too.

But Cullen wanted none of it. He breathed. Just breathed. It was over.

EPILOGUE

'They'll come. If not today, then tomorrow or the next. We have not stopped them.' Aoife the Dread spoke softly, wiping her spear's tip on the tunic of a Roman corpse.

The banks of the Swamp River stank of blood as the sun began to make cracks above the forest canopy to the east. The dead and wounded were scattered in a concentrated area on both sides of the destroyed bridge. Many more drifted like flotsam in the eddying waters below. Crows swirled above all, descending to squabble over their unexpected banquet.

'The king tasked us with slowing their advance,' Kurd Long Limb said. 'We did it.'

'Somehow,' Aoife said, glancing at Cullen. 'Somehow.'

Cullen managed a wan smile. In truth, he felt exhausted and bewildered. Blood caked the side of his face, clogging his eye. He was certain his ribs were broken. He clasped Cassia's hand. She had found him in the aftermath of the fight, as the warriors on the west bank hauled themselves to their feet and the Gauls and Romans on the east slunk back into the woods to join the main column. She had forced her way through the staggering warriors, bouncing from one to the next until she had come to Cullen, throwing herself into his arms so that both fell to the churned grass, lying there, silent, sobbing.

Now they rested with their comrades as morning approached. Aoife's warband watching the roadway. Birds beginning to sing as the fog melted away. Red Beard's beautiful palomino grazing nearby. Cullen would take it for his own.

'They knew, the Dobunni,' he said, thinking of the desertion in the heat of the shield-battle. He dragged up memories of the fight near Cironion. Of the Dobunni the hawks had slain. 'They must have recognised one of the named men from that day.'

White Tal looked up from the elbow wound he had been gingerly dabbing. 'That was Boduoc's revenge.'

'It is not as simple as that,' Cassia said. 'Many tribes have sided with Rome.'

Aoife loomed over them, majestic and terrifying in her furs and iron. 'How can you know, girl?'

So she told her tale. Told of how she had known where the vestige of Ulla's hawks had been stationed, having encountered them that very day, and had run to them with news of the Roman advance over the beaver dam. She had not known it was Cullen and Andoc that she was saving, only that the bridge was key, and so she had screamed at Kurd and shaken Garn and pleaded with Five Thorns, Rues and Tal. And they, in turn, had found Aoife and she, of course, had led the counterattack.

And all that had transpired after Cassia had murdered a king. Cullen could barely countenance it. The lord he had revered all his life. The traitor who had inspired conquest. Berikos deserved his fate, but that did not make the news any more palatable. But that was not the only treachery. For she told, too, of the unguarded conversation between Berikos and his interpreter.

'Which tribes were named?' Aoife said, her glower deepening by the moment. 'Which chiefs?'

Cassia took a long breath. 'Cogidubnus of the Regneses, Boduoc and Corio of the Dobunni, Volisios of the Coritani, Cartimandua of the Brigantes and Antedios of the Eceni.'

That last tribe struck a chord in Cullen's mind. 'Prasutagus,' he murmured.

Cassia glanced at him. 'What?'

He shook his head. 'It does not matter.' But it did matter. Betha had been right.

'They have been wooed by Berikos and Adminios,' Cassia went on. 'Convinced that the legions will overwhelm them, whether they fight or not.' She gave a shallow shrug. 'So why not make a deal and keep their thrones?'

'All those tribes will submit to Rome?' Andoc said, aghast. 'By the ancients.'

'We must retire to the Vaga,' Aoife commanded. 'Warn Togodubnos and Caratacos.'

'We have bought them a little time,' Kurd said, 'thank the gods.'

Garn touched his badger teeth. 'They can assemble a proper horde.'

But from where would the spears come, Cullen wondered, if their supposed allies were, even now, suing for peace? He let go of Cassia and heaved himself painfully to his feet. He walked to the river, the glassy waters emerging from the lifting gloom. A kingfisher perched on one of the spars that had once formed part of the bridge. Absently, he watched it dive, coming back up in a flash, the lolling form of a fish streaking silver through the air. It made him think of the lightning bolts that had accompanied his near death at the hands of Arthmael.

Footsteps padded at his back. Cassia's arms slid around his waist. She kissed his cheek, turning the skin of his neck to gooseflesh. He tilted his head to hers.

'We'll find her.'

'Critheanach is cunning as a weasel,' Cassia said, though she could not entirely mask the note of anxiety underlying the words.

'I'll call my sword Lightning-Strike,' he said, trying to distract her from worry.

'A good name.'

And Lightning-Strike, he thought, had work to do. There were enemies still to face. A Wise One to be killed. A family to avenge.

Up in the branches on the far side of the river, movement caught his eye. Snatches of black and white, glimpsed behind the green of leaves. He lifted a hand in acknowledgement. Then he turned to Cassia, holding her close, breathing deep of her long hair, revelling in her scent and her warmth. The night had brought victory. The Romans had been pushed back, if only for a fleeting moment. He was a warrior of the Isle of the Mighty. The Wolf Scourge, slayer of Branna, defeater of Arthmael and favourite of Taranis. But for now, as the sun rose bright and warm, they were alive. That was enough.

Historical Note

As a self-confessed seventeenth-century nerd, the late Iron Age was not a time in which I ever thought I might set a novel. But then I walked the impressive Roman walls of Silchester, near the Hampshire–Berkshire border, and I read about the incredible archaeology still being found there, from levels below the Roman era: evidence of a more advanced society than previously assumed. A diet that included certain items (olives, wine, shellfish, to name but a few) synonymous with their eventual conquerors. A home life featuring comforts like plates, glassware and expensive, imported jewellery. And the remains of an extensive, planned road network, over which the Romans later laid their own. In short, the people of Calleva, as Silchester was known back then, enjoyed a sophisticated lifestyle, not so far removed from that of their eventual overlords across the sea. It got me thinking, then reading, and, eventually, writing.

I wanted to tell the story of the Roman invasion, but from the point of view of the British tribes, whose existence survives as ghostly marks on our landscape, but who left no written records and whose history and culture is thus reduced to fragments. Pieces of a puzzle. I am not an historian, and I'd never claim to have put that puzzle together, but this book is my reimagining of what those cataclysmic times might have been like for the people that lived them.

A tale like this takes a fair amount of imagination. I would almost go so far as to say that I approached the assignment with a 'world building' mindset, as if I were writing a fantasy novel.

If, then, certain aspects of the story don't quite ring true for individual readers, then I can only apologise.

That said, I have attempted to keep everything about *The Savage Isle* as authentic as possible. The tribes mentioned were all in existence at the time of the Roman invasion (though I have tinkered with some of the spellings to be a little more accurate), and certain characters are a matter of historical record. Cunobelin and his three sons are noted in the classical sources, as is Berikos (often named Verica in modern texts), whose ousting from the Atrebates throne was indeed one of the pretexts for the invasion.

The locations in the book are generally authentic. Verlamion (modern St Albans) was traditionally the major centre for the Catuvellauni, until they subsumed the territory of the Trinovantes. At some point, Cunobelin – called 'King of the Britons' by Roman historian Suetonius – moved his court and mint across to the latter's capital, Camulodunon (Colchester).

The sacking of Calleva is my own invention, but that the town was a thriving Iron Age settlement before the conquest is not in doubt. As part of the empire, Calleva Atrebatum, as the Romans knew it, developed into a major regional hub, and survived as a town into the Saxon period (known by then as Silchester) until it was abandoned around the seventh century. The extensive Roman ruins are well worth a visit.

As for Cullen, he and his comrades are figments of my imagination. But warriors like them most certainly existed, for the Celtic peoples were renowned across the continent for their fighting prowess.

A word on their 'warrior names'. Clearly this is something I have invented for the story, but it seemed fitting that a culture such as this would endow 'war-titles', in addition to birth names. Take the most famous name of the period, for example. Boudicca roughly translates as 'Bringer of Victory'. Maybe her parents gave her that name as a newborn. Maybe she earned it in later life. I reckon it's the latter, and, therefore, she probably wasn't the only one.

Michael Arnold
Hampshire, April 2024

Acknowledgements

Writing this book has been quite a journey, to say the least. I began *The Savage Isle* during lockdown, my Civil War Chronicles series having run aground – my writing career well and truly floundering.

But my wonderful family pressed me to pick up the proverbial pen (well, open the proverbial laptop) and start from scratch. So I did, tentatively. At some point we went for a stroll around the walls of Silchester (Calleva Atrebatum) and the idea for a new series began to take shape.

And here we are. I can hardly believe it.

So, let me start by thanking those aforementioned family members. My parents, John and Gerry, whose unwavering belief in me has always been a source of great strength. My wife, Becca, whose love, patience, encouragement and endless support have kept me grounded throughout this entire process. And special mention to my kids: Josh, Maisie, George and Martha. The best people I know.

I owe a special debt of gratitude to my editor, Craig Lye, whose insightful feedback and keen eye helped transform the rough draft into something I am truly proud of. I can't wait to get cracking on the next one!

Huge thanks to my agent, James Wills, and everyone at Watson, Little, for championing this story from the very beginning. Your enthusiasm, wisdom and hard work have made *The Savage Isle* possible, and I am incredibly fortunate to have you in my corner.

I am also deeply thankful to the wider team at my publisher, Canelo, and their commitment to bringing the novel into the world. Your efforts have been instrumental, and I couldn't have asked for a better publishing experience.

Lastly, to the readers – thank you for taking a chance on this tale. I hope you enjoy it.